Family
Fortunes

Family Fortunes

Anne Melville

DOUBLEDAY & COMPANY, INC.
GARDEN CITY, NEW YORK
1984

All of the characters in this book are fictitious and any
resemblance to actual persons, living or dead, is purely coin-
cidental.

Library of Congress Cataloging in Publication Data
Melville, Anne.
    Family fortunes.
    I. Title.
PR6063.E437F3   1984   823'.914
ISBN 0-385-14833-X
Library of Congress Catalog Card Number 82–45261

Contents

PART I   THE END OF THE SEARCH   1
1946–1957

PART II   LETTING GO   59
1963–1965

PART III   SIVA DANCING   149
1972–1973

PART IV   ANCESTORS   255
1975–1977

THE LORIMER LINE

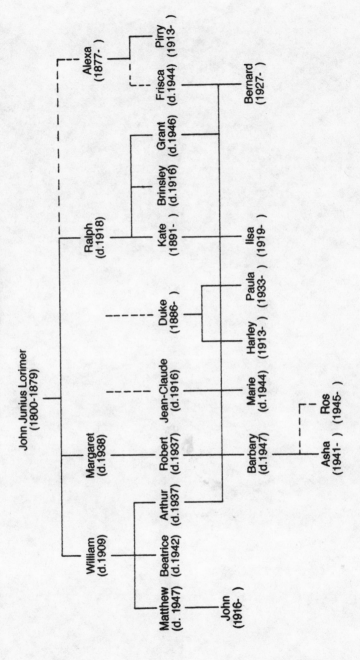

PART I

The End of
the Search

1946-1957

I

I look for a lost treasure. I look at the picture on the wall. I look up a word in the dictionary. I look after the sick baby.

As she struggled with her English exercises, Ilsa Laing hugged more tightly around her the fur coat which her husband had given her on their wedding day in Berlin. London in the winter of 1946 was a cold, cold city. A woman who had grown up in Russia and had spent four frozen winters in Auschwitz and Belsen should have been able to shrug off the deepest frost that England had to offer. But the years of near-starvation had left her thin and anemic. There was no warmth in her blood, yet because coal was rationed she did not feel justified in lighting the fire in the unheated flat until Richard returned from the hospital.

What a long time he was. Ilsa's eyes strayed longingly to a different set of exercise books piled on the piano stool. Her language lessons were a practical necessity, since she would be spending the rest of her life in England. But Richard had also arranged for her to study musical composition and her work for this other tutor filled a deeper need. She wished she could devote the whole day to it.

Music was the mainspring of Ilsa's life, more important to her than physical well-being or emotional relationships. The effects of frostbite meant that she would never be able to resume her career as a concert pianist, but by now she was reconciled to that. The music had moved from her fingertips to her head, and from now on it would be her own music. She would be a creator, not an interpreter of other people's creations. Already she was writing for the piano. But before she could compose for a full orchestra she had a great deal to learn: a different kind of grammar, a new vocabulary. This week's task was to analyze one movement of a Mahler symphony, and she would have liked to come to grips with it at once. But the English exercise must be completed first. "Bread and butter before cake," Richard had commanded, in one of the many phrases which she was struggling first to understand and then to remember.

What could be keeping him? It was more than six hours since he had telephoned from the hospital to say that Tess had had her baby—*his* baby—and that mother and son were both well. Surely Tess would be wanting to rest by now. But that was none of Ilsa's business. She returned her concentration to the list of phrases which must be learned by heart because there was no rule, no apparent logic, to their construction. *I put on my coat because it is cold. I put the book down on the table. I put up my guest in the spare bedroom. I put off my walk until it stops raining.*

More time passed. Disturbed, Ilsa looked first at her watch—like the fur coat, a present from a generous husband—and then at the telephone. But she did not trust herself to use the instrument. It was one thing to accept a call from Richard, who would speak slowly and clearly, and quite another to make herself understood by a girl at a switchboard and a nurse in charge of a busy ward. Lacking the confidence even to try, she pulled on her boots and set out to walk to the hospital.

She knew the way, for she had been to the antenatal clinic there with Tess, linking arms for steadiness as they crossed side streets bumpy and slippery with ice. Now she strode out through a new snowfall which chilled her face even as the exercise of walking restored the circulation to her feet and hands. The hospital was not far away.

She found Richard sitting in the canteen, staring at a cup of tea on the table in front of him. As she sat down opposite, he looked at her with eyes which were clouded and dull, as though a shutter had closed over the energy and enthusiasm and kindness which normally lit them.

"She died," he said. "Tess. She's dead."

Horrified and unbelieving, Ilsa struggled for words. "But you have said—" Even now she did not break the rule which Richard had imposed, that she should speak only in English. "On the telephone you have said—"

"It seemed all right. Fine. Baby yelling. Tess smiling. They let me see her for a bit. Then she needed some stitches. I waited outside. Doctors don't like other doctors watching. Suddenly she hemorrhaged. And they couldn't stop it."

"Hemorrhaged?"

"Bled to death. A woman performing a natural function in a well-equipped hospital in a civilized country. It's something that can't happen. But it did." He pushed the untasted tea aside and buried his head in his hands.

Ilsa looked across at Richard with pity and sympathy. Should she try to comfort him? Kiss him, perhaps? She was his wife, after all, as much as a legal document could make her. But it was Tess who had been Richard's wife in everything but name.

Only four months earlier Tess had stared in dismay at Ilsa as Richard—returning from military service as a medical officer in occupied Germany—introduced as his wife the Russian woman he had saved from a displaced persons' camp. He was not the only man to have made a gift of British nationality in such circumstances, and Tess had found no difficulty in accepting his assurance that the couple were married in name only. She had shed understandable tears at the ill fortune which had sent the letter in which she announced her pregnancy shuttling around Europe and never quite catching up with Richard as he was transferred from one place to another. But she was a girl of character, showing both courage and sympathy in her acceptance of the situation. Secure in the knowledge that Richard loved her, and only her, and understanding that if Ilsa were to be abandoned too hastily she would be forced back to a refugee camp in Europe, Tess had agreed to wait for Richard to obtain a divorce and not an annulment. In the meantime Richard and the woman he loved and the woman he had married had all lived amicably together in his flat until the start of Tess's labor.

The strange friendship which had grown between a British doctor and a Russian inmate of a concentration camp had been wholly one-sided in its practical consequences. Richard had saved Ilsa's life when she was starving. He had comforted her when the search for her mother ended in the report of Katya Belinskaya's death. He had brought her to his own country as his wife, promising to support her until she could make a career for herself in music. And he had arranged for her to have the professional help she needed. Ilsa longed to find something which she could do for him in return. But nothing she could say or do would be any consolation at such a time. She waited without speaking while the first shock of his grief took its course.

At last he raised his head and found a handkerchief with which to dry his eyes. He gave a heavy sigh.

"Might as well go home," he said. "Nothing to be done here."

"The baby?" asked Ilsa.

"The hospital will look after him."

"But—" Uncertain of herself in this situation as in so many others, she wondered what to say. Would Richard reject the baby which had caused its mother's death if the reminder of its existence was pressed too soon? But Ilsa had often heard from her mother—a doctor responsible for a large orphanage—the theory that antisocial behaviour in later life often grew from lack of a mother's cuddling during a baby's first few days in a large, impersonal nursery.

"Will you show me?" she asked.

Richard shrugged his shoulders and led her along tiled corridors to the maternity wing. It was six o'clock, and most of the newly born babies were in the ward, at their mothers' breasts. Only one child remained in the nursery. His back was being gently patted by the nurse who had just given him a bottle, but he had fallen asleep before even finishing the feed. Ilsa and Richard watched as he was tucked back into the cot, and then stood together beside it.

"What shall be his name?" asked Ilsa.

"You mean, what shall we call him?" Richard's correction of her English came automatically. Ilsa repeated the phrase silently in her head so that she would not make the same mistake again, and pondered its significance. Always before when Richard said "we" he had meant himself and Tess, reserving for Ilsa the phrase "you and I." It was a detail which perhaps would only be noticed by someone who was concentrating so hard on the effort to use exactly the right terms in a strange language. Now Richard had made her part of his "we." Had he noticed it himself? she wondered.

Ilsa looked down at the sleeping baby, still exhausted by the effort of being born. The sight did not excite any rush of maternal feeling for the motherless child. She knew already that she could never have a baby herself. It was one of the many consequences of her wartime imprisonment and she had accepted it as a fact, not bothering even to ask herself whether she regretted it. There was nothing to be done about this particular deprivation: and so she had told herself that she could be happy without a child, and believed her own assurance.

It was part of her Russian heritage that she should accept without resentment the hand which fortune dealt out to her. When she was told that her home had been blown up as the occupying Germans retreated from the siege of Leningrad, and that her mother had died in the explosion, she had mourned long and deeply: but in the end she had come to terms even with that bereavement. What was gone, was gone. She must make a new life for herself.

Then the wheel of fortune had turned. Richard opened a door and led her into a new world—but he had never intended to offer her a true place in his own life. If Tess had lived, Ilsa would have slipped unobtrusively away as soon as the legal knots which formally made her Mrs. Richard Laing had been untied. But Tess was dead: and her baby needed, if not a mother, then at least a nurse. Ilsa reminded herself that she must be cautious, ready to retreat as soon as Richard found another woman to love. But that would not happen yet, not while he was mourning for Tess. There was a need here that she could fill. Ilsa flushed with an inappropriate happiness—not at the prospect of taking pleasure in a vicarious motherhood, but because at last there was something she could do to repay Richard for his wonderful generosity.

She tried to stretch out her hand toward the grieving man at her side, to reassure him with a touch, promising that she would do whatever he asked of her. But a distaste for physical contact was yet another consequence of her years in the camps. Richard was her best friend, but there was no sexual attraction to make it easy for her to change the way in which the friendship expressed itself. Perhaps that was just as well. Richard was still in love with Tess.

"Michael," said Richard, answering the question she had asked earlier. "We'll call him Michael."

As though he heard and responded to the name, the baby stirred and opened his eyes—round blue eyes which stared directly at Ilsa, although she supposed he could not yet see her as an identifiable object. Instinctively—and to her own amazement—Ilsa found herself holding out a finger to touch one of the baby's clenched fists. Michael's hand opened, and then closed around her finger, pulling it to his mouth to suck.

Ilsa's heart swelled with compassion. One period of family life had come to an end for her with the official notification of her mother's death. Richard had never pretended to offer any substitute for this. He had given her the chance to devote herself to music in a country which, for all its postwar austerity, offered her a life of comfortable security. It was what she wanted, and she would always be grateful just for that: but it would have been a solitary devotion; a very private life.

Now a different prospect opened before her eyes. Richard's baby needed to be loved, and in caring for the child Ilsa could express her thanks to the father.

No one was ever likely to imagine that Ilsa was Michael's true mother. Just as his father was a big man, so he was a big baby, plump and round and rosy, and the fluffy down on his head was very fair. Ilsa, whose extreme thinness was emphasized by her height, had dark chestnut hair, strained severely down the sides of her face and into a snood on the nape of her long neck. There was something in the angle of her cheekbones and the tilt of her eyes which suggested that one of her ancestors might have come from the eastern territories of the Russian Empire, but her skin was very white and as smooth as though tragedy had never touched her. When she was a girl, her expression had reflected the loving good humor of her family life and the determined concentration with which she established a reputation as a pianist while she was still young. But fear and starvation had changed not just her expression but the very shape of her face. Once she had looked healthy and happy, while now her remote, strained beauty was striking in its appearance but lacking in warmth. But then, since the day when the German soldiers had dragged her away from her mother, there had been no one to expect warmth of her. Until now.

Ilsa bent down and lifted the baby gently from his cot, pressing his cheek against her own. She looked at Richard, allowing her eyes to speak the question for which she could not find the words. Michael burped, sending a stream of watery milk onto her shoulder. She was still wearing the fur, since it was her only warm coat, and Richard hurried to dab away the mess. Smiling, Ilsa shook her head to show that it was not important. She felt his hand press down on her shoulder as he tested whether the coat was dry: then his fingers moved to stroke Michael's head. There was a moment, just a moment, when she and Richard were held close together by their closeness to the baby.

For a little while at least we shall be a family, thought Ilsa—and although she did not say the words aloud, she thought them in English. The past was dead. Well, she had accepted that already. What she had not realized was that she had been living only in a kind of emotional limbo. Now, it seemed, she was ready to emerge and to play whatever part was asked of her in this unusual family grouping. A new life was beginning and, against all expectation, it was to be a family life.

I I

The past is dead, Kate Lorimer told herself as the Red Cross ambulance carried her up the long drive which led to Blaize. But of course that was nonsense. There was no real sense in which anyone could start life again at the age of fifty-six. It might be true to say that the years of her life which she had spent working in Russia had ended in an undoubtedly final manner. But this arrival at her aunt's stately home would be a return as well as a new beginning. She was not coming to live among strangers, but to pick up again the threads of family life which she had broken thirty years earlier, in 1917.

The ambulance drew to a halt and the volunteer driver who had met her off the hospital ship studied a small notice at the foot of the stone steps.

"Blaize School for Young Musicians in the main entrance. Lady Glanville in the west wing," he reported.

"The west wing," Kate told him. Lady Glanville was her aunt, Alexa. She allowed herself to be driven a few yards farther on, but turned down the offer of a wheelchair with a smiling shake of the head. After two months of regular meals in the British zone of Berlin she was not as ill as she looked, and it would never do to make Alexa fear that she had undertaken the care of an invalid. Kate thanked the driver and waited without moving as the ambulance turned and drove away.

The old house was just as she remembered it. Two wars and the passage of thirty years had done nothing to disturb its serenity. The wing which Alexa had kept for herself was the most modern part of the building, added in the reign of William and Mary. Presumably the school had been allowed to take over the original Tudor structure whose main rooms—the great hall, the banqueting hall, the long gallery—might be of some use to an institution but were wholly unsuitable for modern domestic life.

Admission to that central part of the house would be demanded by the pulling of a long iron chain which turned a heavy bell inside the hall, but a modern bell push had been fitted to Alexa's front door in the west wing. Kate stared at it for a moment, gathering her strength for the meeting with her aunt. She was nervous, she realized. Circumstances and the rules which governed the lives of refugees had committed her to her aunt's care, but in a happier world probably neither of them would have chosen to live together. No doubt Alexa at this moment was nervous as well. Kate gathered her courage together with a single deep breath and pressed the bell.

The door was opened. How typical, thought Kate, that Alexa should have held on to her butler through all the years of war and austerity! She checked the inappropriate temptation to laugh, reminding herself that she would still be in a displaced persons' camp if her aunt had not guaranteed support. This was not a time to indulge her sense of the ridiculous. Gratitude must be the order of the day.

And here came Alexa now, not waiting in the drawing room for her guests to be announced, but approaching with outstretched arms. In a moment they would embrace, murmur the first words of greeting. But Alexa paused, unable to conceal her horror at the first sight of her niece. The two old ladies stared at each other in silence.

As far as years were concerned, only Alexa was old. Kate, as she traveled toward Blaize, had calculated that her aunt must have reached her seventieth birthday a few weeks earlier, in the spring of 1947. But as a young woman, a prima donna, she had been a beauty, and no doubt she had inherited a fortune when Lord Glanville died. Whatever money could do to preserve both complexion and figure had been done. It seemed unlikely that even Alexa could have survived two world wars without unhappiness, but whatever anxieties she might have suffered had left no visible signs. The pale skin was tightly stretched over the fine bones of her face, giving her an imperious expression. She was handsome now rather than beautiful, but still recognizably the same person who had wished Kate Godspeed thirty-two years ago.

By contrast, the sufferings which Kate had endured were all too apparent. Although fourteen years younger, she looked far older than her aunt. In the course of the Channel crossing earlier that day she had caught sight of herself in one of the saloon mirrors and studied her appearance dispassionately for the first time in many years. Alexa, she knew, had cause to be shocked. As a young woman Kate had been sturdy rather than slim and later, during the food shortages of many Russian winters, a badly balanced diet had made her fat. By the time she was forty she was overweight and, but for her height, would have looked as dumpy and dowdy as most of her neighbors. But during the past two years, while she searched Europe for her missing daughter, she had learned what it meant to be not merely hungry but starving. As her weight and size diminished, the skin which had once stretched over her flesh became loose and wrinkled. She was still tall, of course, and big-boned. But her face, her neck, her arms, her legs, were all scraggy—and the shapeless clothes which covered the rest of her body were of the kind donated to charities and issued to refugees by people who had already recognized their shabbiness.

Her face mapped the history of her life. Because her father was a missionary she had been born in the West Indies and had never bothered to protect her complexion from the sun: and in the years since she qualified as a doctor her skin had been weathered by the harsh Russian climate. The pain and desolation of losing all those she most dearly loved had etched two deep lines vertically from her nose to what should have been her hairline. Stress and an inadequate diet had played her one other trick. Within the past year her thick tawny hair had fallen out, coming away in handfuls whenever she combed it. Like some grotesque figure in a circus, Kate was completely bald.

None of this worried her. She had never been vain, and she found it easier to laugh at her eccentric appearance than to feel dismay. But she sympathized, all the same, with the effect it must have on other people. It was not surprising that Alexa hesitated now, perhaps not recognizing her guest, certainly appalled by her condition, possibly even nervous that the woman she had rescued from a devastated continent might be bringing with her all the diseases of deprivation.

Alexa's reaction had a surprising effect on Kate. During the past few months—ever since the moment when she had forced herself to accept the fact that she would never see her daughter again—she had become lethargic and dispirited. But now her natural good manners came to the rescue. Alexa had saved her from spending the rest of her life as a refugee. She had a duty in return to give Alexa pleasure in her role of savior. She must present herself as someone who was glad to have been rescued and willing to be helped.

It was a struggle to find the right words to reassure her aunt. For so many years in Russia it would have been dangerous for her true nationality to be discovered that she had forced herself to think as well as speak in her adopted language. As a refugee in Berlin she had painfully reverted to English in the attempt to prove her identity, but had found it almost a foreign tongue.

The effort must be made. She smiled—but kept her distance, so that Alexa need feel under no pressure to touch someone whom she might find disgusting. "Alexa," she said, "this is very good of you."

Once the ice was broken, Alexa swept on toward her as though nothing had interrupted her progress. Kate felt herself being hugged and kissed, more warmly than she would have expected from a woman who before would merely have offered a calm cheek or pursed her own lips formally at the air. "Kate, my dear—I can't tell you— when the news came that you were still alive I could hardly believe it! It's been so long since we even had news of you. Let me take you straight upstairs. Thompson will bring your luggage."

Kate could not resist a smile, and saw Alexa successfully translating it as she led the way up.

"No luggage? No, I suppose not. Well, I hope you'll find everything you need here to start with."

Words failed Kate as she looked around the sunny suite which Alexa was showing her. A large bedroom had been refurnished as a sitting room, with its original dressing room proving quite spacious enough to serve as the bedroom. She was overwhelmed not just by the luxurious size and comfort of the rooms but by the security they offered. For three years she had been on the move, with no permanent home. Even before that, a single room in the orphanage just outside Leningrad had served her as bedroom, living room, office and laboratory. And now Alexa was apologizing that to reach her bathroom she would have to go a few yards down the corridor! Kate sat down on the edge of the bed, uncertain whether to laugh or cry, and her aunt left her alone to adjust herself to this remembered but unbelievable way of life.

After she had bathed, Kate was forced to dress again in the same clothes. Alexa, waiting in the drawing room, made no attempt to be polite about them.

"I'll get my dressmaker round tomorrow to measure you and run up a few basics," she said. "Did they give you any clothing coupons?"

"Yes. Sixty."

"That won't go anywhere. You'll need to spend them on shoes and stockings and that sort of thing. Never mind. Before the war I had a little opera house down by the river. It had to be closed in nineteen-forty, but the wardrobe was well stocked with fabrics for the next season's costumes. We should be able to find something suitable. And I've just bought two surplus nylon parachutes. With a little embroidery they make quite tolerable underwear."

Kate didn't know what nylon was. It would not be enough, she realized, to recover the language she had not spoken for almost thirty years; she would need to learn a new vocabulary, to catch up with everything which had been happening during those years in a world from which she had been totally cut off.

"I'll make one or two skirts and blouses for myself with anything you can spare me," she said. "For the dressmaker, may I wait a few weeks? I'm not usually as thin as this." The words were coming back to her now. An English lady was pouring tea from an English silver teapot in an English drawing room and Kate, absorbing the atmosphere, realized that she would soon be English again herself.

"We shall have plenty of time to talk," Alexa said, handing the teacup. "But do give me an idea of your life, Kate. Just the bare bones of what happened after nineteen-seventeen. We knew that you were in Russia at the time of the Revolution. But for all we've heard since then, you might have been dead for the past thirty years. When the man from the Control Commission called to say that you'd turned up in Berlin, I could hardly believe it."

It was painful for Kate to talk about her life in Russia. But to answer Alexa's direct questions was the best way to avoid more probing of her past. "Do you remember that in nineteen-seventeen you sent me a letter of introduction to a friend of yours, Prince Paul Aminov?" she asked.

"Yes, of course. I sang for him once in his theater palace."

"That palace became an orphanage. It was my home for twenty-odd years. I was its medical superintendent. I never met your friend; he was killed in the Revolution. But I married his brother, Vladimir."

"So! You became Princess Aminova!"

Kate shook her head. "By the time we married he was using false papers. I became the wife of Comrade Belinsky."

"You are a princess," said Alexa firmly—and Kate could not help smiling, guessing how the story would be embroidered as it traveled the circle of her hostess's friends. "What happened to Vladimir?"

"He was executed. It was a long time before I knew that for certain. So many people in those years were taken off to Siberia but came back in the end. So I waited, hoping."

"I'm so sorry, my dear. So very sorry. But"—Alexa hurried on—"before he was killed, did you have children?"

"A daughter. Ilsa." Kate paused, trying to phrase what she wanted to say in a manner which would be definite without giving offense. "I can talk about my husband, Alexa, and the Revolution, and my years in the orphanage, because that's all past history now. But Ilsa—I will tell you once and then, please, I want never to speak of her again. It's too painful."

Alexa nodded her sympathy.

"Ilsa was a musician. So gifted! Before she was twenty she was giving concert recitals. The orphanage was occupied when the Germans invaded Russia in nineteen-forty. They came very quickly. With two thousand children in my care there was no time to escape. Some of the children were Jews. Ilsa hid them—stayed with them in the cellars for three months. But they were discovered." For a moment Kate could not go on. This was the moment which had haunted her nightmares for years but which she could not bring herself to think about in daylight.

"They were all sent to Auschwitz. The children were killed at once. But Ilsa wasn't a Jew. She had to work like a slave, but she lived. When the Russians began to advance she was moved to another camp, Bergen-Belsen. Again, though thousands starved, she survived. I know all that from visiting the camps, reading the lists. After the liberation she left Belsen. She must have tried to get home. But the orphanage had been mined and completely destroyed. The whole village was ruined—abandoned. Nothing there. And at that time, in nineteen-forty-five, I was a thousand miles away with the orphans. There was no one to tell Ilsa where I was, or even that I was still alive. When I got onto the train with the children, no one knew its destination—not even the driver. Where did Ilsa go? No one knows. There were millions of refugees on the roads of Europe. Did she leave a message somewhere? Is there some place she thought I would look for her? As soon as I was able to leave the children I tried to find her. I traced her to Belsen. I went back to our old home. I have left messages in offices, with friends, nailed to trees. She may not still be alive. I saw some of those who were in Belsen on the day of its liberation and I knew that they wouldn't survive for very long. But even if she did survive, I've lost her. In my heart there will always be the hope that somewhere in the world she's alive and happy. But I've had to make my mind accept that I shall never see her again." Kate's voice trailed into silence.

"Did you never tell her about Blaize?" asked Alexa. "About your family—*her* family—in England?"

Kate shook her head. "At the time Ilsa was born the British had sent troops to intervene in the civil war. There was anger in Russia about this. And the British blockade was blamed for the food shortages. Thousands of people starved in the famines after the revolution. It would have been dangerous to let anyone know that I was not a Russian. Especially a child, who might chatter without understanding the risk. So there's no possibility of her looking to England for any family connections."

Kate paused for a moment. Then she straightened her shoulders and held her head high as she looked into Alexa's eyes.

"That part of my life's over," she said. "Perhaps one day Ilsa will take up her career again and I shall read of her performance in a concert review. But until then, Alexa, I don't want to speak her name, or hear it. I shan't ever stop thinking of her. But I haven't come here to sit like a skeleton at the feast. When I asked to be sent back to England, it was because I'd given up the search—accepted defeat. But as long as I don't have to talk about my daughter, you'll find I can be a cheerful companion."

"I understand," said Alexa. For a moment she was silent, and then sighed. "What more can I say than that I'm sorry?" She left the room, touching her niece's hand in sympathy as she passed. When she returned she was accompanied by a six-year-old girl, a slight child with a pale complexion and hair so fair that it looked almost white. The child looked at Kate as she came in—at first curiously and then with some alarm, clutching Alexa's hand for reassurance.

"This is Asha," said Alexa. "Asha, this is your aunt Kate. I told you she was coming. She's going to live with us at Blaize."

"Hello, Asha," said Kate. She did not attempt to embrace the little girl or even hold out her hand to be shaken. Children, she knew, were frightened of freaks. "I look very odd, don't I? I've been ill, you see. But I'm better now, and I expect my hair will grow again quite quickly. What shall I do to cover up my funny head until then? Do you think I ought to wear a hat? Or a scarf?"

Asha stared at Kate with wide blue eyes, but did not answer. For a moment she stood still, rubbing one foot up and down her other leg. Then she let go of Alexa's hand and—still without speaking—ran out of the room.

"Your granddaughter?" asked Kate. She too had some catching up to do. In 1917 Alexa had had two young children: Frisca, blonde and bouncing, and Pirry, heir to the Glanville title and fortune. Asha might easily be the child of one of them—but Alexa was shaking her head.

"No. Asha is my great-niece. When I introduced you as her aunt

Kate, I wasn't giving you a courtesy title. Her father was your brother Grant. He died a few months ago."

Kate felt ashamed that such information should come to her as news. It would be hypocritical to mourn for someone she had not seen since his infancy, but that thought alone reminded her how little she deserved to be received back into the family. Still, perhaps she had earned her reinstatement by the intensity of her wish throughout the past eight years to return to England as soon as it should be possible: to become a Lorimer again, surrounded by all the other Lorimers. Every death in the family deprived her of part of the reassurance she needed, but every new member of it was someone she could love.

"Asha's mother?" she asked.

"She's dead as well. The child's very much alone in the world, except for me."

Asha returned carrying an armful of hats. She dropped them on the floor and then silently handed them one at a time to Kate. Her own school beret brought the first smile to the little girl's blue eyes as it lay flat on the top of her aunt's head. "Too small," said Kate, smiling back.

The next was a wide-brimmed straw which perhaps Alexa kept for hot days in the garden. "Too scratchy."

Number three had clearly been discarded from normal use and handed down to a dressing-up box. Battered out of shape, it was still drunkenly decorated with feathers and veiling. "Too grand."

The last was a printed silk square. Kate folded it into a triangle and laid it firmly along her missing hairline, knotting it at the back of her head. "Very Russian," she said. "Just right. Thank you very much, Asha. Do I look better now?"

Asha nodded solemnly. "Will you tell me Russian stories?" she asked. "Aunt Alexa's run out of stories. She said you'd have new ones for me."

When Ilsa was a little girl—and before such subjects were denounced as decadent—Kate had often soothed her to sleep with tales of bears and woodcutters and magicians in dark forests. She did not wish now to be reminded of Ilsa. But Asha, no longer afraid, was slipping a small hand into hers, offering friendship.

"Yes," agreed Kate. "I'll tell you Russian stories if you'll tell me English ones in return."

Once again Asha nodded. Then she looked from Kate to Alexa and back again. A smile of satisfaction spread over her pale, thin face. "So now I have two aunts," she said.

Kate had received a second welcome to Blaize. She was truly home.

I I I

Alexa heard the sound of the car as soon as it turned off the river road and began the winding climb toward the house. There were times when she felt her seventy years: she had to wear spectacles for reading now, and often when she awoke in the morning her hip ached with what she supposed was an early warning of arthritis. But her hearing was still as perfect as in her youth, allowing her to take almost as much pleasure in listening to music on the wireless or from a record as once she had found in the concert hall or opera house. The car was still a long way off when her keen ear told her that it was not the one she was expecting.

Her grandson was coming for Christmas; but Bernard drove a sports car, fast and noisy. The engine she could hear now was expensively quiet rather than expensively noisy, carrying its passenger up the hill in luxurious smoothness. Alexa moved toward the window to see who was paying the unexpected visit.

It was Leo. Alexa nodded to herself in pleasure as he stepped out of the hired Daimler, cradling a gift-wrapped parcel in his arms. Leo Tavadze in 1947 was a violinist of international repute—a well-dressed man whose fur-lined overcoat emphasized the fact that he was beginning to put on weight—but she had known him before the war when he was a penniless refugee. Because he had made his home in New York, Alexa did not see him nowadays as often as she would have liked, so her welcome was enthusiastic.

"Merry Christmas, dearest Alexa." Leo kissed her on each cheek and then added the third kiss that was a legacy of his Russian birth. "I'm here as a postman—bringing your Christmas present because I don't trust any other mail service to care for it."

Alexa undid the wrappings and opened the box. Inside a cocoon of tissue paper was a glass decanter delicately engraved with a view of Blaize.

"I gave a photograph of the house to a girl who specializes in this work," Leo said. "She's made a good job of it, don't you think?" He was watching anxiously for her approval, but Alexa could not resist teasing.

"So that's how you see me—living in a house that's awash with whiskey!" In the dark days immediately after the war that might not have been a joke. But since little Asha had come to live with her, Alexa had felt far less need of that particular distraction. "It's beautiful, Leo, beautiful. Thank you so much, my dear boy. Sit down while I ring for coffee."

"I have to go," he said regretfully. "I'm not staying in England— only changing planes. I flew in at ten o'clock and I shall fly out at two. There was just time, I decided, to bring this in person—but only just."

"But I want you to meet my niece, Kate, who's come to live with me. She spent all her working life in Russia. There must be places you both know, experiences you have in common." Alexa set down the decanter and went back to the window, looking out to see if Kate was in sight. She had taken Asha out for a walk after breakfast, but they were probably not far away. Leo, though, was gently insistent on his own departure.

"Another time," he said, kissing her hand. "I wanted to see you, if only for a moment. But truly—" He was already moving toward the door when he paused, remembering something else. "I shall be seeing Pirry next week. A Greek millionaire has invited me to play at a private party on his yacht, and I agreed as long as the yacht was kept at anchor in calm water. It will be in the harbor at Monte Carlo— only a little way along the coast from Pirry's villa."

"Give him my love, of course," said Alexa. "And—" It was her turn to pause. But Leo was an old friend of her son's, well aware of the nature of Pirry's household. "And my best wishes to Douglas."

It was hard to express more warmth than that. Had it not been for Douglas, Pirry could perhaps have been persuaded to marry and produce an heir to the Glanville title and estate. Alexa herself could certainly have found some girl to whom the bribe of a title and a position in society might have proved enough to compensate for a less than enthusiastic husband. But it was too late for any arrangement of that kind now. Alexa knew that if she was to remain on loving terms with her son she must accept his friend. And Douglas was a decent chap, steady and loyal. Pirry was better off living quietly in what must be considered a kind of marriage than if he had remained in England as part of the secret, shifting, promiscuous society of men who lived on the fringe of scandal and in danger of imprisonment. "Well, my love to Douglas as well."

It was a shame, though, she thought as she watched the Daimler disappear down the hill, that there had been no time for Leo to hear about Kate, because she came into sight only a few minutes later, scattering crumbs on the balustrade and then retreating back along the terrace so that the birds should not be frightened. Asha clutched her aunt's hand. To judge by her pointing finger, she was telling Kate the names of the birds as they came for their breakfast.

Alexa smiled at the sight of the earnest little girl. Asha allowed herself to be looked after by her great-aunt because that was the proper relationship between someone who was seventy and someone who was only six. But in a quite opposite way she had taken charge of Kate, for all the world as though Asha herself were a schoolteacher and her aunt a new girl, needing to be looked after as well as taught. One of the most delightful moments of every day came at bedtime when Asha—who had started to read when she was only four—read one of the Pooh stories to her Russian aunt and then listened critically as Kate read the same story back to her.

The emergency arrangement was working out better than Alexa had dared to hope. In only a few months Kate's appearance had changed dramatically for the better. Although food was still rationed as stringently as during the war, Alexa's tenants and the manager of the home farm made sure that Blaize was never short of fruit and vegetables, eggs and chickens, rabbits and piglets. So rest and a healthful diet—combined with the strong constitution which had enabled her to survive so many hardships—had helped Kate to put on weight, filling her sagging skin, strengthening her muscles and restoring the old brightness to her green eyes. Alexa had helped to provide her with a wardrobe of sensible clothes, and to complete the transformation Kate had acquired a wig to cover her hairless head. It would have been wiser, in Alexa's opinion, to choose a mousy, inconspicuous shade instead of specifying the tawny red which had been her natural color once. The brightness of the color looked artificially young, emphasizing the lines of her weathered face. But choosing and wearing it had been an important step in Kate's return to society, and Alexa had no intention of destroying her confidence by any word of criticism.

Kate was not yet, though, confident enough to look for work—and that was not surprising. She had qualified as a doctor in England, but that was more than thirty years ago, and during those years she had been completely out of touch with developments in modern medicine. Alexa did not intend to put any pressure on her to find a job until she was ready. As the medical officer in charge of two thousand orphans Kate must certainly have been an efficient administrator as well as a caring doctor. Once she had ceased to feel strange in England, some quite small event might act as a catalyst which would prompt her to take responsibility for other people, and for herself.

The most important lack in Kate's life could never be filled. Alexa understood that neither good food nor health nor employment could do anything to fill the void in Kate's heart which had been left by her daughter's disappearance. Even bereavement might have been easier to bear than uncertainty. If Kate had seen Ilsa killed before her eyes she would have grieved bitterly at the time and probably for the rest of her life—but it would have been a different kind of grief. It was because she did not know exactly what had happened that she had to bottle her feelings up, not knowing whether to hope or to fear. Understanding those feelings, Alexa admired her niece for the cheerfulness which she invariably showed in company.

What a pity it was, Alexa thought as she watched Kate and Asha turn and walk hand in hand toward the house: what a pity it was that the family was not larger. There should be dozens of relations—nephews and nieces and cousins—to welcome Kate and swamp her with that kind of chatter and affection which only family life could provide. Family life, it was clear, was what Kate desperately wanted. It was for this that she had returned to England. But the family was so small!

Alexa stared for a moment at the picture which hung in the place of honor on her drawing room wall. It showed an eighty-year-old man in somber Victorian dress: Alexa's father, Kate's grandfather. John Junius Lorimer had had four children and eleven grandchildren. By any normal progression the family should have continued to expand. But there had been too many deaths in two world wars—too many deaths and too many marriages between cousins and not enough babies.

Never mind. At least there was Bernard, whose two-seater was now roaring up the drive toward Blaize. Because Pirry had been the only child born to Alexa during her marriage to Lord Glanville, that family line was doomed to die out. But before her marriage she had had a daughter, whose son—Bernard—was a descendant of John Junius Lorimer through his father as well as his mother. Bernard would marry soon and start a family, and so, one day—in twenty years or so —would little Asha. The Lorimer family might not be able to provide Kate with the number of relatives she would have welcomed. But it was in no danger of dying out.

The sports car appeared in front of the house and screeched to a halt, sending the gravel flying. Alexa watched as her grandson jumped out and opened his arms to catch Asha as she came running toward him. Bernard Lorimer had inherited a fortune and a baronetcy and a mansion in Bristol from the man whom his mother had married when she was already pregnant: but it was another Lorimer—the baronet's cousin—who had given him his curly bright red hair, his freckled face, his wide grin, and a talent for invention.

Like Leo, Bernard had brought presents with him. He loaded his small, excited cousin with parcels to be carried into the house, but as Alexa came out to greet him he was struggling with something larger and heavier. It was a huge slab of stone bearing a relief carving of an Indian god. At some point in its long history the stone had been cracked, and the mark gave a sly, almost evil expression to the face of the dancing god. Alexa studied it with surprise and some uneasiness, hoping that it was not intended as a gift for herself.

"I'm selling the house," Bernard explained, when all the cheerful excitement of greeting had died down. "It's ridiculous for a National Serviceman with three years at university still to come to own the palace of a nineteenth-century merchant prince. Even if I were to marry and have twelve children we should still only rattle about in it, and we'd never find the servants to look after the place. Bristol University would like to convert it into a hall of residence, so at least the name of Brinsley House will live on. Mother had this stone mounted against one of the walls, so perhaps it should have been left as part of the fabric. But I didn't like the thought of undergraduates leaning their bikes against it and chipping bits off. It was a wedding present to her from Robert, you know—or else a christening present to me. Either way, I felt I ought to keep it."

Robert, as Alexa herself had told Bernard on his eighteenth birthday, was his natural father. He had spent his working life in India and died there without ever seeing his son. Alexa nodded her approval of Bernard's decision to cherish the memento.

"So you want me to give it house room here?"

"If you would. Just till I get a place of my own. Good old Grandmother. I knew I could rely on your hospitable nature."

"Who is it?" Asha had deposited her load of presents inside and now returned to stare curiously at the carving. "Why has he got such a lot of arms and legs?"

"His name is Siva. You spell it S-I-V-A but you pronounce it Shiva. He's the god of creation. He's dancing the dance of creation and he can dance better with lots of legs."

"What's creation?"

"Making things." Bernard swung Asha on to his shoulders and carried her inside. "Have you made a Christmas cake for me? If you haven't, I shall go away again."

Asha nodded happily. "Cook and I baked the cake, but I let Cook do the icing because she's better at it than me. And Aunt Kate made a frill to put round it."

Reminded of Kate, Alexa looked around to see where she was. But she had slipped away, presumably not wishing to intrude on a family reunion. It was a habit of Kate's to disappear whenever a newcomer arrived—a habit which must be broken. Alexa sent Asha off to find her aunt and bring her into the family circle. Bernard was such an easy, cheerful young man that no one could be shy with him for long.

It was Bernard, in fact, who asked the question which Alexa should have thought of herself. They were talking again, over luncheon, of the house in Bristol which was to be sold, the house which was part of the Lorimer family history. Bernard had spent his childhood there and now was proposing to break away from his roots, but for Kate he suggested something different.

"Are you going to look for *your* roots, Kate?" he asked. "Do you plan to return home?"

"This is Kate's home now," Alexa reminded him severely; and at the same time Kate, perplexed, said, "I have no home."

"Your birthplace, I meant. I thought you might be interested in a holiday in Jamaica, to see whether it's changed."

"I hadn't considered—I'd almost forgotten—it's such a long time ago." Startled, Kate considered the question before turning to Alexa. "If I did go back to Hope Valley, would I find any of my family there?"

Alexa knew what she meant. Kate's missionary father and doctor mother were long dead, and so were the sons of that marriage, casualties of two wars. But before he died, her father had acknowledged one other son: the intelligent, brown-skinned boy who had grown up to manage his father's property.

"Duke Mattison is still alive, yes," Alexa told her. "He inherited the Bristow plantation and lives on it with his daughter, Paula. And I remember now, he has some money for you. Your father insisted that a fund must be set up for the day when you came back from Russia. Duke will want to settle with you. It's a good idea of Bernard's. The sea voyage will provide a rest, and if you go soon you'll avoid the worst of the winter. A month or two of sunshine would be the best possible tonic."

Kate's mouth crinkled with amusement. The hardships of her life had not affected her sense of humor, and Alexa realized that it had perhaps been tactless of her to show such immediate enthusiasm for Bernard's suggestion. She had not intended to suggest that a break from their life together would be welcome: but Kate, suspecting this possibility, did not seem to be offended by it.

"I hardly think that an English winter can offer much to discommode me," she suggested gently. "But Duke and I were close friends as children. It would be good to see him again, and to meet his daughter." She smiled at Asha, who was sitting opposite her at the table. "After all, Asha, you have two aunts, so it's only fair that I should have two nieces, isn't it?"

It was clear to Alexa that she would go—not from any sentimental wish to revisit the scenes of her childhood, but from a need to meet

Duke and Paula and enmesh her life in some way with theirs. Family ties would tug her back. Yes, Kate would certainly take a trip to Jamaica.

IV

Almost forty years had passed since Kate had last seen her half brother, and her memory was of a slim, athletic young man. She hardly recognized the elderly Jamaican who was waiting on the veranda of Bristow Great House to greet her. Prosperity and the passing of the years had thickened his body. His curly hair was grizzled, and his skin—which once had been smooth and shining and markedly lighter than that of the other village boys—now appeared darker as well as rougher. But he was smiling as he came down the steps.

"Welcome home, Kate." If he was as startled by her appearance as she was by his, he gave no sign of it. They stood together for a moment, exchanging the first greetings and questions, before Duke took her arm to turn her toward the house. "Come inside. Living so long in Russia, you must feel the heat."

The old plantation house had changed as much as its owner. Built at the end of the eighteenth century as a home for a gentleman, it had fallen into decay after the emancipation of the slaves. Kate remembered it only as a ruin, its upper rooms made rotten by the tropical rain as the shingled roof disintegrated, and its lower floor fouled by birds and goats. Now the house had been rescued and repaired. Roof and floors were sound, white paint sparkled in the sunshine, furniture glowed with polish. From the ceiling of the spacious drawing room a fan was suspended. Its silent revolutions stirred the air, giving the impression of coolness merely by movement. Kate could hear the throbbing of a generator in the background: when evening came it would be possible to turn a switch and enjoy electric light. She could not control an exclamation of astonishment. "What a transformation!"

Duke was pleased as he acknowledged the compliment. "I can understand why Father never chose to live here himself, even though he owned it," he said. "A pastor needs to be near his church and his people. And for a white man to be in the home of a slave owner—that would make him a boss, not the minister. For me it's different. I'm one of them, the lucky one who's found his fortune. I'm proud to live here—and the others, they're proud for me as well."

"So am I," said Kate sincerely. "And glad to see that the old house is a home again." But Duke's comment had stirred a doubt in her mind. "Duke, do the people here know who your father was? I shall want to go into the village, of course, and see whether anyone still remembers me, but I wouldn't like to say anything tactless."

Duke shook his head. "They think Pastor Lorimer left me the land because I knew how to run it and because his sons were dead. I didn't ever say the truth to anyone. It would give a bad name to a good man. When I spoke the word Father to you then, it was the first time since the day he died." He paused. "Soon you're going to meet my girl Paula. She doesn't know that you're her auntie. She can't know, d'you see?"

Kate struggled to conceal her regret. Alexa had told her that Duke was a landowner, a prosperous businessman, someone of standing in his community. But she had not thought of him in those terms as she arranged the trip and enjoyed the voyage. She had come to visit her half brother and to make the acquaintance of her niece. Until that moment she had taken it for granted that Duke would have publicly claimed his position in the Lorimer family, so that his daughter would have been looking forward to meeting an aunt. It was a severe disappointment to learn that she would be welcomed by her niece merely as a guest. Perhaps, before the visit was over, Duke could be persuaded to change his mind.

He called now for Paula to join them and she came at once, carrying a tray of iced drinks to refresh the visitor after the journey from Kingston. Kate watched as the girl distributed the glasses, acknowledged the introduction with a smile and handshake and sat down, very much at ease, to join in the conversation. Both physically and in personality she was more mature than an English fourteen-year-old was likely to be, and more attractive than a Russian adolescent. Tall for her age, slim and straight-backed, she held her head proudly and moved with grace. The tight curls of her black hair were closely trimmed so that her head appeared small and neat. Her skin was darker than Duke's at the same age, but her English inheritance revealed itself in the fineness of her most un-African nose and lips. By any standards she was a strikingly good-looking girl.

Her brown eyes, too, were lit with the same sparkling alertness which had marked her father out from the other village boys from an early age. Kate waited until Paula, after chatting politely for half an hour, excused herself on the grounds of homework to be done: then she commented on this.

"You have a bright daughter, Duke. I remember how clever you were at the same age. Some of her intelligence, like yours, must be inherited from Father. Oughtn't she to know? It seems a pity not to acknowledge it."

"She has her heritage whether she knows it or not," Duke pointed out. "But Father's reputation—when that goes, it's gone forever. It's one of the things people remember, even so long after—how he tried to make girls in Hope Valley get married before they had babies. How can I say to them now, 'Pastor Lorimer, he was a father before ever he was a husband'?"

He spoke with such certainty that Kate was forced to let the matter drop. She had no right to interfere in Duke's life. And already he was moving on to another subject.

"Tomorrow, Kate, when you've rested, we must talk business. They told you in England, perhaps, there's money for you here."

Kate was on the point of protesting, but decided to wait until the next day. If Duke had taken trouble to preserve an inheritance for someone who might not even have been still alive, it would be ungracious to turn down whatever he had set aside without giving him the chance to offer it.

That night she lay awake for a long time in the guest bedroom, listening. As a little girl, in her father's house in Hope Valley, she had often heard in the night the distinctive music which the villagers had inherited directly from their enslaved ancestors—sometimes frenzied and joyful, sometimes heartbreakingly sad. It had permeated her own childhood and later, after her own child was born, she had hummed the syncopated melodies to Ilsa as she rocked her cradle. But tonight there was no music except the shrill chorus of tree frogs and the whispering of the wind through the trees around the house.

In the morning she asked Paula to take her back to Hope Valley, the village which adjoined Bristow plantation. She would visit the church which her father had built and the house in which she had been born. Hope Valley had been Kate's home for the first eighteen years of her life.

It had not altered much, she saw as they approached. The houses were still little more than shacks and the paths between were still steep and muddy. Also unchanged was the number of children of all ages. Babies were tied to their mothers' backs or literally to their apron strings, toddlers scrambled around on the ground, girls helped their mothers around the cooking fires while boys carried water or played with balls or chased pigs and chickens. Paula shook her head disapprovingly.

"Too many babies!" she said. "When I'm grown up I shan't have babies. All these women, they do nothing all their lives except bring up babies."

"And what would *you* like to do when you grow up?" Kate asked her.

"I'd like to be Queen of England," replied Paula promptly. "I know I can't, but you asked what I'd like. I want to be able to *do* things, to get rid of muddles. And there will be a Queen soon, won't there?"

"I'm not sure that she'll be allowed to do much except look regal."

"Well then, I'd like to be a prime minister. In Jamaica, you know, Dr. Lorimer, the women have to look after the families—get the money and do all the work. The men make the babies, but then they go away. Yet it's the men who make the laws and the women have to do what they're told. I don't think it's right. Is it like that in England as well, Dr. Lorimer?"

"Won't you call me Kate? Your father and I are such old friends." She saw the hesitation on Paula's face. "Or if you find that awkward, you could say Aunt Kate. Young people in England often do that when a grown-up is a friend of their parents—think of her as a kind of honorary aunt."

Paula's smile revealed her pleasure. "That's nice. Aunt Kate."

Kate was pleased as well. "How are you going to set about being Prime Minister?" she asked.

"I shall go to England when I'm eighteen," Paula told her. "I want to go to Oxford. If I stay here all my life no one will have respect for me. But if I go to England for my education I shall come back different, more important." She must have noticed in Kate's face an emotion which should have been controlled: doubt, perhaps, or pity. "Didn't you feel like that when you were my age, Aunt Kate?"

"Yes. Just the same. Like you, I wanted to get things done, to make a better world. I decided to be a doctor. Not as impossible as the Queen of England, but not easy, either, for a girl at that time."

"But you did it. And you were happy about it?"

"Yes." Kate hesitated for a moment. "Anyone who's lived in Europe for the past forty years has had to endure difficult times. But I've been a good doctor. Yes."

That had not been her only ambition, and in the others she had been disappointed. But in speaking to a hopeful fourteen-year-old it was important to be encouraging. She smiled cheerfully at Paula as they moved on to explore the village. Together they visited the church which her father had built and the hospital which had been her mother's contribution, and held cheerful conversations with old ladies who claimed to remember Kate. And all the time her determination was strengthening that her niece should not be disappointed in her ambitions.

It was this newly positive spirit which made Kate listen more attentively than she had earlier intended as Duke, later that day, explained how he had interpreted the wishes expressed in their father's will.

"Every year I set money aside for you from the plantation, like Father asked. There was a trust. But after twenty-one years with no news of you, the money came back into the estate. I used it to build a sugar mill. It's called Kate's Mill, so everyone knows it's yours. I can buy it back off you, if that's what you'd like. Or you can keep it, and then the plantation must pay you the milling fees. You can choose."

"I don't deserve it," said Kate. "I don't believe that people should be rich just because their fathers were."

"Rich? This won't make you rich. But Father wanted you to have something. Before he died, he wanted to think about it being yours."

During all the time of traveling to Jamaica, Kate had been resolved to refuse anything that Duke might offer. But the mention of her father affected her. Kate could understand how sincerely he would have hoped that one day she would reappear to take up her inheritance, because she could think of nothing she herself more desired than that Ilsa's disappearance might end in the same way. She reminded herself of her vow never again to hope for something which was impossible. Whether her daughter was alive or whether she was dead, they would never see each other again. If Kate were not to drive herself mad, she must stifle the smallest temptation to say "If. . . ." So she told herself now that Ilsa was not likely ever to profit from her grandfather's hard work—but there was another granddaughter who could benefit.

"This morning," she said abruptly, "Paula was telling me that she wanted to go to England one day, to a university there."

"Not just any university." Duke was smiling. "The University of Oxford. All her teachers tell her, even for an English girl that's hard. For a colored girl, so far away—" He shrugged his shoulders. "But Paula, she wants to set the world to rights one day, and she's made up her mind, Oxford is the key to her kingdom."

"Would you let her go?"

"If she can win a scholarship, she can go and no problem. If she only wins a place, we have to think harder. It would be expensive. But if it can be managed, yes. I'd let her go. I'd be proud. Father was at the University of Oxford."

"I want to help her," said Kate. "While I was on my way here I planned to tell you that I didn't intend to take any of my father's money. But now, I'll accept your offer of the milling dues, so that when Paula is ready I can make a home for her in England and pay her fees. That would give me a lot of pleasure. Will you let me do that, Duke?"

"A young girl, she'd need a home in England," Duke agreed. "I've worried about that. It would be peace of mind for me to know you were there. Not for the money. Just so there'd be someone to care. There's time yet, of course. Three, four years."

Not for many months had Kate felt so happy. She had something to look forward to, a new relationship to explore, the prospect of a life in which she would have her own interests and not exist merely as a dependent of Alexa. Ilsa's place could never be completely filled; but Paula, who had no mother, had as much need of family support as Kate herself. They could help each other. For the rest of her visit she was cheerful, even lighthearted. She had traveled to Jamaica thinking that she was making a journey into the past, but she had been offered a future instead.

As soon as she returned to England she set about looking for some kind of employment—something which would be useful to the sick but might not demand too close an acquaintance with newly discovered drugs or treatments. In any medical service there was always some specialty which was less popular than the rest.

She found it in a geriatric hospital in the north of England, which offered accommodation as well as work. Her tiny flat—like the hospital itself—was bleak: but except for her months at Blaize, Kate had never known what it was to live in comfort, and she was glad to be independent again. The months and years passed quickly for Kate in her hospital while she waited for Paula in Jamaica to grow up.

V

It came as a surprise to Kate to be told in 1951 that she was expected to retire on her sixtieth birthday. Relinquishing her job, she also lost her flat, so was grateful when Alexa came to the rescue for a second time, inviting her to spend the summer at Blaize while she searched for a place of her own. Kate smiled to herself as she accepted. Had she continued to stay at Blaize after her arrival in England, no doubt her aunt would long ago have become heartily sick of her. But she was no longer the drab, resigned refugee to whom Alexa had offered shelter before and there seemed no reason why they should not enjoy a few months in each other's company.

On only her second morning at Blaize a letter arrived from Jamaica. Paula had won her Oxford scholarship and would be coming to England in October. Passing the news on to Alexa, Kate mentioned the pleasure it gave her to know and encourage the younger members of the family. Alexa gave a startled gasp.

"Good gracious! I completely forgot. There's something I ought to have shown you long ago. There may be others, you see." She left the room, returning after what must have been a long search to hand over a crumpled envelope which had already been opened. Puzzled, Kate read the note inside.

"In 1878 a nursery governess, Claudine, who had been employed for a time in Bristol by the Lorimer family, gave birth to a son in France. He was christened Jean-Claude and brought up on a farm called La Chalonnière, halfway between Sarlat and Les Eyzies in the Dordogne. Claudine's husband agreed to bring him up as his own son, so he goes under the name of Grasset. But his father was Ralph Lorimer. Jean-Claude is a Lorimer. Someone ought to know."

"That note was written by my sister," explained Alexa. "She fastened it to her will and then put it away. It was only found on the day of her funeral. There were some pointed comments from the younger generation about the habits of Victorian missionaries! We'd known about Duke in Jamaica, but not about this earlier escapade. Your father seems to have sown quite a few wild oats in his time."

"I'd like to meet him," said Kate. "The boy, I mean. Jean-Claude."

"Hardly a boy. If he was born in eighteen-seventy-eight he must be —what?—seventy-three. And it sounds as if he's never known who his father was."

"I wouldn't say anything. But—" Kate found it hard to explain her need to know that her branch of the family was still alive and would continue to exist after she was dead, and so abandoned the attempt. "Paula won't come to England before September," she said instead. "I've plenty of time to find a flat, somewhere she can join me for the vacations. I can take a short holiday in France. It will be easy to invent an excuse for visiting the farm."

There was nothing to stop her. The travel allowance permitted by the government was meager, but Kate had learned how to travel with an even emptier purse. She left in July with her aunt's note, a French dictionary and a map of France.

With their help she found the farm easily, for it was still owned by the Grasset family. In stumbling French Kate explained her interest, struggling to ask questions which would not seem rudely inquisitive. She was trying to trace the descendants of Jean-Claude, she told the suspicious peasant family, because one of her relations had been a benefactor—a kind of godfather to the onetime governess's eldest son. The Grassets accepted the story, remembering that the farm had originally been purchased with money given as a dowry by a rich gentleman in England.

Jean-Claude, she learned, was dead; he had been killed in the battle of the Somme. But before he died he had married, and fathered a daughter.

"And has she had children of her own?" asked Kate.

"Five children. Two boys and three girls."

Kate smiled with satisfaction. "What is her married name? Where can I find her?"

"She married Pierre Bedouelle, from Limoges. They went to live in Oradour-sur-Glane."

"May I have her address?"

There was a curious silence. At the beginning of the interview both the Grassets had been surly, not prepared to answer questions until they knew the reason for them. But since hearing her explanation they had spoken more freely and in a friendly manner. Kate did not understand why a shutter should suddenly come down on their smiles.

"You know of Oradour?" asked the farmer.

"I have a map. I can find it. But I need to know where her house is."

"Excuse me." Mme. Grasset left the room without explanation. Her husband also rose, bringing the conversation to an end.

"When you reach the village, you will discover. Anyone will tell you."

Kate was forced to accept her dismissal. Not until two days later did she discover the reason for it.

The bus from Limoges set her down at the edge of what seemed to be a building site. There was a cluster of prefabricated huts, apparently being used as temporary accommodation while more permanent homes were under construction nearby. She called to a small boy who had just run out of one of the huts and asked whether he knew where Mme. Pierre Bedouelle lived.

He shook his head. "Not here."

"But this is Oradour?"

"This is New Oradour. Wait." He ran up to a schoolmistress who, surrounded by other children, was emerging from the same hut. To Kate's relief, she spoke good English.

"May I help you?" She listened gravely. "Yes, I know of Marie Bedouelle. She was the dressmaker for the village."

"She was? Do you mean that she's dead? Then why didn't her cousin tell me? Is there some mystery?"

"No mystery, alas. Has no one told you, madame, what happened at Oradour?"

Kate shook her head. She was angry at what seemed to be a waste of her time, but the general reluctance to give a direct answer to her questions made her uneasy as well. The teacher was offering to show her the way to something and Kate followed, perplexed.

The path led them through two fields and over a stone bridge beneath which the River Glane flowed. It seemed a peaceful enough country scene. A few steps more brought them into the main street of a large village. "This is Oradour," said the schoolmistress.

Kate looked in bewilderment from one side of the street to the other. The walls of the houses were of thick gray stone, but they were blackened by fire and the rooms they enclosed were bare and roofless.

"Was it bombed?" she asked. In her wanderings across Europe immediately after the war she had seen the effects of fire storms in Dresden and Berlin. For one horrified moment she even wondered whether perhaps the British, rather than the Germans, had bombed the area after the occupation of France.

"No," said the schoolmistress. "It was not bombed. There was nothing here that needed to be destroyed. A village in the country-side, that was all."

They walked up the street beside the metal tracks of a disused tramway. The silence of the dead village was intense—but in a curi-ous way not a silence at all. Never before had Kate found herself in a place with such an oppressive atmosphere. It was as though the stones of the abandoned shops and houses were trying to speak, and their message was audible to Kate's heart although not to her ears. She found herself breathing faster, needing to control a horror for which she still had no explanation. They turned aside from the central thor-oughfare and came to a standstill. "This is the church."

Like every other building the church was a ruin. The signs of fire were stronger here: it had destroyed not only the roof but part of the walls, leaving only jagged fingers pointing to the sky. Where the altar should have stood, two sticks of charred wood had been bound together to form a cross. Lists of names, the writing protected by glass, were propped on either side of the cross. Kate stepped forward to see them, but her companion held her back. "Now I will tell you what happened in Oradour," she said.

Even after this promise, the same emotion which had sent Mme. Grasset hurrying from the room kept the teacher silent for a moment longer. "The village was visited by the German SS in June nineteen-forty-four," she said at last. "They called all the inhabitants to assemble on the Champ de Foire." She pointed across the main street toward an open space. "At first, I believe, there was no alarm. There had been such assemblies before, to check on identity papers and search for deserters. The children were led out from school by their teachers, the men came from their work, the women from their homes; even the babies had to be carried out. The women and children were brought to the church, here. The doors were closed.

"The men were taken to other buildings in the villages—barns and garages. Then they were shot. Not all of them died in the shooting. The buildings were set on fire while some were still alive. The women heard the shots, the cries. They began to scream. But not for long."

The schoolmistress paused. Kate understood now what she was about to hear.

"The church also was set on fire. First there was an explosion, with smoke which suffocated many of the children. Then machine-gun fire against those who rushed to the doors. And finally the fire. They were all burned, all but one woman who escaped. That is how we know."

"The children!" whispered Kate. *"All* the children?"

"There was one boy who ran away when the assembly was called. He was already a refugee, from Lorraine, and he had learned to be frightened of Germans. He was the only child to live."

"Marie Bedouelle had five children."

"They died with her here. Two hundred and forty-six children were killed. Six hundred and forty-two villagers altogether."

The bones of Kate's body seemed to turn to water. She staggered and would have collapsed if her guide had not caught her and helped her to sit on one of the fallen stones.

"This is why your friends did not want to tell you the story of Oradour. It is too terrible to say, as well as to hear."

For a long time Kate could not speak. "Where are they buried?" she asked at last.

"There are no true graves. The women and children were burned together, in a heap, scrambling on top of one another to escape. Later the Germans threw many of the bodies down a well. It was not possible to separate them. A new cemetery is to be built soon. For now, the bones have been buried in consecrated ground, all together."

"May I see?"

There were photographs, in the French fashion, around the area where the burial had taken place. But not, as normally, of old men and women or soldiers in uniforms. These were family groups, which might include both a baby and its grandmother. Kate found the photograph of Marie and Pierre Bedouelle and their five children, one of them only a few months old. The eldest, a boy of ten, had a lively, intelligent face. Kate searched his features for some resemblance to her father. But what difference did it make if she found one or not? The boy was dead. This unacknowledged branch of the Lorimer line had been most decisively cut off.

"Their house?" By now Kate could hardly speak.

It was a little way away, on the edge of the village. The family had been prosperous, it seemed, owning an orchard and large garden around the house and a car in the garage. The car was still there, sunk on the rusting metal rims of its wheels. In the garden, equally rusty, a pram stood untouched since the day when Marie Bedouelle had picked up her baby to carry him to the assembly. Inside the house Kate could see how the rooms had been used. There was the sewing machine to show where Marie had carried on her trade as a dressmaker. The stove was still in the kitchen, the iron frames of bedsteads had fallen from the upper rooms as the floors burned, a bicycle hung on a wall with spokes tangled like knitting wool.

"But why?" asked Kate.

"Nobody knows. There is another village called Oradour—Oradour-sur-Vayres. It was a center of the Resistance, the maquis. Perhaps there was a decision to punish the Resistance, to make an example. And then a simple mistake. Who can say?"

"Thank you for telling me," Kate said. "I'd like to stay here for a little while by myself now."

"You should not remain too long," the schoolmistress warned her.

For the first time she needed to search for a word. "The ambience, the atmosphere, is not good. No one comes here now except to weep. When you are ready, return to where we met before and I will give you coffee."

"You're very kind." But already Kate had withdrawn into her own thoughts and was hardly aware of the moment when she was left alone. She needed no warning about the atmosphere. From the moment when she reached the church it had chilled her, driving the blood from her head and at the same time sending her thoughts into a whirl as though by their confusion she could reject what she had been told and so in some fashion make it no longer true.

The abandoned pram in the garden made such a fantasy impossible. A live baby had lain here on a summer morning; a warm, soft baby, kicking and gurgling; a great-grandson of Kate's father. Marie Bedouelle must have believed, as she bent to pick him up, that he would be safe in her arms. Instead, she had carried him to his death. Well, at least she had not lived to suffer the grief of her bereavement. It was better to be dead than to suffer such a loss, the loss of a child.

Ten years had passed since Kate saw Ilsa snatched away from her. The building of Auschwitz and the destruction of Oradour were all part of the same horror. War might provide the occasion for such atrocities but could not excuse them. Marie Bedouelle, burned to death, was fortunate. She had suffered pain but had been spared the long-drawn-out anguish which Kate had endured. Parents should never outlive their children. Kate touched the pram with her finger and began to cry, because she had lived too long.

For more than two hours she wandered through the ruined village, sobbing noisily and without restraint, shouting aloud to the ghosts of the murdered villagers, who seemed to press upon her from every side. She wept because everything in her life was dead—her God, her ideals, her loved ones. She had known all that before, but realized now in addition that even a family could die. Marie Bedouelle would have no grandchildren, nor would Kate herself. The only thing which did not seem able to die was Kate's useless, worn-out body. Her pain at the death of Oradour was transformed into rage against her own continued life. By the time the schoolmistress returned anxiously to look for her, Kate was too distracted to remember why she had come to this place or even who she was. She could not live with her thoughts and so she had closed her mind to them. Like a drowning woman she felt herself pulled down into silence and blackness.

Time did not stand still. In the outside world, minutes and days and weeks continued to pass, but Kate was not aware of their passing. She had withdrawn for a little while from the pain of living.

Even after she had in a sense recovered from her breakdown Kate remained in bed, refusing to talk or to read or to show interest in anything she was told. She had no recollection of the hospital at Limoges or of Alexa bringing her back to Blaize. Occasionally she ate some of the food which was brought into her room: more often she allowed the tray to be removed untouched.

At some point during her illness Alexa's son, Pirry, arrived to spend a month with his mother. Kate was once or twice conscious of him standing beside her bed, a good-looking man in his late thirties, elegantly dressed in a white suit. During those first visits he was sympathetic, but the moment came when he must have decided that brutality would be the greater kindness. He came into her room one morning and spoke far more firmly than usual.

"Paula is due to arrive this afternoon, Cousin Kate. You must get up and prepare to welcome her. The doctor tells me that fresh air and exercise now will do you far more good than staying in bed."

Kate turned away, but Pirry would not allow her to evade the conversation; he came around to the other side of the bed.

"You're behaving very selfishly toward Mother. Do you realize that? She's done her best to help you. She's allowed you to regard Blaize as your home whenever you need one. She doesn't begrudge you that—and nor do I." He was reminding her, Kate supposed, that he was Lord Glanville and the real owner of Blaize. "It's not much of a reward for her hospitality if you cut yourself off from everything like this. She worries about you, naturally. I don't see why she should be made upset just because you won't make the effort to behave normally. Don't you think it's time you showed her a little more consideration?"

"You're a fine one to talk about selfishness." It was the first time Kate had spoken for more than a week and her voice, low and rasping, startled her by its unfamiliarity. "You leave her to manage all the property which should be your business. You refuse to give her grandchildren, although you know how much that upsets her."

"My mother has never been one to coo over babies."

"It's nothing to do with babies," said Kate. "It's knowing that you won't be completely alone in the world as you grow older. It's being able to feel that you're part of something, a family, that will live on after yourself. You don't understand, do you, how it feels to long for that kind of security and not to have it?" She sat up, her strength surprisingly restored by the need to communicate her distress. "A family can die, Pirry! Don't you realize that? Even a family like yours, that's been in the history books for a thousand years. The Glanville family will die if nobody cares to keep it alive. As for the Lorimer family, it's almost dead already."

"What about Asha?" asked Pirry. "Or Paula, if it comes to that. I know that you've had a lot of bad luck in your life, Cousin Kate. I know that you would have liked to have grandchildren yourself, and I'm sincerely sorry that you have this unhappiness. But you mustn't project the same feeling onto my mother. She has one grandson, after all. Bernard may not be a Glanville, but he's certainly a Lorimer."

"It's not enough. You know that she needs *you* to have a son; she needs to know that Blaize is safe." Soon after her first arrival in England, Kate had learned from Alexa the details of the entail which tied Blaize to the Glanville title. If Pirry should die without an heir, it would all pass at once to a cousin. And if Alexa were still alive she would have to leave her home, for there was no love lost between the two branches of the family.

"That's not really any concern of yours, is it?" Pirry's voice was still pleasant, but the firmness in his eyes made it clear that he was not prepared to discuss the matter further.

"No," Kate agreed. "It's not my concern." She allowed herself to sag back into the bed. "And perhaps you're right. What's the use of having children when people kill them? The world is full of murderers. Five little children, burned to death. All five at once. A mother should be able to protect her children. Five little children, screaming, and no way to help them. My daughter called out, and I couldn't help her. They took her away. I had to watch. You're right to be selfish. It's better for the children that they're never born. Never to be born is best."

She turned away from Pirry again; his sigh of exasperation was audible but did not dispel the lassitude induced by her despair. Nor did Paula's arrival in the bedroom later that day rouse her to anything more than a mumbling apology.

"I promised to have a home for you. I'm sorry. I've let you down. You'll have enough money. But I can't—I'm sorry, Paula. I'm not well."

"I see that." Paula's voice was soft and sympathetic. Kate turned her head. Her dark-skinned niece, eighteen years old now, was even prettier than at their last meeting, tall and slim, straight-backed and graceful. Kate could feel proud of such a niece. But she remembered in time that for the sake of a dead man's reputation she was not allowed to claim the relationship. If Duke had permitted her that pleasure, she would have made more effort now to keep her past promise. Instead, she continued to mumble what was intended as an explanation of her illness.

"It was like Pompeii," she said. She had spent a fortnight's holiday in Italy the previous year. "Oradour was like Pompeii. Silent streets and deserted shops and abandoned objects lying where they were left. But then, not really like Pompeii. Accidental death is horrifying, but there's no malevolence in it. Different from murder. At Pompeii I saw fear lying in the ash. But at Oradour I could hear the screams trapped in the stones."

She raised her head and found that she was alone. Just outside the door Pirry, who must have led Paula away, could be heard apologizing on her behalf.

"You see how it is. It seems to have unhinged her mind. I'm sure she'll be better soon. But for the time being—it's hard for you, when you were relying on her."

"I don't need her." Paula's voice was clear and self-possessed. "In Jamaica she was kind and interested—and it made my father's mind easy to know she was here. But he doesn't need to learn any different, so he'll go on feeling easy. There's a room waiting for me in college. She's not obligated to help me, after all. I'm nothing to her. Just the daughter of someone she knew forty years ago."

"I'm your aunt!" called Kate. Why should she care what anyone now thought about her father, who had been dead for so long? But already Pirry and Paula had moved out of hearing. Unsteadily, because it was so long since she had had a proper meal, Kate left the bed and began to search for clothes. Someone had put her wig away in a cupboard; it took her a little while to find it. By the time she had dressed and packed and made her way downstairs, Paula had left.

"Pirry's driving her to Oxford." Alexa made no attempt to conceal her disapproval of Kate's behavior. "Why are you carrying your suitcase, Kate?"

"I'm leaving. You've been very kind to me and I've taken advantage of you. I'm grateful for all you've done, very grateful indeed. But I mustn't impose anymore. It's best for someone who's lonely to be alone. I'll keep in touch with you, of course. And with Paula as well. I know I've behaved badly. But you won't have to put up with me here any longer. May I phone for a taxi to take me to the station?"

"Certainly not," said Alexa. "You can't possibly leave. Where would you go? You need company until you're feeling better again. Put that down and take off your coat and have a drink." She poured her niece a whiskey almost as large as her own.

Kate had no choice. She accepted both the drink and the instructions because she did not feel strong enough to cover the distance to the railway station on foot. But very early next morning she came quietly downstairs to call a car for herself, and by the time the rest of the household assembled for breakfast she had gone.

VI

The last Saturday in August 1957 was to be an exciting day in the household of Dr. Richard Laing. On his way down to breakfast Richard paused for a moment outside the door of his wife's bedroom, wondering whether to wake her early for once so that she could enjoy every moment of it. But probably she would not thank him for the disturbance. Unlike Richard himself, who was at his best in the mornings, Ilsa liked to work late into the night, when both the house and the city were still. There was a housekeeper to provide breakfast for anyone who wanted it, and so Ilsa rarely rose before eleven in the morning.

But in spite of Richard's own consideration, today was to be an exception. Ten-year-old Michael bounded up the stairs and threw open the door.

"Wake up, Ilsa. Come on. Have you forgotten what's happening today?"

Richard watched in amusement as Ilsa struggled into wakefulness and allowed Michael to hug her. It was unlikely that she would have forgotten what was in store, for this was the day on which her symphony was to be given its first performance. That in itself would have given her pleasure enough, but there was more. It was to be included in a Promenade Concert and televised. Millions of people who had never heard even the name of Ilsa Laing would tonight listen to her music. Richard, whose name was well known in his own sphere—as a specialist in allergic reaction—was pleased and proud that his wife was at last to have some popular recognition of her hard work in the past ten years. She was already highly regarded by the musicians who had studied and mastered her difficult music, but tonight's concert would mark a significant step forward in the growth of her reputation.

Ilsa herself knew that. She was smiling as she pulled herself up in the bed, although she could not resist a friendly grumble at Michael's impatience. "There are still ten hours to wait, you know."

"What d'you mean? They're here already. The set was delivered ten minutes ago and now the van with the aerial has just pulled up outside. The men will need to know where you want everything to go."

Ilsa caught Richard's eye and the two adults burst out laughing.

"I see," said Ilsa with mock seriousness. "Do you know, Michael, just for a moment I thought you were excited about my concert!"

Richard could tell that she was not hurt by her mistake. For over a year Michael had been complaining—sometimes with indignation and sometimes with pathetic descriptions of his deprived status—that he was the only boy in his class at school whose home did not contain a television set. Ilsa, who adored Michael, was never able to refuse him anything he wanted and would have succumbed to the campaign long ago. But Richard had held out against it, and it had been cunning of the boy to plead that, since Ilsa was to appear on the screen that evening, she would want to be told how she looked.

"The set is to go where the chess table was before," Ilsa said now.

"As for the aerial, the men will find the best place for that themselves."

"I'll go and help them." Michael turned to dash downstairs again, but Richard held him back for a moment.

"Before you go there's something I want you to promise."

"You mean about finishing my homework before I watch anything? I've promised that already."

"This is a different promise. You're not to take the set to pieces and put it back again until Ilsa and I have had the chance to see at least one program."

The ten-year-old laughed protestingly as he hurried off, but Richard would have been surprised if his son had not considered the possibility. Both at school and in his private hobbies Michael was a peculiarly one-track boy. He wrote only pedestrian English and was a duffer at Latin and French; he had no talent for painting and no interest in music. But he could juggle figures in his head with ease and accuracy; and while other boys tinkered with bicycles, Michael preferred to solve invisible problems, working out what was wrong with something he could only imagine. Such things as wireless and television and the telephone, which Richard took for granted and Ilsa—he suspected—still regarded as magic, were for Michael a source of endless fascination.

The two adults were still laughing as Michael ran downstairs: but with his departure something more than just his physical presence was removed. It was Michael, and only Michael, who could bring that particular look of loving warmth to Ilsa's eyes. More than eight years had passed since Richard—already married to Ilsa—had fallen in love with her. The calm beauty of her face and the smooth whiteness of her skin, strained so tightly over her slender body, had proved unbearably exciting then, and still excited him now. But even on the night when she had become his wife in fact as well as in name, he had never been quite sure whether she shared his passion or merely accepted it.

Richard knew that Ilsa would always be grateful to him for bringing her to England—and that she would never do anything which might lose her the pleasure of caring for Michael. But although she never refused his lovemaking, she never took any initiative herself.

He understood her reserve. There had been too much tragedy in her early life. In particular, the traumatic parting from her mother must have left her insecure, perhaps frightened to love in case she should lose her lover. And she had seen so many diseased and decaying bodies that she had become fastidious, almost disgusted by the touch of flesh upon flesh. With Richard himself, because they were loving friends even before they became lovers, she did her best to control the instinct to shrink away, but of course he was aware of it. In a curious way it strengthened his desire for her. One day, he promised himself, he would not merely possess her but would feel her for the first time dissolve in his arms, giving herself up to love.

Perhaps even tonight. The concert would be a major event in Ilsa's life. She would be excited and glad to share her excitement. He would make sure that there was champagne waiting on ice when they returned for a celebration. Ilsa would reach out spontaneously to touch him with all the warmth and tenderness which she already demonstrated to Michael.

Richard smiled at his own daydream and saw Ilsa glance at him in amused curiosity.

"A penny for those happy thoughts," she said.

He leaned over her in the bed and kissed her lightly on the lips.

"You can have them free," he offered. "I was thinking that this is going to be a red-letter day for Ilsa Laing."

VII

That same August Saturday was also a red-letter day for Paula Mattison. As the organist brought to an end the indeterminate meanderings with which he had filled the last two minutes and broke into the Wedding March, Alexa, in the front pew, turned her head to watch as the bride came past. Slim and straight-backed, Paula looked beautiful in a high-necked cream dress whose cut emphasized the slenderness of her hips. Alexa, who had helped her to choose it, nodded approvingly. Paula had style.

Pirry had style as well. Elegant and distinguished in his cutaway coat as he escorted the bride to the altar, his eyes sparkled with pleasure in the occasion even while his step was one of measured dignity. Alexa sighed inwardly to herself at the sight. If only it were for his own wedding day that her son had dressed like this! But there was no point in regretting the impossibility of such a picture. Pirry was playing the part of the bride's father because Duke Mattison was too ill to travel from Jamaica.

No one had ever told Paula that she was a Lorimer. She did not know that Pirry was her cousin and Alexa her great-aunt. But Alexa had felt a kind of responsibility for her ever since the chaotic day of her arrival from the West Indies. Kate's collapse and failure to keep her promises had long been understood and forgiven both by Alexa and by Paula herself, but even after Kate's recovery it had proved easier to offer from Blaize than from Kate's tiny flat the kind of support and vacation hospitality which was needed by a student with no home of her own in England.

What began as a practical offer had grown into a friendship. Paula was a girl after Alexa's own heart: intelligent and ambitious. She had been the only colored girl among the undergraduates of her generation at Oxford and this singularity attracted not prejudice but a kind of stardom. Almost without effort she became the girl who knew everyone and everything worth knowing there, and used her information to begin a career as a journalist even before she graduated. This was perhaps the reason why she failed to achieve the First-class degree which was expected of her: but it certainly helped her to move into Fleet Street without the usual provincial apprenticeship. During her earliest months in England she had talked about going back to Jamaica when she was qualified to be of some use to the people there, but in recent years nothing had been heard of this plan.

Alexa enjoyed both gossip and political argument and it was for her own sake as much as Paula's that she had encouraged the Jamaican girl to treat Blaize as her home. She had, in fact, offered to hold this wedding there. Since the music school was on holiday in August the banqueting hall could have been borrowed back for the reception. But the parish church was too tiny to contain all the guests on the groom's list—and because Paula and Laker had met at Oxford they had a sentimental wish to be married there. "In Laker's college chapel," Paula had said, laughing; and for a moment Alexa had felt hurt, thinking that a chapel could be no larger than the church at Blaize.

But Laker's college, it transpired, was Christ Church, and his chapel a cathedral. This was a large and a very smart occasion.

Although the wedding itself was taking place in Oxford, Alexa had cast herself in the role of mother of the bride. It was from Blaize that the invitations had been sent out and to Blaize that presents had poured in. Paula had made no secret of her gratitude—and for more than the physical advantages of using Blaize as a base. James Laker-Smith, who was just about to become her husband, came of a good family and had been to a good school and had ambitions to become a Conservative member of Parliament. In spite of all this he was not a snob. But it was likely that his parents would have felt an initial dismay at the news that he was to marry a black girl. Alexa hoped that some of their doubts had been assuaged as they discussed arrangements with a dowager baroness, saw the bride's guests ushered to their seats by Sir Bernard Lorimer, Bart., and watched the bride herself arriving from one of the most beautiful mansions in the home countries, to be given away in marriage by the fifteenth Lord Glanville. Alexa was not a snob any more than Paula and Laker were, but she had never felt any hesitation about flashing titles in front of those who were foolish enough to be impressed by them.

Beside her, her great-niece sighed in admiration as Paula passed. Asha was too old to be a sweet little bridesmaid, too young to be an elegant adult. The straw hat she wore sat uneasily on her long straight hair: nor did her spectacles do anything for her appearance. Sixteen was an in-between sort of age. She had lost her wide-eyed childish appeal without yet having achieved the prettiness of a young woman. But Alexa did not despair of her. There was plenty of time yet before she need step onto any kind of social stage.

When it was Asha's turn to marry, Alexa promised herself as the service got under way, she should have a real country house wedding —a feast of flowers and food and dancing to fill the ballroom with beautiful women again, just as in the old days. But that was all in the future. At the moment the sixteen-year-old's life was that of a schoolgirl—a clever and hardworking schoolgirl—who applied herself with determination to whatever she undertook. Asha's big day this August had been celebrated in the previous week when her 0-level results arrived, for she had attained the highest grade in every subject. Yes, a clever girl. No doubt about it.

The only other recent wedding in the family had been Bernard's; but that, of course, had been in the hands of Helen's family. The marriage was a success, as far as Alexa could tell. No sign of babies yet, but there was plenty of time for that. Helen, cool and capable and always well groomed, had given up her job before the wedding, devoting herself since then to the care of her house and husband. That was an old-fashioned attitude these days; certainly Paula had made it clear that she intended to press on with her own career. But it must mean that Bernard had a comfortable existence as well as a beautiful wife.

Helen and Bernard were sitting behind Alexa in the second of the family pews, but where was Kate? Her current job as a doctor's receptionist kept her busy for five and a half days a week, but on Saturday afternoons—and for this occasion above all—surely she must be free. This was not a moment, though, at which Alexa could turn around. She waited until she had witnessed the signing of the register and then paused for a moment before returning to her seat to scan the congregation.

Yes, Kate was there, sitting near the back. Perhaps she had not felt smart enough to take her place with the rest of the family. Alexa could see that she had made an effort to dress up. She was wearing a hat, although it was the wrong sort of hat. Her appearance was neat and bright. For a woman who was not interested in how she looked it was a creditable show, but probably even after so much care she had worried lest she might be letting Paula down in such company. Alexa herself was fond of Paula, and was well placed to provide practical help: but Kate loved her.

The reception after the service was held in one of the college quadrangles. The afternoon was hot and the wedding rituals tiring. There were guests to be greeted, photographs to be taken and speeches to hear. Alexa was glad when she could relax on the lawn with a glass of champagne. She could see Kate looking around, preparing to slip away; but Paula had noticed this as well, and took her hand to hold her back.

"Are we allowed to know where you're spending your honeymoon?" Kate was asking as Alexa joined them.

"At Bristow. I've had news that my father's illness is more severe than he told me. In Jamaica, to be seventy-one is to be an old man. I want to see him again before—before he dies."

"As bad as that!" Kate's face revealed her dismay, and Paula squeezed her hand apologetically.

"I'm sorry, Aunt Kate. I ought not to upset you with bad news on a happy day. I know he was a friend of yours from a long time ago."

"He's my half brother," said Kate, startling Alexa by the announcement. It was Kate herself who had always insisted that Paula could not be told the truth of her relationship to the Lorimer family, but it was Kate now who was making the relationship precisely clear. "My father was his father as well."

"You're telling me that Pastor Lorimer was my grandfather!" Paula stared incredulously at Kate.

Kate nodded. "When you see your father, don't let him know I told you. He's never wanted anyone in Hope Valley to find out, in case it hurt a good man's name. But for a long time I've wanted you to know."

Paula still needed a moment before she could believe what she had been told. "It's not unusual, in Jamaica, not to know the name of your grandfather," she said. "But all the same, I've always hated not knowing about my family." She threw off her astonishment and her eyes danced with pleasure as she embraced Kate warmly. "Thank you, Aunt Kate. I'm so glad that you're a real Aunt Kate, not just a courtesy one. And then—" She turned toward Alexa.

"I'm you great-aunt," Alexa told her, and there was more kissing and laughter.

"So Asha must be my cousin!" Paula exclaimed. By now her shock had given way to amusement. "What a joke! What a pair we make!"

It was certainly hard to believe that the two young women were related as they stood smilingly side by side. By Jamaican standards Paula was far from black, but her skin was a dark shade of brown, while Asha's was as pale as could be. Alexa had never known any other girl whose complexion was so translucently fair, and the ash-blond hair which had inspired her christening seemed also to be almost without color.

Still laughing, Paula hugged Kate again. "I won't tell my father what you've said," she promised. "But it's a second wedding present you've given me today, Aunt Kate. The present of a family. What a day! A new husband to go away with, and a new family to come back to."

Alexa smiled with satisfaction. It was not only Paula who had acquired relations today. Now that the family link had been acknowledged at last, it would be possible to think of Paula as a Lorimer. Her children, although they would bear the name Laker-Smith, would be part of the Lorimer line.

Kate, she could see, was happy as well, smiling widely under the unsuitable hat. Alexa knew that nothing would ever bring true contentment to Kate's heart except the discovery that her lost daughter was, after all, alive somewhere in the world. She had no other ambition: the job she had found to occupy her after her retirement from hospital work was no more than that—a way to pass the time. But she seemed contented with it, and could laugh at herself enough to suggest to Alexa that their relationship was an easier one now that they no longer lived in the same house. She concealed her feelings about her daughter and lavished her affection on Asha and Paula. So the announcement she had just made was no small thing. When Kate returned to England ten years earlier it was to take up again the threads of whatever family life was still left to her. By her public acknowledgment of Paula's place in the family she had strengthened her own links with that kind of contentment. Alexa nodded to herself in satisfaction. This was Paula's big day: but it had been an important day for Kate as well.

VIII

In the evening of that same Saturday Kate let herself into her little flat and sighed with relief as she pulled off the wedding hat and kicked off her shoes. It had been a tiring day—not just because of all the traveling, but because she found any kind of social occasion a strain, even such a happy one as this. She still kept all her family links alive, of course, but apart from that all her free time was spent on her own. That was her own choice and she was content with it: but it had the one unfortunate consequence that any kind of party caused her as much anxiety as pleasure.

Her decision to live alone did not mean that she lacked human contact, for she was dealing with people all through her working hours. But Kate knew well enough what Dr. Morley's patients thought of her. They sat in rows in the surgery waiting room with nothing to do except stare at the receptionist until their turn should come. There was plenty of time for them to study her lined face, her dowdy clothes and the auburn wig which was not only too bright a color for a sixty-year-old woman but refused to stay in its proper position.

Her own hair had started to grow again: that was the trouble. She had never known whether it was the malnutrition of the war years or the trauma of accepting the loss of her daughter which had caused her hair to fall out in 1947. Whatever the reason, the loss had seemed permanent; but in the spring of 1957, for no reason that she could understand, a white fuzz had made its appearance all over her scalp. In a few months' time perhaps she would be able to do without the wig. Meanwhile, reluctant to discard it but no longer able to fit it snugly on to a bald head, she found herself tugging at it like an ill-fitting hat under the contemptuous gaze of the neat young women with their sniffing children on their laps.

The patients were frightened of her as well as contemptuous, especially when they wanted Dr. Morley to make a home visit. Kate knew that her manner on the telephone was too brusque. She found it hard to conceal her impatience with the triviality of most of the illnesses which the doctor was called to attend. During two world wars she had seen so many people die, and in such pain, that she had little sympathy with anyone who could not endure a small discomfort until morning. Sometimes the patients complained to Dr. Morley, telling him that it was none of Miss Lorimer's business to decide whether or not their need was urgent; and sometimes, uneasily, he mentioned the complaints to his receptionist, making it clear that he would have to take the responsibility for any misjudgment on her part—but at the same time assuring her that she had never yet made a mistake.

Kate knew that he could not press the criticism too far: she was too useful to him for that. As soon as he discovered that she had few friends and rarely went out, being content to sit all evening in front of her television set, he had offered her a flat in the basement of his own house, rent-free in exchange for her almost permanent availability to answer the telephone. She was expected to take down details of what were claimed to be emergencies and to pass them on to him.

Occasionally Kate wondered whether she ought to reassure him by revealing that—on paper, at least—her medical qualifications were as good as his own: but on the whole she suspected that he would be embarrassed by the discovery. In any case, it was because she no longer considered herself competent to practice as a doctor that she had applied for this humbler work after her breakdown at Oradour.

Although the patients might look down on her and Alexa was un-disguisedly horrified by her way of life, Kate herself was content with her day-to-day existence. Nothing would ever heal the ache in her heart for her lost daughter, but she had just enough family life to save her from loneliness and enough good humor to make her solitary life perfectly acceptable. So many people in the world were worse off than she was that even in her unspoken thoughts she would have been ashamed to feel sorry for herself.

When she asked to take one of her rare days off to attend her niece's wedding, Kate had promised to be back by half past seven. Punctually at that time she reported her return to Dr. Morley and switched the telephone through to the basement flat. She put the kettle on to boil and turned on the television set. It was an old set with a small screen and, because it offered no choice of channels, Kate never bothered to discover the program in advance. She left the set on all evening. If there was anything of interest she watched it. If not, she still watched it, but knitted at the same time.

Tonight she had arrived home, it appeared, in time for the begin-ning of an orchestral concert—one of the Proms. The work to be performed had presumably been announced before she switched on; by the time the picture appeared on her screen the players were tuning their instruments. There was a second's silence and then a burst of clapping from the audience as the conductor appeared. Kate went back into the kitchen. To watch a concert added nothing to the pleasure of listening to it: the cameras would move fussily around, picking out individual players and their instruments and distracting attention from the balanced orchestral sound. She heard the quick double tap with which the conductor demanded attention and silence, but remained in the kitchen, waiting for the kettle to boil. The wedding reception had provided her with quite as much food as she ever ate in a day; a cup of tea was all she needed for the evening.

The music surged into the little flat, overflowing from the dark basement sitting room into the even darker kitchen and illuminating them both with a sunlight of the spirit. The sound enveloped her in comfort in exactly the way in which, as a child, she had felt herself wrapped and comforted by the balmy warmth of the Jamaican climate. So close was the texture of the music that it seemed to transform the humidity of her island birthplace into this other medium, heard instead of felt. Presumably it was only her imagination, but could she not hear beneath the swirling strings a faint syncopation, as though drums were beating in the distance? It added a jungle rhythm to a motif as familiar, though long forgotten, as a hymn tune, and reminded her of the lullabies which the women of Hope Valley sang to their babies in the darkness while Kate and her brother Brinsley lay awake, listening.

Kate had passed the same tunes on to her own baby, although she was careful only to hum them, realizing that it would be dangerous for Ilsa to hear any English words. By now Kate had forgotten the words herself, but she was not mistaken, surely, in recognizing some of the themes. She found herself humming again, remembering—for once without bitterness—the day when she had left Jamaica as an eighteen-year-old. It had been a day when her eyes were bright with hope and enthusiasm, her step firm and springy and her heart filled with a passionate determination to help those less fortunate than herself. Briefly now, as the music swelled, her heart swelled again with it.

The kettle was boiling. For the moment or so Kate busied herself with the making of a pot of strong tea. It would need to brew for five minutes. While she waited, still in the kitchen, she returned her attention to the music.

The first movement must have ended while she was rattling the lid of the teapot, and now the mood had changed. Drumbeats and syncopation, comfort and jollity were replaced by the melancholy notes of a single violin at first plucked in sad halftones and then soaring heart-breakingly upward, as though the music was stretching itself through the darkness of night to touch the stars. It brought back another memory, as distant and unexpected as the first and just as poignant: the memory of a night during the Serbian retreat of 1916 when she huddled in a blanket on a high pass of the Albanian mountains, wondering whether she would live through the cold of the night, whether she could survive another day on the march. How astounded Dr. Morley's patients would be if they knew what adventures their despised receptionist had enjoyed and endured in her youth. Did every old woman, Kate wondered, every passerby in the streets, hold in the memory such intense excitements and such deep sadnesses as those she had experienced in the distant days of war and revolution?

One of the Serbian soldiers on that freezing December night had drawn his bow across the single string of a gusle, using the same poignant halftones as the violinist at this concert. Every man on that retreat had known that he might never see his country again. The music expressed the heartbreak of them all. On that winter night the mournful Slav music had been fixed forever in her memory by the intensity of the musician's emotions and her own love for her companions. What she was hearing now was not the same tune, but unmistakably it expressed the same mood.

She had been sad on that evening, expecting never to see her friends again even if they survived the retreat. Her life, when she looked back on it, contained too many departures, too many farewells. But at least, thought Kate as she poured the first cup of tea, this composer who had so unexpectedly touched her memories with his music was not likely to penetrate the privacy of the two separations from which she had never recovered. She raised the cup to her lips but, before she could take the first sip, the mood of the music changed once more.

It was not possible, she thought. Her eyes widened unbelievingly as the plaintive note of the single violin faded away and the whole orchestra, in a dramatic crescendo, swept her in sound out of the tiny, dark basement flat and into the limitless Russian countryside. She felt herself flying over snowfields and forests. But no, she was not flying, she was in a train, traveling on and on, and all would be well as long as the train did not stop. She willed the music to continue, pressing it on as it whirled like a snowstorm, with each wild flurry embracing more and more of a landscape without horizons. It was from a train in the middle of a snow-covered Russian forest that her husband had been dragged away, never to be seen again.

Kate's heart beat faster, thumping the blood against her eardrums so that she could hardly hear the music. It could not be a coincidence that a symphony should run so exactly parallel with her life. A single flash of recognition, one familiar theme to recapture a mood, would be usual enough. That the same work should contain two such musical memories was unlikely but not impossible. But three! How many people in the world could there be who had absorbed the music of Jamaica, Serbia and Russia?

Kate searched for an explanation and gave herself a choice. It was possible that she was, at last, going mad. Ever since her Oradour breakdown she had been conscious of the danger. It was to avoid the risk which complete solitude would have held that she had applied for the job as Dr. Morley's receptionist. Or could it be that she was dying? The pounding of her heart suggested the possibility. Perhaps it was not only a drowning man who relived his whole life in its last few seconds. Some other physical change might have the same effect.

There was a simple enough test. She had only to move, to step from the kitchen into the sitting room, to see whether the orchestra was still playing and to concentrate on listening to the sound. If what she heard was only in her head, then she must look also to herself for the explanation. But if, against all probability, her life had in some extraordinary way been set to music, there must be a rational interpretation. She did not in fact move, but waited for what she knew was coming. It was certain that she had never heard this work before, but with an equal certainty she could predict how it would end. Whether she was hearing the music or imagining it would make no difference to that.

It came exactly as she had expected. The symphony had opened with one lullaby, which Kate had known once but almost forgotten. It approached its end with another, which she would never forget. As the orchestra faded to a whisper, a balalaika began to play the tune which Prince Vladimir Aminov had composed during Kate's pregnancy, ready to welcome the baby he had never lived to see.

Ten years had passed since Kate last allowed herself to indulge in hope. Tears flooded her face as she allowed the unfamiliar emotion to overwhelm her. She did not notice that the untasted cup of cold tea slipped from her hand, shattering on the floor and splashing her ankles. All her concentration was directed toward the moment when the symphony would end and she would hear the name of the composer.

The sound of the balalaika died away. There was a single shrieking chord from the whole orchestra. A moment of silence. The enthusiastic applause of a young and generous Prom audience. Pressing against the wall for support, Kate made her way back into the sitting room.

The conductor was bowing. He shook the hand of the leader of the orchestra. He waved all the players to their feet. And then, with one arm outstretched, he hurried to the side of the platform. When he returned, he was accompanied by a woman.

It was too much to bear. Kate's head was spinning and dizziness forced her to stand still in the doorway. This must be the composer, and the composer must be Ilsa. No one else knew the tune of that last lullaby. And yet for a moment Kate could not be sure. The daughter who had been snatched away from her sixteen years before was a sturdy twenty-two-year-old, strong and healthy even after three months spent hiding in the cellars with the Jewish children. The woman who moved forward now, tall and thin in a narrow evening dress, looked older than Ilsa should have done. Her hair—it was impossible on the black-and-white screen to tell whether it was a dark chestnut color—was strained sleekly back off a white face whose skin stretched too tightly over the bones. Kate's first reaction, in fact, was that of a doctor rather than of a mother. This woman, whether she knew it herself or not, was ill.

Now the camera offered a close-up—only brief, but long enough for Kate to recognize the high cheekbones and slightly tilted eyes which Ilsa Aminov had inherited from her father. There could be no doubt about it. Kate had found her daughter again.

Above the continuing sound of the Promenaders' applause came an announcer's voice. "You have been listening to the first performance of the Cradle Symphony, by Ilsa Laing, played by the BBC Symphony Orchestra in the Royal Albert Hall."

It was a miracle, Kate thought, struggling like a swimmer to keep her thoughts clear above the maelstrom swirling within her head. A miracle that Ilsa should be alive. A miracle that the discovery should be made in such chance fashion. Through the more familiar miracle of television she was actually looking into her daughter's face. And soon, very soon—although it seemed unbelievable, she could not doubt it—they would meet again.

The program was ending. In the Royal Albert Hall the audience continued to applaud and the players to bow, but the camera was withdrawing, retreating backward as though from the presence of royalty. The figures on the platform became too small and too blurred to see. In a moment they would disappear.

Kate's rational mind knew perfectly well that she would have no difficulty in making contact with Ilsa. She could telephone the BBC, the hall, the orchestra. But there was a moment, as the picture faded, in which her thoughts were no longer rational. In the darkest hours of her years of loneliness there had been more than one occasion on which she had feared that despair might unbalance her mind. She hardly had time to recognize in these last few seconds that her reason had snapped at last, because it was not misery which overwhelmed her but bliss, the redemption of a lifetime of hardship and much sorrow by a single experience of pure happiness. Her daughter was alive, and so Vladimir Aminov lived on as well and Kate herself would never completely die. She flung herself at the vanishing picture, her arms stretched wide to clasp it, to embrace Ilsa and hold her back. Beneath the weight of her unsteady rush, the television set staggered and toppled, and they fell together to the floor.

At the coroner's inquest three days later Dr. Morley gave evidence that he had identified the body of the old lady in the ginger wig as that of his late receptionist, Miss Lorimer. But there was an unexpected intervention from an even more elderly lady, elegantly dressed in black, who announced herself to be Lady Glanville and desired it to be put on record that the dead woman was a doctor and that her correct title was the Princess Aminova. The young reporter from the local papers, doing his routine round of the courts, sniffed a good story but found no one willing to provide more details.

Nor were the facts of the princess's death any clearer than those of her life. Neither the firemen who had carried her out of the blazing basement nor the doctor who had examined her body could say whether she had died from electrocution, from suffocation or from burns. So the coroner certified that death was due to misadventure and left it at that.

He was wrong. Kate Lorimer, mother of Ilsa Laing, had died of joy.

PART II

Letting Go

1963-1965

The February of 1963 was as cold as any of the frozen months which had provided Ilsa Laing with her first experience of a British winter in 1946. But in those days of postwar austerity not even money had been able to buy comfort. Now, by contrast, Ilsa's home was provided with twentieth-century luxury behind the distinguished Regency façade of a Nash terrace overlooking Regent's Park. Richard was successful in his career and generous in spending his high income. His wife could have anything she asked for. But of all the pleasures on offer, the one which Ilsa most appreciated was the luxury of unlimited hot water.

The years of filth and freezing conditions which she had endured as a young woman in a concentration camp were a long way behind her now but might still explain her obsession with cleanliness and her delight in warmth. She liked both to begin and to end each day by luxuriating in a hot, deep bath. Today was her birthday: the extra length of this morning's bath time was a birthday present to herself.

The water was cooling. Ilsa reached to turn on the hot tap again.

"Ilsa! Ilsa, you're going to be late!"

The anxiety in Michael's voice came clearly through the bathroom door. Ilsa smiled affectionately at the sound. The sixteen-year-old boy was almost as obsessive in his regard for punctuality as she was in her need for hot water.

"The interview is to be recorded," she called back. "It's not going out live. So the time is not too important." Nevertheless, she stretched to release the water and began to prepare herself for her morning's engagement.

Michael was staring out of the window as she came into the bedroom, took off her robe, and stepped into the dark-red dress which she had already laid out. To be wearing evening dress at half past nine in the morning felt strange; but the televised interview would be shown in the evening, immediately before a concert to be relayed from the Royal Festival Hall.

"Will you zip me up, Michael?" Esther, who could normally be asked to help, was at this time of day busy with her responsibilities as housekeeper. As careful in this task as with the scientific experiments which absorbed him at school, Michael put one hand underneath the zip as he drew it up, to be sure that he would not catch her skin.

"You're getting thinner," he told her. "This dress was tighter last time I helped you." He fastened the hook at the top of the zip. "You should eat more. You didn't come down to breakfast."

Ilsa laughed at the accusing note in his voice. "I never come down to breakfast."

"But it's your birthday. Had you forgotten? You should have come to be given your presents."

Ilsa never forgot the date—and because tonight's performance of her Third Symphony was billed as a birthday tribute, there had been more reminders this year than usual: but she had long since ceased to think birthdays important. Now she was dismayed at hurting Michael's feelings. She set down the mascara which was to add the last touch to her makeup. Even if it made her late, she must not rush any gesture that he wanted to make. But he was holding nothing in his hand: nor could she see anything unusual in the room. He smiled as he saw her eyes searching.

"Richard's checking his lecture notes in the study and mustn't be disturbed before lunch," he said. Richard was shortly due to leave for a medical conference in the United States. He had arranged to stay on after it for three months, studying developments there in his special field of allergy, and then to give a series of lectures in Australia before returning home. "But my present's outside," Michael added. "You can see it from the window."

The front of the Laings' house faced directly over Regent's Park.

But Ilsa's bedroom was at the back. It overlooked a small private garden in which the housekeeper's husband, combining the duties of gardener with those of handyman, struggled against problems of excessive shade and air polluted with exhaust fumes. She looked out of the window. The sheet of snow which had covered the lawn six weeks earlier had been disturbed only by birds scrambling for the crumbs which Michael threw out. Aboveground, nothing but the brave golden stars of a winter jasmine gave any promise of a spring to come. But at the far end of the garden was a black mound which had not been there the previous day.

"It's municipal sludge," said Michael. "Happy birthday!"

"Municipal sludge!" For once Ilsa did not need to act astonishment. "What is municipal sludge?"

"Well, you see, my first idea was to buy a climbing rose and plant it for your birthday. But Rundle said that it would never do, because the soil was too tired. From being used over and over again for a couple of centuries, he said. Then I read about this sludge. The council makes it by turning refuse into a kind of manure, and it reacts chemically with the soil—so if we dig it in and leave it for a bit, I may be able to give you the rose for Christmas."

"Michael, I adore you! Has any other woman in the world been given such a marvelous present. Municipal sludge!" They fell into each other's arms, laughing. "Thank you, my darling. As soon as I get back we'll go out together and smell it. And now I must get the interview over." She grimaced to show her distaste for the prospect.

"Why are you going to do it?" asked Michael. "I know you hate talking about yourself."

Ilsa gave a wry laugh. "Would you call my music popular, Michael?"

"Well—"

"No need to pretend. Most people who listen to concerts care only for three or four old favorites. Beethoven, Mozart, Brahms, Tchaikovsky. A few have moved into the twentieth century—for Mahler, perhaps. If you ask a man in the street the name of any composer alive in England today, he may possibly be able to remember Benjamin Britten. But no one else, I promise you. 'Ilsa Laing? Never heard of her.'" Ilsa had been dialing the number of the local taxi rank as she spoke and now asked to be picked up at once.

"And you see," she went on, "this is a problem which faces every composer now that princes and patrons are out of fashion. If an artist paints a picture, that picture exists as soon as he has finished it—even if he never finds a buyer. But although I can create a piece of music on paper, the music doesn't come alive until it's interpreted, and to pay the musicians there must be an audience. If I'm to think of my music as a form of communication and not merely as a self-indulgence I have to use every means I can to interest audiences in my compositions. Most people, unfortunately, are more interested in the composer herself than in her work, so that's where I have to start."

"What are you going to talk about, then?"

"The interviewer will ask me about my childhood—because if he has done his homework he will know the answers already. And I expect he will ask how I physically set about the task of composition. People are obsessed by the mechanics of creative work. Do I rule the staves myself, use pen or pencil, sit at a piano, play before I write? Very few people are capable of talking intelligently about contemporary music. If he proves to be one of them it will be a pleasant surprise. A *considerable* surprise."

There were to be no surprises. So much was made clear in the preliminary chat before she was taken into the studio. Ilsa waved away the sandwiches which represented standard BBC hospitality, but accepted a cup of coffee and drew on a cigarette as her host leaned forward in his chair to discuss tactics and provide reassurance.

"This won't be an *aggressive* interview, Mrs. Laing. My intention is to give you the cues, in a sense, so that you can tell the viewers what you think will interest them. We'll come to a discussion of your music —and how you see your place in British musical life—in the second half of the program. I plan to start with the history"—he glanced down at his notes "—the very *dramatic* history of your life. If there are any private areas . . ."

"My husband is a physician. A specialist. He has his own clinics— the Laing antiallergy clinics. I'm sure you know about the silly doctors' rules which regard any public mention of a speciality as advertising. I can talk about him at the time when we met, when he was in the army, but not about his work now." Richard had been at pains to impress this on her when the letter from the BBC first arrived.

"And in your own life? For example, I know that some ladies don't care to specify their age . . . ?"

Ilsa's laughter lightened her low, husky voice. "I was born during the Russian Civil War. I first composed music during the siege of Leningrad. I said goodbye to a career as a pianist when I lost two fingertips in Auschwitz, building a railway in below-zero temperatures. Every event of my life is tied to some event in history. If the matter of age is important to them, it will not take your viewers very long to do the arithmetic. In nineteen-sixty-three I am forty-four years old. You may ask me the question directly if you wish."

She had already noticed that the fluency with which she spoke English came as a relief to him. After seventeen years in the country only an occasional intonation or slight formality in her choice of words betrayed her foreign origins. Now he relaxed even more obviously. "I was told I might find you reticent," he confessed.

Ilsa leaned forward to stub out her cigarette. "The time to be shy was when the invitation arrived. It was not possible to half-accept. I made the decision, so—" She gestured the wholeheartedness of her acceptance with her hands. "I'm fortunate: there are no skeletons in my cupboard. Misfortunes, yes, certainly; you have them already written on your little cards, no doubt. If you press too hard, perhaps you could make me cry. But not blush." She knew, though, that she would not cry. For very many years now her emotions had been wholly under control.

That did not prevent her from feeling a stab of annoyance as—face powdered and chair adjusted under the hot studio lights—she listened to the musical extract which had been chosen to introduce the program. She thought of herself as a composer of atonal music. The Cradle Symphony was untypical of her work: it was sentimental and old-fashioned. But she saw that it must have seemed a useful lead into the story of her life, and answered the first, obvious question without any indication of resentment.

"Yes, my own cradle, you might say. It was based on the tunes my mother hummed to me during my childhood. I wrote the symphony as a kind of requiem for my mother—although for all I know she may still be alive."

She saw his eyes flicker as he wondered briefly whether to explore

that hint of mystery; but he was not a man to take risks. He continued to work chronologically through his notes.

"You were born in Russia?"

"Yes, in a village outside Leningrad. It's called Pushkin nowadays."

"Were your parents musical?"

"I never knew my father. He died before I was born. My mother
was a doctor. Not musical in any professional way, but valuing music.
I was brought up in an orphanage, because my mother was its medical
superintendent. But the building had been a palace once, belonging
to a family of the old nobility, and one of her triumphs was to preserve a piano—a very good piano—through a time when anything
which would burn was being chopped up for firewood. She wanted
me to be a musician. But she never had to force me. It came naturally."

She allowed the questions to lead her ploddingly on, past the early
recognition of her talent as a musician, her training at the Leningrad
School for Musically Gifted Children, her first recitals, her first foreign tour. But when they reached the invasion of Russia in 1941 she
became uneasy about the bland pace of the questioning.

All her answers were true. When the Germans overran her village
and occupied the orphanage, she had hidden in its cellars for three
months with those of the orphans who were Jewish, and it was in that
silent darkness that she had first known the urge to compose. But
there was something false about the smoothness of question and answer. The interviewer—because he was facing her at this moment,
knowing that she had survived—did not seem to understand how
unlikely survival had seemed at the time. She had expected execution
when she was discovered in the cellars, and reprieve had condemned
her instead to years of slave labor. Sickness brought her to the very
brink of death in Auschwitz; and later, after the retreating Germans
transferred the inmates to the camp at Bergen-Belsen, starvation had
taken her for a second time almost past the point of no return. It was
difficult now for Ilsa, expensively dressed and speaking out of a prosperous background into the comfortable drawing rooms of her viewers, to give a true impression of how it had felt to endure those years.
Looking back on them, the interviewer might suggest that her story
had had a happy ending; but at the time it had been impossible to
imagine any ending at all except that of a squalid death.

"And after the liberation, did you return to the Soviet Union?"

"I tried to go back home, to look for my mother. But the whole village had been destroyed. The Germans exploded mines under every building as they withdrew. I was told by an official that my mother and all the remaining orphans had been killed when the orphanage was blown up. I'm not sure now that I was told the truth. The Germans who were quartered in the orphanage showed no mercy to the Jewish children, certainly. And they were harsh to me, although by their rules I suppose I deserved it. But they had seemed to respect my mother—and I can't believe that they were such monsters as to murder so many innocent children. There were many such horror stories told, and at that time it was easy to believe them because our hearts were filled with hatred. Later on, I had doubts, and tried hard to find out what might have happened instead. But it was impossible. No one had records of possible evacuations during a time of chaos. And the Soviet Union is a huge country. It's easy to become lost. My mother may at this moment be caring for a new generation of orphans somewhere in the east, in the new lands; but I have no way of finding out."

"So how did you come to live in England?"

"You could say that was a romantic story. . . . "

"You could say that was a romantic story."

In the drawing room of his Nash home that evening, Dr. Richard Laing stood up abruptly. "It's time we left, Ilsa," he said.

Michael turned his head only briefly to say goodbye, before returning his attention to the television screen. Ilsa knew that nothing she was about to say in the recorded interview would come as news to him. He had heard many times the story of how his father, arriving with the British troops to liberate the prisoners at Belsen, had stared in horror at the skeletal figures inside the electrified fence. By his medical care he had saved the lives of hundreds of them, but one in particular he had picked out from the first moment—guarding her from the dangerous generosity of the soldiers who were shocked into distributing their personal rations, and gradually building up her strength until she was able to assist him as an orderly. No doubt Michael did indeed believe what followed to be a romantic story; but

Ilsa understood why her husband was not prepared to remain in the room while she lied.

During the twelve years or so in which they had lived together as a happily married couple Richard might have found it acceptable for her to speak of a romance in 1945 which in fact had only blossomed in 1949. But the warmth of those years had ended on the day when Ilsa had discovered him using his consulting room for a purpose which could have caused him to be expelled from his profession—for the woman with him had been not only one of Ilsa's friends but a patient under Richard's care. Ilsa had not betrayed him to the British Medical Association, but the sense of her own betrayal had left her deeply hurt.

The current state of her marriage, however, was not one of the matters which she had been prepared to discuss in the interview. Had he stayed to hear the rest of it, Richard would have been embarrassed by nothing but the fact that he could recognize what she was concealing. But he was right to say that it was time to leave. The concert—to be transmitted live from the Royal Festival Hall—would follow immediately after the recorded interview.

Four hours later Richard drove her home again in silence. Ilsa was excited by the evening. It was not just that the audience had applauded and that the conductor, over a celebratory drink afterward, had been enthusiastic. Before every first performance she suffered from a kind of stage fright—a terror that the music she was about to hear in the concert hall might not be the same as the music she had originally heard in her head. No amount of trial recording or attendance at rehearsals could reassure her. Only a full-scale performance could provide the electric certainty of success. At the end of the symphony she had been certain. But Richard did not speak.

"You didn't like it," she said as he unlocked the front door and stood back to let her go in. She went straight up the first flight of stairs to the drawing room.

"Technically it was very good." Richard poured himself a brandy and soda and raised his eyebrows interrogatively in her direction.

Ilsa shook her head. "But?"

He frowned over a choice of words. Lighting a cigarette, Ilsa watched his restlessness.

"There was something missing. There was no feeling, no heart. You're growing very cold, Ilsa."

"Myself, or my music?"

"Are they different? When you wrote the Cradle Symphony—"

Ilsa made a gesture of annoyance. "That was years ago. I felt the need then to express a particular emotion. I used an old-fashioned romantic style because it seemed appropriate. It was a side street, a tributary, which has nothing to do with the main flow of my music at all."

"Perhaps that's what I'm complaining about. Perhaps I'm just an old-fashioned romantic who likes to have his emotions touched. I understand what you're trying to do with your atonal music. I can even appreciate it in an intellectual kind of way. But with every year that passes I find it more difficult actually to *enjoy*."

"I'm not writing for anyone's emotions. My music—except for the Cradle Symphony—comes through my head. I don't *feel* it. I'm a channel of communication, that's all. There's a sense in which the music exists already. My work is to organize it, to write it down."

"I'm not sure that that's a wise attitude. You're cutting yourself off from life, Ilsa. I admire your dedication, the hours you spend at your music. But you ought to spend more time with *people*. You should have more friends."

"I have Leo."

"I sometimes think that your affection for Leo is directly related to the amount of time he spends outside the country."

"And Michael. And you."

"Yes?" Richard, still prowling, glass in hand, turned to face her. "Do you expect this way of life to continue forever, Ilsa?"

She glanced up at him, wondering whether she should be alarmed. "For Michael's sake—"

"Michael's nearly seventeen. He's experimenting with his own relationships. We may be doing him more harm than good to live a deception. Do you want him to believe, on his wedding day, that this is how married people live?"

"He's never seen anything but affection between us."

"You mean that he's never seen us quarrel. Do you think he doesn't realize that it's only because we don't care? I need more warmth in my life, Ilsa."

"I think from time to time you've found it."

"Because I've been driven. . . . I don't regard myself as a philanderer. What happened three years ago was because I was tired of being—well, tolerated instead of wanted. And since then, you haven't so much been punishing me, have you, as indulging your own taste for privacy? It can't go on."

Ilsa waited in silence to hear what he proposed.

"I shall be away on this jaunt until June. Plenty of time for us both to think about things. You must decide what you want. We'll talk about it when I get back." His voice dismissed the subject for the time being and he sat down, his restlessness assuaged by the attempt to clear the air. As he set down his glass, he glanced at the note pad beside the telephone. "A message for you," he said, tearing off the top page and handing it across.

As she took the sheet, Ilsa was still considering her husband's ultimatum, and a moment or two passed before she looked down. But what she read brought her to her feet, her eyes widening with an even greater shock. Unable to speak, she handed the paper back to Richard.

At the top of the page, carefully printed, was an unfamiliar telephone number. Michael had written a message underneath.

"Ilsa, someone called Lady Glanville phoned. Says you don't know her. Sounds pretty old. Will you ring her back as soon as poss. She wants you to come and see her at Blaize (her stately home, I rather gather) tomorrow morning. She's just been watching your TV interview and says she can tell you what happened to your mother."

I I

"Ten years!" repeated Ilsa incredulously. "For ten years we were both living in England, and didn't know it!" Had she been alone, she would have cried her anguish aloud. As it was, she could only fumble in her handbag for her cigarettes. "Do you mind if I smoke, Lady Glanville?"

The old lady on the sofa facing her made an almost imperceptible movement of her shoulders, which Ilsa interpreted as indicating sympathy but disapproval. Breathless with the shock, she took two or three quick pulls on the cigarette and then threw it into the fire.

What she had just learned tempted disbelief. Yet Lady Glanville had been too definite in her statement to permit of any real doubt. On the telephone she had refused to do more than promise information at a face-to-face meeting, but she had wasted no time after Ilsa's arrival at Blaize before making her announcement.

"Your mother was my niece. When she came to live here in nineteen-forty-seven she told me all about you, and how she had failed to find you after the war. Everything you said in that interview agrees with her story. There's no possibility of mistake." With the meticulous memory of the very old, Lady Glanville had detailed Kate Lorimer's life story from her birth in Jamaica until her loss of contact with the family after 1917; and then again through the last ten years of her life.

She had explained, as well, why it was that Kate had felt her British background to be a danger to herself and her child. "At first it was because she had great ambitions for you. It was necessary, she thought, for you to be a good citizen, with nothing unusual in your background. And later, when she began to plan a return to England, she was afraid that if you knew of her intentions you might show anxiety, which would alert the authorities. Afterward, of course, she was angry with herself on that account."

"The last ten years, in England, was she happy?"

The old lady's delicate hands gestured her inability to give any assurance. "She felt in need of a family when she came here. You could say, perhaps, that she was looking for another daughter. She found two nieces with whom she tried to develop a close relationship. But I don't believe, really . . ." The frail hands fluttered again. "She wanted you, and she had lost you. She had the satisfaction of knowing that she did useful work. But no, I can't say that she was happy."

The television interviewer had not been able to make Ilsa cry, even when he probed the most terrible years of her life. But she was near to tears now—tears of frustration at a missed opportunity as well as of distress. For a moment she had to struggle for breath as the realization of her loss overwhelmed her.

In an attempt to calm herself she stood up and crossed the room.

Between two long windows, a console table was covered with photographs in silver frames. Ilsa bent down to study them, expecting them to represent members of the family and hoping to see her mother there. But the first to catch her attention was the face of a friend of her own, who could not possibly be related to Lady Glanville. Later she would ask why Leo Tavadze should have been signing his likeness with love and gratitude, but for the moment there was only one question she wanted to put.

"Have you a photograph of my mother, Lady Glanville?"

"I'm your great-aunt, you know. You could call me Aunt Alexa. But I expect you find that rather a sudden relationship. Well, your mother would never allow herself to be photographed in those last ten years. But I guessed you'd ask that question. I looked through my old albums last night. At the end of nineteen-fourteen, just before she left for the war, Kate had a picture taken to send to her parents. I have a copy of it." It was ready on a table beside the sofa: she held it out to her guest.

Ilsa's last sight of her mother had been of a distraught woman, screaming aloud in an unknown language—it must have been English, Ilsa realized now—at the sight of her daughter being dragged away to imprisonment. Even before that, bereavement and responsibility and an unbalanced diet over many years had made her mother's face heavy and lined with worry. Now Ilsa found herself looking at a handsome young woman in her early twenties, with a clear complexion, shining eyes and a wide, smiling mouth. Her long, thick hair framed the strong features of her face and everything about her expression proclaimed her confidence in herself and in the work she was about to undertake. It was the face of someone who expected to be happy and who could have no conception of the hardships which lay in wait for her.

As Ilsa stared at the photograph, her heart seemed to tear painfully apart, as though it were breaking not metaphorically but in reality. The emotion which flooded her body robbed her of breath; or else the room had been suddenly drained of air. She felt herself suffocating and, as she gasped for breath, her head began to swim. Like someone clinging to the end of a twisted rope she fell, spinning dizzily, into blackness.

She awoke—but it was not a usual kind of awakening—to find

herself lying on a chaise longue in an empty room. For a few moments she coughed, trying to clear her throat, and the sound must have acted as a signal, for the door of the morning room opened. The elderly gentleman who came in spoke with a polite, almost tentative voice; but Ilsa was accustomed to look at the hands of strangers and saw firmness and competence in his.

"Mrs. Laing. I'm Dr. Mason. Lady Glanville asked me to have a look at you."

"She shouldn't have troubled." Ilsa sat up and managed to control her cough. "It was stupid of me to faint. But I had had a shock."

"Alexa told me. Not the details, but the fact that you'd had news to upset you. This is no trouble. Not a professional call. I come to have lunch with her every Sunday. When she telephoned, it was to suggest that I should bring my little black bag with me." He was unfastening it as he spoke, and hanging his stethoscope around his neck.

"There's nothing wrong with me, thank you very much."

"Then I hope you'll allow me ten minutes so that I can pass that reassurance on to Alexa. She was worried." He wound a wide band around Ilsa's arm as he talked and pumped air into it to check her blood pressure. She opened her mouth to protest, but was overcome by another fit of coughing.

"Nasty tickle. Does it bother you much?"

"Only when I wake in the morning, as a rule. My husband tells me I smoke too much."

"He could be right. How many?"

"Oh, forty or fifty a day."

"He *is* right. Could you not cut that down?"

"If I saw the need." A few moments of coughing a day, a slight breathlessness, had always seemed a small price to pay for the comfort which smoking brought her. A cigarette was part of her routine of concentration when she was working. It gave her something to do in company and prevented her from feeling lonely when she was alone. The habit, formed in the chaotic months after the end of the war, when cigarettes were the currency of friendship, had become part of her way of life.

"May I look at your hands?" He studied her fingers without making any comment on the mutilation which had been caused by frostbite. "Now would you slip off your blouse? And cough. And again. And breathe deeply. More deeply still, if you can." Ilsa felt the small cold circle pressing into her skin. "Have you always been as thin as this, Mrs. Laing?"

"Not always, but for a long time. As a girl I was quite plump. 'Sturdy' was the word my mother used."

"And since then?"

Ilsa heard the question, but did not answer it immediately. The casual mention of her mother had upset her again, but this time she was determined not to let her emotions affect her. During the war she had been starved. And afterward, when it might have been expected that she would eat voraciously, the self-control that Richard had taught her in the first days of liberation had become another habit. She had found herself regarding food almost with disgust, and ate in order to stay alive, but not for pleasure. "I haven't much of an appetite," she said.

"Let's hope that Alexa's cook can change that." Dr. Mason put the stethoscope back in its case. "How long is it since you last had a complete medical check?"

"Many years. I'm never ill. And my husband is a doctor, so—"

"From my own experience I know that doctors recognize illness everywhere except in their own families. Unless it falls into their speciality, and then they see it where it doesn't exist. I think you should let someone look at your chest, Mrs. Laing. Take an X ray, I mean. I'll give you a note to a hospital. Or you may prefer to go to your own doctor. And if you could cut down on the cigarettes in the meantime, that would help you to find out whether the coughing diminishes as a result. Now then, I'm to ask you to come and have a drink before lunch as soon as you feel up to it."

Ilsa returned to the drawing room just as Alexa was accepting a generous glass of whiskey from a good-looking man of about fifty. His stylish, although casual, outfit of pale-blue slacks and polo-necked sweater, with a navy-blue blazer, covered a trim figure, and only the thinness of his carefully combed sandy hair gave a clue to his age, for his suntanned face was smooth and unworried. He smiled at Ilsa with a mixture of friendliness and curiosity as he waited for Alexa to introduce him.

"Ilsa, my dear, this is my son, Pirry. Pirry, your new cousin, Ilsa Laing."

Ilsa had not yet come to terms with the discovery that she possessed an English great-aunt. No doubt it followed naturally enough that she must expect to find herself part of a complete family; but her bewilderment must have shown on her face, for Pirry laughed sympathetically as he raised her hand lightly to his lips.

"I stayed out of the room while Mother was breaking the news, so that you wouldn't feel completely overwhelmed by unexpected relations," he said. "But I couldn't wait any longer to tell you what a privilege it is to find myself connected with you. I'm a great admirer of your work."

Ilsa gave an astonished laugh. "It's almost as unusual for me to meet someone who admires my work as to find myself with a new cousin." Warmed by Pirry's open charm, she accepted a glass of sherry and felt her strength flooding back after her brief collapse.

"You and I share the same birthday, it seems," Pirry told her. "Not the year, but the day. Yesterday's concert was a birthday tribute, wasn't it, for you? And the reason why I was in England and able to listen to it on the television was that I always visit Mother for a few days when it's *my* birthday. So we're both Pisceans. Both creatures of water. Generous and sympathetic and self-sacrificing. Talented in music or art and philosophic about accepting the ups and downs of life. Naturally I'm only emphasizing our good points."

"You surely don't believe in all that nonsense about the stars, Pirry?" said Alexa accusingly.

"Certainly I do. What can be more satisfactory than to learn that one's character has been fixed forever at the precise moment of one's birth, so that there's no point in making the slightest effort to improve and all one's imperfections are the fault of one's mother. If you think that my consumption of champagne is overenthusiastic, you should have given birth two days earlier, to make me a reserved, intellectual Aquarian. Now, cousin Ilsa, if you would turn round, you have yet another cousin to meet. But this is positively the last—for today, at least. This is Asha Lorimer."

Asha was a tall young woman in her early twenties, with a transparently pale complexion and straight, shoulder-length hair so fair that it seemed almost colorless. The severity of the spectacles she wore contrasted strongly with the luminosity of her skin, becoming almost a disguise; but behind them her blue eyes were as lively as Pirry's.

"Like Pirry, I kept out of the way," she said as she shook hands. "You can't have the faintest idea who I am, can you?"

"Let me explain." Alexa was drawing wavering lines on a sheet of paper, but broke off to point to an oil painting of a somber Victorian gentleman which hung above the display of photographs. "That portrait there is of my father, John Junius Lorimer. He had four children. I was the youngest, by many years. Your grandfather, Ralph Lorimer, was my brother. He went out to Jamaica as a missionary and had three children. One of them—Kate—was your mother. Another one was Grant Lorimer, Asha's father. So your mother was Asha's aunt."

"And are there more to come—cousins, I mean?"

"Not many," Alexa told her. "Not enough. But I have a grandson, Bernard."

"You're forgetting Paula," Asha reminded her. She turned back to Ilsa. "Paula Mattison, the journalist, is a relation of yours as well. When Aunt Alexa said that our missionary grandfather had three children, she was thinking only of the white ones. But he had black descendants as well."

"I'm impervious to shocks by now," said Ilsa, seeing that Asha was watching for a reaction. "When I woke up this morning I had no blood relations anywhere in the world. And now, without warning—"

"But too late for the only one you wanted." Ilsa found herself being hugged in sympathy. Undemonstrative herself, and averse to being touched, she was unable to respond with any movement of her own, but she warmed to the girl who so quickly understood how much more important was the beloved mother lost than the strange relations gained. Asha proved equally sensitive to her dislike of embraces and moved away without fuss. In any case, the sound of a gong drew them all to the dining room for lunch.

Ilsa spoke little as the meal progressed. When she had had time to collect her thoughts there would be many questions to ask, but she had still not recovered from the shock of discovery. Alexa, however, would not allow her guest to isolate herself. She posed a fighting question.

"Do you believe in mixed marriages, Ilsa?"

"Oh, really, Aunt Alexa!" protested Asha, while Pirry grinned at her sympathetically and Dr. Mason looked down at his plate with the concentration of a man who did not propose to get involved in what was coming.

"My own marriage could be described in that way," Ilsa said cautiously. "My husband is British."

"Well, so are you."

"Not by birth. Not by upbringing. I'm Russian. I can't alter that at a moment's notice simply because I learn I have an English grandfather."

"But neither you nor your husband is black? And you share the same religion?"

"Ranji is not black," said Asha. "And you know perfectly well, Aunt Alexa, that if he hadn't come from a Christian family he would never have been sent to my grandmother's mission school. I love you very dearly and I was delighted to come here for Pirry's birthday— and to meet a new cousin—but if you're going to keep on at me about Ranji I shall start making excuses next time you ask."

Ilsa saw the old lady draw breath to continue what was clearly a long-standing argument, so she came to the rescue with a question of her own.

"Since my mother was born a British subject, her marriage as well as mine must have been of mixed nationality," she said. "You never met my father, I suppose, Aunt Alexa?" She did not find it easy to use this form of address, but was rewarded by the success of her change of subject.

"I knew his brother. In my youth I was a prima donna. I sang for Prince Paul once in his theater palace outside Leningrad—of course, it was St. Petersburg then, before the Revolution. That palace became the orphanage in which your mother worked. Perhaps she never told you that? Your father was Prince Vladimir Aminov, you see, and to be the daughter of a prince was dangerous, I suppose."

Ilsa set her coffee cup back on its saucer, aware that her hand was trembling. Her father had been a soldier named Belinsky, a hero of the Civil War. Or so she had always believed.

"I'm more grateful to you than I can express for what you've told me," she said. "But I don't think I can listen to any more news today. It's not just news, you see. It's discovering that nothing was what it seemed. Having to abandon all the certainties of my past life." Suddenly she could not even speak, but buried her head in her hands, struggling to control herself. Once again it was Asha who reacted with quick sensitivity.

"May I ask you for a lift back to London, Cousin Ilsa? When I came to Blaize last night for Pirry's birthday dinner, I planned to leave straight after breakfast. Naturally I couldn't resist the chance to stay and meet you. But I ought to get back as soon as possible."

"Of course." Ilsa managed to recover her composure sufficiently to thank her hostess, her great-aunt. "I hope you'll allow me to visit you again. There are so many questions—but I need a little time."

"I quite understand, my dear." Unlike Asha earlier, Alexa did not force embraces on her visitor, but remained seated as she said good-bye. Pirry's touch was light and cool, as though he understood Ilsa's dislike of being tightly gripped, but his eyes were still bright with a sympathetic interest. Dr. Mason, standing a little apart from the family in order not to intrude, held out an envelope.

"I took the liberty of scribbling this note," he said. "I've addressed it to John Simpson because I happen to know him and respect his work. But of course you could give it to your G.P. if you preferred."

"Thank you very much." Ilsa was polite but uninterested as she put the envelope into her handbag. Her brief collapse was the least important incident in a dramatic day.

Outside the great house, she lit a cigarette, sighing with satisfaction after she had inhaled. The driver of her hired car—for Ilsa had never learned to drive—held the door open; but she paused to study her surroundings. The day, although bright, was still very cold. The rhododendrons which lined the long drive between Blaize and the river were weighed down with snow, and the pale sun of the afternoon was not powerful enough to melt the frost on the woodland trees. The thick white carpet which covered lawns and terraces isolated Blaize in silence and stillness. Stepping in the tracks which the car had made, Ilsa moved to the side of the house and looked down over the gentle undulations of the parkland. Beneath an old and beautifully shaped oak tree, fallow deer clustered around a bale of forage which had been thrown across from the boundary of the home farm to keep them alive. Nothing else in the landscape moved.

"In Russia, too, we knew this silence—the silence of the snows," Ilsa said. "You know"—she turned to face Asha "—the grounds of the palace which became our orphanage were laid out in the style of an English park. It was fashionable amongst the nobility at the end of the nineteenth century to clear part of the evergreen forest and to landscape the area like this. Almost every evening my mother used to stand outside for a few moments staring at the trees—the English trees. Perhaps they reminded her of Blaize. Perhaps she often used to think about her life here. Yet she never spoke of it. Never." She sighed again, gesturing Asha toward the car. "Well," she said as they drove off together. "Tell me about Ranji."

"Nothing to tell," said Asha. "He's just a friend of mine. Indian, as you probably guessed from the name. I always fight Aunt Alexa when she says he's black, but it's true that he's quite a dark brown. He's a student at the London School of Economics—which I reckon is pretty impressive for someone who was born in a tiny Indian village. I admire him. He's terribly clever, but I think he finds London a bit daunting. The sheer size of the city. He needs someone to make him feel at home. Anyway, I like him."

"And this is not approved?"

Asha gave an exaggerated sigh. "Aunt Alexa brought me up. She has the right to fuss over me as though she were my mother. But she doesn't understand how things have changed since she was young. She's ambitious for me in a way that I'm not for myself. I'm a teacher —and in her book, teaching's a second-rate profession. And if I have to do it, I ought at least to get a job in some classy private school, teaching the daughters of the upper crust, instead of in a multiracial comprehensive. Then, no doubt, I could marry the wealthy brother of one of my pupils and move in the right circles for the rest of my life."

"I didn't have the impression that Lady Glanville was a snob."

"No. Sorry. I shouldn't have put it like that. You're right, really. She's not a money snob and she's not a title snob. But she *is* an achievement snob. An elitist. She was immensely famous herself when she was young. All the Lorimer women for the past hundred years have been high achievers—and now you come along, and you're a high achiever as well! Because Aunt Alexa's so old, everyone she likes has arrived at the top already. She doesn't realize that young people may need a little time to get there. If she'd let herself get to know Ranji, she'd realize that he has all the ambition that she'd like to see in me. He's determined to be rich and successful one day. But you're not interested in Ranji. Nor in me, more than to be polite. It's too late, isn't it, for you to accept us as your relations?"

"My mother was older when she came back to England."

"Ah, but she was *looking* for us," explained Asha earnestly. "Everything else had let her down. Being part of a family was tremendously important to her. What she really wanted was to find you, of course, but as a second best she needed aunts and cousins and nephews and nieces. She hoped too much of us sometimes, and perhaps we didn't always live up to it, but there was never any doubt about what she wanted. It's different for you. Of course you must be curious about what happened to your mother, and sad at not seeing her. But as far as the rest of us are concerned, yesterday you didn't even know we existed. You haven't emerged out of nothingness as Aunt Kate did. You've got your own family, your own life."

Ilsa glanced at her young cousin's serious face. It was tempting to protest, to express interest, to make some gesture as spontaneous as Asha's own embrace earlier in the day. But many years of controlling her feelings had left her unskilled at forming new relationships and she could not easily throw off the habit of restraint. Besides, it seemed to her that Asha had spoken the truth.

"Yes," she agreed. "I have my own life."

I I I

"I'm here on business," said Asha, calling on Ilsa without notice in the Easter holiday, a month after they had met at Blaize. "Educational business. I could have done it over the telephone, of course, but when I saw where you lived, I couldn't resist the temptation to come and snoop. I've always wondered what these houses were like to live in. They look so grand from outside."

"Someone who was brought up at Blaize is surely not impressed by this. It's different for me. My mother had just one room for living and sleeping and working, and as a child my only territory was a bed in an alcove off that room, with a curtain to draw across."

"It was in a palace, all the same."

"When a palace is occupied by two thousand people, it ceases to be palatial. Would you like to see over the house?"

"Yes, please."

Ilsa laughed at her cousin's frankness and gave her a conducted tour of all except the housekeeper's basement flat. "As you see," she pointed out when they returned to the drawing room, "a large part of the house consists of the hall and stairwell. Our heating bills are astronomical."

"Is your husband very rich?"

"Yes." Ilsa did not resent the inquisition. At Blaize she had been given information, and no one had spoiled the occasion by asking questions in return. But it was natural that her relations should be curious. "He's a specialist in allergies, and he owns two clinics. One is in the country: patients come from all over the world, sometimes for very long stays. Everything in their diet and environment is controlled —even the air. The other clinic is in London: for consultations and tests and diet control. It may take a long time to discover exactly what is causing an allergic reaction, but Richard always succeeds in the end. That's satisfying for him, and satisfying for the patients as well, so they don't seem to mind paying high fees. Of course, the expenses of running the clinics are very high. And the tax bills also. But after all that"—she waved her hand round the elegantly furnished drawing room—"there is enough."

"Lucky you. Well. To business. For my sins, I have to help with careers at school. I don't deal with the individual interviews, but every week I have to find someone to give a talk to the children who are in their last year. Once a fortnight I'm producing a thoroughly useful person to talk about the sort of job which most of the children will in fact end up doing—someone from a bank, or Marks and Spencer, or the army, or a secretarial agency, or our local furniture factory, or London Transport; you can imagine the sort of thing. But on alternate Thursdays I try to introduce some new idea. And I wondered if I could persuade you to give a talk on being a composer. Not a lesson— not telling them *how* to compose. Just describing what it's like as a career."

It took Ilsa only a few seconds to consider the request and reject it. "Composing music is a vocation, not a career," she said. "My kind of music, at least. None of your pupils, Asha, will ever have heard of me.

They will never have listened to my music. They won't want to be like me, so how can I inspire them? You need someone who writes pop songs, or television jingles. Start with the music which the children would like to compose before introducing them to a man who does it."

"That's half the point. All the composers I know about are men. Except you. I want a woman. It's part of the process of jolting the children's ideas. For at least three of next term's talks I want to produce a woman who's the tops in her own field—to stop the boys believing that women are no good at anything serious, and to show the girls that a woman can make a success of almost any career."

Ilsa laughed sympathetically, but did not change her mind. "I understand that you hope to make your pupils ambitious, but I suppose they will all have to earn their own livings when they leave school."

"Yes."

"Then I'm the worst possible example. No one can earn a living by composing works for the concert hall—which is all that I do. Well, perhaps half a dozen people in the world; not more. If you studied a list of contemporary composers, you would find that one or two had a private income, others earn money as conductors or instrumentalists, or teach, or write scores for films or television."

"And you?"

"I live as a parasite on my husband's income," Ilsa confessed. "His earnings give me the time I need to do exactly what I like. I'm not expected to contribute to the family expenses; if I were, we should have had some hungry days! I'm not ashamed of being so dependent; I'm grateful. All through history creative musicians have looked for patrons. Mine happens to be Richard Laing. I suspect that isn't precisely the message you're trying to preach."

"No," agreed Asha honestly. "Independence is the name of the game. The girls I teach take it for granted that there's always going to be someone else to tell them what to do. They don't realize that their ideas are out of date already. I want to put them in control of their own lives."

"You can't imagine yourself being dependent on anyone, then?"

"Oh yes. One day I'd like to get married and have children, and I don't agree with those women who have a baby and promptly hand it over to a child minder. But I think it's important to taste indepen-

dence before you give it up. And anyway, I wouldn't think of marriage as dependence. My husband and I would be bringing up our
children together: it would be his job to provide the money and mine
to provide the care."

"How delightfully old-fashioned of you!" laughed Ilsa. "And speaking of children"—she had heard the slamming of the front door,
followed by whistling on the stairs, and waited for Michael to appear
—"let me introduce Michael to you. Michael, this is Asha Lorimer,
one of my new cousins."

Asha looked surprised as she shook hands with Michael and chatted
for a few moments about the chess tournament in which he had just
been playing. "You didn't tell us you had a son," she said to Ilsa.
"Well, of course, we didn't ask you; too busy pushing the names of
strange relatives at you to spare time for the ones you had already. It
makes it even sadder that Aunt Kate never knew what happened to
you. It was the thing that upset her most, believing that she hadn't
got any descendants. If she'd only known that there was not only you,
but that she had a grandson as well!"

"Except that actually," began Michael. He caught Ilsa's eye, as
though uncertain whether it would be in order to continue, and
changed his mind about what he had intended to say. "If you'll excuse me," he mumbled. "I'm supposed to phone the match result
through."

He disappeared at speed, and Asha stood up. "Well, I've failed in
my mission, so I'd better be off. Don't bother to come downstairs; I
can see myself out." She stepped toward Ilsa, preparing to kiss her
goodbye, and then checked herself. "Sorry," she said.

Ilsa wondered why she was apologizing and then remembered that
at their last meeting she had stepped back from Asha's embrace.
"You're very observant," she said. "I'm the one who should say that
I'm sorry."

"Not important." Asha was smiling. "Some families are kissing
families and some aren't. As an orphan, I got a lot of fussing when I
was a little girl, so I developed the kissing habit young."

"I suppose we're all conditioned by our childhoods. You were an
orphan brought up in a loving family. I was a loved daughter brought
up in an orphanage. My mother couldn't favor me in front of the
other children, so she only kissed me in private. It was a special treat,

not a normal gesture. But that's not so important. I would really like to feel myself part of your family, to adopt your habits. What stops me—" Ilsa paused, glancing at Asha to guess whether she would want to hear, and collecting her strength to go on.

"The day that the British troops came to Belsen," she said, "I was following Richard through the camp. I had just met him for the first time. We passed some soldiers who had dug a pit and were pushing bodies into it with their shovels. Richard was horrified; he was horrified by everything he saw that day. He tried to prevent me from seeing. And he was horrified again to realize that I wasn't shocked— because this was a familiar sight to me. At least, I believed at the time that I wasn't shocked. It was later, after I came to England, that the nightmares began. At night, I would see again the people I'd met during the day. Fat, healthy, smiling people. But in my dreams they would be naked, and when I touched them—"

She stopped abruptly, unable after all to describe how it had felt, even in imagination, to reach out to firm flesh and feel her fingers breaking through into rottenness. Nor could she confess that it was not always a nightmare—that sometimes even by day, confronted with real people, she had hardly been able to control her terror that she might reach out and find herself shaking a fleshless hand.

"Is it still like that?" asked Asha.

"No. Michael cured that part of it. Seeing him as a baby, watching him grow, *knowing* that his body was healthy, I could never have nightmares about him. As he grew up, I was able to accept other people for what they seemed. But never myself." The nightmare had changed direction. Now she recoiled from the touch of strangers in case they should discover the rottenness within herself. And yet she was perfectly healthy. It was all an illusion.

"Was there no one who could help you?"

"If I'd met my mother again . . . To be held by the one person . . . but it's too late for that now. Richard wanted me to see a psychiatrist. Since I'd allowed him, as a doctor, to restore my body, he didn't see why I should object to letting someone else heal my mind."

"And did you?"

"It's hard to explain. When you've been near to death, or in pain, or in danger over a long period, you learn to put yourself somehow outside your own body—so that you don't care what's happening to it." Ilsa wondered whether it was possible for someone so young and safe to understand. "By the time the war ended, I was living only in my mind; my mind was myself. And the music came from my mind. I couldn't afford to let anyone meddle with it." She gave a gasp, half of laughter and half of dismay. "I've never put that into words before. How self-centered it sounds!"

"You really are a Lorimer," Asha told her.

"What's so distinctive about Lorimers?"

"Single-minded determination. Devotion to whatever talent they may possess. Once upon a time the Lorimer family was immensely wealthy, I'm told. That old man in Aunt Alexa's portrait owned a bank in Bristol. But the bank crashed and he lost the whole of his fortune. Ever since then the family fortunes have rested on talent and ambition. And I don't mean fortune just in the sense of money, but of happiness as well. Lorimers are only contented in terms of success in whatever field they've chosen. You're a composer, and you don't care about being happy as long as you can compose. Or rather as long as you're composing, you *are* happy. Is that right?"

Ilsa was taken aback by the speed with which her young cousin had summed her up. "Are you telling me that every member of my new family is so single-minded? Yourself, for example?"

"Oh, I'm a freak by family standards," Asha said cheerfully. "Devoted to the pursuit of happiness, you might say. Ordinary happiness. I enjoy teaching and one day I shall enjoy being married. But I'm never going to be best in the world at anything. Quite different from you. You're the genuine article—a hallmarked Lorimer."

"I wish that were true. I'd like to feel that I belonged. But it's not easy. I've already had to discard everything I thought I knew about my parents. To go further, to become part of your family, I feel that I'd need to let go of everything I take for granted in my present life—to be born again. Do you understand?"

"Yes, I do. And why should you want to try? I'm only suggesting that in one sense you belong already. The Lorimer genes have an identity of their own. Without knowing anything about your son, I'd guess that there's some sphere in which he's determined to succeed."

"That's true. He wants to be an astrophysicist and reorganize the universe. But—" Ilsa hesitated and then made up her mind. "But he's not in fact a Lorimer. My husband's son, but not mine. That's what he was going to say a few minutes ago—that he's not my mother's descendant by blood."

"Oh." Asha considered this for a moment. "Perhaps that makes it less sad that Aunt Kate never knew about him. Ilsa, I mustn't keep you any longer. I'm sorry you won't inspire my fifth form to write symphonies! 'Bye for now." She moved toward the door, raised her hand in cheerful farewell and ran lightly downstairs. As the front door closed behind her, Michael came back into the room.

"Was that an awful gaffe?" he asked. "I thought it would be all right to tell Asha since she's part of the family. But then I could see that you didn't want me to. I stopped in time, didn't I? She didn't realize."

"I told her," said Ilsa. "After you'd gone. You were quite right. It's a family matter, but she's family."

"Is it for my sake that you like to pretend?" asked Michael. "Just because I'm illegitimate?"

"Not for your sake at all." Ilsa had recovered from her moment of uncertainty and was smiling again. "Entirely for my own. I want to take full credit for all your brilliance and charm. I want to think of myself as your mother—your *real* mother."

"But you can't—"

"No, of course I can't. Not in any logical way. All the same—" For a moment she was serious again. "Self-deception can take a surprisingly powerful grip. Admitting the truth to Asha meant letting go of an illusion."

"But it hasn't changed anything," Michael reminded her. "You still adore me and I still adore you—and all the more because you chose to look after me when you didn't have to. I'm at a notoriously difficult age, you know. Boys of sixteen drive *real* mothers to distraction. Under any normal family setup you and I would be at each other's throats by now instead of indulging this mutual admiration."

"Oh, Michael!" Ilsa stubbed out her cigarette and hugged him. Michael had always been able to make her laugh.

"You're all right, are you, Ilsa?" he asked. "I know it was tactless of me to start blurting things out, but for a moment you looked as though you were going to faint. And you really are getting terribly thin."

"I'm perfectly well." The words seemed truthful as she spoke them. Later that day, though, Michael's question prompted her to stare critically in the glass and then to step on to the weighing machine in Richard's bathroom. Richard was a big man who weighed himself every week in order to diet or exercise away any extra ounces. But Ilsa's weight had not changed for years—or so she had thought. Now, as the marker steadied, she saw that she had lost twelve pounds. And she had not been overweight before.

It was not important, but it reminded her of the letter which Dr. Mason had pressed into her hand at Blaize. She had done nothing with it because her temporary collapse had been an isolated incident, explicable by the unusual circumstances. But the doctor—like Michael—had clearly wondered whether something was wrong. And it was true that she had found her cough more troublesome since Dr. Mason drew her attention to it. She looked for the letter.

Mr. Simpson, it appeared from the address on the envelope, was a hospital consultant; and the letters after his name revealed that he was a surgeon as well as a physician—not the sort of man to be interested in a patient who needed only a bottle of cough mixture. Ilsa spent a moment considering the significance of this.

How should she best assuage her growing uneasiness? She could go to her general practitioner and take his advice. Or she could wait for Richard to return and recommend the best man in the field for a private consultation. But which field? That was the first thing to discover, and it suited her mood that she should be in a sense anonymous—not Dr. Laing's wife, but an unknown woman on the outpatient list of a National Health Service hospital. Quickly, before she should change her mind, she telephoned to make an appointment.

IV

At Ilsa's first visit to the hospital Mr. Simpson had been jolly as he read her letter of referral, asked the routine questions and made the routine tests before dispatching her to the X-ray department. At the second visit his manner was more serious, but still reassuring. There was, it appeared, yet one more test to be done, under anesthetic, requiring her to come into the hospital for a day. At the third consultation Mr. Simpson was jolly again. Ilsa suspected that he was about to lie to her.

"I hope," she said, "that I can trust you to tell me the truth."

"Truth implies certainty," he answered. "Not everything in medicine is clear-cut. And most people distrust opinions which allow of no argument."

"What I distrust is evasion," Ilsa told him. "I wouldn't have come to you in the first place if I had wanted not to know. You wrote to my husband, Mr. Simpson, asking him to see you. As it happens, he's abroad at the moment." Because Ilsa had been kept waiting for her first appointment, it was June by now and she expected Richard home the next day: but she saw no reason to reveal this. "I deal with his personal correspondence when he's away. I was upset to discover that you proposed to talk to him before you saw me again."

"What do you want to know, Mrs. Laing?"

"My husband is a physician," Ilsa told him. "He doesn't specialize in diseases of the chest and he doesn't specialize in cancer. But he's kept all his medical textbooks. I spent an hour in his study after I'd read your letter to him."

"If I may say so, Mrs. Laing, that was an unwise thing to do."

"Perhaps." Ilsa shrugged her shoulders. "But it's too late for me to forget what I read. So nothing you tell me will be more alarming than what I'm already suspecting."

"And what is that?"

"I think that in the X ray you were looking for carcinoma of the bronchus. And in the biopsy you were testing for metastasis." She had memorized the terms as she checked through what Richard's book called the presentations, with a mixture of recognition and incredulity.

"Almost anyone reading a medical dictionary can convince himself that he's suffering from some illness or other. It's usually quite imaginary. Your self-diagnosis is incorrect, Mrs. Laing."

"Then what is the correct one? It's my body that we're talking about. Must I return to the books?" She could read in his eyes that his reluctance to answer was because he believed that she did not genuinely wish to know, and became impatient. "I know that the English like to pretend that death doesn't exist, Mr. Simpson. But

I'm not English. I'm Russian. I acknowledge death as a part of life. It's not the recognition that I must die that makes me angry, but the feeling that other people know more than I do about my own life. I want to be in control. I need to know the facts."

There was a short silence: but probably, she thought, he had decided to believe her.

"Let me ask one more question first, Mrs. Laing. I ought to have put it to you earlier, but the possibility it raises is not often found in a professional woman like yourself. Have you ever in your life had any contact with asbestos?"

"I don't think so."

"It could be a very long time ago. Think right back."

"I don't even know what it looks like."

Mr. Simpson opened a drawer of his desk and passed across two sealed glass jars. "Have you ever been near any fibers like this?"

Staring at one of the jars, Ilsa searched the past with her memory—so successfully that she shivered with cold on the warm June day. "Not that color," she said slowly. "More gray. But"—she paused until the picture was clear in her mind—"when I was in Auschwitz, I helped to lay a length of railway track. And after, when it was finished, to unload wagons which came along the track. They were building a waiting room next to the crematorium. There were sacks of building materials. Cement and other things."

"They were sealed?"

"Yes. But dust came through. And sometimes they fell and split. They were too heavy for us, you see."

"And some of the split sacks contained fiber like this?"

Slowly, unbelievingly, Ilsa nodded. "But Mr. Simpson, that was twenty years ago! And only for a few weeks!"

"It's a time bomb," the consultant told her. "And your smoking has made the clock tick a little faster. Sometimes it's as long as forty years before the effect of exposure becomes obvious."

"So what *is* the effect?"

"There's a pleural tumor. It is, I'm sorry to say, malignant."

Ilsa had asked for the truth and had promised to believe it. But this particular truth was impossible. Surely.

"That can't be right," she protested. "I don't believe—I'm perfectly fit. I don't feel ill at all."

"What you mean is that you haven't felt any pain," Mr. Simpson said. "One of the problems of treating mesothelioma is precisely the absence of pain for such a long period. There's none of the early warning which we can hope for with other illnesses. But you have had warnings, you know. Your coughing is one. And perhaps you've forgotten how it feels to breathe really deeply. You say you don't feel ill, because any change has been very gradual. But it may be almost twenty years since you were truly well."

Ilsa stared at him for a long time without speaking. Her face still registered disbelief, but in her stomach she was afraid. "Can you operate?" she asked at last.

"I'm afraid it's too late for that."

She gave a sigh of reluctant acceptance. "So I would have been just as well off if I had never come to you."

"A moment ago you said that you wanted to hear the truth."

"Perhaps I only meant that I didn't want to know I was hearing a lie." She tried to laugh at herself. "I don't want you to tell my husband or anyone else, Mr. Simpson. I'd like to choose the time myself." She prepared to stand. "Well—"

"You can't walk away yet, Mrs. Laing. I can do a lot to help you—to get rid of the cough and to ease your breathing. I shall want to see you regularly; and if you have any discomfort I want to know about it at once. There's no need for you to suffer any pain. I'll prescribe some tablets now, though it may be a long time before you need to use them. Later on you can have something stronger."

There was one more question to be asked. For all her earlier strength, Ilsa could not put it, but Mr. Simpson was experienced and sympathetic enough to guess what she did and did not want to know.

"You can do a lot to help yourself," he told her. "Keep out of smoky rooms and streets full of traffic fumes. Don't go out in fog. And I'll make two specific recommendations. Every cigarette you smoke helps to shorten your life. Most doctors nowadays would agree with that statement. I personally would go further and say that if you stop—not cut down, but stop—you can add a little time, recover some of what you've lost."

Smoking had been one of Ilsa's pleasures as a young woman, one of her deprivations during the years of imprisonment. And after the war cigarettes had represented freedom and a form of wealth. Since her marriage to Richard she had never needed to be without a pack. Nevertheless, she felt confident that her will was stronger than her addiction. If she decided to give up the habit, it could be done. She reserved the decision for later consideration.

"It's less easy for me to be dogmatic about my other belief," Mr. Simpson confessed. "Over the years I've had to give this prognosis, or something like it, to a good many patients. Some of them give up on the spot. I try to persuade them that they have years of good life ahead, but it almost seems as though they want to move straight into hospital and die. And because they want it, it happens. But there are others who have unfinished business. There's no valid medical reason why a mental determination to achieve something should slow down a physical invasion of the body. But it often happens."

"Determination to live, do you mean?"

"That's how it may present itself. But the cause is usually more specific. A scientist has set his heart on finishing a piece of research. A young mother needs to care for her children until they're a little older. An old lady knows that her husband is dying and won't leave him to do it alone. Don't go back to your husband's books, Mrs. Laing. Don't start studying all those charts which pretend to show expectations of life. It's too easy to forget that every average has to have a top figure as well as a bottom one. Remind yourself that you're exactly the same person that you were an hour ago. The facts haven't changed. Only your knowledge of them."

That was not, in the circumstances, a very comforting statement. But the consultation was not over. There was more advice to be given, prescriptions to be written and explained. Controlled again after her outburst of disbelief, Ilsa listened, accepted, expressed polite gratitude, queued at the hospital pharmacy, departed.

Outside her house she paid off the taxi but did not go inside at once. Instead, she crossed the road and walked through the park at a pace brisk with anger. "It's not fair!" How often, as a little boy, had Michael flung that accusation at her, his small body bursting with resentment. Ilsa, consoling him, had never contradicted the statement. From the moment of conception, life was unfair to everyone. But it was difficult to resist a feeling of bitterness now. She was in the prime of her life. It was hard to be brought up short just when her talent was gaining recognition. Had she not already suffered more in her lifetime than most people? Surely she deserved a little longer to prove that her survival had been worthwhile.

Calming herself, she turned into the rose garden. The June roses were at their best, still firmly shaped and delicately colored, their petals not yet staining or twisting or falling. Ilsa paused in front of a formal bed of Peace and marveled at the perfect form of each blossom and the subtle variations of color—from cream to crimson, from primrose to peach. Had she ever properly appreciated the beauty of a rose before?

On this warm summer day, the scent of the roses was as soothing as their shape and color. The better to appreciate it, Ilsa drew in a deep breath and at once found herself coughing uncontrollably. Passersby —men and women who had already enjoyed twenty or thirty years more of life than she could expect—stared curiously or sympathetically as she clutched at the back of a park seat for support and gasped her way through the attack. Only after several moments was she able to breathe normally again.

She sat down, waiting to recover, and remembered another day when she had breathed deeply. At the age of twenty-three she had been hauled out of the cellar in which she had been sheltering a group of Jewish children. After three months with no sanitation and little ventilation, the atmosphere was foul, and there had been a few seconds in which the relief of filling her lungs with cold, pure air had kept at bay her fear of what might happen next. Then the German officer in charge of the orphanage had pointed his pistol at her head.

"I could shoot you," he told her. "Now. Here. I have the right."

Ilsa had stared at him steadily, defiantly, refusing to be afraid. Terror came later, as she was dragged away to join the children on their journey into the unknown—a terror not of death but of a life no longer under her own control. There was a sense in which she ought to think of herself not as unfortunate in hearing a death sentence now, but as lucky to have lived so long. She had had twenty years of borrowed time.

Another memory—triggered perhaps by the need to recall her past for Mr. Simpson. This time she was lying on a bunk in Auschwitz, dying of typhus and dysentery—too weak to recognize that a brusque order to report to another hut and accept a change of work represented a chance of survival. The girl on the bunk above—Sigi Holzer, now long dead—had bullied Ilsa back to life, her voice reverberating inside an empty head. "If you've given in, you might as well go on the fence, choose your own death. But if there's someone you love, something that you've dreamed of doing with your life, you've got to stay alive. For as long as it takes."

"Going on the fence" meant flinging oneself against the electrified wires: it was the only means of escape from Auschwitz. Ilsa, painfully, had remembered her mother and the music which was already creeping into her mind. She had chosen to live—and for a little while, before better working conditions could have their effect, nothing but that choice had kept her alive.

What she had been told in Mr. Simpson's consulting room was not dissimilar to the urgent words with which Sigi had urged her into activity. She still possessed the will to survive, for there was so much to be done: music to be written, friendships to be left in good repair. Her mother was dead: it was too late to weep over that final parting. But there were other relationships which needed attention. Richard had served notice before he left that he was not happy with things as they were. Ilsa resolved without hesitation that he must be given whatever he wanted. This was no time to bear grudges.

Ilsa glanced at her watch and stood up. The immediate timetable of her life was not changed by Mr. Simpson's verdict, and Leo would be arriving at her house very soon. Three months earlier, curious to know why her friend's photograph should stand in Lady Glanville's drawing room, she had left a note for him at the Connaught Hotel, knowing that as soon as he was in England he would read it and get in touch with her. He had telephoned the previous evening.

There was one gesture to be made before she returned home. She felt in her handbag for the two packs of cigarettes which she always carried and tossed them into a litter bin. She was making a bargain with fate, following the doctor's advice and expecting a reward, to be measured in weeks or years. But now it was time to put her clouded future out of her mind and discover how much Leo knew about her new family, the Lorimers. In particular, there was one question to be asked. Had he ever met her mother?

V

"The Glanvilles saved my life," said Leo. "If it hadn't been for Pirry Glanville, I should have died. And if it hadn't been for Alexa Glanville, I should have gone mad."

"You need to explain that." Ilsa, while mentioning that she had seen her friend's signed photograph at Blaize, had given no reason for her unexpected interest in Lady Glanville and her family.

"I was living in Vienna at the time of the Anschluss," Leo reminded her. "My wrist had healed, but I had no money or work or reputation."

Ilsa already knew of the hard times which Leo had faced in his teens. Born in Russia, he was a boy prodigy on the violin. But before his fifteenth birthday, his Jewish mother disappeared in one of Stalin's purges. His father, being a Georgian, must have believed himself safe; but the motor accident in which he died a few weeks later was hard to explain. Whether or not it had been expected that Leo would also be in the car, at the age of fourteen he found himself the orphaned son of disgraced parents, with a hand and wrist so badly injured that it seemed unlikely he would ever play the violin again. His homeland had ceased to be proud of him, and he in turn no longer felt safe in it. Vienna provided a refuge; but not for long.

"My papers were unconvincing," he continued. "The one thing they showed clearly was that I was Jewish. To be a Jew in Vienna in nineteen-thirty-eight . . . ! I was to be sent to a labor camp on my eighteenth birthday. Pirry smuggled me out of Austria three weeks before that. He took a big risk for me. If you've met Pirry, you may think he looks soft. Such a charming man! Always smiling, as though nothing were important. But underneath—well, he saved my life. And took trouble afterward to make sure that I could stay in England."

"And Lady Glanville?"

"I shall never forget Alexa's face when Pirry asked if I could stay at Blaize." Leo rocked with laughter at the memory. "So thin I was in those days—half starved. Shabby. Anxious. And seasick; there had been a storm in the Channel. A miserable specimen. And Alexa, of course, thought I must be Pirry's latest lover." He gave Ilsa a sideways glance. "Do you know about Pirry? That he's a queer?"

"I didn't, no." Ilsa had little interest in sex. She lacked both instinct and curiosity about the inclinations of the men she met. In any case, Pirry had been introduced to her as a relation, not a potential partner. "It's not important. Go on."

"Well, Alexa was horrified at first. But if you know her, you'll realize she's not one for half measures. Once it had been explained, she let me stay at Blaize. Gave me a practice room. Understood that what I needed was time and a lack of interruption. Soon I was able to play again, as well as before. But then the war began and I was declared to be an enemy alien! No one was sure whether I was Russian or Austrian—but what matter? In nineteen-thirty-nine, either way I must be an enemy. So I was interned."

"And the Glanvilles rescued you again?"

"Pirry was already in the army. It was Alexa who made a fuss on my behalf, pointing out how ridiculous it was to suppose that a Jewish refugee would do anything to help Hitler. And why should the British taxpayer keep someone who could support himself if he was allowed to go off to New York? Luckily I already had a United States quota number. But it was Alexa who made it possible for me to go."

"So when you came back to play in England after the war, did you sometimes visit her at Blaize?"

"Yes, of course."

"And did you ever meet a relative of hers there—Dr. Kate Lorimer?" According to Alexa, Kate had spent several years in residential work; but between appointments she had stayed at Blaize for weeks at a time.

"Once or twice, yes. She may have been there more often, but she usually stayed in her own suite when Alexa had visitors."

"But you saw her?"

"Yes, in passing, from time to time. An old lady in a ginger wig. And now, Ilsa my dear, it's your turn to answer a question and explain why I'm undergoing this interrogation. What's your interest in the Glanvilles?"

"The old lady in the ginger wig was my mother," said Ilsa.

"Ilsa, my darling!" More quickly than might have been expected in a man who had left his thin days far behind, Leo moved to sit beside her on the sofa, his arm holding her close. "How cruel of me! I'm so sorry. I didn't know."

"Nobody knew." Ilsa felt drained by the mere fact of revealing what she had discovered.

"I'm so sorry," he repeated. "Your mother! And you never saw her in England? I know how much it would have meant to you. If only Alexa had told me more about her niece's background. Or if Dr. Lorimer herself had been willing to talk. But I suppose it was painful for her. And it would never have occurred to me that an English-woman might be your mother."

"Nor to me, of course. Well, it's too late now to be upset."

"But you *are* upset." His grip tightened around her shoulders. Ilsa, suffering from the shock of the consultant's news as well as from Lady Glanville's earlier revelations, allowed herself to sink into the comfort of his embrace. Comfort was all she needed, and all Leo was offering; but it was unfortunate, all the same, that this should be the moment when Richard came unexpectedly into the drawing room. Unfortunate, too, that Ilsa should be startled by his arrival into jerking away from Leo as though she felt guilty.

"Richard! We weren't expecting you back until tomorrow!" But that was a mistake as well; a tactless greeting to a husband returning after so long an absence.

"I left Melbourne early to avoid a strike. Don't let me disturb you. I've been on the move for thirty-six hours, given too much to eat and too much to drink, and I'm never any good at sleeping on planes. I'm going straight to bed now. By breakfast time tomorrow I'll have my body clock in sync with British Summer Time. Give Michael my love when he comes in, Ilsa, but persuade him that I'd rather not be disturbed." He nodded pleasantly at Leo and went upstairs.

"Richard!" Ilsa, dismayed, hurried after him. It was less than an hour since she had resolved to welcome her husband home with the warmth he wanted. Richard waited for her on the landing.

"I really am very tired," he said. "Completely flaked out, in fact. Pretend I'm not here. Coming home tomorrow, as planned." He bent to kiss her lightly on the lips and then went into his bedroom and closed the door behind him.

In the drawing room Leo, unworried, was smiling. "I hope Richard isn't a jealous man," he said. "It would rile me to be suspected of something that I've never in fact been allowed to enjoy. I'll leave you to make your peace with him. But I have two tickets for Glyndebourne on the last day of June. Will you join me?"

"I'd be delighted." She held out her hand, expecting him as usual to raise it to his lips, but instead he took her in his arms, and his kiss comforted her for a second time.

Leo Tavadze was the man whom Ilsa might have loved, had she only known him earlier in her life. They had met soon after the war, introduced by music. Seeking an interpreter whose reputation could carry the burden of her unknown name and difficult music, Ilsa had sent the score of a violin concerto to the famous soloist in New York. On his next visit to London he asked her to call at his hotel, and they found themselves immediately in sympathy.

On the face of it, they were very different. Ilsa's sufferings at the hands of the Germans had left her tightly controlled, while Leo had celebrated his escape from a concentration camp with laughter and good food and wine in pleasant company. He had grown plump, while Ilsa was thin: his expression was good-natured where Ilsa's was cool: his eyes shone with enthusiasm while Ilsa's neutrally observed. When he fell in love with her—and it happened very quickly—he pressed his suit with exuberance, followed by overacted despair. When Ilsa found herself beginning to love him in return, her defense was to withdraw, to force coldness into her voice as she reminded him that she was married. At the time she had seen this as an example of fidelity, and only later wondered whether she had genuinely resisted temptation, or had never felt it. Leo had been her closest friend for the past thirteen years, and he provided the second exception to her dislike of physical contact. She could accept Michael's hugs because she had known his healthy body from babyhood. She was equally at ease with Leo but for a different reason. They had both been refugees: they had both suffered. In a smug, safe world they had in common the memory of insecurity as well as the veneer of success.

As he held her in his arms that afternoon, Leo must have believed that he was comforting Ilsa only for the loss of her mother. He could not have guessed at the other void which had just opened beneath her feet. That night she lay awake for a long time, keeping very still, as though by listening to her body and taking it unawares she could find some evidence that Mr. Simpson had told her the truth. But it seemed that only one of his statements was immediately confirmed: she felt no physical difference from the day before. Only her mental state had changed. She saw the future as a clock out of control, its hands whizzing madly around and around while her mind raced to keep up with it. From now on, everything would be either unimportant or urgent.

Building her bridges with Richard was one of the urgencies, yet she was unprepared when he came into her bedroom early in the morning. Refreshed by more than twelve hours' uninterrupted sleep, he was ready to begin the new day with the sunrise—while to Ilsa, who had been awake until three in the morning, it was still the middle of the night. Feeling the side of the bed tilt beneath his weight as he sat down, she struggled to open her eyes. Her chest was heavy and her throat thick: she needed to sit up and establish her diurnal pattern of breathing. But Richard, looking seriously down at her, was demanding her full attention.

"Too early for a night bird like you, I know," he said. "But I've got something important to tell you. While I was in the States, I was asked if I'd set up an allergy clinic—a new Laing clinic—in Oregon. There's a lot of investment money around for private medicine. It's an attractive offer—giving me a share in a custom-built clinic equipped to my specification—in return for the use of my name and methods and my own presence there for the whole of the first year and three months in each subsequent year."

"What about your work here?"

"I've got good people on the staff—people I've trained myself. Like any sort of detective work, most of my treatment depends on a meticulous routine of tests rather than the flair of one man. I could leave the clinics here in sound hands while I'm establishing the same routines over there. I believe I could make myself useful in the States. And it would be highly profitable."

"So you've decided to go?"

"Yes. That makes it all the more important for me to ask the question which I put to you before I left. You've always said that you could compose in a cupboard if you needed to, so there shouldn't be any problem about a mountainside in Oregon. I hope that you'll agree to come with me. But first of all, we need to have a talk."

Ilsa had had three months to consider the ultimatum he had put to her on her birthday, but it was the hour in Mr. Simpson's consulting room which had concentrated her mind. Richard had been so good to her in the past, and she was so grateful to him, that she must repay her debt now by giving him whatever he wanted—whether that proved to be a divorce or a new beginning to their marriage—without reserve.

"I know you were hurt when you found out about Penny," he said. "I apologized to you then, but you haven't been able to forgive me, have you? For three years. Well, now I'll say again how sorry I am that I upset you. But this time—"

"I'd like—" Ilsa paused to clear the huskiness from her throat. "I'd like to explain *why* I was hurt. It wasn't just jealousy. It was the humiliation of being deceived. I think I could have lived with the discovery if Penny had been a stranger. It was thinking of her as a friend—looking back afterward and remembering all the times when I'd chatted and smiled without guessing. To be kept out of a secret has a curious kind of hurtfulness. But you're right that three years is too long to bear a grudge."

"Are you saying—?"

"I'm saying that I'm sorry for overreacting." She was almost tempted to laugh as she saw the astonishment in his eyes. This was not the answer he had expected. But after only a second, surprise was banished by tenderness.

"So can we start again?" His hand touched her cheek softly, stroking it as though to test whether she would shrink away.

"Is that what you want?"

"Of course that's what I want." He leaned down and began to kiss her, gently at first but then with a sudden passionate force. Ilsa willed herself to relax the tenseness which so often in the past had spoiled their lovemaking. She needed to breathe deeply, but the weight of Richard's body was pressing down on her congested chest while his tongue filled her mouth. So important did it seem for her to give herself to Richard without reserve that for a moment she managed to resist the panic of suffocation. But her muscles tightened: she felt herself choking, unable to breathe at all. It was necessary to push him away as she began to cough.

This was the most violent paroxysm she had yet experienced. Gasping for breath whenever she could, she got out of bed and, supporting herself against the wall, staggered into the bathroom where the linctus which Mr. Simpson had prescribed was waiting. By the time Richard followed her in she was sitting on the bathroom chair with her head buried in her hands and her breath coming in short, wheezing gasps. "Sorry," she said. "Terribly sorry."

Richard's smile was disappointed but affectionate as he looked down at her. "You really should cut down on your smoking," he said, as he had said often before.

"I've given up. I stopped yesterday. It seems unfair that such an effort shouldn't be rewarded by immediate relief. Sorry, Richard."

"Come back to bed." He piled up the pillows so that she could sit with their support at her back. Then for a second time he sat down on the bed. "We'll wait until tonight. What do a few hours matter? And perhaps in any case it would be tidier if I were to speak to Penny first. Finish everything off neatly."

"Penny? You've still been seeing Penny?"

"Not since I went off in February. But before that, yes, of course. You may have found it easy to behave like a nun for these last three years, but you didn't imagine that I'd been living like a monk, did you?"

"But—" Ilsa found herself stammering with the need to adjust her earlier decision to a situation which she should have anticipated. A few hours earlier it had seemed incontrovertible that gratitude should express itself in the restoration of a loving marriage relationship which would offer Richard pleasure now, and later would comfort him with the thought that before she died they had ended the coolness which had grown between them. But it would be no kindness to let him end a love affair which might last him for the rest of his life for the sake of only a year or two with a sick wife. "That's not necessary, Richard. I told you, it was the humiliation before. If I know about it, that's different. I want to give you something, not take something away. I'd like to feel that you had her love as well as mine."

"I'm a one-woman-at-a-time man," Richard said. "And you'd hardly suggest that I should invite Penny to follow us to America for the pleasure of watching you and me settle in together. She knows that I want to make my peace with you. She knew before I went away. I think, as a matter of fact—" Richard hesitated before deciding to continue. "I think she'd like to find a husband now, and have children. She's not getting any younger."

"Does she want to marry you?"

"Obviously she sees that she can't."

"I should put it the other way." Ilsa got out of bed again and put on her dressing gown. "Do you want to marry *her*, Richard?"

"I don't care to live alone. I want to live as a married man. Well, I *am* married. To you. This is what I want—to live with you again, as we did before."

"But I'm not sure—"

"Only a moment ago you said—"

"I thought you were lonely." Ilsa began to pace the room. "I felt a responsibility. I wanted to end this coldness, as you asked, so that we could be friends again. For the rest, I'll try, but—I don't think you ought to send Penny away."

"For Christ's sake!" In his working life Richard was endlessly patient. Perhaps because such control did not come easily to a man who by nature was emotional, his temper was quick to flare outside the clinic. "Can't I have a mind of my own? First you refuse to share me with Penny and then you insist on it. What do you want, for God's sake?"

"I want you to be happy. You've been so generous to me. I'm looking for a way to be generous in return."

"Your generosity presents itself as something very much like rejection. Have you ever loved me, Ilsa? Not just waited to do your duty as a wife, but longed for me to hold you? God, you're so beautiful! But why do you think I needed Penny in the first place? Because you've never behaved with any warmth or shown any passion. You gave me what you thought I wanted because you were grateful, I suppose—for being helped back to health, for being rescued from Europe, for having the time and money to indulge in an unprofitable profession. Well, gratitude is a very cold emotion. And I never asked you to be grateful. Only to love me. Do you love me? Show me. Now."

He snatched her fiercely into his arms and pressed her head back with the force of his kiss. The position was uncomfortable, but this time it was not a fit of coughing which made it impossible for Ilsa to respond. Instead, her body stiffened with a pain in her chest which increased as though a band of steel, encircling it, was being steadily tightened. Only a day earlier she had told Mr. Simpson that she had felt no pain. When he gave her the tablets he had known, she supposed, that this would come, but she was unable to move to reach them. She needed Richard now as a doctor; but the pain was so intense that she found herself holding her breath, and could not speak.

Aware of her rigidity, and misunderstanding it, Richard pushed her away with a mutter of exasperation, so that she staggered and fell on her knees beside the bed. A little time passed before she was able to exhale and then, with a series of exhausted grunts, begin to breathe normally again. She expected Richard to speak, perhaps understanding what had happened: but when at last she was able to raise her head, she saw that he had already left the room.

For some time, collapsed on the bed, she was unhappy, needing someone in whom she could confide. But Richard was a compassionate man, and the truth would hold him at her side. Rather than leave his wife to be ill alone, he would send Penny away. However comforting that might be for Ilsa herself, it would not be fair to tie him in such a way—and this unfairness, unlike the other, she had the power to prevent. As her strength and courage returned, she recognized that she must let him go.

V I

Leo was too fat and Ilsa, these days, too easily tired. They laughed at each other as they struggled up the slippery grass of the downland. Leo had booked two rooms in a hotel near to Glyndebourne, so that they could avoid the long drive back to London after the opera. This arrangement held another advantage: that they would be able to change in comfort before the performance, while other operagoers were struggling into their dinner jackets behind some Sussex hedgerow or arriving at Victoria Station in midafternoon wearing evening dress. There was nothing wrong with that part of the plan: but in addition they had agreed to spend the whole day in the country.

"Such an expedition makes it appear faintly possible that I'm not in the peak of condition," Leo admitted, mocking himself. "If one leads the life of a decadent townsman, one should lead it consistently. Whose ridiculous idea was this, that we should *walk?* And I an American now!"

Ilsa joined in his laughter. She had never thought of herself as temperamental, but nowadays could hardly keep up with her own changes of mood. Today she was euphoric, putting out of her mind everything Mr. Simpson had told her. Since Richard's departure there had been no return of the terrible pain in her chest; and, as the surgeon had promised, abstinence from smoking had combined with the linctus he prescribed to effect a dramatic reduction in her coughing. There were times—and this was one of them—when she felt sure that there was nothing wrong with her.

"I hope Richard doesn't mind you deserting him for the night like this," said Leo—taking for granted, no doubt, an answer quite different from the one he received.

"He doesn't even know I'm here. He deserted me first, rather more permanently."

Why had she told Leo that? His surprise at hearing the words could not be any greater than her own at speaking them. They had emerged without premeditation, but to Leo her statement must have sounded like a significant declaration. His silence suggested that he was seriously considering implications which she had not intended.

"I shouldn't have said that. I don't know why I did. It's only happened since I last saw you, and perhaps I haven't come to terms with it yet. The official story—for Michael's benefit—is that Richard has gone back to America to start a new clinic; and I have to keep a home going in England for Michael himself while he's still at school. He's taking his A-levels and the Cambridge scholarship examination this year. That version's true enough, but it implies a reunion which isn't likely to happen."

"Does that upset you?"

"As a marriage, it ended three years ago. One must always feel sad, I suppose, to fail in a relationship. But I hope—" She and Richard had had two meetings in the past three weeks. They had both been businesslike and polite. There was no reason why they should quarrel now and perhaps, if there was time, they could become friends again. Anxious to end this conversation, she turned to lead the way down the hill toward Leo's hired Daimler.

At the door of her room in the hotel, Ilsa looked at her watch. They must be in their seats at Glyndebourne before half past four. "I shall take a bath," she said. "But I'll be very quick."

"No rush. I'll come for you in about forty minutes." Leo went to his own room, farther down the corridor.

Ilsa unpacked her evening dress and hung it up before going into the private bathroom. Above the sound of splashing water a few minutes later she heard the door of her bedroom open and close. She went back to find Leo standing there.

"Ilsa my dear." He sat down on one side of the bed, stretching out his hand so that she also had to sit in order to reach it. "Is it really necessary for us to go to the opera? *The Magic Flute*, after all! What is it, when all is said and done? A Masonic publicity stunt. A fantastic vehicle for a few extravagant displays of vocal pyrotechnics. All very well to pass the time when no more satisfying experience is to hand, but—the evening will be interminably long. And it's not as though we can't imagine it all, is it?"

Ilsa hesitated. But why not, she thought; why not? How could she pretend to be surprised, when she had given him what he must have seen as an invitation? Although she felt no passionate excitement, Leo might not expect this of her. He probably saw it as an opportunity for them both to demonstrate the love they had felt for each other as friends for so long. Why not? "Then let us imagine it," she said, smiling at him with gaiety in her eyes.

Leo flung himself backward on the bed, pulling her with him.

"You're wearing your beautiful dress." His free hand waved toward the gown of emerald silk hanging on the back of the door. "You are the most beautiful woman at Glyndebourne today, as I am indubitably the most distinguished man. I begin to see the advantages of imagination over reality. Everyone stares as we step with dignity from the Daimler. We wander through the gardens. The wilderness is especially attractive today. The salvia, though, I find out of keeping."

"Ah, but the delphiniums!" exclaimed Ilsa. "The wonderful shades of the blue garden! Have we time to walk round the lake?"

"I think not now. The first warning is about to sound. Our seats are upstairs, in the front row. The young man next to you will be seeing the opera for the first time, I suspect. He is reading the synopsis of the plot with great attention. A wise precaution, if I may say so, sir."

"Ssh!" said Ilsa. "Whatever happens afterward, the overture at least makes sense."

"Um pum pum pum pum pum diddle diddle, *um* pum pum pum pum pum," began Leo, and Ilsa joined in lightly, faster and faster until she ran out of breath. "Quiet!" she commanded, and they were happily silent for a few moments.

"The supper interval," announced Leo at last. "I left the hamper so generously provided by the Connaught in the sunken garden. So! Caviar, cold duckling and orange salad, and—naturally—strawberries and cream. Even a refrigerated ice pack for the campagne. A simple meal, but I trust it suffices."

"Even an hour and a half has been hardly long enough. There's still no time for that walk round the lake."

"Back to our seats. The plot grows even more preposterous. But Pamina has completely won my heart. How delightful that at last a slim waist is regarded by opera directors as being almost as important as a beautiful voice."

They were quiet again until Leo gave the signal to applaud. Ilsa stretched lazily on the bed. "There's no point in hurrying to the car. We shall still have to wait before we can get out of the field."

"But this is still part of the evening," Leo reminded her. "This snake of expensive cars, nose to tail along a country lane. As we wait for our turn the leader is climbing out of sight, over the hills and far away. Soon he will be racing along the empty roads to London, whilst we need make only this short journey to Lewes. The night porter lets us in, and we walk up the stairs together." He turned his head to look at Ilsa.

"The evening is over," she said. "We're back where we started. My bath is running. And unless I turn the tap off soon, the manager will be knocking on the door, complaining of a flood."

"Be very quick."

Ilsa nodded her head and went into the bathroom. Just in time, she pulled out the plug and turned off the tap. The two actions took less than a second, but that was long enough for a doubt to be born in her mind. She took off her bathrobe and used it to wipe the condensation off the full-length mirror. With critical eyes she studied her own body.

She was too thin. Perhaps that had also been true when Leo first fell in love with her years ago; but then, covered by expensive clothes, her thinness had disguised itself as elegance. Without their concealment she looked bony. Her thighs, not sufficiently firmed out by flesh, were unhealthily pale; there was a gauntness in the hollows beside her collarbone; and the skin of her shoulders and breasts, whose whiteness had always been part of her cool beauty, was becoming somehow gray. No, surely, that could not be true; it must be only the new condensation of the steam as it blurred her image on the glass. But nothing could explain away the scrawniness of her long body. How could Leo possibly love a woman like this—and by daylight, now, in the afternoon? Could she bear to see disappointment in his eyes?

And there was something else: a deeper doubt. How often in the past had her old nightmare come between herself and Richard—the irrational terror that he would somehow break through the superficial skin of her beauty and touch the rottenness and decay within. At the time it had seemed merely a fantasy, but now it was true. Her body was indeed unhealthy and imperfect, and she could not bear to offer it to Leo. There could be no question about the depth of her affection for him. But they had missed their chance of loving each other thirteen years earlier: it was too late now.

Leo was still lying on the bed when, once again wearing her bathrobe, she came back into the room and stood still, not knowing what to say.

"Leo, my darling," she began, and then shook her head helplessly, trying to laugh at her own incoherence. "Leo, I'm so sorry—I just don't feel—I can't—"

He held out his hand and she went over to sit on the bed beside him—just as she had sat, laughing, only a short time earlier.

"You don't love me?" he asked.

"I love you as much as ever—oh, more than before. But perhaps that was never in this way. I'm frightened of changing whatever it is that we've shared. I want to stay as I am with you. To be not less, but not more either." She could feel his hand squeezing her own and then releasing the pressure, although perhaps he was not conscious of the movement. Then he drew her down to kiss him. It was the moment when he might have held her fast, refusing to accept her reluctance. But instead he was gentle, stroking her hair and neck: and when he allowed her to sit up again she saw that the smile in his eyes was understanding.

"You don't mind!" she exclaimed. "You're not angry at all. You didn't really want me, did you?"

"I wanted exactly what you wanted, and to find that you want it too is the most wonderful thing. I want us to stay as we are."

"Then why—?"

"You told me that Richard had left you. It was something you might have kept secret, and so I knew that the news must be important. I misjudged the type of importance, that's all. I thought I must choose either to advance or to retreat. I couldn't bear to lose you—to think that you might look elsewhere for comfort. And of course"—he laughed aloud—"the prospect of making love to you was extremely pleasant. I'm only confessing, since you've given me the lead, that I'm just as comfortable not making love."

"What a lazy man you are, Leo!" It was a measure of her relief that she dared to tease him.

"Well, you see, Ilsa, there's no one else like you in my life. If you were to become one of the women I've slept with, something would certainly have been gained, but also something would have been lost."

"Then you shouldn't have pretended."

"There was no pretense. One can prefer one course of action without necessarily regarding the alternative as anything but delightful. I know what you mean, though. Perhaps the best thing about this delightful day is that you trusted me enough to be honest."

Ilsa was silent. She had not, after all, been completely honest. In the three weeks since she heard the doctor's verdict on her health she had longed to confide in someone: to tell the truth—to say directly, "I'm dying." Michael was too young, and Richard had not waited. She would never be able to tell him now, for fear that pity would bring him back against his true wishes, or that guilt at abandoning her would turn his new life sour. She had hoped to look to Leo for comfort, since he had been her confidant for so many years. But when it came to the point, she saw that she could not disturb his comfortable life with such a confession. It was the end of another illusion. She had already recognized the limitations of her own love for Leo. Now she was forced to acknowledge that Leo's love for her had its own restrictions: he would not want to be burdened with the truth.

"I love you, Leo," she said. It was curious, and sad, that she should speak the words for the first time now, just as they ceased to be of importance.

Leo kissed her. There was no passion in the kiss, no desire, and there never would be again; but they were both happy with it. He looked at his watch.

"You know," he said, "if I dispense with an extra shave, I could be dressed in ten minutes. Could you step into your magnificent gown in the same time? Because it might still not be too late for the opera."

VII

The message from Asha Lorimer was brief and surprising. "Can you come to tea on Saturday? Please try. Four o'clock." Ilsa, curious, decided at once that she would go.

The address was in the Portobello Road, whose antique shops and stalls were thronged with tourists and browsers. Recognizing that it would be quicker to walk the last hundred yards, Ilsa dismissed her taxi at the end of the road. She rang the bell on a shabby door squeezed between two shops. Inside, footsteps hurried down a flight of stairs and the door was opened by a young man with a dark skin and an intelligent face. "I am Ranji," he said.

As they shook hands, Ilsa remembered the name from her first visit to Blaize, when Alexa had nagged Asha about her young Indian protégé.

"Shall I lead the way?" he suggested. In any case, there would hardly have been room for Ilsa to squeeze past him. She followed him up the dark, narrow stairs and through a second door, and was agreeably surprised to emerge into a large and very light living room. Perhaps the brightness was due to the absence of curtains—and the impression of size to the paucity of furniture.

"We were given possession only yesterday," explained Ranji. "And we thought it would be sensible to redecorate before moving our furniture in." Like Ilsa herself, he pronounced each syllable with more precision than a native-born Englishman and there was in his intonation a very slight lilt, resembling that of a Welshman; but apart from that he spoke English perfectly. Ilsa was just working out the implication of what he had said when Asha appeared to confirm her conclusion.

"My dear, how lovely you look!" Ilsa's compliment was sincere. Asha's long and very fair hair gleamed as though each strand had been individually polished, and her pale face for once was flushed. She wore a dress of silky turquoise which clung round her slim waist before flaring out into a swirling skirt which seemed to crackle with an excitement of its own. She laughed with a mixture of delight and disappointment as she saw Ilsa look at her left hand.

"Oh! You've guessed! Yes, Ranji and I were married this morning."

"Congratulations!" Was this an occasion for kissing the strange young man as well as her cousin? Yes, it was, although he was as shy about receiving the gesture as she was in making it. "And to you, Mrs.—?"

"Mrs. Ranjidambaram. Isn't it a mouthful?" Asha giggled happily. "My pupils will never get their tongues round it. I shall go on being called Miss Lorimer at school. Like an actress with a stage name. Ilsa, I want to explain straightaway why we didn't invite you to the wedding itself. The thing is, I'm afraid Aunt Alexa isn't going to approve. She'll come round to it, of course, but for the moment . . . So we didn't tell her in advance, in case she got worked up. And if we didn't tell her, we couldn't tell anyone else in the family. Because she'll phone everyone up and ask why she wasn't warned. We didn't think that would be fair to people. This way, you can all truthfully say that you didn't know. Well, when I say all, I mean you and Bernard and Helen. Paula's working on a story in New York and Pirry lives in France. Look, do sit down. The last people left this enormous sofa behind because they couldn't get it down the stairs. Heaven knows how they got it up."

Asha was chattering out of nervousness as well as excitement, Ilsa realized as she accepted the seat. "Remind me about Bernard. You did tell me, I know, but I was so worked up about my mother at the time that I didn't take it in."

"Bernard's a Lorimer, like I was, not a Glanville like Pirry. He's a research chemist with his own lab near Cambridge. He's terribly clever and terribly rich. He hires all the brightest chaps coming out of the university and works with them himself, and he's got his own factory so that whenever they come up with some wonder drug they can churn it out themselves and put the profits back into inventing something else."

He arrived at that moment, a tousled, bright-eyed man in his late thirties. Whatever he spent his money on, it was certainly not clothes, Ilsa thought—but their crumpled, casual style was appropriate to the rest of his appearance. His red hair was curly, and any attempt which he might have made to control its springiness was wrecked by his habit of running his fingers upward through the curls. His face—soft and friendly—was almost as crumpled as his clothes, etched with deep lines in unexpected places. They were lines of thought rather than worry, Ilsa decided, watching as he hugged Asha affectionately and then turned to acknowledge the introduction to herself.

"No Helen?" asked Asha.

"She's in hospital for a couple of days, I'm afraid."

"I'm sorry. Nothing serious, I hope."

" 'Observation' is the word. Hoping to clear up something that's been dragging on. No, not serious, just a nuisance. Women are very complicated, aren't they?" He addressed this remark to Ranji. "Asha, you haven't finished the introductions."

"I was just coming to that. This is Ranji. My husband."

"My God! Have you really done it! Grandmother will be furious! Oh, not about you, I don't mean," he said, shaking Ranji's hand vigorously. "It's just that I'm sure she was longing to give Asha a real send-off. The last of the great country-house weddings. Borrowing back the school's part of the house for a day during the holidays. I can see it now: the ballroom back in use, with half the county invited, and the banqueting hall laid out with expensive presents, and photographers and bridesmaids, and the bride sweeping down the aisle of the village church, wearing the family jewels and hundreds of yards of white tulle. A cake to be cut and lots of speeches full of almost-dirty jokes. Confetti and champagne and tin cans tied to the car. How could you rob her of all that, Asha!"

"You're making a very convincing case for this morning's registry-office affair," Asha said. "And cake and champagne at least we can have. Sit down, Bernard, while I fetch a few things."

He sat next to Ilsa and talked about her mother, guessing that this was what she would like to hear. Ranji hovered nearby, smiling to indicate that he was part of the conversation despite knowing nothing of the subject. The party appeared to be complete and they were all surprised when the doorbell rang.

"Ranji, will you?" called Asha from the kitchen. "It can't be any-one for us, because no one knows we're here, so send them away."

As Ranji disappeared down the stairs, Asha pushed in a laden trol-ley, on which a homemade wedding cake held pride of place. She had made cucumber sandwiches as well, delicately thin triangles with their crusts trimmed off; and scones still warm from the oven; and jam tarts; and brandy snaps filled with cream; and a chocolate cake layered with butter icing. "Good heavens!" exclaimed Ilsa, who never ate tea. "What a feast!"

"I can't cook anything sensible," Asha explained. "Aunt Alexa let me go into the kitchen and pester the cook for a lesson whenever I liked, but I always asked to be taught sweets or cakes. My real special-ity is fudge." She turned in surprise as Ranji returned with a compan-ion. "Pirry!" Asha flung herself into her cousin's arms. "I didn't know you were in England. What marvelous timing! You've arrived just in time to celebrate my wedding. The first champagne cork is about to pop."

"Wedding? Did you say your wedding?"

Ilsa and Bernard smiled at each other as Pirry recovered from his astonishment and was introduced to Ranji. His nature appeared to be a placid one, for by the time he had murmured all the right phrases and turned to Ilsa, his startled expression had been replaced by the warm smile which she remembered from their first meeting.

"I'm delighted to see you here, Ilsa. I was intending to get in touch while I was in England because I have a request—but later, perhaps." His expressive face revealed anxiety as he watched Ranji preparing to open the first bottle of champagne. "The world," he murmured sotto voce to Ilsa, "is divided into those who were born with a champagne cork between their fingers and those who were not. Ranji!" he called more loudly. "I must insist now on being regarded as the bride's father. Allow me to take charge of the drinks, in order that you and

Asha can hold hands bashfully while we drink to your future happiness."

"Now you see why we didn't want to be married at Blaize," laughed Asha as Pirry's practiced hands set the champagne flowing. "We knew we shouldn't be allowed to organize anything for ourselves."

"Never do anything for yourself if you can find someone else to do it for you. Here's to you, then, Asha and Ranji. Health and happiness. No, you can't drink to yourselves. You have to wait until you toast the guests."

Only a few moments earlier Ilsa, like Bernard, had felt sorry that Asha should have deprived herself of a party that she could remember all her life. But Pirry threw himself with such gusto into the role of life and soul of the party that the tiny gathering was magically transformed into the right social occasion. Appropriating the roles of bride's father and best man, he and Bernard told the kind of stories that Asha had hoped to escape, laughing at their own jokes while they ate a hearty tea. Their boisterousness was kindly meant and Asha, flushed with happiness as she shared a cushion on the floor with her husband, joined in the laughter out of gratitude for their tact in turning the tea party into a celebration. It was left to Ilsa, herself an outsider in the family group, to realize that Ranji was not only excluded from their family references but shocked by some of their jokes. But he did his best to share in the fun, smiling at each of them in turn.

When they had emptied the plates of scones and sandwiches, eaten token slices of rich fruitcake and finished off the champagne, Pirry stood up to leave.

"But you haven't explained how you come to be here!" exclaimed Asha.

"That's easy. I called at your old chummery and was given your new address."

"But why today? I mean, it's marvelous to see you. But you couldn't possibly have known it was a special day."

"Well, I happened to be in town and I wanted to have a chat. To make some plans for Mother. But it can wait."

"It doesn't need to wait. We're all family here." Asha's arm tightened round Ranji's waist.

Pirry looked around the room and then sat down again. "Yes, of course," he agreed. "All family. Well, I've come to look for somewhere Mother might live. Not now, but sometime in the future."

"Why does she need anywhere?" demanded Asha. "The wheelchair business isn't serious, you know. She can potter about the house and garden perfectly well. And she's had one of those chair lifts installed to take her up the stairs on her bad days. She'll never leave Blaize."

"Unfortunately, there are some circumstances—highly remote, but needing to be considered—in which she might have to leave."

"Only if—" Asha checked herself and stared, startled, at her cousin. "Pirry, you're not ill, are you?"

"Definitely not. Fit as a fiddle. It's because Mother would ask exactly that question that I need to move with circumspection."

"But if there's nothing wrong—"

"I'm not ill, but I'm prepared to recognize that I'm not immortal, either. A few weeks ago, the chap I was swimming with suddenly had a heart attack in his own pool and sank like a stone. Only forty-six—four years younger than I am. I couldn't help thinking that if it had been me instead, it would have left Mother in an awful mess. I may believe—I *do* believe—that I'm good for another thirty years. But I don't propose to give up any of the things I enjoy. I shall continue to eat good meals and drink good wine, occasionally in excess, and I ought to recognize the possibility that the clock might suddenly stop. Put it this way. It can't do any harm for me to take a few precautions, and I shall feel easier when it's done. I do have a responsibility to Mother, after all."

"Yes." Suddenly Asha did not look happy anymore. She turned to Ilsa to explain. "Blaize is entailed, you see. And Pirry hasn't got any children. There's a branch of the Glanvilles hovering up in Scotland, just waiting to move in."

"You mustn't believe everything Mother tells you," Pirry said mildly. "I know Mother doesn't like them much, but they're an ordinary decent lot. It's not their fault that the entail will operate in their favor one day. However, it's certainly true that my cousin will eventually inherit Blaize. Not only the house, but the whole estate, and the rents that go with it. Also a capital fund which was set up after the

Park Lane house was bombed. So there would be two separate problems over Mother. The money problem and the housing problem."

He looked around the room, smiling pleasantly. "You shouldn't have asked me about this, you know. Weddings and funerals bring together the same people and very much the same food and drink, but their atmospheres aren't compatible. Even when the funeral is as hypothetical as this one. Are you sure you want me to go on?"

Nobody spoke; but Ilsa, watching Asha's face, saw her nod.

"Well then, I've dealt with the money. I've bought Mother an annuity. It came quite cheaply for someone who's already eighty-six; how is a mere actuary to know that she's indestructible? And I have a life assurance policy going in her favor. She could invest the proceeds to provide more income, or spend the capital a bit at a time—at five thousand a year, say, it would last her till her hundredth birthday. That should do, I hope. I don't want her to have any anxiety. But I have responsibilities in France as well."

"So are you going to buy her another house?" asked Asha.

"Not a whole one. I don't see the point. Agreed, Mother's managed marvelously until now, but it's bound to get more difficult. She won't want to deal with staff, and she won't want so much space. Have you read about these country mansions which are being converted into homes for elderly people? You buy a couple of rooms, good-sized rooms, and put your own furniture in them. There's a manager to see that they get cleaned, and you can eat in the dining room and enjoy the grounds and it's only a question of money, not responsibility. In a place like that, Mother could feel that she was still living in some kind of style, but there'd be someone around to notice if she was ill. This is really why I came today, Asha. To ask whether you thought it would be a good idea for me to buy into something of that sort—and whether you'd come with me to inspect a suitable place. Because if the situation were ever to arise, I should rely on you actually to deal with it. You haven't quarreled with her, have you, about this marriage?"

Asha shook her head. "She doesn't know that it's happened. She may be angry at first, but I expect she'll accept it when she realizes that it can't be changed. She may cut off from me for a bit, but I shan't ever cut off from her. After all, she's been almost as much of a mother to me as she has to you."

"That's my girl!" Pirry stood up again. "And having thus effectively put a damper on the conversation, I'll leave you to share the first washing-up of your married life. Ranji, my dear chap, I do apologize for flinging you into a caldron of family affairs like this. But the feeling of being stifled by in-laws is an essential ingredient of any wedding day. I hope the other essential ingredients prove rather more enjoyable." He hugged Asha warmly and left her to start her honeymoon. Ilsa and Bernard followed him down the stairs.

VIII

Down in the Portobello Road, Ilsa automatically looked around to estimate the chance of finding a taxi, but Pirry put one hand on her arm and the other on Bernard's. "One more drink," he said. "The pubs will be open now. And I feel the need to dissipate the gloom."

"If you're genuinely as fit as you claim, what is there to be gloomy about?" asked Bernard suspiciously.

"Oh, it's nothing to do with myself. But that marriage! A mistake, don't you agree? You'll come with us, won't you, Ilsa? The quickest way to feel part of a family is to join in the postmortems."

Ilsa was not by nature a gossip, but the circumstances which had precipitated her into this unknown family were bound to make her curious. "Why are you so sure it's a mistake?" she asked, after they had settled themselves at a table with their drinks. "I hardly know Asha and I've never met Ranji before, so I can't make any judgment myself."

"None of us—except my grandmother—has met Ranji before," Bernard told her. "That's a bad sign in itself. A girl who felt confident about her choice would want to show him off, surely."

"I'd find it simple to describe the kind of man Asha *ought* to have married," said Pirry. "She was only six when she was orphaned, and my mother was already seventy when she took charge of her. So Asha has had no experience of normal family life. She should have married the son of two happily married parents so that she could adopt his way of living. One has to learn from observation how married people cope with each other. Instead, she's picked a man whose relations are thousands of miles away—a man from a different culture. She probably doesn't know what he expects of a wife, and in a foreign country he may not know himself."

"That means that they'll have to work harder at their marriage than most people," Ilsa agreed. "But won't it be easier, in the circumstances, that neither of them has a pattern to which they must conform? They'll make their own pattern."

"Possibly. But there's another thing. Asha's parents were cousins. She's a Lorimer through both sides of her family. Bernard will agree with me that all the Lorimer women seem to have certain characteristics in common. Different talents, but always a great deal of determination."

"I remember Asha telling me that herself," Ilsa agreed. "Positive achievers, I think she called them all."

"Yes. Well. Because Asha's been brought up by a woman—my mother—who was genuinely famous in her youth, she may feel that she can't, doesn't *want* to live up to whatever is expected of her. But she's an intelligent and efficient girl. What she does, she does well. At the moment she may believe that she isn't ambitious and that it's enough to show her independence by escaping from Mother. But one day the Lorimer genes will prove too strong for her. She'll start to organize her own life. And then—in my opinion—she'll need to have a husband whose own life is sufficiently well organized for him to stand up to her; otherwise he'll just go under. And what has she chosen? Someone younger than herself. Still at university, so he hasn't got a job or much money. Someone who may or may not meet prejudice on account of his color, but who certainly hasn't got the kind of contacts to give him a good start. In other words, an insecure young man."

"You're assuming that Ranji isn't a strong character," said Ilsa. "Do we know him well enough to be sure of that? As you said yourself, *any* young man may be overwhelmed by a mass descent of his wife's relations. And you seem to be assuming also that in a happy marriage the husband must always dominate the wife. Is it so terrible if the wife should prove to be the stronger of the two?"

Pirry looked startled, while Bernard burst out laughing. "You're forgetting that our cousin Ilsa is a Lorimer female as well."

Pirry joined in the laughter against himself. "And also forgetting that the nature of my own domestic arrangements hardly qualifies me to pontificate on the holy state of matrimony. I met my own life partner in a prisoner-of-war camp," he explained to Ilsa. "His name is Douglas and he represents the responsibilities in France I mentioned earlier, because I've lived with him ever since the war. Minds are broader outside England." He was watching to see how she reacted. Leo had already revealed Pirry's inclinations and she felt no disapproval. It was none of her business how he chose to live. Her own family life might be crumbling about her, but she did not yet have any feeling of belonging to this one.

Bernard was the first to leave, and once again Pirry put out a hand to hold Ilsa back.

"There's something I want to ask you. And I shall be so desolated if you say no that I hardly dare put it into words."

"What is it?"

"Have you ever thought of writing an opera?" he asked. "Not a grand opera, a Covent Garden affair. But something suitable for television. That's a new medium which ought to be creating its own art forms. An opera which was a mixture of studio singing and film background could be exciting."

Ilsa had never considered such a project and allowed her face to reveal the fact.

"I wondered whether we might collaborate," Pirry continued. "You may or may not know that I earn a little pin money from my translations of various gloomy Scandinavians and Germans. And as my mother's son, I've been brought up with opera. I do know about some of the technical problems. It seemed to me that *The Lady from the Sea* would have possibilities—Ibsen's play. The two kinds of water, the sea and the fjord, could be part of a television production in a way which would be impossible in an opera house. At the moment I'm still organizing the structure, to make sure that it would work technically and dramatically. Before I start on the actual libretto, I need to know whose music I'm writing for. Yours would be exactly right. Leo gave me his recording of your violin concerto as a Christmas present ten years ago, and since then I've bought everything of yours that's on disc. Even before I knew of our relationship I was wondering whether I might approach you."

"I don't know the play." Ilsa was neither encouraging nor discouraging.

"It's about freedom of choice. The heroine, Ellida, has to choose between two kinds of life—calm-water life and open-water life, you might say, with two men tugging her in different directions. You'd need to use two styles of music which in the end could be reconciled —as though the sparkling introduction to your piano concerto were dancing about on top of the adagio theme from the Cradle Symphony and gradually becoming absorbed in it. I'm quite sure you could express all the variety of moods which would be needed. If I were to send you the scenario when I've finished it, perhaps with the libretto for a specimen scene, would you consider the project?"

At their first meeting, overwhelmed by the news about her mother, Ilsa had paid little attention to Pirry, assuming him to be a well-to-do dilettante, pleasant enough but possibly shallow in his tastes. His businesslike concern for his mother's welfare had already altered that impression. Now he was inviting her to consider him a fellow professional, and his knowledge of her work was flattering.

"No need to answer at once," he said. "I'll give you a ring before I leave England. And you needn't commit yourself to more than a look at the scenario even then. Now, may I drive you home?"

"Would you like to come in?" Ilsa asked ten minutes later as they drew up in front of the Nash terrace.

"If it isn't an intrusion, I would very much like to see the room in which you work. Because if this opera project were to take off—I hope I'm not pushing too hard, but I really have set my heart on it— we'd need to develop a kind of telepathic communication. I'd want to be able to imagine you at work."

"You'll be disappointed." Ilsa led the way in. "You may expect something grand, looking over the park. But I like to have no distractions at all. I could work best in a prison cell without a window."

Pirry looked round the small, dark room. "Will you sit as though you were working?"

Ilsa sat down not at the piano but at her drafting table, and tilted its surface to the angle she preferred. "Does your house in France have a music room?" she asked.

"Yes. Very large. Some friends and I play chamber music there, so we need the space. One wall is all glass, opening onto a terrace with a view of the sea. *Very* distracting, I'm afraid you'd find it. But I hope you'll come to see it one day, all the same." He was still staring intently at every detail of the room.

"I'd like to see your scenario," Ilsa told him impulsively. "It's a new idea, writing an opera. But it could be exciting."

"Marvelous!" Pirry's eyes lit up with such enthusiasm that he seemed to be not older than Ilsa, but far younger. He took hold of her by both hands and raised her to her feet. "Marvelous!" he repeated.

"I'm not promising anything. Only that I'll consider it. But, Pirry—" She stopped, astounded by the realization of what she was going to say. "I would need to see it quite soon. I may not have very long to work on it."

"You mean that you're expecting another commission?"

"No. I mean that I'm ill. I have a kind of cancer."

Pirry was still holding her hands. Ilsa, who normally so much disliked being touched, had not freed herself because his mood of excitement transmitted itself to her through the contact. Now, through the same channel, she felt his exhilaration changing abruptly to shock and sympathy. "My dear Ilsa! I'm so sorry!"

Ilsa gave a short, surprised laugh. "I've been keeping it a secret. Even my family doesn't know. Nor Leo, although he's my closest friend. But I suddenly wanted to tell someone."

"Thank you." His grip on her hands became painfully tight, and he used it to pull her closer, so that by their nearness they shared a moment of sadness. His voice was quiet as he asked, "Does it frighten you?"

Ilsa shook her head. "Not now. For a little while when I was first told, yes. Although even then it was anger more than fear. I suppose one always asks, Why can't I have a little longer? But it has to happen sometime, so . . . I told you because I wouldn't like to begin something and then—"

"No," said Pirry. "You told me because we are going to be friends. You knew that we must start with honesty and trust. It must be important to you, if there's a time limit, to believe that whatever you do should be worth doing. Are you sure—?"

"I can't be sure until I see what you have in mind," Ilsa told him. "I need to find out whether I'm in sympathy with it. But I have a premonition that what inspires you will be inspiring to me as well. I shall look forward—very much—to hearing from you when you're ready."

I X

Less than a week after Pirry mooted the idea of an opera, Ilsa was commissioned by the BBC to compose a brief choral piece for a concert to be televised on St. Cecilia's Day in honor of music's patron saint. The invitation was accompanied by five poems, chosen in the hope that one of them might provide inspiration.

"Who is Humbert Wolfe?" asked Michael, reading the poems while Ilsa considered the invitation. Since Richard's departure she was making an effort to appear at breakfast every morning.

"I don't know. I haven't heard of him."

"He wrote one of these. It's a conversation between a fiddle and a bow about the fiddler. I like the way it ends:

> " 'And if of dust he shapes this brittle
> lift of the wings, this song's one petal
> that shines and dies, is it not just
> to suffer for song, o singing dust?
>
> " 'His was the choice, and if he wake us
> out of the wood, but will not slake us,
> thus stirred with the stars, at least we know
> what pain the stars have,' says the bow.

"Neat. Do you suffer for song, Ilsa?"

"For me it's the other way round," she said. "I suffer when the song is silent."

"Will you take the commission?"

"Yes. But I shall have to move fast; November's only four months away."

She chose the Wolfe poem, not only because Michael liked it, but because the words gave her the excuse to slash through the choral texture with dramatic phrases played on a violin. She worked hard in the next few weeks and was pleased with the result.

"Will you come with me to the concert, Michael?" she asked on the morning of St. Cecilia's Day: she had been sent two tickets for the studio performance.

"I can't really spare the time, if you don't mind."

Ilsa was disappointed; yet while the final rehearsal and the concert itself were in progress she would not have been aware of having a companion; and by the time the performance ended she was too tired to talk. She should have been hungry, because she had stayed in the studio between rehearsal and performance to scribble down ideas. But the thought of the canteen was unappealing. A more attractive way to restore her energy would be a refreshing bath at home. As soon as she had thanked the performers, she made her way up the stairs from the underground studio and straight out of the lobby.

A single step outside showed her that no taxis would be on the road that night. A dense wall of fog pressed against her face, irritating her eyes and throat in only the brief second before she turned back through the swing door to consider what to do. But the distance from the studios to her home was not really very great: Michael had frequently teased her with the statement that she could walk it in half the time she spent waiting for a taxi. She gave a little sigh, a small grimace, and then pulled her scarf across her mouth and nose before stepping outside for a second time.

The air was very cold and surprisingly wet. This was not an old-fashioned pea-souper, not darkened by smoke or made poisonous by chemical effluents as in the first years after the war; but it was dense enough to be stifling. Breathing through the scarf, Ilsa felt that she was suffocating; but when she pulled it aside she at once began to wheeze and cough.

She covered her mouth again and tried to hurry; but so closely did the fog press against her eyes that she experienced all the anxiety of a blind woman lost in unknown territory. At first she could feel her way along the walls or railings of the street, but then she had to cross the wide road which lay between her and the park. She strained her ears as well as her eyes, but the fog muffled sound as well as obscuring vision, and the few vehicles which were still on the road appeared without warning out of the silence. Inside the park the problems were greater, for there were no walls to guide her. To take a shortcut across the grass was to risk losing all sense of direction. With one arm extended in front of her to warn of obstructions or other pedestrians, she made her way cautiously around the outer circle.

Long before she reached the house she was coughing. She closed her mouth, trying to control the irritation; but then it shook and rumbled inside lungs which were panting for air. When finally she leaned against her own front door, she surrendered to the violence of the attack for a few moments while summoning the strength to turn the key in the lock. Staggering inward with the opening door, she was only just able to push it shut before collapsing on the stairs to rest. It had taken her almost an hour to cover the short distance home.

The hall light was on, but the rest of the house was in darkness. Presumably the Rundles were asleep in their own flat. Michael might be asleep as well, or perhaps still working at his books. Ilsa drew on her remaining strength and hauled herself up the first flight of stairs to the drawing room. Sitting down on the sofa, she huddled inside her fur coat and brought her noisy, shallow breathing gradually under control.

For those first few minutes she was glad to be alone, but soon she became resentful of the silence. Where was everybody? The Rundles should have stayed up, anxious for her safe return. And Michael— why did Michael never come to her concerts? It was unforgivable of him to take so little interest in her work. She should be discussing the music with him now: the house should be full of light and warmth and friendly conversation. If she had company, she would not feel so ill.

Allowing anger to overcome her exhaustion, she stood up and turned on all the drawing room lights. At once, as though she had rung a bell, Michael appeared in pajamas and dressing gown.

"I was listening for you," he said. "I was worried about how you were going to get home, but I couldn't think of anything to do."

"There wasn't anything. It was lucky I was in walking distance. But the fog's given me a tickle in my throat. Would you fetch the bottle of brown medicine from my bathroom?"

After she had taken a strong dose of the Brompton's mixture she was able to relax. Her breathing came more easily and her heart, which had been pounding with anxiety and exertion, gradually steadied.

"How did the concert go?" Michael asked. "I've been feeling mean all evening about not coming. It's the scholarship exam next week that's the trouble. All the time when I'm not working for it, my brain keeps asking me questions I can't answer, so that I have to dash straight off and look up my notes. I couldn't have listened to the music properly. But I should have gone, all the same, shouldn't I?"

Ilsa smiled at him, affection driving away her fear of collapse. Michael was as tall as herself, but in his camel dressing gown he looked as cuddly as a four-year-old, with the same expression of earnest perplexity. Except in schoolwork, he was young for his age.

"I would have liked your company," she admitted. Breathing was still an effort, but she could control it well enough to talk. "Concerts are like coffee: an acquired taste. If you go regularly, you'll begin to enjoy them one day. And then you'll be cross with yourself for not starting sooner. Tonight, of course, you needn't have pretended that you expected to appreciate the music. It would only have been a gesture of family solidarity."

"Sorry," he said.

"Well, I hadn't realized the Cambridge exam was so close. I thought it was at the end of term. So we each have our own dragons to fight. I have to listen to a first performance in a concert hall, while you'll face your crisis in an examination room with nobody to applaud. All the worry and none of the fun. Never mind. The day you know enough to send the world spinning into a black hole, I'll take my turn to stay away."

"You're cross about my not going, aren't you?"

"Not cross at all. I could have pressed you harder to come, but I thought it was better to let you decide. You decided wrongly and you studied your decision and saw that you were wrong. That's one mistake you won't make again. It's all thoroughly satisfactory."

Michael's worry was banished by a boyish grin. "How appallingly lazy you are, Ilsa! You even make me bring myself up."

"And a very good job you're making of it. Michael, you're not worried about this scholarship exam, are you? It's only a trial run. You're still young. You'll have another chance next year."

"The school calls it a trial run because they don't like to muck up their percentage of honors with failures. As far as I'm concerned, it's the real thing. I want to start at Cambridge next October."

"Why are you in such a hurry to grow up?" asked Ilsa, smiling.

Michael sat down on the arm of the sofa. "Almost all the important discoveries in science nowadays are made by people under thirty," he said earnestly. "It's as though after that one's brain loses the ability to make—what would you call it?—the creative leap. Intelligence starts going downhill from the age of about seventeen. So it's a kind of race, you see, to acquire as much knowledge and good judgment as you can while you've still got the brains to move on from what's already known. Does that sound cocky? I don't mean it to. But if I turn out to be any good, there may not be much time."

"If you turn out to be any good, you may end up by making time run backward for you."

They laughed together, but Ilsa began to cough again. Michael's cheerful company had distracted her but now, as she tried to stand, she was once again conscious of her exhaustion. Michael, however, had remembered something he wanted to tell her and did not notice.

"Ilsa, I tried to watch the concert on the box and it wasn't on."

"What do you mean? It must have been."

"No. No picture at all. Just a blank screen and music. Not your music, either."

"Wasn't there any announcement?"

"There might have been at the beginning, but I didn't switch on until I thought they'd have reached your piece."

"I suppose there was a technical fault. Or perhaps someone important has died. Churchill, it could be. How infuriating." It was not often that Ilsa could hope for a large audience for her work, so she had reason to be annoyed by this lost opportunity.

"Yes. Rotten luck. Well, good night." He gave her a smacking kiss on the cheek and went up to his bedroom at the top of the house.

It took Ilsa longer to reach her room. The effect of the Brompton's mixture had worn off more quickly than usual and as she climbed the stairs she was only able to take a series of quick, shallow breaths. Her lungs were full of fog which bubbled up, filling her throat, drowning her from within. "We are the water people," Pirry Glanville had said. Now water was choking her, dragging her down into an invisible ocean. She sat on the edge of the bed and bent down, trying to force out the fog. The effort triggered off her coughing again.

To the turbulence in her lungs was added the agonizing pain which she had experienced once before, when Richard was in the room. It tightened across her chest, pinching her heart and knotting her muscles in spasm. She heard Michael rushing down the stairs from the floor above and thought that he must have heard her groans—but as he burst through the door it was clear that his arrival was a lifesaving accident.

"I put the radio news on," he said breathlessly. "President Kennedy's been shot. He's—Ilsa, are you all right?" He did not need to wait for an answer. Ilsa heard him lift the telephone receiver to summon the doctor and allowed herself to collapse.

When she opened her eyes again, Michael was still next to her bed, but everything else had changed. There was a mask over her face, and tubes dripped into an arm which was tightly strapped down. When she stared at him, he seemed oddly out of focus. He said something that she could not hear, and a uniformed nurse appeared at his side. Their two faces blurred and faded again.

This must have happened several times, for sometimes Michael was not there and sometimes there was a different nurse. Once she thought she recognized Mr. Simpson, and more often, more certainly, their family doctor, Dr. Wainwright. It was Dr. Wainwright who gently drew her out of the twilight and back to full consciousness. Without remembering the intermediate stages, she found herself one day propped up against a mound of pillows and breathing without the help of oxygen.

"You'll be all right now." Dr. Wainwright was studying the record of her pulse and temperature. "Back to normal quite soon."

Did he know what "normal" meant? "What happened?" Ilsa asked. Her voice, out of practice, emerged as a croak.

"A bad bout of bronchitis is what I told Michael."

"True?"

Dr. Wainwright sat down. "No. But according to John Simpson, you didn't wish your family to be informed about your health."

"He told you."

"There are rules about specialists passing their findings on to GPs. Or etiquette, at least. How could I treat you without knowing? I was sorry to read his notes. We've been working on this together. You can thank him for pulling you through."

"Through what?"

"A pleural embolism. It could have killed you."

"Will it happen again?"

"You'll have to be careful. As soon as you're well enough to travel, I'd recommend you to go somewhere warm and dry. Now, do you feel up to seeing Michael? He's been worried."

He came into the room as soon as the doctor had left, and gripped her hand tightly. "Shouldn't you be taking your exam?" she asked.

"I finished that ages ago. The results came out last week."

"How did you get on?"

"Trinity offered me a place. I'll be starting in October."

"Oh, darling!" He had hoped for a scholarship. "That's my fault. You must have been worried all the time you were doing the papers."

"You're supposed to congratulate me! Most people don't get accepted at all. As for the scholarship, that's not important. Cambridge has a civilized system of offering extra awards to people who do well in their first year. I'll pick up something then, you'll see."

"But, Michael, if it's all settled, how long have I been ill?"

"Five weeks," he told her. "Dr. Wainwright kept you sedated to stop you coughing. He explained it to me so that I wouldn't think you were in a coma. Now he thinks you're stronger, so he's cut down on the drugs. That's why you've woken up so suddenly."

"Five weeks!"

"Yes. You've missed Christmas. Would you like your presents now?"

"Just yours," she said, and allowed him to dab her wrists with the scent he had bought.

"I'll tell you who sent the others. Then you can look forward to seeing them tomorrow, when you're strong enough to enjoy them." Neatly cutting string and paper, he took off the outer wrappings of the parcels and discovered one that was not a Christmas present, but a typescript. "From Pirry Glanville," he reported, reading the signature on an enclosed letter. "It looks like a play."

"He wants me to write an opera," Ilsa explained.

"Are you going to?"

"I don't feel up to it." There would not be time. All the same, she asked Michael to leave the libretto within reach.

The next day she was a little stronger and found it easier to talk. "I phoned Richard, of course, to tell him you were ill," said Michael. "He asked if he should come back. I don't know whether I said the right thing. He'd explained to me before he left how important it was for him to stay out of England for a whole year. Something to do with tax. He was ready to dish that, but I thought you wouldn't notice whether he was here or not while you were having all those drugs, so I suggested he waited until you could talk to him on the phone yourself."

"You said I had bronchitis?"

"Yes. I explained about the fog."

"You were quite right not to bring him back. In fact, you should have gone out there for Christmas."

"He did invite me. But I didn't want to leave you."

"Why not go now?" suggested Ilsa. "If you've won your place at Cambridge, there's no point in staying on at school. You could have an interesting six months in America. Richard might get you a research job to do at his new clinic. Or at least give you some lab work." Most seventeen-year-olds might choose to fill a gap between school and university in more frivolous fashion, but Ilsa knew that Michael was only happy when he was working.

"No. I'm going to stay with you."

It took Ilsa only a moment to decide what to say. "Lord Glanville has invited me to stay with him on the Riviera, so that we can work together on the opera. That will take a long time—a year, at least. If you were away at the same time, we could close up the house."

"I thought you weren't going to do the opera."

"I was still dopey when I said that yesterday. Dr. Wainwright has told me to spend the rest of the winter in a warmer climate. Pirry didn't know I'd been ill, but his invitation is perfectly timed. If I accept, you and Richard will know that I'm comfortable and well looked after. And as soon as I'm strong again, I shall want to get back to work." She could see that he was tempted but still doubtful. "Go on," she urged. "It will take a little time to get an American visa, and you'll need a letter from Richard to guarantee your support. Phone him up today and tell him that you'd like to come, and that I'm better. Too croaky to talk on the phone, but better."

"Sure?"

"Sure," she said; and to prove it she opened the libretto of *The Lady from the Sea* and began to read.

At their two brief meetings she had found Pirry's personality attractive. He had charmed her into expressing enthusiasm for his project, but the excitement of a new commission soon after their last encounter had taken the edge off her interest. Would his work prove sufficiently professional to tempt her again? The fortunate timing of his invitation was not enough in itself to make her uncritical.

On her first reading of the typescript she was concerned only to judge whether the story was sufficiently dramatic, the characters inspiring and the production technically possible. But even at that stage the conflict between the wild strength of the seafarers and the more placid lives of those who lived on the fjord excited her with its musical possibilities—just as Pirry had promised. When she opened the folder for a second time she could already feel herself retreating into the state of mental isolation which invariably preceded the first stirrings of creativity. This was, after all, a challenge she could accept. She had the ability to do the work. All she needed was time.

On the last day of December Mr. Simpson visited her. "I warned you about fog, you know," he said.

"Yes. I'm sorry." Earlier, she had intended—if she ever saw him again—to ask him why he had bothered to save her life. What was the point, she would have asked, of dragging me back just to go through it all again before too long? But the question remained unspoken because an answer had already presented itself. There was still something she wanted to do. She was going to write an opera. She was going to write it with Pirry and in the process, she felt sure, she would find her place in the family she had discovered less than a year earlier. She had let both Michael and Richard go, but there was still somewhere she could belong.

X

Ilsa found it easy to understand why Pirry had chosen *The Lady from the Sea* for his first libretto, for the sea was his own natural element. Sailing was his passion and swimming his regular exercise. From every window of his villa on the headland of a small cape there was a view of the Mediterranean. He owned no beach, for the promontory was high and rocky; but a zigzag stairway led down to a jetty from which he could dive directly into deep water, and also to a large sheltered boathouse. Here were moored his two racing yachts, the much smaller single-handed Snipe which he kept for relaxation, and the motorboat which he and Douglas used for workaday trips to Nice or Monte Carlo during the summer months when the coastal road was choked with tourists.

When Ilsa first arrived from England, weak from her illness and tired by the journey, there was no question of her joining her host on the water. In any case, the weather was blustery and she had been warned to keep warm. But as the spring sunshine began to sparkle on smoother water and little by little her energy returned, she accepted his invitations to go out for an afternoon when there was no racing. As a girl she had sailed in the Gulf of Finland and, although she now lacked the strength to control a boat, or even to crew, her body instinctively knew how to lean and balance as Pirry jibed or turned close into the wind.

On racing days it was Douglas who went out with Pirry, while Ilsa watched—if the course was near enough—from the gazebo on the tip of the headland. The two men had been living and sailing together for almost twenty years, and Ilsa wondered at first whether Douglas might be resentful when she arrived for a long stay. But his protective attitude toward Pirry made him pleased that the long-planned opera was to take shape at last, and she found him friendly and welcoming. He was a sturdy man in his early sixties, with iron-gray hair and a thick mustache; he spoke little and was always busy.

"Duggie doesn't appreciate our sort of music," Pirry had said at their first introduction. "He raves about some pop group called the Beatles and is deaf to the charms of Beethoven. But he can tune any kind of engine to sing a sweet song. And he understands all these newfangled electronics. He's longing to set up a multiple tape deck— whatever that may be—in the music room for you, so that you can build up layers of sound and judge the effect." Douglas had smiled, glad to have his sphere of interest delineated and making it clear that he would not interfere in Ilsa's work.

Her days quickly constructed their own timetable. In the early evening she discussed details of the opera with Pirry over the champagne cocktails which he had prescribed to cure her lack of appetite. After dinner he would sometimes come into the music room with her for an hour, but for most of the night she worked alone, with only a single spotlight to pierce the blackness and only the steady surge of the sea against the rocks to disturb or inspire her. Morning was her time for sleeping, in the guest cottage a short distance away from the villa. Afternoons were for relaxation—although even then she was still thinking about the opera, her mind alert to recognize and remember any new idea. Never far from her thoughts was the fear that she might not have long enough to finish the work.

There were good days and bad days in these months which she spent as Pirry's guest. Mr. Simpson had kept his promise to see that any pain was controlled. Approving of her move to a better climate, he had provided her with a liberal first supply of drugs and instructions, and a long letter to be passed on to Pirry's medical adviser, Dr. Lequesne. Her ill health had been clear enough when she first came out to France—clear even to Douglas, who was not told the truth of it. But the spring restored her strength to such an extent that sometimes she wondered whether Mr. Simpson could have been mistaken. She allowed herself to hope but was never tempted to slacken the pace of her work. The summer was hot, and she was well enough to accept a visit from Michael in September. When she waved him goodbye for the start of his first term at Cambridge, she was confident that he suspected nothing. Leo, too, came to stay at the end of a European tour. He had been for many years a regular visitor to Pirry's villa and now was delighted to find two of his closest friends living under the same roof. His arrival brought an extra glow of happiness to the household, as each member of the trio took pleasure in observing the warm relationship between the other two.

With the coming of winter, though, her sense of well-being began to fade. Although she coughed less violently than a year earlier, there was a thickness in her chest which made breathing a painful struggle. Her neck, too, had become stiff, making it difficult to sleep comfortably. Not that she cared about sleep any longer. Finishing the opera was all that mattered.

As the end of the year approached, it was possible to be optimistic. By now Pirry had nothing to contribute but encouragement, for she had completed the setting of the libretto. What remained was the orchestration of a storm scene and the composition of the overture— left until last so that it could incorporate the themes which were to follow. Christmas Day came almost as an intrusion, and as soon as it was over she returned to the score.

Pirry and Douglas had planned a party for New Year's Eve. They would use the music room for dancing and, because Pirry had ambitious plans for decorating it, Ilsa worked in the guest cottage for the three days before the party. The change of routine disturbed her concentration and she could feel the pace of her work slowing. Her brain seemed muddy and confused: she could no longer hear the music clearly in her head. Perhaps, she thought, the drugs she was taking were dulling her wits. In order to test whether this was the case, she abandoned them.

The regimen laid down by Mr. Simpson and continued by Dr. Lequesne was designed to anticipate pain rather than merely relieve it after it began, so only when she ceased to take the medication did she realize what she had been spared for the past twelve months. The drugs had laid a flimsy veil over her mind, but a far more potent block to inspiration now was the tightness in her chest. It began as a dull ache but gradually increased in strength. She was unable to eat, unable to work, unable to think of anything but the pain. As she crouched in agony over the desk at which she had been working, her muscles locked themselves into rigidity and her brain had lost the key to unlock them. The telephone, directly linked to the villa, was only a few feet away. She could see it, but was unable to move a hand to reach it.

It was Pirry who rescued her, calling at the cottage half an hour before his party was due to begin and needing only a single glance to see what was wrong. Like a baby, Ilsa felt herself first picked up and then set down on the bed. Pirry kept his arms around her while she struggled to speak. In brief gasps she explained how idiotically she had deprived herself of her drugs.

"What will work fastest now?" he asked.

"Injection. Pethidine. Bathroom." Until now she had been taking diamorphine by mouth, but the stronger drug had been waiting for just this kind of emergency.

He unfastened her dress and helped her off with it. By now the pain in her chest was so intense that Ilsa was finding it difficult not to cry. Pirry's expression, as a rule pleasantly easygoing, was grim with sympathy as he hurried into the bathroom. She heard him washing his hands before he came back with the hypodermic syringe and an ampule. "I'll do it for you," he said, studying the dosage and checking it with her. "I'm used to giving Duggie jabs for his asthma." Sitting on the edge of the bed he swabbed her skin, slid in the needle with a smooth firmness and pushed the plunger home. Removing the needle, he pressed down on the spot for a few seconds, and even after relaxing his grip did not move away. Ilsa guessed that he was going to wait until the drug took effect and was grateful.

"I brought a bottle of champagne so that you could see the new year in over here if you didn't feel like company," he said. The casual note had returned to his voice: by a friendly chattiness he was reassuring her that the emergency was over. "But pethidine may not be an approved ingredient of a champagne cocktail. So perhaps you'd better let the old year slip away without celebration." He took hold of her hand, squeezing it gently. "But I hope you'll remember nineteen-sixty-four as one of your good years, Ilsa. It's been marvelous for me, and all because of you. My cousin from a cold climate."

Ilsa tried to smile, and Pirry looked down at her as though perplexed by his own thoughts. "It's odd, you know." He was still chatting inconsequentially, to pass the time. "I was brought up by women. My father died when I was only five or six, and after that the household seemed to be entirely female. My mother, my aunt, my sister, a host of female cousins. The Lorimer ladies. I wouldn't have minded them being so successful themselves if they hadn't been so determined that I should be talented as well. I was to do something worthwhile with my life, and do it energetically. But I never was energetic, I fear. The world is divided between those who see life as the raw material for achievement and those who regard it as a finished product. I admired them all, the Lorimer ladies—but collectively, as a family, they've always terrified me. I'm not a misogynist: a lot of my best friends are women. All the same, I feel as though I've been frightened of women all my life."

"Not your mother, surely."

There was a long silence, as though he were putting the question to himself for the first time.

"There's a special feeling about inheriting a title," he said. "You do sometimes wonder why you were born. My mother's always made it clear that she would accept any kind of wife for me, if only the marriage would produce—not just a baby, not just a son, but an *heir.* It makes me wonder about myself. My father was in his fifties when I was born. His first wife had been an invalid. When he married Mother—oh, I'm sure they loved each other. But it's difficult not to believe that the wish for an heir came into the contract somewhere. I wasn't born for my own sake. I was born so that I could be the next Lord Glanville and cut out my uncle Duncan. The world is divided another way as well: between those who simply live and those who inflict life on others. My mother had that power over me: the most terrifying power of all."

"But you love her."

"Oh yes, I love her dearly. But then there's this ridiculous business of the entail, which adds a certain guilt and resentment to the package. Not only did she give me life, but she makes it essential for me to go on living, because my death would diminish her in a very literal way. And just suppose—sometimes I have a nightmare. I love Duggie as well, you see. But suppose something happened—the house on fire, perhaps, and I could only save his life at the cost of my own. What would I do, Ilsa? Somewhere along the line I've lost the right to love anyone more than my mother."

He sighed, and for a few minutes neither of them spoke. Then Pirry returned to the thought from which mention of his mother had diverted him. "But it *is* odd, you know. You're a Lorimer lady, aren't you, Ilsa? Quite as talented as any of the others. As formidable, even. How does it happen that I'm not frightened of you?"

"It's because I'm cold. Self-centered. Interested in nothing but my music." Ilsa was quoting what Richard had said—without bitterness, because she believed it to be true. She added her own contribution for good measure. "And not possessive. I'm no threat to you."

The pethidine was taking effect now, flowing through her body. Pain receded, leaving behind a blissful weightlessness. Pirry's fingers, moving delicately over her skin, soothed her toward sleep, but a new thought startled her into alertness again. It was true that there was no way in which she could threaten Pirry, and perhaps it was because he did not threaten her that she felt so much at ease with him. From their first meeting she had known that he would never desire her body, never wish to explore it, probing its rottenness. Yet when he had pressed the needle into her body—a body invaded by a real and not an imagined malignancy—he had shown no embarrassment and she had felt no disgust. And how he was stroking her almost like a lover, and she found only comfort in the contact. From Richard, all too often, she had shrunk away; but Pirry's touch in this dozy, happy twilight of the mind filled her with a kind of love. "Pirry!" she said, her voice incredulous with the discovery.

With the empathy which had made their working collaboration so sensitive and successful, Pirry understood what she meant. "I don't understand it either," he said. Briefly his hand tightened on her bare shoulder and he leaned over to kiss her on the forehead. "Happy New Year, Ilsa," he said. "Go to sleep now. I'll see you again in nineteen-sixty-five."

XI

Now a sense of urgency possessed Ilsa. She had been given a warning. Her body might withstand the attack of disease for some time yet, but for how much longer would the clarity of her mind survive? She worked all afternoon as well as through the night, sleeping only for three or four hours each morning. Meals were brought in, but she had little appetite. Dr. Lequesne, summoned on New Year's Day to approve the injections which she now needed regularly, had offered to find a private nurse: but Pirry, with only a quick glance at Ilsa, turned the offer down and himself provided all the care she needed.

The need for haste drove Ilsa to abandon her usual method of working in the music room. She moved from a writing table to the piano and made use of the recording devices which Douglas had installed. If she failed to complete the composition herself, a competent orchestrator would be able to understand her intentions from the tapes. Pirry, too, was drawn into the work. As she wrote one line of music she dictated another to him. He was in any case determined to stay close at hand, ready to give her an injection every three hours.

And then, at nine o'clock one morning, the opera was finished. Pirry jumped to his feet, exclaiming with excitement, as Ilsa signed her name on the score. After sitting for thirteen hours almost without moving she was unable to straighten herself at once. Her hands climbed from his waist to his shoulders as though she were pulling herself up a ladder; but when at last they were standing face to face, neither of them could speak for laughing.

Beneath the excitement she was very tired. She allowed Pirry to help her back to the cottage and then, unusually, slept right through the day, waking in the evening with a dry mouth and a head which spun dizzily as she sat up in bed. It was hunger, no doubt; she had eaten nothing for twenty-four hours. Moving carefully, she bathed and dressed and made her way across the lawn to the villa. Even before reaching the drawing room she could hear the sound of hysterical laughter. She arrived at the glass door and stared inside.

To the music of the radio, Pirry and Douglas were dancing. Since Ilsa had known them, their behavior together had never been anything but dignified, but now they seemed to be caricaturing themselves—flirting, mincing, giggling. Pirry was wearing the maid's frilly white apron tied around his waist. When they caught sight of her Douglas collapsed, still laughing, into a chair, while Pirry—showing no embarrassment—came over to slide open the door and help her inside. He opened a bottle of champagne which was waiting in the ice bucket and filled three glasses.

"Time to celebrate! To *The Lady from the Sea!*"

Ilsa was too happy to worry about whether it was wise to drink on an empty stomach. But after the toast she looked at the men in mock disapproval. "I have the impression that you two started celebrating some time ago."

"That was something quite different," Pirry told her, laughing. "Your husband turned up while you were asleep."

"Richard! Here?"

"Yes. Tell her, Duggie."

"Pirry was out sailing," said Douglas. "He'd told me that you weren't to be disturbed after working all night, so it seemed simplest to say that you were out as well. I was changing the oil in the Porsche —wearing my dirtiest overalls—and Dr. Laing obviously thought I was the chauffeur. He started pumping me about what went on here. Not quite the gentlemanly thing to do, in my opinion, gossiping to servants! He made it pretty clear what he was after. He'd been expecting you to divorce him, apparently, but you hadn't; so he'd come to find out whether he had grounds for divorce himself. After all, you appeared to have been living with Lord Glanville for the past year."

"So what did you tell him?" But Ilsa could already guess.

"He heard Pirry come up from the boathouse. "Is that Lord Glanville now?" he asked. "Yes," says I. "I'll fetch her." So I nip over and put Pirry in the picture, and he grabs Jeanne's apron and the pan that she's stirring and out he prances and within five minutes Dr. Laing's got the message that he'll have to look elsewhere for his guilty party."

"If you *want* him to divorce you, we can go back on it, of course," said Pirry more seriously. "It would really set my friends chattering if I were to be cited as a corespondent. But since there aren't any genuine grounds, it seemed simplest to make that clear, and even to exaggerate just a little."

"Just a little," agreed Douglas happily. Both men began to giggle again.

"But he wants to talk to you," said Pirry, refilling Ilsa's glass. "There's something about his girlfriend hoping to have a baby. I didn't like to ask whether there was any urgency. I suppose you were going to divorce him for desertion after two years and not for adultery, were you?"

If Ilsa had thought about it at all, she had dismissed the subject of divorce as unsavory and unnecessarily upsetting to Michael. It would be humiliating to undergo questioning about her private life. But behind that distaste had lain her belief that the tumor in her chest would end the marriage more decisively than any judge. "Is Richard coming back?" she asked.

"Tomorrow evening. Of course, if you don't want to see him—"

"I'll see him. He's right: it's time to be businesslike." She shrugged the matter off as the celebration continued. But later, when Pirry had seen her back to the guest cottage, she returned to the subject. "When Richard comes back, I don't want him to know that I'm ill."

"Why not? It would stop him bullying you."

"He won't do that anyway. You don't know him, of course. He's a kind man. Sentimental. He may be angry with me now, but that's my fault. If he ever learns that I was already ill when he walked out—and that I knew it—he'll never forgive himself for going."

"Why should you worry about his feelings?"

"Because I owe him so much for his kindness—and his love—in the past. So don't say anything, will you? Not tomorrow, or ever."

"Just as you like," said Pirry. "But—"

"But what?"

"Nothing. Sleep well."

Ilsa's puzzlement lasted only for a few seconds after he had left. As she brushed her hair she stared at her face in the glass and the reason for Pirry's doubt stared back at her. Even were Richard not a doctor he would know as soon as he saw her that he was looking at a dying woman. Makeup could perhaps camouflage the black sockets of her eyes and the unhealthy color of her skin, but she would not be able to conceal her hollowed cheeks or the lines which pain had etched above her nose and at the corners of her mouth. Richard would look at her and be first of all dismayed and later, when he had had time to think, guilty.

She could refuse to see him, of course, or go away. But that would be cowardly—and already an alternative solution was insinuating itself into her mind.

For the second time since her illness had revealed itself she remembered a conversation in Auschwitz, the fervent whispering from the bunk above her head. "Choose your own death," Sigi had urged. Ilsa herself, many years later, had spoken the truth in demanding truthfulness from Mr. Simpson. "I want to be in control." No amount of self-control could now keep her alive for very much longer, but this one power still remained: she could choose her own death. She could go out to meet it in a place and at a time of her own appointment and make of it a positive act rather than a suffering.

The satisfaction of holding that power, as throughout a wakeful night she approached a decision, was the only argument which carried weight. To consider Richard's feelings, to spare herself physical pain and the mental anguish of knowing that she could no longer create music, to save Pirry from having to watch as she became weaker—all these were trivial points, relevant only because there was nothing on the other side to balance them. Brought up in a godless society, she had never felt any need of religion. Her life was her own, to live as she could or end as she pleased. She could make a kindness out of her death, and she would be doing no one any harm. Why should she deny herself this last pleasure of choice?

It must seem to be an accident. Her bathroom cabinet was full of the drugs she had been prescribed, and the villa's private bar was well stocked with alcohol. But Pirry had been giving her injections for the past three weeks, and to take an overdose might expose him to trouble. In such a case, too, the nature of her illness would be revealed to Richard at an inquest. How could she contrive that Pirry would be able to keep his promise and guard the secret of her condition?

It was easy to think of an answer. For a little while she explored it with her mind and saw no objections. She lay on the bed without attempting to sleep, deliberately recalling all the most vivid memories of her life and from time to time shivering with delight and excitement like a young girl on the night before her wedding. Every moment now was to be savored.

The next morning Pirry came to give her another injection. "I'm driving into Nice," he told her. "Shall I take the last pages of the score to be photocopied?" Throughout the year he had taken this precaution with previous batches, in case the original sheets should be lost or damaged.

"I'll sort them out for you," Ilsa said. "One or two discarded pages may be mixed up with the final version." She led the way to the music room, walking more easily than for several days. Pirry commented on this.

"Well, the pressure's off. It was a strain, getting it finished."

"Does it leave you feeling sad or happy, now it's done?"

"Oh, happy. Yesterday I was too tired to be sure, but now—I think it's good, Pirry. You know, I should never have thought of attempting an opera if you hadn't persuaded me. I'm very grateful."

"Grateful! I can hardly believe my luck that you agreed. Can we do it again, Ilsa? This has gone to my head. I'd like to write a libretto from scratch, instead of adapting someone else's story. A modern plot. How about an opera in which the main character is a house? Families move in and out, there are squatters, and terrorists holding hostages. There could even be a ghost."

"A singer to represent each wall." Ilsa entered into the spirit of the fantasy. "The four walls acting as chorus while the inhabitants change. Oh, Pirry!" Recognizing the desperation of his attempt to provide her with a new incentive for survival, she hardly knew whether to laugh or cry. "Dear Pirry!"

"Dear Ilsa!" He stepped forward and took her in his arms. As they stood close together, Ilsa could feel the comfort of his affection and concern warming her body. She hoped that her own excitement was communicating itself to him in turn.

When the moment of closeness was over, Pirry looked at her with mischief in his eyes. "If Richard was peeping through the window then, all his suspicions—or hopes—will be confirmed," he said. "Well, I'll be back in time for lunch. Goodbye."

"Goodbye." That was perfect, Ilsa thought as Pirry left the music room—to part, not quite casually, with love and laughter. There would be nothing for Pirry to regret.

She sat down and began to write to Michael at Cambridge: a cheerful letter which would give no hint of her intention but would make her love for him obvious. Her pen moved with more generous strokes than usual as she described her pleasure at completing the opera. "And now the sun is shining, tempting me to an hour on the sea in Pirry's yacht," she wrote. "I expect to see Richard this evening, so I'll finish this later and add his news as well as the rest of mine. Goodbye for the moment." She addressed the envelope and left that and the letter untidily visible. Then she went back to the cottage to change.

By the time she was ready, Pirry had driven off in the estate car and Douglas was working on the Porsche again.

"I'm going to take the Snipe out," Ilsa told him. "An appropriate treat to celebrate finishing the opera." The Snipe was the only one of

Pirry's boats which she could hope to manage single-handed; and, because he sailed it every day that he was not racing, she could hope to find it already rigged.

"It'll be cold in the wind." But Douglas could see that she was sensibly dressed, and it was not in his nature to tell other people what was best for them.

It took Ilsa a little while to make her way down the zigzag steps to the boathouse, and the effort of pulling on the fixed rope which drew the little yacht out of the protected water was almost too much for her. But as the Snipe emerged from shelter and reared up under the attack of the wind, she gave a gasp of triumph.

Almost at once, though, she realized that she lacked the power to control the yacht on a day of such blustery weather. It would be an accident after all! She laughed aloud at the discovery and felt her body flooding with an excitement more passionate than either love or life had ever aroused in her. To prolong the ecstatic anticipation, she determined to hold a safe course for as long as she could. The wind carried her across the bay and she was able to make one successful jibe to turn back toward the cape. But now it was necessary to tack. Her arms began to ache and her breath panted into the chill January wind. The Snipe, tilting dangerously, raced back through the icy black water. With a correct instinct, Ilsa threw her weight outward. But her strength was draining away fast: she would not be able to hold the little yacht close to the wind for very much longer.

At this distance from the headland she had a view of the villa and its gardens. She saw Pirry appear from the side of the house and run to the top of the steps—Pirry, whom she had never known to hurry! He searched the bay with his eyes, looking for her, and even at this distance the attitude of his body revealed his anxiety.

Intoxicated with self-induced exhilaration, Ilsa let go of the tiller for a moment to wave; but Pirry, dashing down the steps, did not see the gesture. She began to lower her arm, but something had knotted in her chest and she could not move, or even breathe. A pain fiercer than anything she had previously experienced squeezed her heart; but it was not important, for now a wave surged against the rudder which she no longer controlled, pressing it in a new direction. As the Snipe hesitated, tossing its head in the spray, rearing over each wave and smacking down again into the trough which followed, the wind seized its chance to snatch at the far side of the sail. Doubled up in agony, Ilsa lifted her head and saw the boom sweeping toward her.

As cold as the snow in the land of her birth, the icy water snatched at her breath and pressed a freezing finger on her heart. The pain exploded and died. Without any struggle, Ilsa released her hold on life and disappeared.

XII

It was on the morning of Sir Winston Churchill's funeral that the telephone call came from France to the flat in the Portobello Road. Considerate in all his arrangements, Pirry had made sure that should there ever be bad news, Asha and not his mother would be the first to hear. He had been efficient as well. For many months a folder had been lying in a drawer of Asha's desk, listing addresses, telephone numbers, details of the emergency plan already drawn up for Alexa. The international operator made the connection and Asha listened in silence as Douglas, tearful but straightforward, told her what had happened. Pirry was dead. He had died, it seemed, in an attempt to save Ilsa's life.

Hardly able to believe the news, she repeated it to Ranji. "I must go to Blaize," she said, and he nodded in sympathy. "I'll take a bag. I shall probably need to stay the night with Aunt Alexa."

"Then I should come also." They had not spent a night apart since their marriage.

Asha shook her head. "It's not the right occasion, darling." Under the disguise of peremptory orders for some errand to be performed, recent telephone calls from Blaize had suggested that Alexa was preparing to forgive Asha for her secret and unsuitable marriage. But she had not yet brought herself to mention Ranji's name. She was pretending that he did not exist; and Asha had been equally well able without using words to make it clear that she would not visit Blaize again until she could bring her husband with her. Still, this was not the right moment to stand on principle. "You go and watch the procession, as we planned, and tell me about it tomorrow." They had been intending to join the thousands who would be lining the funeral route to St. Paul's.

Asha could tell that Ranji was not happy with the arrangement, but the need to arrive alone at Blaize was so clear to her that she gave him no chance to argue. Instead, she turned back to the telephone and made a call to ensure that the suite of rooms bought by Pirry would be ready for Alexa as soon as she chose to move her furniture in. Then she called Bernard.

"Did you ever meet Ilsa's son, Michael?" she asked when she had told him the news. "He's up at Cambridge. Douglas wondered whether one of us could break it to him about his mother. It's bound to be a terrible shock, and a long-distance call from someone who's practically a stranger would be a bleak way of hearing."

"I'll drive in and see him," Bernard promised. His home and laboratory were only just outside Cambridge. "Do you know his college?"

"Trinity, Douglas said." Asha thanked him and hung up. There was nothing more she could do in London. She kissed Ranji lovingly and set out for Blaize.

The curtains of the drawing room were closed when she arrived and for a moment, as she waited for the door to be opened, Asha wondered whether the news of Pirry's death had preceded her. But it was only that Alexa preferred to watch television in darkness. The state funeral, with its many stages of ceremonial, was scheduled to fill the screen for most of the day.

"Sit down," Alexa commanded, showing no surprise at the visit. "You haven't got television in that flat of yours, I suppose."

"No, we haven't." Thus provided with an excuse for coming, Asha saw no need to be abrupt in breaking the news. As she sat down, she looked to see what was happening. Inside St. Paul's the coffin had been set in position for the service; there was a momentary pause, filled with the sound of organ music, while the pallbearers moved away.

"You've missed the procession," Alexa said. "And the arrival. There was a nasty moment on the cathedral steps when we thought we were going to lose another ex-prime minister. Attlee must be almost as old as I am. Over eighty, anyway. Too old to be carrying coffins about. And Winnie was no lightweight, either. All well, though."

The words were flippant, but her voice was husky with emotion. As the service began, Asha found herself sharing the same mood. The sentiment engendered by the occasion was so intense that it seemed to burst out of the black-and-white picture, filling the room. The camera's eye rested silently on kings and presidents and generals inside the cathedral, or searched the crowds outside for the faces of weeping women and men whose eyes were fixed on distant memories.

The service ended, the procession re-formed, the dignitaries scattered. The coffin was carried on its way again; this time, down to the river. In the distance, as the launch which now carried it drew away from the bank, a row of tall dockland cranes dipped in tribute to the occasion. The silent movement and elegant line of their dark silhouettes provided an unexpectedly poignant moment of beauty. Alexa abandoned the pretense that she was not affected.

"Turn the sound down, will you?" she asked. "But keep the picture." She blew her nose and took off her spectacles so that she could dab her eyes.

"It's not just the man, you see," she tried to explain as Asha obeyed. "After all, to someone your age, what was he? A party politician who drank too much and lived too long? Or a page out of a history book? But to anyone older he represents a time and a mood. Those dockers who dipped their crane jibs just then—Bolshies to a man, I wouldn't be surprised. Saw him as their class enemy. Voted him out of office after the war. Quite prepared to use their industrial power to bring him down again after he got back, even if it brought the country down with him. But those same dockers fought for the same country in nineteen-forty. What we're burying today is a reminder of the time when everyone in England was on the same side as everyone else. You hear people say sometimes that the best years of their life were in the war, and it seems sad that that could be true. But I can understand it. I expect almost everyone in England has been watching this today—on television if they can't get to London —or listening on the radio. And I can remember the last time that happened—a whole nation sharing a single emotion, concentrating on a single event."

As though she had spoken a cue, there was a change in the picture on the screen. Presumably the coffin was out of camera range: it was possible to deduce that the interval was being filled with recordings of Churchill's most famous wartime orations, illustrated by the events which had occasioned them. The picture now was of the beach at Dunkirk, with its long lines of soldiers stretching into the sea, waiting to be rescued while German planes swooped over them.

"That was the time," said Alexa. "We didn't have television then; at least, I didn't. We all listened to the radio. Every moment we could, for six days. The hottest days of summer. Pirry was there, you know, at Dunkirk. He almost got away. But the ship was sunk under him. That's how he was captured. Five years in a prisoner-of-war camp. I often wonder if things would have been different if . . ." She stood up, stiff and unsteady after her day of viewing. "I must phone Pirry. Now. He calls me every Sunday evening, but I'm not going to wait. I want to talk to him."

She was turning toward the telephone. Asha, moving quickly, stood in her way.

"You've been crying too," said Alexa. "I didn't notice, in the dark. You shared the feeling, then, in spite of being too young to remember?"

"I shared it, yes. But that's not why I was crying. I didn't come here just to watch television, Aunt Alexa. I've brought bad news."

"About Pirry?"

"Yes." Asha had had all day to rehearse it, but still found it difficult to say the words. "Pirry—he's dead, Aunt Alexa."

"Pirry! Pirry! He can't be. How?"

"In the sea. After a sailing accident, Douglas said."

Alexa sat down, suddenly, as though her legs had ceased to support her. Asha held her hand tightly, not daring to speak. The old lady who had wept for Churchill's passing sat dry-eyed and stiff-backed as she tried to believe that her son was dead.

"It's not possible. That idiot Douglas must have made a mistake. Pirry's been sailing all his life. He doesn't have accidents. And he's a marvelous swimmer. After being sunk at Dunkirk, he swam for hours back to land. Tell me it isn't true, Asha."

"Douglas said the sea was terribly cold. He didn't actually see the accident. But he thought Pirry might have got a cramp. Or else that he died from shock when he hit the icy water. Oh, darling, I'm so sorry." Asha searched for words of comfort, but could find none. She sat in silence, gripping Alexa's hand, while a long time passed.

Meanwhile the television screen continued silently to record the

day's events, and in the end it was a change of scene which distracted
Asha's eyes. Churchill's coffin was on a train now. The camera followed the train out of the station, through a cutting, over a bridge,
between rows of small, smoke-blackened houses, on and on until it
was so far away that the railway lines seemed on the point of converg-
ing. She knew that in fact it was on its way to the family resting place
in the village of Bladon; but without the commentary to interpret the
picture it seemed as though the train were disappearing into a sym-
bolic infinity. The rituals of mourning were coming to an end. She
released Alexa's hand for a moment and turned the set off.

Alexa's voice pierced the darkness of the room with a chilling calm-
ness. "I'd like to walk round the house. Will you phone through and
tell Mr. Jamieson?" For the past twenty years Alexa had made her
home in only the west wing of Blaize. She had the right at any time to
visit the school which occupied the rest of the mansion, but always as
a matter of courtesy gave notice of her wish to do so. "And make an
appointment for me to see him tomorrow. Pirry got those people up
in Scotland to agree to the lease. The school will be given good
notice. But it may have to go in the end. Mr. Jamieson will want to
start looking round."

Both women blinked as Asha turned on the light before moving to
the telephone. "It's a holiday weekend," she reported after the call.
"Mr. Jamieson's away until Sunday evening. The caretaker said to
give him a minute while he switches the lights on at the mains for
you."

"Where will they go?" Alexa wondered aloud. "And where shall *I*
go?" At last her self-control shattered. "Asha, what am I going to
do?"

In 1947 Alexa had led a five-year-old girl through the door which
led from her private wing to the school building. The journey had
been intended as a treat, the offer of a new kingdom to explore. But
Asha, frightened by such an expanse of unknown territory, had cried
for her dead mother: it was the first clear memory of her life.

Alexa, on that day, had promised to look after the orphaned child
and had kept her promise faithfully. Now it was time for the debt to
be repaid. It was Alexa, eighty-seven years old and devastated by
bereavement, who was lonely and afraid; and Asha who must take the
responsibility for her happiness.

"There's a place waiting for you," she said. "A sort of country flat. Terribly nice. It's all arranged. I'll take you to have a look at it. You can move in whenever you choose—the day after Pirry's funeral, if you want to." The elderly gentleman on his Scottish estate who had already, unwittingly, become the sixteenth Lord Glanville, was unlikely to play the part of a Victorian villain and turn a helpless old lady out into the snow. But if Alexa was determined not to be beholden for a moment to the new owner of the title and estates, Asha intended to relieve her mind of any fears. She brought Alexa her stick and took her other arm. Together they passed through the door leading to what had once been the state apartments.

The building was cold, and empty with the special hollowness of rooms from which a community is temporarily absent. Still supporting Alexa, but careful not to intrude on her thoughts by speaking, Asha allowed herself to be taken to the ballroom. It had been used for a concert before the school dispersed, and no one had yet tidied away the rows of chairs or the violin stands on the low platform.

"We had such marvelous occasions," sighed Alexa. "I remember the very first ball I attended here. It was in nineteen-five, long before Pirry was born. Before I had any thought of ever living at Blaize. Piers already wanted to marry me, but I was in love with someone else. We danced together here. I was beautiful in those days. But that's dead as well."

Had the shock induced a sudden rambling senility in the old lady? Perhaps, Asha decided, this period of reminiscence was an essential part of mourning. It was necessary for rituals to be observed. For Winston Churchill, the ceremonies of state: for Pirry the memories of a mother in a house peopled with ghosts.

Alexa sighed and shook her head sadly as she moved on and began slowly to climb the oak staircase up to the long gallery at the top of the house. It was the school library now: but, apart from the clutter of bookshelves, hardly changed since Tudor days.

High along the paneled wall hung a row of portraits, of thin-faced men with long noses. "The Glanvilles belong with the house," said Alexa without regret. "Except for these two. These are mine."

It was late in his life that she had commissioned a portrait of her husband, for he was already silver-haired when they married. Like his forebears he was tall and thin, but showed none of their superciliousness: his eyes were kind and intelligent. The portrait was a conventional one of a man in formal clothes. Beside it, Matthew Lorimer's painting of Pirry on his twenty-first birthday seemed at first glance to be not so much a portrait as a burst of sunlight. The young man's red-blond hair and fair skin emerged from a golden background so subtly that the final truth of the likeness was startling by comparison with the first impression of random brushstrokes.

"He was such a pretty boy." Alexa stared at the picture. This was what she had come to see. "He and Frisca, both beautiful children. And both dead. Both my children dead before me. It's not supposed to happen that way. You promised, Pirry. You promised to stay alive."

She was weeping at last, but after a few moments she gave a deep sigh, seeming to bring herself under control.

"Pirry always thought that I was afraid of leaving Blaize," she said. "But it was never my house. Always his. I wasn't brought up here. I looked after it because I hoped one day he'd come and live in it himself. I wouldn't have minded moving out then. But now—" She shivered. "I don't like things to change. I wanted to go on as I was. What's going to happen to me now, Asha?"

"I'll look after everything, Aunt Alexa. You don't have to worry."

"It was never the house," Alexa repeated. "Not the bricks and mortar. But Blaize was a home—the heart of the family. Not the Glanville family, after Piers died: the Lorimers. They all came here, to live or stay. Well, what's left of the family now? Ghosts, that's all. A house full of ghosts. So many deaths, and no births anymore. When are there going to be babies in the family again? Why should I want to stay here? I can entertain you all in a bed-sitting-room. You and Bernard and Ilsa and—Why didn't Ilsa telephone? She was staying with Pirry. She ought to have phoned directly, to tell me what happened."

"Ilsa died as well, Aunt Alexa. In the same accident."

Alexa was silent for a moment, but then looked up again at Pirry's portrait. Asha could tell that she did not really care about this second piece of news. She had lost a son and a great-niece at the same time, but had only tears enough for one of them.

Even Asha had been too deeply affected by Pirry's death to spare much thought for Ilsa. In silence she remembered the woman who had appeared almost from the dead in such an extraordinary way to take her place among the Lorimers. Until today, it had seemed that she had no part to play in the history of the family, that they had not loved her enough to make her feel that she belonged. She would never be one of the ghostly memories of Blaize. Yet Pirry must have cared for her; and her death had set in train a series of events which she could not have anticipated. As Alexa continued to stare brokenheartedly at the picture of her son, Asha thought about her pale, cold cousin and shivered in the unheated gallery. She took the old lady's arm again.

"Let me take you back into the warm, Aunt Alexa," she said.

PART III

Siva Dancing

1972-1973

I

There were no special visiting days in the country house which had been Alexa's home for the seven years since she was forced to leave Blaize. Although the companion Asha had found for her was a trained nurse, able to support her through the infirmities of old age, the converted mansion was not a nursing home. Alexa's suite of rooms was her own and she could entertain her friends there whenever she chose. But she had few friends left. She herself was ninety-five by now, and almost everyone who had once been close to her was either dead or too old to travel. Only Asha and Bernard visited her regularly. They came on Saturdays—her companion's free day—rarely overlapping but never leaving her without a visitor. It was clear enough to Alexa that they took pains to agree to a timetable between themselves so that she would never be disappointed.

If this proved to be one of Asha's days, the conversation would be about school affairs. Last year Alexa had listened with amusement to her great-niece's description of all the problems and disasters which followed the amalgamation of her school with another one to form a huge comprehensive. Now, with the beginning of a new school year, Asha would have a new class of children in her care. Thirty unfamiliar names—many of them foreign—would during the next few months take on characters of their own: the clever one, the wicked one, the unpunctual one, the neglected one. Alexa looked forward to following their progress.

It was more difficult for Bernard to make his work sound interesting. Alexa knew nothing at all about science. Although she could share her grandson's excitement as he described each new discovery in the laboratory which might—after years of testing—cure or control some disease, she did not understand the details. And although she gathered that the company which manufactured and distributed the drugs was extremely profitable, she did not know much about business either. Every time Bernard used the word "drug" she thought he meant cocaine or heroin and only with an effort remembered that he was talking about medicines.

It could have been worse, Alexa reminded herself as she pottered unsteadily around her sitting room, touching the flowers which were already perfectly arranged or checking the contents of the tea tray. On one occasion Bernard had brought with him Ilsa's boy, Michael— a friendly young man whose blond beard reminded her of some of her early beaux in the first decade of the century. She had asked *him* about his work, and he had started off by explaining the theory of relativity with the intention, apparently, of describing how he intended to bring it up to date—until her obvious incomprehension had brought his explanation to a halt. Bernard, on his next visit, had described the young man as a genius, but had never brought him again.

In the first years after Pirry's death and the move from Blaize Helen had usually accompanied her husband on his visits, but several months had passed since Alexa had seen her last. She had been ill and then, to end several years of discomfort, had gone into the hospital to have a hysterectomy. That was three weeks ago, but once again Bernard was alone when he arrived on this autumn Saturday in 1972.

"Helen sends her love," he said, stooping to kiss his grandmother and unwrapping the chrysanthemums he had brought. "But I made her stay in bed. She's still feeling very groggy. And the operation seems to have left her feeling depressed, even though she admits that there's nothing to be depressed about."

"It's always a hard time for a woman when she accepts that she can't have any more children. Or any at all," added Alexa pointedly.

"There was nothing sudden about that. We agreed long ago—"

"Choosing not to do something is different from knowing that you have no choice." In spite of her great age, Alexa expressed her opinions as sharply as ever. "You realize what it means. I shall never have any descendants now."

Even as she spoke she recognized the logical flaw in her argument. Helen would never be a mother, but there was nothing to stop Bernard himself from becoming a father. Alexa stifled the thought that was almost a hope. In her own beautiful and bohemian youth as an opera singer she had sown her fair share of wild oats. But Bernard had not inherited his grandmother's impulsiveness. He was a devoted and almost certainly faithful husband whose childlessness was deliberate. In past discussions he had done his best to explain his belief that to inflict life on a human being was an act of selfishness—and that in any case the world was overpopulated. Alexa had pointed out in reply that it was far from being overpopulated with Lorimers, but recognized that she had lost the argument long ago.

"Asha will have a baby one of these days," he assured her.

"It will be brown." Alexa made no pretense of being liberal in her views on miscegenation. "Not a descendant of mine, either. In any case, how long does she expect me to wait? I can't live forever, you know."

"Of course you can." Bernard gave his grandmother an affectionate kiss and opened the briefcase he was carrying. Alexa smiled to herself in amusement. She had long ago realized that her grandson always prepared a topic of conversation before he came to visit her, so that he would not need to spend too much time discussing Alexa's fellow residents or staff. Today—judging by the leaflets he produced—the subject was travel. "Tell me which of these holidays you think Helen and I would enjoy next spring." He spread the brochures in front of her. "I wondered about Russia—Moscow and Leningrad. You've been there, haven't you?"

"Seventy years ago I sang before the Tsar," she agreed. "But it was different then. Palaces and jewels. All you'll see now are collective farms and orphanages. Besides, spring isn't the time for Russia. There's slush everywhere when the snow starts to melt. You should go in October. Leningrad in October, with the trees turning color and the sun shining, is the most beautiful city in the world. At least, that was true when it was St. Petersburg."

"October's too long to wait. How about India, then?" He picked another brochure from the pile and showed it to her.

"India? People don't go to India for holidays. They go there to work. Your father worked in India. He died there." She checked herself, momentarily anxious. Did Bernard know that his real father was not the man who had married his mother? Yes. She remembered now. She had told him all about Robert Scott on his eighteenth birthday. She watched Bernard as, reminded of that conversation, he wandered over to the collection of family photographs arranged on his grandmother's piano and stared at the picture of two young cousins holding hands on the terrace at Blaize: his mother and the father he had never met.

"I've never really understood," he said. "You've always said that they were very much in love. Why didn't they marry?"

"Sometimes it happens that two ways of life are simply not compatible, not with the best will in the world. Your mother was a marvelous dancer—a star. She needed theaters, bright lights, the life of a big city. While Robert—it was more than simply that his job as an engineer was out there. He was in love with India."

"Is that possible? To be in love with a place?"

"He tried to explain it to me once, afterwards. As though there were some kind of magic about it. India was a passive country, he said —never asking for anything, just waiting, accepting what was offered or enduring what was imposed. And casting some kind of spell which made it difficult to escape. It didn't ask to be loved or hated, and yet everyone did love it or hate it. That was what Robert found, anyway. He was one who loved it. It didn't make much sense to me, talking about magic, any more than it did to your mother at first. But she seemed to understand in the end. She had to let him go back. But she couldn't bring herself to go with him, even though you were already on the way."

"Odd," said Bernard, and Alexa smiled affectionately as he gathered the scattered brochures together. Her grandson was too level-headed to describe a working environment in terms of magic. But curiosity was part of his character as well. It was curiosity, meticulously channeled and controlled, which had made him so successful as a research chemist. And although he had given no hint of his decision now, Alexa strongly suspected that curiosity about the spell which had bound his unknown father would draw him next spring to visit India.

I I

Michael Laing had his own methods of communicating with the outside world. The cottage to which he had retreated after completing his doctoral thesis was less than forty miles from Cambridge, but he had not given its address to any of his friends, so he received neither mail nor visitors. Once a month he picked up letters which had been addressed to him at his old college, usually discovering with pleasure that they were already out of date and so needed no answers. He had removed the bell from his telephone receiver, so that he could make calls himself but not be interrupted by others.

But although the cottage was in many ways primitive, it contained machines which would have caused the agricultural laborer for whom it was built in 1820 to mutter about witchcraft. Michael not only had his own computer terminal but also possessed a facsimile transmitter which he used to exchange pages of notes with one collaborator in Switzerland and another in Massachusetts. He had set aside three years of his life in which to concentrate his research into time and space without the distraction of earning a living even in a university astrophysics department. During this period he was prepared to accept support from his father because he sincerely believed in the importance of his work, but he was naturally concerned to keep his living expenses as low as possible. Living as frugally as any medieval scholar and in as much isolation as any early Christian hermit, he allowed himself only one social engagement each week. Every Sunday he had lunch with Helen and Bernard Lorimer.

Seven years earlier, at their first meeting, Bernard had been the messenger who brought bad news to the young undergraduate, but in spite of that had become a friend. Michael would never forget the couple's kindness as he struggled to come to terms with the shock of Ilsa's death. They had opened their home to him as though he were their own son and, as his intimacy with them grew, Michael enjoyed an unaccustomed warmth of family relationships. His father now was permanently settled in the United States, but even at the time when they all lived together he had been aware that Richard and Ilsa, equally talented and busy, were attached not so much by their love for each other as by the love of each for Michael himself.

Bernard and Helen were quite different. They were in their forties and had been married for almost twenty years, but they were still in love with each other. Michael could tell that from the way in which Helen would touch her husband as she passed him, and from the light in Bernard's eyes as he looked at his wife.

In other respects the couple had much in common with Ilsa and Richard. Helen, like Ilsa, was tall and slim and well groomed in appearance, calm and efficient in behavior—although she devoted herself not to music or any other career but to providing a comfortable life in a beautiful home for her husband. Bernard was incapable of dressing as smartly as Michael's father, but he was as dedicated and as successful in running his pharmaceutical business and research as Richard was in the very similar enterprise of his allergy clinics. Although Michael had not been born into the Lorimer family and had been sixteen before he discovered even his adoptive link with it, he felt completely at home in the household of Ilsa's cousin.

Had the Sunday arrangement not been such a regular one, he might have been tempted to stay at home on a February morning in 1973 when freezing rain made his motor bicycle a dangerous form of transport. But the pleasure of their weekly chat, even more than the promise of a glowing fire and an excellent meal, drew him as usual across the damp, flat fenland—to be rewarded by an unexpected invitation from Bernard while Helen was out of the room making the coffee at the end of the meal.

"Would you like to come to India with me next week?"

Michael looked at Bernard in surprise. "But surely Helen—"

"She doesn't feel up to it after all," Bernard said. "I can see it was a mistake on my part to choose this kind of holiday. I booked it well ahead in the hope that it would be a treat she could look forward to. No one warned us how long it would take her to recover from the hysterectomy. It seems to have knocked all the stuffing out of her. It's four months now, but she still gets tired very quickly. So she doesn't feel she could cope with the heat and the food and the traveling."

"Can't you just cancel?"

Bernard shook his head. "We had to decide before the new year whether or not to confirm the booking. Helen hoped that another few weeks might make all the difference, so we went ahead. Now that she realizes it would be too much for her, she's taken it into her head to go to a health farm instead."

"I've put on pounds since I came out of hospital," Helen said, returning to the drawing room as a signal that the coffee tray was ready for Bernard to carry in. "And all my muscles have melted away from disuse. I need to be starved and slapped and generally put back into shape."

"That's nonsense, of course." Bernard kissed her on the top of the head as he brought in the tray. "But it leaves us with the situation, Michael, that I've paid a large sum of money for a holiday for two people. Since Helen is going to disappear to the health farm in any case, I might as well take off as planned. That leaves an empty seat on a plane from London to Delhi and back from Bombay to London. Since the bed that goes with the package will be in my room, my choice of companion is restricted. Helen might not approve of me asking a female. And from my own point of view, I need someone I can boss about to some extent. No smoking and no snoring: that kind of thing."

"I smoke," said Michael.

"Not if I forbid you to, you don't."

Michael laughed as he considered the tempting invitation. His budget rarely allowed him a holiday. But he was not at his best in hot climates and preferred to spend the limited time which could be spared from his work climbing mountains rather than sight-seeing in cities. He was not sure that he would enjoy traipsing round India with a group of strangers from whom it would be difficult to escape. "Would you expect me to stay with you and the party all—"

Bernard interrupted the question. "I wouldn't expect anything. Package holidays suit me because I spend most of the year making decisions and being responsible for other people, so just for a couple of weeks I like to leave all the organization to someone else. I'm inviting you to pick out whatever parts of the package would suit you. You can ditch the rest. No skin off my nose."

Michael made up his mind quickly. "I've always wanted to go trekking in Nepal," he said. "I'd be immensely grateful for a flight to Delhi if you really wouldn't mind me leaving you there and taking off by myself."

"Fine. That's settled, then. The group will be flying back from Bombay at the end of the tour, so you'd have to make your way there, but that should be simple enough."

"No problem," said Michael, putting on an Indian voice and grinning with delight. "What nice people you are. I can't think what I've done to deserve you." But if he had really not known, Helen's affectionate hug would have given him the answer. She would have liked to have a son of her own who came home every week for Sunday lunch. Her home was always so clean and tidy that perhaps in her younger years she had been reluctant to expose it to all the mess that came with babies and young children. Or perhaps the ill health which in the end had made her hysterectomy necessary had even earlier made childbearing impossible for her. Michael had never thought it any of his business to inquire or even to wonder why she and Bernard had never had a family, but he was absolutely sure that now, when it was too late, Helen regretted her childlessness.

Michael had spent the first eighteen years of his life enjoying the love of a woman who was not his natural mother. He knew how to accept such love and how to give it. He kissed Helen now in thanks for her husband's generosity, and felt the warmth of her pleasure in return.

I I I

"Give my love to the Taj Mahal," said Helen. She clung tightly to Bernard as he kissed her goodbye at Heathrow. "And be good," she added.

"When am I anything but good?"

"When have you ever been allowed to face temptation alone? Every other member of the party may prove to be a widow looking out for an unprotected man." But she was smiling, unworried.

Bernard smiled back. Somewhere inside the airport at this moment were nine or ten strangers who at the end of eighteen days would have become acquaintances. It might even prove possible to strike up a casual holiday friendship with one or two. But there was no danger of any of them proving a threat to his marriage. He gave her a last kiss and made his way to the check-in desk.

Michael was there already, conspicuous in the queue from the size of his backpack and his heavy mountain boots. They had agreed earlier not to travel together; and not only because Michael preferred to sit in the smoking section of the plane. A man of forty-six traveling with another man in his twenties might need to explain the relationship if it were not to be misinterpreted, and the effort would hardly be worthwhile when they would next have to explain that Michael was deserting the party at Delhi.

So Bernard was on his own as he began the process of identifying his fellow travelers—an easy task, in view of the garish orange luggage labels provided by the travel agency. He was not good at remembering names and so concentrated hard as introductions were made. Helen had been right to promise him widows as companions, for there were two traveling together. Mrs. Farmer was tall, smart and blue-rinsed. Mrs. Mostyn was short, fat and mousily fair.

The tall, erect man in his sixties with thick white hair and toothbrush mustache was Colonel Alderton, almost certainly ex-Indian Army. His daughter, Daphne—being taken, no doubt, to see where her father had won the war—was a solidly built young woman in her early thirties. Ten years ago she must have been pretty, and not all the prettiness had faded. Now there was a hopeful anxiety in her expression as her eyes flickered over the other members of the party. She was hoping for company of her own age, probably—and especially for an unattached man.

Perhaps Dr. Ibbotson would fill the bill: a Yorkshireman, ten years younger than Bernard, and also traveling alone. There was no other possibility, for as the party filled up its seats in the plane only two more males appeared. Mr. Hunwick was very definitely half of a married couple, while Stephen Clyde's unsuitability for Daphne was of a different kind. Bernard, shaking hands, studied his appearance with frank enjoyment. He was beautifully dressed in a suit whose color graduated from a rich purple at the shoulders to a pale pink at the ankles. He wore purple suede shoes with stacked heels and his curly blond hair had come straight from a hairdresser. It came as a distinct surprise to hear him say that the seat still empty was for his wife, who had only just flown in from Ireland and was waiting for her luggage to be transferred.

She arrived a few minutes later, coming up behind Stephen Clyde and touching his shoulder gently. Bernard could see the young man's expression of pleasure as he rose to greet his wife. But if he had not used that word a moment earlier, Bernard would have been hard put to it to guess the sex of this last member of the party. Even as it was, his stare was doubtful. It was possible that Stephen might put his own meaning to terms.

In the end he accepted that she was a woman, nearly flat-chested but not quite. She wore a black sweater and slacks—sensible for traveling but not becoming. She was older than her husband, and far less beautiful. Her straight black hair appeared to have been cut at home with the help of a ruler. Its thick fringe, almost touching her eyebrows, gave her face a flattened, primitive appearance. She wore no makeup. Nothing about the other members of the party had struck Bernard as unusual, but about Mr. and Mrs. Stephen Clyde he felt very curious indeed.

She stowed her coat and cabin bag away and sat down opposite Bernard. The plane was one in which half the seats faced forward and half back. Bernard, in the front row of the nonsmoking section, was facing the first row of smokers.

"Gitta Clyde," she said to him, stretching out her hand as she introduced herself. Her voice was low and the handshake she offered was a firm one, her strong fingers clasping his own rather than allowing themselves to be encircled.

"Bernard Lorimer." There were occasions in his business life when Bernard found his title useful and, because Helen liked being Lady Lorimer, he made no attempt to conceal it on social occasions. But he had never felt that an inherited baronetcy was anything to boast about and so did not emphasize it on occasions such as this.

"Are you traveling alone, Mr. Lorimer?"

"Yes." He caught Michael's eye but managed to refrain from smiling. "My wife is recovering from an operation," he explained, glad that Gitta Clyde's question had given him the opportunity to make clear his marital status so that he would not have to bother about it again. "I enjoy traveling, but she's not so keen even at the best of times, and she felt the heat would be oppressive while her health was still below par."

"Why do you like to travel?" The question was so blunt as to be aggressive, and Bernard stared at Gitta Clyde for a moment without answering. He indulged his own curiosity as much in social life as in the laboratory; he had always been a man who asked questions. His companions on this tour were interesting to him now mainly because he knew nothing about them. One of his minor pleasures would be to study his fellow travelers and consider what made each of them tick. So it was clearly unjust that he should resent interrogation of himself by someone with an equal curiosity. "I find traveling restful," he answered.

His inquisitor gave a quick, hard laugh. "Then you haven't read the itinerary! All those flights at five o'clock in the morning!"

"Mentally restful, not physically. Nothing important is going to happen. I spend most of my working day making decisions and choices and every decision has consequences—sometimes important ones. But nothing that I may decide to do in the next eighteen days will have any permanent consequence at all."

"Everything that happens has a consequence," she said. "When you board the plane for the flight back, you won't be the same person. You're bound to have changed."

"Not all changes have significance," he suggested; and then, deliberately lightening his voice to bring the conversation to an end, "But I grant you, by that time I shall no longer be a man who hasn't seen the Taj Mahal."

His tone discouraged further discussion of the subject and, as the plane took off and climbed and turned, he was able to open his book. Opposite him, Gitta sat without occupation. Every time he glanced up, he found her staring at him. No doubt it was only his position immediately facing her which condemned him to her scrutiny, but awareness of her continuing gaze was a distraction, interrupting his own concentration. Gitta's face lacked mobility. All its character came from her dark, almost black eyes. With them she seemed to be considering him feature by feature, their directness making it impossible to outstare her. When she lowered her gaze, it was only in order to consider more of him than his face, studying him almost as intently as an artist might study a model. He tried by the force of his own look to turn her eyes away from him; and failed.

The plane flew steadily through the night. City lights, mountain snows and black, invisible deserts fell away below and behind them. Bernard made no attempt to sleep. He accepted the drinks and meals which were offered and then sat back without fretting at his wakefulness, relaxed in the darkness. On his left, the two widows turned from side to side in a restless doze, while the doctor and the beautiful young man in two of the facing seats slept soundly. Immediately opposite him, Gitta continued to stare.

Bernard closed his eyes and thought of Helen. Helen, elegantly beautiful at last night's party, warmly beautiful afterward in bed, and still beautiful now, no doubt, among the fat women of the health farm. Only when he opened his eyes, startled by some shudder of the plane or the sudden loss of height which heralded a refueling stop, was the picture of his wife and the memory of his love for her shattered by the personality of the woman who faced him. The blackness of Gitta's clothes and hair and eyes made her almost invisible in the pale light of the cabin, but her pale face was visible and he could tell that, like himself, she was making no attempt to sleep. No doubt her dark eyes were still staring at him, but he was no longer irritated by their aggression. The holiday had only just begun. Soon he would know as much about her as she had already discovered about him. When he ceased to be curious, she would have no further power to disturb him. He closed his eyes again and waited for India to arrive.

I V

Bernard had chosen his tour for the amount of sight-seeing it promised. He was not to be disappointed, for early on their first morning in Delhi the local guide led them on an extensive exploration of the Old City. By the time they had explored the grounds of the Red Fort and the Mogul Gardens, lingered in the bazaar streets off Chandni Chowk and made their way to the great mosque, the sun was high in the sky and all the members of the group were beginning to flag in the unaccustomed heat. Mrs. Mostyn and Mrs. Farmer took a cursory glance at the mosque from a distance and demanded refreshment. The others moved slowly on while the guide was pointing out a silk factory which would offer tea as well as sales talk, but were halted by an urgent entreaty.

"Take off your shoes, take off your shoes." The guide hurried to catch up with his flock and prevent them from misbehaving. "This is Jama Masjid, mosque of great holiness. All must take off shoes."

Mrs. Hunwick gave a screech of protest. Long before he arrived in India Bernard had decided that to be fastidious here would be pointless, but he had some sympathy with her disgust on this occasion. Between the street and the raised courtyard of the mosque was a flight of steps, lined by rows of beggars who vigorously waggled their amputated stumps as they chewed and spat. Birds, resting on an archway above the steps, contributed to the general uncleanliness, and a small boy—covered with sores around which flies clustered— was at this moment urinating on the bottom step. Mr. and Mrs. Hunwick decided to join the tea drinkers in the silk factory.

Those who remained were given a short lecture on the mosque and then allowed time, if they wished, to climb one of its minarets. Dr. Ibbotson led the way up the tall, pencil-slim tower, followed by Daphne.

Inside the minaret there was no light. As Bernard, in third place, climbed the steep spiral steps, the blackness and narrowness of the shaft combined to induce claustrophobia. And when at last he emerged into the dazzle of daylight, it was to discover another hazard. The top of the minaret was flat: four slim pillars supported a pointed canopy, but except for them there was no form of guard rail. Anyone emerging from the staircase who took more than two steps forward would immediately find himself on the way down again. The three tourists cautiously sat around the edge of the staircase opening, their legs dangling down. But even then Daphne did not feel safe. Her grip on Bernard's arm unbalanced him, increasing his insecurity to the point of vertigo. In the narrow streets of the Old City immediately below, women in bright saris flitted like butterflies around the bazaar shops, thin men in white hurried on busy errands and boys wobbled on bicycles through the crowds. Seen from above, the movement seemed purposeless but continuous: if one individual came to a halt, his stillness was immediately concealed by the surrounding bustle.

In an attempt to steady his head, Bernard searched for a stationary object on which to fix his eyes and caught sight of Gitta Clyde. Alone among the thousands of moving people she was sitting quite still in an open area just outside the courtyard of the mosque, the fixed center of a shifting circle as small boys surrounded her, begging, selling, or offering their services as guides. She appeared to be taking no notice of them. Instead she stared up at the top of the minaret. Bernard wondered why she had not come up with them. If he were to wave, she would see him. But waving was a gesture which assumed a more lighthearted friendliness than they had yet had time to establish. In addition, it would disturb his balance still further. Deciding that he had had enough of this uneasy perch, he began a careful descent.

It was a relief to return to the open courtyard, in which Stephen Clyde was taking photographs of small children. Outside its precincts, Bernard put on his shoes and gave a coin to one of the four beggars who claimed to have been guarding them.

Gitta Clyde, from her position at the bottom of the steps, watched with an amused smile. "You're letting the side down," she said as he went over to join her. "The colonel insists that we shouldn't give anything to anybody."

"I haven't the temperament to give money to a beggar as a reward for nothing but begging," Bernard admitted. "But I'm prepared to pay for anything which can be described even remotely as a service. By the standards of these people I must be immensely rich. It doesn't cost me much to offer what may mean a lot to them."

"It costs you your privacy. You've established yourself as a honey-pot, so here come the flies."

"I shall concentrate on talking to you and refuse to notice them," he said. But this was not as easy as it sounded, for small hands plucked at his arms and shriveled women who were perhaps still young thrust their puny babies in front of his face, muttering words that he could not understand, although their import was clear enough.

"Why do they do it?" he asked, honestly amazed. "Millions too many people here already, and so much poverty! Why does a woman like this bring another baby into the world with no hope of supporting it?"

"Perhaps she doesn't know how to prevent it," suggested Gitta; but Bernard shook his head.

"That would have been true twenty years ago. In the villages it may still be true now, for all I know. But Delhi is the capital city of a country committed to a birth control program."

"You may be giving India credit for more efficiency than it can achieve. Or for more intelligence among its people than they possess. You may even be assuming a wish—in the family, not the country—that doesn't exist. It can't be easy to change overnight a belief that has held a society together for centuries—that the main purpose of a woman's existence is to bear children."

"When a woman is as poor as this and it's so obviously in her best interest—" began Bernard; but Gitta was shaking her head.

"This isn't a sphere in which logic rules," she suggested. "Women need to have children. All women, unless they're cowardly or selfish, recognize that need. They need to create and they need to possess. It's rich women, not poor ones, who can afford to acquire substitute possessions and who can think of other things to create. A poor woman—a *really* poor one like these—may never possess anything in her life except her own baby. And it's the only thing she's able to create that requires absolutely no capital investment."

Bernard stared at his companion, but her flat, expressionless face gave no clue as to whether or not she was seriously putting forward what seemed to him an extraordinary point of view.

"I can't accept that," he said. "I think you were nearer to the truth earlier on, when you talked about the attitudes of society. I agree that in very many societies, certainly including this one and until recently our own as well, the pressure on women to have children is strong. So strong that many of them may well feel they have no option. But if a woman is given a true choice, as happens more and more in England nowadays—if she has the same opportunities as a man—then she's just as likely as a man to decide that what she wants is a career rather than a child."

"Not many men make that decision," Gitta pointed out. "Most men decide to have both a career and a child. And most women might well decide exactly the same if they were truly given the opportunity. But how many of them are? Most have to make a choice. And most choose to have children, even when the choice seems to their disadvantage."

"But not all," Bernard said.

"We may be defining choice in different ways. Do you have children yourself?"

"No."

"And if that's from choice, would it be impertinent of me to ask whose choice?"

Yes, the question was impertinent. Bernard saw that it emerged logically enough from their conversation, but there was a stiffness in his voice as he answered. "My wife and I agreed, naturally."

"You agreed finally, I'm sure. But one of the two of you would have to raise the subject first. I can see that I *am* presuming. So I won't press the question. I'll guess instead. 'My dear,' you said, 'there are too many people in the world already. It would be selfish of us to add to their number. And we could live more comfortably without encumbrances.' And your wife, because she loved you—and because a reluctant father is a blight on any child and its mother—agreed that you were speaking the truth. She did not, however, suggest that you should have a vasectomy, because secretly she hoped that you might one day change your mind. Nor did you yourself volunteer for the operation, which might have proved inconvenient or even briefly painful. Instead, you expected her to go to the family planning clinic, and trusted her never to risk your anger by proving forgetful."

This exercise of the imagination came so near to the truth and was expressed with such contempt that Bernard stood up angrily, brushing off the beggars who surrounded him and the boys who were trying to clean his shoes. Gitta did not move, but looked up at him, her black eyes momentarily enlivened by mischief.

"I've been unpardonably rude when all you expected was a little holiday chitchat," she said. "You must put it down to the classic resentment of the woman who is childless by accident for those who are childless by choice. You'll find the rest of the party in the silk shop over there. Tea and Seven-Up are being served."

Half a dozen small boys prepared to tug him into either the right shop or one of its competitors. Bernard allowed himself to be borne away, and did not look back. For the rest of the holiday, he promised himself, he would find a less prickly companion than Gitta Clyde.

V

By the fifth day of the tour Bernard had learned as much as he wanted to know about most of his companions. He had been quick to decide which of them were to be avoided whenever possible: Mrs. Hunwick, perpetually grumbling about Indian standards of hygiene, and her husband who—pleasant enough in his own right—rarely escaped from her: Mrs. Mostyn, always the last to arrive and the first to flag, demanding seats and drinks: and Mrs. Farmer, interested only in shops and prices and incessantly discussing both in a high-pitched Kensington voice.

Stephen Clyde at least was quiet. His only fault as a member of a group was his devotion to photography: he tended to lag behind the party when it was on foot and to ask for the car to be stopped when they were on the move. Bernard did not greatly object to the delays. The reason why he had made no effort to establish any kind of relationship was the resentment he still felt at the rudeness of Mrs. Clyde.

Of the others, Colonel Alderton had proved to be a surprisingly congenial companion. Far from displaying a know-all authority, he was reticent, almost shy—even confessing in an endearing manner that he was at a complete loss how to treat the hotel servants. It no longer seemed right to shout at them in the old way; but no other approach, he pointed out regretfully, produced any results. Bernard enjoyed his company, but to sit with him for a meal or in a car meant accepting Daphne as well.

By now, over a glass of duty-free whiskey with the colonel, Bernard had learned the details of Daphne's domestic situation. Her husband had left her to set up a separate establishment with his receptionist, and for the past two years she had been sustained by anger. But now that the divorce had come through, her husband had remarried while she had no new partner. Her attempt to put a brave face on the situation concealed but did not cure her depression.

Bernard could sympathize with a woman who felt herself to be unlovable. It was her need to establish a pretense of intimacy, no doubt, which resulted in her compulsion to touch. She lost no opportunity to take Bernard's arm, or Dr. Ibbotson's; but even when she appeared to be flirting, her manner was tentative. She posed no danger to Bernard's peace of mind, for she would not risk a new rejection and she knew that he was married. Even if she hoped for a brief holiday affair to restore her battered self-esteem, she would wait for him to make the running.

She would wait in vain. It would take more than a week or two of absence to make him forget Helen. Gitta Clyde had come uncomfortably near to the truth in her cutting picture of their decision to remain childless: but what she had not taken into account was that a couple who made such a contract were bound to recognize its special obligations. Both Helen and Bernard had worked throughout the nineteen years of their marriage to keep it alive and exciting: and fidelity was part of the bargain.

Daphne offered no temptation, so it was for her sake rather than his own that Bernard, while not rudely avoiding her company, did not allow himself to be seen seeking it. It would be a pity to raise her hopes, that was all. Whenever possible he sat with Dr. Ibbotson, a general practitioner from the north of England, whose comments on what they saw were pleasant and practical but who also recognized that there was no need to talk all the time.

After two days in Agra, with the Taj Mahal seen and photographed in every possible light, there was to be a day trip to visit the temples of Khajuraho. Bernard was ready early and was enjoying the peace and coolness of the hour before sunrise when Mr. Hunwick came out to join him in the garden.

"The wife's staying behind today," he said. "Not feeling too good."

"I'm sorry."

"This dysentery thing, you know."

"Oh. Delhi belly."

"Is that what you call it?"

"It's the colonel's phrase. He expects us all to succumb."

"Well, I hope not. It's a nasty thing. The heat and the strange food, I suppose. And dirt. It gets the wife down a bit. I've a bad conscience, as a matter of fact. Dragging her out here. No one really enjoys a holiday for someone else's reasons, I suppose."

"What *were* your reasons?" asked Bernard. He had already decided that the two widows had come to India so that they could say they had *been* to India: this was just one in a series of expensive holidays with which they passed the time. But that conclusion would not fit the Hunwicks, who were clearly less prosperous.

Mr. Hunwick laughed as though not expecting to be believed. "My father was a medical missionary in Bombay. Long time ago, of course. Gave it up when I was born. But never forgot the ten years he spent here. Talked about it all the time. I wanted to see for myself. Perhaps that's why the dirt doesn't worry me as much as it does the wife. The more filth I see, the more right it seems that my father should have worked here. God knows, they still need doctors badly enough."

"Someone ill?" asked Dr. Ibbotson, joining them in time to hear the end of the sentence.

"Not so as to bother you. Though I must say, I'm surprised you admit to being a doctor on your holiday."

"We were talking about our motives for coming to India," said Bernard. "Why did you choose this trip, Dr. Ibbotson?"

"The same reason as the colonel." Dr. Ibbotson pulled up a chair. "Drawn irresistibly back to a place which infuriated me for almost every moment of the time when I lived here. I don't know what it is about India. Some kind of spell. Sooner or later it seems to pull everyone back."

There were two elements in that statement to startle Bernard. The doctor was using almost exactly the same phrase that Alexa had attributed to Robert Scott—the phrase that indirectly had drawn Bernard himself to India. But for the moment he picked up the more obvious cause of surprise. "I didn't realize you'd been out before."

"Well, never to Agra. And only for a day to Delhi, coming off the plane. I didn't have any money last time to travel around. I came through V.S.O. just for a year, after I qualified. I was interested in deficiency diseases and trying to decide whether to specialize or go into general practice. A year out here gave me a lot of experience. There was a famine that year, just as there is now."

"*Is* there?" Bernard was surprised. "I hadn't heard that."

"The doctor I worked for fifteen years ago runs a hospital in Udaipur now. I wrote to tell him that I'd be passing through and he told me the situation in his letter back."

"Are you liable to become involved again?"

"Gracious, no. I'm here on holiday. My reason for coming is tourism—to see the sights I missed before. And speaking of tourism, our cars seem to have arrived."

Two hours later, as the group walked together from the airstrip at Khajuraho into the grassy area beside it which was scattered with stone temples of all sizes, Bernard glanced at Mr. Hunwick and smiled. His guidebook described the temple sculptures as erotic, but Mrs. Hunwick would certainly have regarded them as disgusting and might well have forbidden her husband to look. The attack of Delhi belly had done him a good turn.

Every inch of the outer wall of each temple was covered with carvings. Bernard hardly bothered to listen to the guide, but studied what appeared to be a definitive set of illustrations, in stone, of all the possible positions for copulation—including those for coupling with animals. Not all the examples were of much practical use in modern society, for some required the help of servants in order that one partner should be held up in the air, head down, while other poses looked to be attainable only by contortionists.

Stephen Clyde was having a field day. He had brought a tripod with him, and the largest of his many cameras, and was preparing each shot with care. Like Bernard, he made no attempt to keep up with the guide. His devotion to photography might well be his reason for choosing the trip, for India offered a plentiful supply of contrasts: it was easy to feature a beggar and a palace in the same shot.

As for Mrs. Clyde, she had perhaps—like Mrs. Hunwick—come only to keep her husband company. Bernard considered that thesis and rejected it. Quite apart from the fact that the Clydes were rarely to be seen together, Gitta was not a woman to borrow anyone else's reason for doing anything. She must have some purpose of her own; but just as he was beginning to speculate about it, she came up to join him.

"I owe you an apology," she said abruptly. "Last time we spoke together, I was very rude. I've been waiting to say that I was sorry, but you haven't let me get near you—and I'm not surprised. It was an unforgivable way to behave."

"That's all right." Bernard approved of the fact that she realized the need for an apology, but saw no reason why he should be effusive in accepting it.

"I live in a remote part of Ireland," she said, as though this accounted for her behavior. "Monday to Friday Steve works in London. So I'm on my own most of the time. I haven't been on a package tour before. That first day in Delhi, it came as a shock, realizing that I'd be tied to the same crowd of people for the next eighteen days."

"We were the crowd who upset you, were we, just the nine of us? Not the millions of Indians all around?"

"I can escape from them. They have no curiosity about me. But you and the others, I'm attached to you, and you all want—well, I've got the feel of it now. But you caught me when the lack of mental privacy first hit me. I shouldn't have taken it out on you. I'm sorry."

She turned toward him as though appealing to him to accept the apology. She was not a woman who used her mouth for smiling, and her face was almost as devoid of expression as at their first meeting; but the dark blankness of her eyes had been replaced by something which he could interpret as sincerity. He nodded in a manner which she could take as an acceptance of her explanation. He was prepared to start again with her, because he was still curious.

"Why did you decide to travel with a group?" he asked.

"Money. One has to be really very rich, doesn't one, to travel independently to a place like India. This whole package—hotels, food, guides, the lot—doesn't cost much more than I would have had to pay, as a single traveler, for the air ticket alone."

"And what made you choose to come to India?"

"There are things I want to see," she said. "A series of visual impressions to imprint on my eyes and transfer to my memory."

"Like the Taj Mahal?"

"Well, *not* the Taj Mahal. But that kind of thing."

"Why not the Taj? A visual impression if ever there was one. What's wrong with it?"

"It's dead," Gitta said. "Beautiful, but dead. That's reasonable, I suppose, considering its purpose, but it makes the effect unstimulating."

"What does it lack?"

"Movement, I think. Energy. Or at least the kind of tension that suggests two equal movements held in balance."

"You talk like an architect."

"I don't know anything about architecture."

"What *do* you know about? Do you have a job? What do you do?" To ask the questions directly should be the simplest way to satisfy his curiosity. But Gitta seemed determined to protect her privacy.

"You're expecting me to put myself into a category for you," she said. "If I were to tell you that I was a milkmaid—or a judge—then from that moment you'd see me only in terms of your own picture of a milkmaid or judge. I don't care to be labeled by my profession."

Gitta spoke with the same brusqueness which had annoyed him in Delhi, but by now he was becoming accustomed to her manner. This was not the moment, though, to continue a conversation which could only be a distraction from what they had both come to see. They walked together, threading their way between the temples and staring upward at the carvings, until their guide brought the whole group to a halt.

They had reached the largest of the temples, a great cathedral of stone which rose in a series of domes and pinnacles to a tower and spire at one end. The guide led the way into a series of dark chambers whose inner walls were almost as richly carved as those outside. This building, he announced, was dedicated to the god Siva.

"Who is Siva?" asked Mrs. Mostyn. Bernard gave a mental sigh. Quite apart from the fact that this information had already been provided in both Delhi and Agra, he had already discovered that all their local guides were overeducated young men, taking any work they could find while they awaited their opportunity to become professors of philosophy. Mrs. Mostyn's question was an invitation to practice a lecture.

"Siva," said the guide, leaning himself comfortably against a statue in a manner which confirmed Bernard's fear, "is one part of the Hindu trinity of gods who together form the Trimurti. This I believe is a concept easy for you as Christians to understand: one in three and three in one. The whole of life is divided amongst these three gods in many different aspects. Brahma is the creator, Vishnu is the preserver and Siva is the destroyer. Translating this to the elements, Brahma is earth, Vishnu is water and Siva is fire."

"It seems odd to worship a god of destruction." Mrs. Mostyn, having given the cue for the lecture, was now interrupting it.

"Was not your own god Jehovah a destroyer?" asked the guide. "Only from the destruction of chaos could the earth be created. And it must be understood that Siva destroys evil as well as good. For one example, he is the destroyer of disease, and for this reason is worshiped also as the god of medicine. His sign is the bull, and in this form he tears away the curse of infertility. To destroy one aspect of life is to create its opposite."

Bernard allowed his attention to wander and his eyes to study those of the interior carvings which could be seen in the dim light. They reminded him of the relief of the dancing Siva which leaned against the wall of his garden in England. That carving had been taken from just such a temple as this, he supposed, sent back to England by Robert Scott, the man who had loved India more than Bernard's mother. Bernard—who had been so interested in discovering why everyone else in his group had chosen to come to India on holiday—was reminded that part of his own reason was the wish to understand this obsession on the part of his natural father. So far he had had no success. His holiday was full of interest and enjoyment, but he was an outsider, a foreigner, in a way which cut him off from the life of the country: he observed it, but did not feel its pains or excitements. Whatever the fascination was which had drawn back Colonel Alderton and Dr. Ibbotson—and Robert Scott as well, in the year of Bernard's own birth—it had not yet revealed itself to him.

Disturbed by what he saw as a lack of receptivity in himself, and oppressed by the darkness of the temple, Bernard abandoned the guide and his lecture and groped his way out into the bright sunshine. Stephen Clyde had not interrupted his photography even momentarily to follow the group into the temple; and when Gitta came out onto the smooth grass only a few seconds after Bernard, she glanced at her husband but did not disturb his concentration.

"A time for using one's eyes rather than one's ears," she commented as she moved past Bernard with her heavy, unfeminine tread.

"What's the guide on about now?" Bernard quickened his pace to walk beside her.

"Elaborate parallels with the Greek and Roman gods to show that there's only one religion in the world. Siva is Pluto, god of the underworld, lord of the spirits, dancing on the bodies of the slain. But I mustn't mock. I take it that Siva is your patron—the god of medicine."

"I prefer to claim the protection of Vishnu, the preserver," Bernard said. "I doubt whether Siva would accept me as a votary if he were to discover how many millions of contraceptive pills my factory turns out each year."

"Ah yes, you're the antifertility man." But her attention was not on the conversation, but on the sculptures. Bernard moved with her around the temple, which was more richly ornamented than any of those which they had studied earlier. Gods and goddesses, kings and queens, soldiers and their horses, musicians and dancers, all marched in friezes around the group of towers. Lovers experimented in even more complicated postures than had been seen outside the smaller temples. Stone courtesans, often wearing nothing but a necklace, primped and powdered and enticed.

"Do you think there was ever a time when Indian women had breasts as enormous as that?" Gitta asked. "The young girls nowadays all seem so slender."

"The breasts on display in *Playboy* every month represent one man's taste," Bernard pointed out. "There can't be many girls with such a figure, and yet the magazine's readers may have come to think it the norm. For all we know, these amorous ladies could all be carved from one favorite model of the sculptor—or they could represent his own ideal. What puzzles me more is whether, if there *was* a model, she was expected to take up every pose. This one, for example." He pointed at the image of one particularly well developed female who had bent her leg up behind her and leaned her shoulders back until she could grip her ankle, apparently in order to study the sole of her foot. "Could a woman bend back like that?"

"Easily," said Gitta. She considered the stone figure of the courtesan. Then slowly but smoothly she moved into the pose and held it. Her blouse, pulled tightly across her chest, revealed nothing which even remotely compared with the two unnaturally round, high globes on which she had earlier commented; but her long cotton skirt fell from her waist in the same line as the stone drapery of the carved figure, making her briefly as graceful as the woman she was imitating. Just for a moment, as she continued to hold the position in perfect balance, she seemed to Bernard to have become a different person from the ugly woman he knew. He had thought her clumsy, because of the heavy way she walked, but the movement of her arms and body was delicate and perfectly controlled as equally slowly she returned to a normal standing position.

He struggled for a moment to put a name to what he had recognized in the unexpected combination of grace and muscle. All his curiosity about Gitta had returned. She was the only member of the party whom he did not yet understand at all. He might not have much interest in, say, Mrs. Farmer, but he found it easy to imagine her way of life. He could see her visiting a certain type of shop, could guess at the standard of the bridge she would play in the afternoons, the theaters she would choose to visit in monthly outings. Her entertaining habits, the library books she read, the drink, carefully occasional, with which she cheered an evening of depression—all these details were part of a pattern which he did not need to have explained.

Gitta Clyde, by contrast, from the moment of their first meeting, muddied her own pattern with every word she spoke. But that last silent moment seemed to contain a clue. He put his guess to her as a question.

"You moved then like a ballet dancer," he said. "Did you have that training when you were young?"

For a moment Gitta hesitated. Then she said, "Yes, I did," with an abruptness which made it clear that there were to be no supplementary questions, and walked away.

Bernard enjoyed his small triumph. It was always a good moment when he felt able to put a label on a stranger. This one, of course, was incomplete. It was clear that Gitta Clyde was not a dancer now, and probably had not been one for many years. A single piece of information about her past life did not reveal much about her present activities—nor did it, in itself, make her interesting to Bernard, who never went to the ballet. But it was a start, a small crack in the shield she held up against the curiosity of strangers. Sooner or later, he would begin to know her better.

V I

Udaipur, the colonel promised as the group boarded a plane at Jodhpur, Udaipur would be different.

By this time, twelve days after the beginning of the holiday, all the members of the party were beginning to tire. There had been too many five-o'clock awakenings for six-o'clock departures; too many long journeys in cars which became ovens when the windows were closed but filled with dust if they were opened. The places to which their itinerary had taken them—Fatehpur Sikri, Jaipur, Amber—had been chosen for the beauty of their palaces but were equally memorable for heat and dirt. Udaipur, however, would be different.

"Why?" asked Bernard as the little plane circled Jodhpur once and then flew steadily south.

"Water. Udaipur is built on water. Every garden has its own well. The city stretches along three lakes, and the water gives the place a kind of sparkle. I came up here for a leave once. Invited by the Maharana to stay at the monsoon palace in the hills. Hunting, you know. A long time ago, but I've never forgotten it. His grandson's gone into the tourist business, they tell me. Converted half a dozen palaces into hotels. He certainly had enough to spare."

The flight was short and a local guide was waiting to welcome the party, mentioning nervously that there had been a change in the choice of hotel. His nervousness was justified. Mrs. Farmer spoke for the party as she demanded an explanation. From the beginning she had appointed herself unofficial guardian of the typed itinerary, each day checking the places visited against those which had been promised. Her meticulousness did not stem from particular knowledge of the items which from time to time she found to have been omitted, nor to any special enthusiasm for them; but she believed in getting what she had paid for. She pointed out now that the party had been promised accommodation in the luxury hotel—once a palace—which stood on an island in the middle of a lake, that this represented the high point of the tour, and that no change would be tolerated.

The rest of the group was on her side, although glad to leave to one person the unpleasant task of quarreling. This guide was less fluent in English than others they had had, and less forceful. He flung out his hands in partial surrender.

"We will go first to the hotel to which you have been transferred. From there you will see the difficulty. If any of you still wish to change, there will be no problem." He hurried them into the waiting cars, which drove them through a line of foothills and then steeply up to a high plateau before pulling up in front of a brilliantly white-washed building of spacious design. This, the guide announced, was their revised destination. Like the lake hotel, it had at one time been a palace. The party stepped out onto the terrace, no longer sure whether to maintain the complaint. It was clear that they would be comfortable here, and cooler on the ridge than down at lake level. Only the colonel was in a position to say whether the original choice of hotel would have been better.

What the colonel said at that moment was "Good God!" The others came to join him on the edge of the terrace. They looked together at the view. "The hills should be green," said Colonel Alderton. "Never seen those hills when they weren't green. Never been as bad as this even at the end of the hot season—and that hasn't begun yet."

He was staring across the plateau to the farther side of the ring of hills. The monsoon palace in which he had once spent his leave could be seen perched picturesquely on a height, but the slope beneath it was covered only with a parched and dusty brown scrub. And there was worse than that. Bernard remembered how his guidebook had enthused over the lakes which curved around the wall of the city, describing them as the jeweled necklace of Udaipur. The lake palace, a cluster of white marble domes and courtyards which covered the whole of one of the small islands, should have seemed to float like a pleasure ship on the sparkling water. Instead, it was now surrounded by mud. The lake was empty.

"Two weeks ago we have taken a group to the lake palace hotel," the guide told them. "They have complained very much of flies and the smell. Also there is a problem with stealing, because now it is possible for children to reach the hotel by walking when it is dark. We have made this change for your convenience, but there was not time to tell your agency in London."

Graciously Mrs. Farmer withdrew her objection, even going so far as to express gratitude for thoughtfulness. Dr. Ibbotson came to stand beside Bernard.

"I'm spending the rest of the day with the medical officer I worked under in my V.S.O. year," he said. "He moved here five years ago. He's taking me to see his hospital in the afternoon and for a meal with his family in the evening. But to start with I've asked him here for lunch. Would you care to join us?"

Bernard accepted with pleasure. During the previous twelve days his contact with the people of India had been restricted to shopkeepers, waiters, taxi drivers and guides, and he welcomed the prospect of conversing with a professional Indian. He kept his distance for the actual moment of reunion, watching from the end of the terrace the emotional hugging which took place as soon as Dr. Chandra leaped from his car. Only after a few moments did he stroll along to be introduced to the plump, jolly man whose English had been perfected while he was qualifying at St. Thomas's Hospital in London.

Dr. Ibbotson had ordered a curry to be prepared in his guest's honor. It was a disaster—chunks of tough meat in a tasteless and watery sauce. This was taken by Dr. Chandra to be a fine joke.

"The last legacy of British rule!" he announced. "Young boys who were taught by officers' memsahibs to make brown Windsor soup and pink blancmange are now the senior cooks in our tourist hotels. They provide European food to avoid complaints and have never learned to cook anything else. Naturally, they do not eat the meals they cook. In the evening they go home to a good curry prepared by the women of the household. Vegetable curry, not meat. In Udaipur we grow fine vegetables, fresh and full of nourishment. In good times, that is."

"Tell me about the water," Bernard said. "Is the situation as bad as it looks?"

"Worse. Worse." The smile faded from Dr. Chandra's face. "At this time of year the depth of water in our lakes should be twenty-four feet. The hills should be green and the goats grazing in the high pastures. Well, you have seen how it is instead."

"How has it come about?"

"Three years ago there were only twelve inches of rain in the monsoon instead of thirty-five. That was bad, but not too bad. Because of the lakes, we in Udaipur have a reserve for such emergencies. But the next year, two years ago, the monsoon failed absolutely. Nothing. Such a failure occurs one year in perhaps thirty. It is always a disaster, but a man need expect it only once in his working lifetime. And then, last year, the real catastrophe. Five inches only of rain fell. Enough to make the seed sprout, but not to let it grow. And because of the past years, there are no reserves of food left."

"So what will happen?"

"I estimate that before the end of September twelve percent of the people in my area will be dead. Of these, some are already old and would die in any case. But ten percent will die of famine."

Bernard, appalled, could think of nothing to say—and even before the discussion began he had lost his appetite for the meal.

"I have spoiled your pleasure in the day," said Dr. Chandra, noticing this. "You must forgive me. We have an agricultural problem and we have a medical problem, but also we have a political problem. Every province must fight all the others for its share of relief. For many weeks it has been necessary for me to press my claim to the government in Delhi—to compile statistics, to submit reports. I have a duty to put a case as strongly as I can. So it becomes difficult for me not to make a political speech even on a social occasion like this."

"What you say is horrifying." Bernard could hardly believe the scale of the impending tragedy. "You know, if twenty people in England are killed in a coach crash, or fifty youngsters die in a disco fire, the newspaper headlines shriek 'Disaster!' And yet here you are telling me of a disaster which will affect unimaginable numbers—you're saying, I take it, that hundreds of thousands of your people will die of starvation—but no newspaper in England has even mentioned it yet. And when it happens, it will probably be described in a factual half column and then forgotten."

Dr. Chandra shrugged his shoulders. Now that he had stated the alarming facts, his own passionate involvement seemed to fade. "Every question must be considered from two sides. I have told you that twelve percent of our population will die, and this is true. But then, we all must die, and none of us can know when. Who can claim as of right that he should still be alive next year? Those who die in the hot season of this year will not need to die in the hot season of the year after. When the end is the same, why should the time be considered so important?"

"That's not a point of view which you can expect any European to share," suggested Dr. Ibbotson.

"Because Europeans are afraid of death," Dr. Chandra reminded him. "For many centuries we have despised you for this, and so we have no right now to come on our knees, asking you to help us postpone for a little while the deaths of some of our people."

"That can't alter the reaction which, as Europeans, we're bound to feel," suggested Bernard. "It seems wrong that we should come as tourists just to stare at the country and then simply go away again."

"Not at all. The government has decided not to beg for charity, but we hope to earn help from outside on a businesslike basis. We need your tourist money, desperately we need it. It is the lack of foreign currency which will kill my twelve percent. The food exists in the world. There is wheat. There are powders made from milk, from soybeans, from fish, even from petrol. What we lack is the ability to pay for it. So"—he smiled, as jovial again as though no problem existed—"you must be happy while you are here. We hope that you will visit our shops and buy our gold and jewelry. And most of all we want you to tell all your friends when you return what a beautiful place this is. That is why—although unfortunately we cannot conceal the mud in the lakes or the dryness of the farmland—we shall do our best to keep our dying children out of your sight."

The lunch lasted far longer than was justified by the food, and by the time the two doctors left for their visit to the hospital, the rest of the party had already been taken by car on a city tour. Bernard looked down from the hotel terrace and decided that he could cover the same ground on foot. Although the sun was still dazzlingly bright, there was a sufficient breeze to make it seem a pleasant afternoon for walking.

He had reckoned without the appalling smell. Long before he reached the bottom of the slope it became clear that—probably for centuries—the citizens of Udaipur had been using their lakes as public lavatories and that the temporary absence of water had done nothing to change their habits. Once inside the city wall he abandoned his plan to keep near the lake and instead plunged into the labyrinth of streets. Somewhere in this area there was a palace which had been converted into a museum instead of into a hotel. Bernard turned in its direction and came face to face with Gitta Clyde.

Her appearance was a surprise only in the sense that he had not known she would be in that place at that time. It had become clear early in the tour that it was almost impossible for any member of the group to escape from the company of the others. Using the same transport to take them to the same places, they all had the same list of sights to be seen. Gitta and Bernard both chose when possible to explore on foot and alone, but it was inevitable that their paths should cross.

Today she seemed pleased to see Bernard, if only to communicate her excitement. "Isn't this a wonderful place!"

"Is it?" Bernard was taken aback. Even away from the lake, the city stank. He associated the smell with dirty, wind-swept subways or the darker corners of shabby tenements. Because of it he had felt that he was walking through a slum and had hardly bothered to use his eyes. His concentration had in any case still been on the conversation with Dr. Chandra.

Now, commanded by Gitta's sweeping hand, he studied the street in which they were standing. On the dazzling white walls of the simple mud houses, he noticed now for the first time, pictures had been painted. It was these, apparently, which so much delighted Gitta.

"This one is to celebrate a marriage," she said, pointing to the wall which she had been considering when Bernard first caught sight of her. On either side of the door was a fantastic animal, painted in bright, clear colors but decorated so elaborately—rather in the style of a medieval book of hours—that the subject was not immediately recognizable. "The elephant is for happiness and the horse is for prosperity. And look over there."

Above the door of a similarly humble house across the street a large clay relief was attached to the wall. It depicted a man and a woman and a variety of birds in bright primary colors liberally outlined and dotted over in black. Both the modeling and the coloring were primitive, but Bernard was prepared to concede that the effect was striking.

"Everywhere else, we've been shown old glories which have been allowed to decay." Gitta's excitement added an unusual animation to her voice and her eyes. "But this place is still alive today. Have you been to the shops yet?"

"No."

"Come with me, then." She led the way with a briskness which in such heat was a sufficient sign of enthusiasm. Bernard looked around curiously as they turned a corner. He had already become used to the manner in which all shops of a single trade were grouped in the same street. This was the first time, though, that he had seen an extensive area devoted to nothing but brightly painted wooden toys.

"I would have thought they were slightly overestimating the city's demand for playthings," he suggested, as he looked down the long row of open doorways, each displaying toy soldiers and puppets, miniature rocking cradles and popguns, nestling dolls and tiny farm animals.

"These are workshops," Gitta said. "Factories more than shops. I should think traders come from all over India to buy. Just watch this old man."

They stepped inside one of the tiny shops. The young boy who rose to greet them squatted down again in response to Gitta's gesture. She must already have spent some time on the premises, for she held aside a curtain before moving confidently farther inside.

In a workroom at the back of the building a very old man, his skin stretched tightly over his bones, was carving a small horse. He had almost finished the piece and with great care was patterning the mane to give the impression that it had been plaited.

"You see," said Gitta. "The whole town is busy making things. Creating unique objects. Don't you think that's exhilarating?"

Unwilling to admit that he failed to share the excitement, Bernard picked up a finished carving which stood waiting for someone to paint it in the bright yellow, red and black of the goods in the shop. "This one," he said, "is exactly the same."

"Not exactly. It's got a wicked look in its eye instead of a docile one."

Bernard studied the two horses again and still failed to see the difference. He shook his head, disagreeing with her. "You called this a factory, and of course you were right," he said. "Hardly a fast-moving assembly line. But the old chap is making copies of a prototype just as a Ford worker does. An object can be handmade without being a work of art. Give this to a child and it wouldn't matter to him whether it were mass-produced on a machine or carved like this at the rate of four a day."

"I agree it may not matter to the customer," Gitta said. "But it matters enormously to him." She nodded her head in the direction of the old man. "He's *making* something. Not just pushing a button for money. Maybe he's run out of new ideas now, because he's so old; but he still has the craft. He can make an object that's going to be loved. There's pride in that." She gave a quick laugh. "We have a different mood, you and I. I'm high and you're low. I can tell that we're not going to agree."

"Does he speak English?" asked Bernard.

"No. The boy in the front shop can manage a little. He was the one who explained about the wall paintings. But the old man not at all."

"Then I'll tell you why I feel low. It's because I've just learned that by the end of the next six months this old man will almost certainly be dead." He passed on part of what Dr. Chandra had told him. It seemed to make little impression on Gitta.

"He's very old," she pointed out. "Even if they'd had a good harvest last year he might not survive the next few months. But what I'm trying to tell you ought to make you less gloomy on his account. This man is a maker. A creator." She took the unpainted horse from Bernard's hand and began to stroke the smooth wooden flanks with her thumb. "When he goes, he will leave behind him sons, and a grandson, and thousands of wooden toys which wouldn't have existed without him. No one completely dies if he has something to leave behind. It's the thought of that kind of survival which makes life worth living. And it's the people who don't think life is worth living who most resent death. If you were to tell this man now that his death is approaching, you might even find that he would be contented."

"Your attitude has a lot in common with Dr. Chandra's. I'm afraid it doesn't convince me, though."

"Because you've never made anything!" exclaimed Gitta. "Not even children. There's never been a moment when something has taken shape which could never have existed except for you, and when you've been able to call out, 'This will last after I'm dead, and because of that it doesn't matter if I die tomorrow.'"

She spoke with passion, and the silence between them as she ended was charged with tension which she broke at last with a sigh. "I'm sorry. That was unfair. Of course you've made things. Cures for diseases. I can see that this talent seems a small one to you. All I'm trying to say is that to him it's probably very important."

"Yes," said Bernard. He was impressed not so much by what she said as by the fervor with which she expressed herself, but he found it hard not to take offense at the personal attack. Turning away, back to the shop, he picked up a bright-yellow popgun, dotted with black in the local style. A push on the handle forced out a cork on a string with a satisfactory pop. A purchase would represent a kind of rent for the use of the workshop as a debating chamber; and Helen had so many godchildren that one among them was bound to be of the appropriate age. "Have you visited the City Palace yet?" he asked Gitta while he waited for his choice to be wrapped.

"Yes. I was on my way back from it when we met."

"Then if you'll excuse me . . ."

"Of course." They were polite strangers again. Bernard was glad that he need not continue in her company. Gitta appeared to have no normal, middle-of-the-road social conversation. Either she was silent or else she was aggressive. There had been absolutely no need for him to have an opinion on the artistic significance of a small wooden horse; but now the consciousness of violent opinion beneath the flat, expressionless face would make it difficult for Bernard to enjoy a mindless tourist meander with her beside him. As he strolled toward the palace, he was content to be alone.

VII

Bombay had a character of its own. Here, nakedly, metropolitan India revealed itself, offering the tourists little beauty to distract their eyes, but rather the realities of life lived on the borderland of death. Sharing a taxi with Mrs. Mostyn and Mrs. Farmer, Bernard sat in silence during the headlong drive between shanty towns which edged the road from the airport—decrepit huddles of corrugated iron and sacking surrounded by fetid swamp water. Bombay was the last stopping place on their itinerary. He was enjoying the tour, but at none of the cities they had so far visited had he felt any touch of the magic which, according to Alexa—herself unable to believe in it—had held Robert Scott in thrall to India. It seemed unlikely that this sprawling, overcrowded city would be able to cast any such spell.

"We shall be able to do some shopping here," said Mrs. Mostyn as —skidding the wrong way around a rotary at sixty miles an hour—the taxi left the shantytowns behind and hurtled through a shopping area. Bernard did not bother to listen as the two widows resumed their familiar click-clacking comparisons of goods and prices, but he was glad of the reminder. He had picked up one or two small trinkets for Helen as they went along, but she would expect one larger present. Should he choose jewelry? Or would a sari be more acceptable?

In the end, on the afternoon of the next day, he bought both. With a pair of gold earrings in his pocket and two lengths of gold-flecked silk in a packet under his arm, he found a seat on the edge of the Maidan: two teams of schoolboys were playing football in a midafternoon temperature high in the nineties. With only half his attention on the game, he conjured up a mental picture of Helen, beautiful Helen, with gold earrings dangling and wearing a dress made of the silk he had bought. The strength of his desire to be with her at that moment was disconcerting and, to control it, he set himself the task of making plans for the remaining three days of the holiday. These, according to the itinerary, were to be spent at leisure in Bombay. But Bombay did not have the appearance of a city with much entertainment to offer the visitor. He had visited the Elephanta Caves with the rest of the party that morning. What else was there to do?

The memory of Elephanta provided a possible answer. Throughout the morning's trip their guide had referred to other caves and other statues: larger, more artistic, covering a more extensive area, altogether more impressive. Ajanta and Ellora were the names most often repeated—not close to Bombay, but accessible. Bernard moved off in search of a tourist office.

The young man behind the counter was smart and helpful, agreeing that this was an expedition which should on no account be missed. "But is only one plane each day, sir. Leaving at ten minutes past six in the morning for Aurangabad. And to return, the same plane departing from Aurangabad at seven-forty."

"That's fine. I'll go tomorrow and stay two days."

"I regret, sir, that tomorrow's flight is fully booked. Half an hour ago I have endeavored to find a seat for another passenger, but with no success. In three days' time I can obtain for you a seat."

"In three days' time I shall be in England. Phone the airport." Now that he had decided to go, he was not prepared to be obstructed. The young man shrugged his shoulders and did as he was told. The flight was still fully booked.

"How long does the journey take by train?"

"Unfortunately, sir, there is no direct connection. It would be necessary to change from one train at one o'clock in the morning and to wait until four o'clock for the train on the narrow-gauge line. And the same on returning. You would have insufficient time for your sightseeing in Aurangabad."

Cross with himself and with the agency—because they should have suggested the expedition before he left England and booked it for him in advance—Bernard walked out of the air-conditioned office without a word. Then he was ashamed of his ungracious behavior. The young man was not to blame and had tried to be helpful. But he did not retrace his steps. Instead, still annoyed, he made his way back to the hotel.

His irritation with the small frustration was not assuaged by a preprandial drink in his room. It increased his annoyance to find that the hotel had set aside a single table for the group's evening meal, so that he could not even nurse his bad temper in silence. It was sufficiently obvious for Dr. Ibbotson to ask what was bothering him.

"A hiccup in the tourist system," Bernard told him. "I spent the afternoon trying to get myself out to Aurangabad tomorrow." Already he had forgotten how very recent was the idea, how unreasonable his expectation that empty seats should be waiting for his use. "But it can't be done."

"Why not?"

"The plane's fully booked. There are hundreds of empty hotel bedrooms waiting for tourists, apparently, but only one small daily flight to fill them. And I must say I don't fancy another three days in Bombay. I find the humidity oppressive. Still—" Putting his annoyance into words to some extent helped to relieve it. He changed the subject and joined in the general conversation with a determined show of cheerfulness.

At the far end of the restaurant a band began to play a Western quickstep and at once Mr. and Mrs. Hunwick rose to their feet. The rest of the party watched in surprise as they proved themselves to be stylish ballroom dancers. Dr. Ibbotson looked across at Daphne. "I can't match that," he said. "But would you—?"

Daphne was on her feet before he had finished the invitation. On Bernard's right hand Stephen Clyde also stood up—but not, as Bernard at first supposed, to dance with his wife. Instead he murmured something in her ear and left the restaurant.

Bernard turned his head to look across the empty place and found Gitta staring at him thoughtfully. She was just about to suggest something to him. Making a guess at what it might be, he thought it only gentlemanly to get the question in first, and asked her whether she too would care to dance.

"I don't dance," said Gitta in her usual blunt style.

Bernard looked at her in surprise. He moved into the seat which Stephen Clyde had vacated, so that they need not shout. Once they were sitting close together, the loudness of the music insulated them from the rest of the party, making it possible for them to talk privately. "When we were at Khajuraho you told me that you were actually a dancer."

"A scientist ought to be more precise about attaching an answer to the question which preceded it. I agreed that I'd trained as a dancer. But that was years ago. I haven't danced since I was seventeen." She looked into his eyes with the directness which he found so disconcerting. "I don't look like a dancer. I don't move like a dancer."

"When you took that pose, copying the statue, you moved in an unusual way. Like a woman who knows where her muscles are and what each one can be expected to do. Not many people understand their own bodies in quite that manner."

"So you labeled me as a professional dancer?"

"Not now, of course."

"Of course not." Her laughter mocked herself as well as him. "Well, now or then, you were wrong. Something very heavy fell on my foot when I was seventeen. Ever since then my left shoe has been filled with metal. It's a very serviceable sort of foot. I can stand on it indefinitely. I can walk on the level as far as anyone else. I can climb stairs and ladders, more slowly than other people. But I can't swirl effortlessly round in waltz time. And if I were to tread on my partner's toes by mistake, he'd feel it."

How could he have failed to notice? Bernard asked himself. He had certainly observed that she had a firm stride, heavier than that of many women, and less graceful—but it was in keeping with her personality and not unusual enough to be remarkable. What he should have realized was that he had never seen her legs, for she invariably wore either trousers or a long skirt. And when the rest of the party took off their shoes to visit a mosque she had always stayed outside.

While he was considering this, Gitta returned to the subject which clearly had been on her mind before he interrupted her. "I've got a spare seat on that plane," she said abruptly. "If you're really keen to go, you could have it."

"You mean that you're not using it?"

"We had a ticket each, Steve and I. It's the place I'm most anxious to visit—almost the whole point of the holiday—so we arranged the trip through the agency before we left England. I shall be going tomorrow. But Steve—Steve's found himself a boyfriend. He had his hair done yesterday and was swept off his feet by a beautiful sixteen-year-old barber. He asked me this morning whether it would worry me to travel alone. So his ticket is up for grabs. Would you like it?"

"Very much. Very much indeed. You don't seem very bothered. About your husband, I mean."

Her flat, sallow face turned toward him, enlivened for once by a glint of mischief in her eyes. "Well, it's not the first time."

"You don't care?"

"People have different sorts of marriage. This is the kind that suits Steve and me. Me more than him, in fact. I don't regard marriage as important. But Steve is useful to me, as well as being my best friend. A marriage contract is as good as any other kind for keeping our interests together."

"Are you trying to shock me?" Bernard asked. "I don't believe any woman is as cold-blooded as that."

"Perhaps you only know nice women. Most women are givers. I

happen to be a taker. It's important to recognize one's category honestly."

"I don't agree with your generalization. Most women are takers."

"That's nonsense. You're talking about money, but money's not important—and you're out of date anyway. I give Steve money, but that doesn't make me a giver. I'm talking about emotions. Almost all women have an emotional need to give. That's why they hang on to their men, so that they have someone to give to. One can take from anyone, casually, but one can only give within a relationship."

"Give what? Take what?"

"Anything," said Gitta. "Love, sex, friendship, inspiration, support, sympathy. Anything that needs a human being as its vehicle. I take it all and move on. So I can't complain when Steve does the same. It's better than that, even. It makes me all the more free."

Bernard did not bother to understand what she was talking about. Instead, he smiled at her gratefully. "Well, as far as I'm concerned, you're a giver," he pointed out. "A good fairy, making my wishes come true. Waving your magic wand."

"You're laughing as though you don't believe in magic!"

"Well, of course not." He looked at her, startled. "Do you?"

"I have an Irish grandmother. How could I not believe?" She was teasing, but only just. "Well, I do believe that wishes of a certain kind come true. There's a degree of spiritual intensity which earns its own reward."

"I'm not sure that I've deserved this particular reward. Two days ago I'd hardly heard of Aurangabad. There can't be much spiritual intensity in a sudden whim to go sight-seeing in a particular place."

"Perhaps the intensity will come afterwards. Who knows what may be waiting for you in Aurangabad? Or perhaps the caves, Ajanta, Ellora, are wishing to see you even more strongly than you wish to see them."

"You're the one who's talking nonsense now."

By her laughter she seemed to agree, but then reminded him that he would need to be up at four-thirty the next morning to catch the plane. He saw the sense of going early to bed, but found himself kept awake by the questions which swirled through his mind. He wanted to understand Gitta Clyde and found it frustrating that she should so deliberately refuse to give him any clues. How much—like the metal foot—had he not until now even suspected about her? What did she do with herself all day in Ireland while her husband was amusing himself in London? Why had she refused to answer that question when he put it to her directly? What was the aspect of her life which would explain everything about her but which he had not yet been allowed to glimpse?

As a young man Bernard had held the theory that central to every human being was some ruling passion, which might inspire to great achievement or, frustrated, be a cause of misery: something which could be dulled or suppressed by age or circumstance but could never altogether die. Later, he had begun to wonder whether this view was fashioned too particularly by the undoubted talents of his relations, and had tactily begun to exclude women from his generalization. With only a few exceptions—which included his mother and grandmother and all his aunts and cousins—women, he suspected, were more prone to embrace the enthusiasms of others. Their passions were for people, or else were of brief duration. Long before middle age enveloped them, they settled merely for staying alive and preserving their family relationships. Was Gitta a member of this dull—although no doubt happy—group? He found it impossible to think so; and yet he was quite unable to identify any talent or enthusiasm which might provide the clue to her character.

Even when at last he began fitfully to sleep he was unable to escape from Gitta. One of the carvings he had seen in the Elephanta caves that morning had represented Siva, vertically divided to be male on one side, female on the other. The androgynous figure had disturbed Bernard, who preferred people to be unmistakably of one gender or the other; and now in the troubled darkness of his dreams he seemed to see Gitta Clyde's flat and unstimulating body moving backward into a shadowed cave to merge into the carving of Siva as though she, like the god, was at the same time male and female. She was behind the stone, or inside it, and thrusting to burst out again. Bernard supposed himself to be watching, powerless to help but unable to leave. He was conscious of a throbbing of energy within the dead gray stone of the carving. Then with a crash the metal foot kicked its way through and the stone shattered into pieces. The telephone was ringing by his bed to tell him that it was half past four.

VIII

Tired after his restless night, Bernard was in no mood to chat to Gitta as the plane rose from Bombay Airport into the darkness. Only as the sky flushed with a delicate dawn light did he shake himself awake and ask about the program she had arranged.

"The two sets of caves are in different directions," she told him. "We shall do one trip each day. There's due to be a guide waiting at the airport with a car. Since we're having breakfast on the plane, I'd prefer to drive straight off to Ajanta, rather than waste time checking into the hotel. Would that suit you? It would mean that we could get the driving over before the heat really builds up."

Bernard nodded his agreement; he could sense her excitement and eagerness to be on her way. Without understanding the intensity of her mood, he realized that what they were soon to see was what primarily had drawn Gitta to India.

The road which took them across the Deccan plateau was lined on each side by women who split large rocks with hammers again and again until they were left with a pile of small stones. The bright colors of their saris and the animation of the children who carried away the flat baskets of stones made the sight resemble an unusual form of picnic; but this was relief work, the guide told them. A family working together could earn three rupees a day, just enough to buy its ration of food.

"The soil looks rich," commented Gitta—for the fields they passed were furrowed with black volcanic earth.

The guide agreed, but pointed at a dry riverbed, its course marked by a crazy paving of mud which had baked and cracked in the sun. Beside it cows and goats still wandered, impelled by a distant memory of past lushness to drop their lips toward the bare soil. The story here was similar to what Bernard had already heard from Dr. Chandra. These stone-breaking women were the wives of small farmers who in normal times were prosperous. But here too the monsoon had failed last year for the third year running. The cotton crop had survived, but there would be no food for the summer. Already the village wells were empty and for the next four months, as the sun grew steadily hotter, the only water would come from government tanker trucks.

Bernard remembered the statistics he had been given in Udaipur and wondered whether the same forecasts applied here. But tact and sympathy restrained him from pressing the question directly. One couldn't, in cold blood, ask someone what percentage of his own friends, relations and neighbors would be dead before four months had passed.

The car came to a halt on the dramatic edge of the plateau, where the land fell sharply away before stretching to the horizon as a flat, parched plain two thousand feet below them. It was from here, the guide told them, that a party of British officers had seen the panther which they were hunting spring down the edge of the plateau and then disappear into the cliff face of a river gorge below.

Although it was already possible to see the caves which had been discovered when the hunters pursued their quarry, there was a good deal of driving to be endured before they reached the spot. The road zigzagged down through this wild, stony area.

"What is it that made you particularly want to come here?" Bernard asked his companion.

"Two different reasons for the two separate expeditions," Gitta told him. "What excites me about the paintings we're going to see today, in Ajanta, is the knowledge that they existed for centuries without anyone suspecting they were there. For thirteen hundred years no one saw them; but they existed all the time. Don't you find that fascinating?"

"And tomorrow?"

"Ellora!" Gitta spoke the word with awe and repeated it once as though it were some kind of spell. "Ellora!" Then she spoke more briskly. "Tomorrow is tomorrow. Don't let's spoil today by thinking about what we're going to see next."

They arrived at Ajanta, leaving the car beside a deep gorge which a river, now dry, had cut into the shape of a horseshoe. A steep climb brought them to a point halfway up the side of the gorge, where a railed path had been built out from the cliff. Bernard looked curiously at the long line of carved stone doorways cut from the cliff face. "They don't look like caves," he said.

"It's a misleading word," Gitta agreed. "This is all artificial. The stone was cut out from the middle of the rock to form Buddhist temples. As no doubt our guide will tell us in detail."

Their early start had made them the first of the day's parties to arrive, so as they stepped curiously through each elaborate entrance into one of the huge dark spaces carved out by Buddhist monks almost two thousand years earlier, they were alone and could examine in a leisurely way the paintings which covered the temple walls and ceilings. Holding up electric lamps with large reflectors to illuminate the frescoes, the guide described at length the religious precepts or princely ways of life which they illustrated. Gitta wandered away, preferring to see the work through her own eyes. Bernard, continuing to listen, wondered how long the paint would survive the invading atmosphere of human breath and sweat.

By the time they reached the far end of the gorge the day had become very hot and they were tired. By now, too, the area was crowded. A large party of Japanese blocked the path, photographing with equal enthusiasm the painted temples and the ruff-necked monkeys performing gymnastics on the cliff face. It took Bernard and Gitta some time to edge their way back and relax in the shade of the tourist restaurant.

"You were describing the delights of discovery," said Bernard when they had ordered curries and soft drinks. "I suspect you left out the chief one. It's not just the satisfaction of seeing inside something for the time. It's knowing that there's nobody else around when you do it. But I'm annoyed with myself for not knowing about these caves before I left England. I would have read up about them."

"When you *did* hear about them, at Elephanta, why did you want to come? And have your anticipations been fulfilled?"

"I have no feeling for art," Bernard admitted. "And very little for history. I had no true anticipations."

Gitta laughed with mischievous amusement. "Then why on earth go to the extra trouble and expense?"

"Because I'm a proper tourist. A rubbernecker. I need to be told what I ought to see, but then I make sure of seeing it. I can rest or go shopping just as well in London as in Bombay. I come on holiday to be entertained, and a long journey is only justified when the entertainment is something which couldn't be found in any other part of the world. Looking at pictures or palaces is only an excuse for taking a break from my work; but I like the excuse to be genuine. Ajanta qualifies triumphantly. And from the respectful voice in which you mention it, I suspect that Ellora may be even better." But Gitta was still not prepared to be drawn on that subject.

The journey back to Aurangabad was even hotter and dustier than the morning's drive. After they had arranged the next day's departure time with the guide in the lobby of the hotel, Bernard looked at his watch. "We could take a siesta and have a late dinner," he said. "But I feel more inclined to stay awake now, have dinner at the earliest possible time, and then go early to bed." He took it for granted that they would eat together—and that Gitta, like himself, would be feeling the effects of their early rising and the hot car journeys.

While Gitta disappeared into her room, Bernard lingered for a moment outside his own door, looking around. The old colonial hotel, with its spacious, easygoing atmosphere, fitted his mood perfectly. A wide balcony, shady and cool, ran in front of the rooms on the upper floor of the two-storied building, serving as a corridor as well as a sitting-out place: pots of flowers alternated with pairs of old but comfortable cane chairs. Shabby though the hotel might be, it was neither more nor less than he had expected anywhere from India. In it he could unwind, throwing off his tiredness and feeling himself alone. Gitta's nearness did not impinge on his solitude, for there was nothing intrusive in her personality. He could seek her company or ignore it, and she would hardly notice.

Entering the bedroom, he smiled at its run-down appearance. This would have had Mrs. Hunwick organizing a group protest; but it was clean enough, and large. All the same, even to Bernard it seemed a pity that the hotel should not show off its country's crafts. Why were there not beautiful local rugs on the well-scrubbed floor instead of narrow strips of worn green carpet; sheets of fine lawn instead of roughly laundered thick cotton; woven curtains from cottage industries instead of drooping squares of Lancashire print; a handmade pottery ashtray instead of a gimcrack circle of molded glass?

Well, it was not his business to teach India how to sell herself. On the far side of the bedroom he found a door leading to a huge and cobwebbed bathroom. The water in the rooftop tanks had been too thoroughly warmed by the sun for his shower to be refreshing, but it enabled him to remove the dirt and sweat of the journey. By the time he had dressed again, in clean clothes, he was in tune with the atmosphere of an unhurrying country.

Later, strolling through the hotel gardens, he found the remains of a tennis court. The grass had long since died, but the earth had been meticulously raked level before the sun baked it dry. Frayed snakes of wire dangled sinuously from each green Slazenger post, but he felt sure that there had been no net for many years. Far from seeing this as a sign of inefficiency he accepted as reasonable the thought that no one in his senses would come to this particular spot in order to chase little balls in the eye of the sun.

In other respects the hotel's gardeners had made an effort not rivaled indoors. The brown lawn was patterned with flower beds whose roses and bougainvilleas, stocks and African marigolds, were—in spite of the drought—being treated at this moment to bucketfuls of water. Just around a corner, a pair of appreciative goats whose tethering strings trailed broken behind them nibbled a row of newly watered ferns. Bernard wondered whether to shoo them away. Then he mentally shrugged his shoulders, as doubtless the gardeners would have done, and went inside.

Dinner that evening proved not to have been worth the effort of staying awake. After a single mouthful Gitta put down her fork, although Bernard continued for a little longer to explore the stew in the hope of finding something edible.

"Don't you feel guilty about leaving food when there's so much hunger outside?" he asked.

"The more I leave, the better the cook's children will eat tonight, I imagine."

Bernard remembered how calmly she had listened—both in Udaipur and again this morning—to the details of the drought. "It doesn't worry you, does it?" he asked.

"What?"

"The fact that a famine is on the way."

"If I could prevent it, I would," Gitta said. "But I can't carry all the failings of nature on my own conscience. I'm not an engineer, capable of building dams. I'm not an agriculturalist, able to plant trees. I see the need. But I'm personally incompetent to do anything about it. When I get back to England I shall give money to famine relief, but perhaps you don't count that."

"No," said Bernard. "That's a practical reaction, and very admirable. But you don't *feel* anything, do you? Thousands of people are going to die here, and you don't really care."

"Death is built into life. If nobody ever died, there would be no room for anyone to be born."

"That's the sort of thing I mean," said Bernard. "Those are simply words. I was talking about feelings. You don't care."

Gitta considered the accusation and accepted its truth. "I suppose you're right. My life is self-regarding. No man's death diminishes me."

"We're not talking about one man's death, but thousands. Millions perhaps."

"I'm not affected by numbers." Gitta spoke definitely. "The label of disaster may be useful to a newspaper or history book, but it doesn't make any difference to the sufferer. No individual can die more than one death, however terrible the famine."

"You haven't got your values right," Bernard told her. "It isn't dying that's the terrible thing. It's losing. Bereavement. If you were a mother, watching six of your children die one after the other, you wouldn't feel like that."

"If I were a mother I wouldn't be me," Gitta retaliated. "And who are you to talk? You're the man who doesn't believe in creating."

"I try to preserve." Bernard pushed his plate to one side, donating his share of stewed mutton gristle to the starving millions outside and watching without enthusiasm as it was replaced by a generous helping of red jelly.

"Yes, of course." Gitta gave him the smile of a woman who is anxious not to quarrel and yet reluctant to abandon her argument. "But if nothing was ever created, there would be nothing worth preserving. Or you can put it the other way round. If you consider something worthy of preservation, it was right that it should have been created in the first place."

"Oh, come, where's the logic in that? I may disapprove—I *do* disapprove—of large families of unwanted children. I make pills which I hope will have the effect of limiting the number of births. I support every attempt which is made to discourage feckless women from producing their seventh, eighth, ninth child. But on the day the ninth child is born, then it has the right to claim the support of my laboratory in keeping it alive."

"You're sentimental!" Gitta was laughing at him, although not unkindly. "Do you think the coffee will be worth waiting for?"

She stood up, taking his answer for granted. They went straight to their rooms, although it was still early in the evening; but in spite of his tiredness Bernard walked up and down the shabby strips of carpet for a while, ruffled by the conversation. It had been a mistake to discuss an important topic in personal terms—especially since their personal knowledge of each other was inadequate. Clearly, for example, Gitta did not realize that the isolation and recognition and testing and production and marketing of a new drug was itself an act of creation. Something existed as a result of his work that had not existed before. With that gap in her understanding, she could not legitimately attack him.

His information about her was even less complete. Had she any creative talent at all? Women often compensated for childlessness by making cakes or gardens, church hassocks or flower arrangements. Any discussion concerning relative values was meaningless until he knew what she believed to be important.

Perhaps the next day would provide a clue, he told himself as he turned off the light and went to bed. He remembered the special voice in which she had spoken the word Ellora. Perhaps tomorrow she would allow him to understand her a little better, if only by accident. And if she didn't, that was not important either. In three days' time they would be back in England and he would never see her again. Such a thought had carried Bernard through many tedious holiday moments in the past. However boring or infuriating his fellow travelers might be, the moment inevitably came when he could say good-bye to them for good. With that thought to cheer him, he could be as boring or infuriating in return as he chose. Not that he wished to annoy Gitta. It would be enough if he could find out why she had come.

I X

The drive to Ellora next day was shorter than that to Ajanta. This time the road passed by ruined palaces, crumbling forts, onion-domed tombs which glared in whitewash in the middle of parched fields. They saw one steep hill whose sides had been cut away to form a cliff; above this, massive stone walls surrounded a hill castle, decayed but dominating. Bernard leaned forward toward the guide.

"Can we stop here for a moment?"

"On the return journey is better, sir. When the tourist bus arrives at Ellora, the temples will be crowded. If we journey straight on we shall have an hour there before this time."

That made sense, and Bernard saw that Gitta was in a hurry to get on. Her anticipation filled the car with energy, pressing the driver to abandon his sedate country style and dash with Bombay brio toward their destination.

"What's the difference between Ajanta and Ellora?" Bernard asked Gitta half an hour later. They were standing together in a bleak, deserted area, waiting while the guide bought their permits. Bernard found the atmosphere disturbing, even a little eerie. The air was too quiet, too still. Somewhere nearby, presumably, the guide was cheerfully chatting with the guardian of the place, passing over money and perhaps accepting refreshment, but in disappearing he had left behind no impression that he would ever return. Bernard waited for Gitta to reply. What he really wanted to discover was why today's visit was more exciting to her than yesterday's, but he guessed that the more impersonal question was likelier to reveal the answer.

"At Ajanta the temples were cut from the middle of a vertical cliff as caves," she reminded him. "But the Ellora temples have been carved down from the top, as well as inwards, out of the solid rock. The people who made them could leave a roof on the main part of a temple but cut away the rock all round, from above, to produce an open courtyard—and then excavate the inside of the temple itself. So that what looks like a free-standing building is actually all chiseled from the rock, working from the top downwards."

"And what's the significance of that?"

"Who's looking for significance? Different styles, that's all. But it does have one consequence. At Ajanta, where nothing was exposed to the weather, the decoration was in the form of painting—which has in fact deteriorated. Here, it's carving—and the Deccan rock is very hard. It should look much as it did when it was newly carved."

"Something else that was hidden, waiting to be discovered?"

She glanced quickly at him as though she agreed with what he said but suspected that he might not have intended the interpretation she put on his words.

"The finished caves have always been known. But—" She paused. It was not that she was unsure of herself, but that she seemed doubtful whether or not to share a secret belief with her companion. "You could say, I suppose, that everything in nature—a piece of stone or a human being—has its own potential hidden inside it. Quite often the development is botched. But when the true potential emerges—when the relationship between the second stage and the basic material is perfect—there's a special quality, a special atmosphere. Ellora has that reputation, for a kind of perfection. Not necessarily perfect carving in any absolute sense. But a perfect transformation from a rocky hill to—well, to what we're just going to see. Here's our guide back again."

They followed him along the dusty path, but Bernard felt the conversation to be unfinished. "And why should the prospect of seeing a perfect transformation be so important to you?" he asked.

Gitta, impatient to arrive, shrugged her shoulders as she strode along. "Different things inspire different people. A painter may have a special model. A poet may need a muse. What *I* find inspiring is the sense—" But she abandoned her answer as they arrived on the brow of a ridge and looked across a narrow valley. "Here we are," she said, and breathed the word softly again. "Ellora."

In spite of what she had described to him, Bernard felt his eyes widening at the unexpectedness of the sight. As at Ajanta, the temples curved along the side of a cliff, but the resemblance ended there. Of the many façades, in a variety of elaborate styles, one in particular caught the eye. Near the center of the curve a flight of steps led up to a row of pillars which flanked the dark entrance to a cave. A huge Hindu figure, as high as the pillars, lounged nonchalantly at one side. A frieze and a row of smaller pillars continued the façade upward for a little way, but above that the face of the cliff remained uncut. From the foot of the steps, no one would be able to guess what lay inside.

From this high viewpoint, though, they could see the complete temple. As Gitta had explained, the top of the cliff had been cut away to form a courtyard, leaving a complex of towers and chambers in its center. Stone elephants ornamented the courtyard, and around it two-storied galleries were cut into the stone. As a building erected in the normal way from the bottom it would have been impressive enough: as a single piece of rock carved out from the top it was almost unbelievable.

"This is Kailasha." The guide could guess what they were studying. "Twice the size of Parthenon of Greece. Now we go down."

He led the way into the valley and up the other side. Bernard would have liked to go at once to the Kailasha, but was outvoted. The guide preferred to work along the row in order that his clients could appreciate the chronological development of styles; and Gitta, like a child, chose to save the greatest treat until last.

The crowd which came on the tourist bus had been and gone before at last, hot and foot-weary, Bernard and Gitta stepped inside the courtyard of the Kailasha and studied the carvings on the outside walls of the temple.

"Do you like the style?" Bernard asked.

"Which style?" Gitta seemed happy but not exactly satisfied. "It's such an extraordinary mixture. The mass of the temple presses down, but the towers float up. There's a whole wall carved with a military campaign, which must have been intended to be educational, and yet those stone monkeys leaping about on the roof are a lighthearted joke. What I can't feel here is a sense of the religious center. The other temples were less impressive, but they did have an atmosphere of worship. Perhaps it will be different inside."

Side by side they walked into the first chamber and came to a standstill in front of a relief carving. It showed the same androgynous Siva that they had seen two days earlier depicted in the Elephanta cave. For a second time Bernard was disturbed by the concept.

"You don't like it?" asked Gitta, sensitive to his mood.

"I prefer people to be one thing or the other."

"Yet none of us, surely, is wholly masculine or wholly feminine. We're all in various shades of gray."

"It's fashionable to say so. But misleading, I think."

"What sort of god do you worship?" she asked. "All male or all female? Or do you not see a difficulty? If you started to write down the attributes you considered male or female, you'd realize how much you're influenced by temporary or geographical fashions."

"You'd hardly deny a physical difference."

"I'd deny its importance," Gitta said. "Except in the limited spheres of copulation and reproduction and suckling. And there are gray areas even there." She did not wait for him to comment but moved on to a second chamber, and a third, each darker than the one before.

The last and highest of the halls overwhelmed them by its size. The solid-rock ceiling was cut to represent wooden beams, pressing heavily on the rows of pillars which pretended to support them. The stone floor, polished with wear, reflected a little light near the entrance, but the farther end of the chamber was dark.

"If you will please be keeping to one side, I will illuminate the Siva lingam," said the guide, and obediently they moved away from the doorway. A large mirror outside was lifted and turned to catch the sun, directing its light into the chamber. Gitta and Bernard, keeping to one side of the beckoning silver path, followed it in. They stopped at the same moment as a dark recess at the farthest end was revealed.

For a moment neither of them spoke. Bernard was embarrassed to have a woman beside him as he stared at the phallus in the center of the shrine. It was three feet high, cut from the same rock as the rest of the temple, but startling in its smoothness in a place where all available surfaces were intricately decorated with carving.

Gitta's silence, he felt, had a different cause: she seemed to have been struck dumb by awe. "We've found the center at last," she whispered. "The eye of the temple." Stepping forward, she moved her hand softly over its surface. Bernard found the gesture insupportable.

"Don't touch it," he said—and then apologized for his sharpness. "I'm sorry. But it's obscene."

"What's obscenity?" asked Gitta. One finger still rested on the stone but—perhaps in deference to his outburst—she checked her stroking movement. "Something intended to shock? This may be shocking to us, but was it intended so? I doubt it."

Bernard could not answer her question. He was excited, with an excitement which had no object. There was nothing about Gitta, whose behavior here was as matter-of-fact as usual, to stimulate him. The lingam's obscenity lay in its startling ability to arouse a purposeless lust which had no possibility of satisfaction.

"It's the paint," he said unconvincingly, since she seemed to be waiting for an answer. Three thin lines of red encircled the top of the lingam like a necklace. He moved forward on the pretense of examining them more closely, but also in the hope that at close quarters the stone would prove to be nothing more than a shape. "Or is it blood? Whatever it is, it's not old. Do you think this is still used for something? I could imagine . . ."

He did not like to finish the thought, but Gitta looked up at him and laughed. "Yes, I could imagine as well. Shall we go?"

"One question. Is this the thing you came here to see?"

Gitta shook her head. "No. I don't know exactly what I expected to find. I just hoped . . ." She allowed the sentence to fade away. "Well, whatever it was, I haven't found it. The atmosphere is here, but . . ." She made an effort to laugh at her disappointment.

The guide, watching from the entrance to tell when they were ready to leave, swung the mirror to show the way out. This time the brightness of the reflected sunshine moved around the outer wall. Bernard felt Gitta's hand suddenly gripping his arm, holding him back.

"It's here after all," she said softly; and then called to the guide. "Will you point the light back here? That's right. Hold it!"

There were a few seconds of unsteadiness as the guide propped up the mirror at the angle which Gitta had requested, so that he need not stand holding it. When he moved away, the beam pointed straight at a stone figure on the wall.

It was Siva again—the twentieth representation, probably, that they had seen in the past three hours. It was not the most beautiful or even the most perfect; in fact, it had been mutilated. It reminded Bernard strongly of the stone relief which had been his christening present from Robert Scott, for that too was imperfect, cracked in a manner which added an element of slyness to the mouth of the god. But even if it had lacked that element of familiarity, Bernard would have understood why it should arrest Gitta's attention.

It was the pose which made such a dramatic impact. Siva was dancing, his body arched backward to a degree which was humanly impossible. The carving—in depth less than a statue but more than a relief—was simple, even primitive. No sculptor who took the human skeleton seriously could have portrayed such a position, yet into it he had injected a controlled energy which pierced its way out of the dull, hard surface. Within the pose was concentrated the power which surrounds an arrow in a drawn bow, with all the stillness of a cat in the second before it pounces, when the movement is already assembled in its body. Bernard's own muscles tensed as though to resist an attack. Only after a little while did he realize that this might be a reaction to his companion's fierce grip on his arm. Gitta herself appeared to be in a state of trance.

Bernard studied the carving in detail, until he was able to isolate the element of shock. Siva was male, but the pose he held was female. Gitta might not have agreed, but Bernard found the figure more disturbing even than the one in which a physical difference had been marked by a central line.

"An even more impossible position than the one I set you at Khajuraho," he said. "I don't imagine you could bend like that, could you?"

The only light was that reflected on the wall. In spite of her closeness, he could hardly see Gitta. But he was aware of her reluctant return to awareness of his presence as she looked in a new way at the carving, studying its lines.

"I should need support." She was still gripping his arm just above the elbow. Now she moved her hand down until it held his, and brought it to the small of her back, the palm flat against her spine. "If you move, there'll be a nasty bump," she warned him.

As she arched her back, Bernard needed to press against it with all his strength. She moved with a controlled, yogalike slowness, forcing her shoulders backward. Although Bernard had asked her to do it, he realized that he must stop her. His reason told him that he did not want Gitta but—so soon after the sexual stirring aroused by the Siva lingam—she was too close for him to be sure of remaining reasonable.

"Stop it," he said. "You'll hurt yourself." He pushed her upright again, disturbing her balance so that she staggered slightly. "I need some fresh air. I'll wait for you outside."

Hurrying into the courtyard, he sat down on the stone foot of an elephant to wait until Gitta emerged from the shadows. She looked pale, but seemed unflustered.

"Let me ask you again," he said, as they drove away from the site. "You didn't know what you were looking for. But you knew when you found it. What was it you found? And why did you look for it here?"

"Ellora!" She had spoken the word before with exactly the same tone of incantation. "Haven't you ever had magic words in your life? Someone wrote a poem about that sort of thing. I can't quote it, because I've never been able to remember the words that were magic for him."

"Chimborazo, Cotopaxi." Bernard understood at once what she meant, but allowed her to complete the explanation.

"That's it. Well, Ellora was one of my words. The seed has to be sown very early in childhood, I think—so far back that one forgets. I've certainly forgotten how I heard of Ellora. At first, it was just the music of the name. Later, I read books and studied pictures. All my life I've wanted to come—but this was the first time I could afford it. When you long for something for years, it's tempting to invest it with significance, isn't it? To expect something more than just another trip. You're sure that you're going to find something special at the foot of the rainbow, even if you haven't the faintest idea of what it may be."

It was unusual for her to speak with such excitement. What she was trying to explain was surely caused by more than the fulfillment of a childhood ambition. "And that particular carving?" he pressed.

"Oh, I don't know. Haven't you ever looked at someone, a woman, a stranger, and felt winded? Without any rhyme or reason?"

Bernard did not answer. Had they genuinely shared an emotion, he wondered, or had the reaction of one infected the other? He was glad when the guide interrupted to ask whether they still wished to visit Daulatabad.

"What's that?" asked Bernard.

"The hill fort you were noticing this morning, sir. This city was fortified in the fourteenth century. The Shah Tughlak forced one million of his subjects to march here from Tughlakabad, the Delhi of that time, so that this should become his capital."

"And what happened to it?"

"Sir, after seventeen years there was no more water. They marched back to Delhi again."

Bernard was tempted to comment that the Indian people seemed fated to be victims, whether of a mad shah or an implacable climate. But he only said that yes, he would like to stop.

Gitta left him to climb the hill alone. Perhaps the path was too steep for her. As he explored the abandoned city, Bernard found himself unable to bring it to life even in his imagination: his ignorance of its history was too complete. The huge walls and steep streets were impressive, but no more than that.

Turning back toward the car, he saw Gitta standing in a riverbed—as dry as all the others—which must once have acted as a moat. She was surrounded by a group of small boys trying to sell her something. Each held out an old tobacco tin whose contents rattled as they were shaken. As Bernard approached, she dismissed all but the eldest boy. A bargain had been struck. She handed over money and received what seemed to be money in return. Bernard came close to look.

She had bought two coins. One was of silver, elegantly decorated. The other, which looked much older, was a coppery brown and very thick.

"This is from the reign of Shah Jehan," she said. "You know, the Taj Mahal man. And this is from Shah Tughlak, who built this place. Or so the boy says." She held the coins flat on the palm of one hand, passing the fingertips of her other hand over them to encircle the edges and touch the surfaces as though she were reading Braille.

"Do you collect coins?" he asked.

Gitta shook her head, continuing to stroke her purchases.

"Then what's the attraction? Do you use them psychometrically? I mean, do you feel now that you're in touch with Shah Tughlak?"

She shook her head a second time. "Not with him. I don't imagine he ever touched this. But perhaps with the man who lost it in the river. Or even with the boy who found it."

Bernard looked at the boy. He was dressed as well as any Indian village lad not actually in school uniform, wearing clean although faded blue shorts and green short-sleeved shirt. His back was very straight and his thin legs, barefooted, were planted on the dusty ground in a definite manner, a little apart. His brown eyes were alert as he watched his customer, trying to calculate whether the transaction was at an end or whether a word at the right moment would produce further benefits.

In that brief second, when the boy was balanced and ready to move, but remained still, Bernard felt for the first time that he was on the verge of understanding Gitta. As though he were in a dream, all sound receded and he found himself looking at the Indian through Gitta's eyes. Then the boy moved. The energy which had been momentarily pent up was released as he offered another coin from his tin.

"Memsahib, memsahib, this coin of Aurangzeb, very fine, very old."

Gitta flicked him aside, breaking the spell. Something in the dry riverbed had caught her eye; she bent down to pick it up.

"What have you found?" asked Bernard.

As she held out her treasure he stared curiously at the ugly brown object. It looked like a potato—a potato attacked by blight. If he were to hold it and squeeze, its rotten intestines would squirt over his fingers in a brown and foul-smelling stream. Common sense told him that it could not in fact be any kind of vegetable; but still he was reluctant to touch.

"Take it," said Gitta.

His fingers closed on it lightly, careful not to press. But it was hard—a pebble, like all the others in the riverbed. Its shape was in no sense beautiful—just a vague roundness with a surface broken by an acne pitting and a warty knobbiness. He handed it back, his eyebrows raised in question.

"You don't recognize it?" asked Gitta.

"As what?"

She knelt down in the riverbed and set her discovery on a flat rock. Using another rock as a hammer and a thinner flake of stone as a chisel, she split the pebble with a single neat tap. Before the two sections could fall apart, she pressed them back into their original roundness.

"You've seen the Taj Mahal," she said, standing up again. "And so have thousands of other tourists. But nobody has ever seen the inside of this stone. You're the first. It's been waiting millions of years just for your eyes. And if you were to destroy it, no one would ever see it again. It's a private present for you."

She put the stone into his hands and closed his fingers around it. Bernard looked down at the ugly object. Then he moved the two halves apart. The center was hollow, but inside the brown shell was a stratum of many-faceted pyramids which glinted in the fierce sun—almost, but not quite, like a bed of diamonds. He tilted the two halves from side to side so that the pointed teeth sparkled with light.

"What is it?" he asked for a third time.

"Quartz. Do you like it?"

"It's extraordinary," he said. "That it should exist at all, and that you should find it inside something that looks like a bad potato. Are you a geologist?"

For a moment, as Gitta's strong fingers closed his own over her gift, there had been a current of friendship between them. Now her laughter annoyed him into realizing that he had spoilt the moment with his question.

"You're still looking for the label to stick on me, aren't you? No, I'm not a geologist any more than I'm a dancer. When you meet a woman traveling with her husband, isn't it enough for you to think of her as a wife?"

"No," said Bernard definitely. "At least, not in your case. Mrs. Hunwick is a wife. A housewife. I'm sure she polishes furniture and cleans the bath and arranges flowers and cooks nutritious meals for her husband and loves him in a cozy way: and for her that's enough. You have a different aura—as you're well aware. I told you before, you could stop my guesses by telling me. I'm only trying to understand you."

"Perhaps I don't want to be understood. I know who I am and what I am. Why should it matter to me what you think?" Once more she took his hand in her own. The two halves of the stone lay open on his palms. "The quartz was there all the time, whether you recognized it or not," she pointed out. "It didn't make any difference to its nature when you thought it was just an ordinary stone."

"You mean that the facts aren't altered by the label even when the label's wrong. But surely that makes it all the more important to get the label right. When I first saw you with your husband, I suppose I might have thought that you were just a wife tagging along; in the same way that I thought this"—he looked down at his open hands—"was merely a potato, ugly and diseased. But I would have been as wrong in one case as in the other. And with that sort of misunderstanding between us, how would we ever have been able to communicate?"

"You have a nice line in comparisons," she laughed. "You've decided that I'm a stone, and hard—although still ugly and not even good to eat. But I could say that I was a stone all the time. It wasn't the fault of this"—she touched the quartz briefly before dropping her hands back to her sides—"if you looked at it from too far away."

"We're still not in communication. To talk about a stone is as misleading in its way as to talk about potatoes. How does one find out whether it has a core of quartz?" He kept his voice light, but he intended the question seriously and he could sense that Gitta recognized this. She did not answer at once, but began to walk toward the car.

"It's a dangerous proceeding," she said at last. "You can't be sure by looking and you can't be sure by touching. You have to close in and crack down. And then you could find yourself with nothing but a broken pebble—or, of course, a broken hammer."

She turned toward him and smiled, as though to say that he should not take her seriously. Bernard found it difficult to smile back. She was warning him away. He could assure himself that the warning was unnecessary, but the fact that she had pointed out a danger tempted him toward its edge. As a member of a tourist group Gitta was insignificant: ugly and standoffish—but only because she did not care to present herself as interesting. Now, alone with him, her rejection of any camouflage made her strength of character as conspicuous as the ugliness. He was certain that such a strength must derive from a core of identity to which he had not yet penetrated. But how could he come closer to the truth when she would not allow herself to be approached by questions?

They had reached the car by now. The driver rose from the patch of shade in which he had been squatting and opened the door for Gitta. Bernard went around to the other side. He wrapped the quartz carefully in his handkerchief so that it would not chip and put it into his pocket. The car jolted back on to the road.

X

After a late lunch, Bernard took a siesta. With a whole subcontinent slumbering around him, this manner of passing the afternoon was not laziness but correct behavior. Waking at five o'clock, he ordered afternoon tea for two to be brought to the balcony. The request for a meal he had not taken for years—and a drink that he mildly disliked—gave him for a second time a sense of appropriate action.

The tea tray had arrived before he appeared, showered and dressed, outside his room. Gitta sat beside it, wearing the sleeveless white blouse and floor-length wraparound skirt in which she would spend the evening.

"Will you pour?" he asked, checking the tray as though he were playing Kim's game: teapot, milk, sugar, cups, saucers, spoons. In this country one could not take anything for granted. But it was all there, complete with two grayish slices of Madeira cake.

"No. You."

Her offhand rejection of the woman's role ruffled him and he picked up the metal teapot without reflecting that the handle might be hot. Gitta, meanwhile, had raised a pair of binoculars to her eyes.

"What can you see?" he asked, shaking his burned fingers. Somewhere nearby were the minarets and dome of the mausoleum which Aurangzeb had built for his wife. But Gitta's target was closer to hand.

"Birds."

At first Bernard thought she meant the huge kites which hovered on ragged wings above the hotel garden. Then he saw that all the trees were crowded. Green long-tailed parakeets darted between the leaves which they exactly matched. A wagtail nodded on the bare finger of a frangipani; a tiny weaverbird rested on the top of a mango tree. There were others which he could not identify.

"Those are bulbuls." Gitta passed him the binoculars so that he could see the flashes of red beneath their tail feathers. "And there's a pewit in the same tree. At least, that's what I'd call it—I suppose it may have another name here."

"Do you make a special study of birds?" he asked her, recognizing without the help of magnification the golden feathers of an Indian pheasant which was making its leisurely way across the drive.

"I love the shape of birds. Cormorants. Eagles. Marvelous." She looked at him mischievously. "But I'm not an ornithologist either."

Bernard smiled back. "It's all right. I think I've given up."

To save them from pursuing that subject, three crows landed clumsily on the railing of the balcony. Their blue-black feathers were glossy with health, their black beaks strong, their bodies plump. Bernard—remembering all those human bodies which would soon lack food—was shocked when Gitta tossed a piece of cake toward them.

There was no fighting. One crow caught and stood on the prize, arching its body in profile to the onlookers as it bent to eat. One of its companions turned to stare directly at Gitta, its black eyes demanding rather than pleading. The other, more indignant, opened its beak in half profile to complain. They were briefly still: a set piece. Bernard laughed at an incongruous thought.

"Joke?"

"It's as though they're posing for a bust. Do you know that painting of Charles the First? The head from three angles?"

"Yes, I know it." She looked at him as though he had said something to surprise her. But when, after a silence, she spoke again, it was Bernard's turn to be startled.

"I'm going back to Ellora. I want to see that temple again. The Kailasha."

"It's impossible," Bernard exclaimed. "If you don't catch tomorrow's plane to Bombay, you'll miss the flight for London."

"There's tonight. I could go now."

"It's half past five. By the time you've found a car and driven there, it'll be dark."

"It will be more exciting in the dark. A different atmosphere. I'll borrow a torch from the hotel." She stood up, and the long skirt swirled around her ankles with the same energy which flashed from her eyes. Bernard, alarmed, stood at the same time, to stop her.

"Gitta," he said, and his use of her Christian name for the first time passed unnoticed by them both. "I don't think you should. The guard won't let you in. And it's a lonely part of the world. You could find yourself in trouble."

"The guard will settle down for a quiet night in front of his fire," said Gitta. "If he does see me, he can be persuaded to let me pass. His job is to make sure that nothing is harmed or stolen. I don't mind him keeping an eye on me. As for trouble, I don't think so. I find the nature of the Indian people unaggressive. I should be surprised if rape was their daily diet."

Her confidence briefly checked Bernard's doubts: but then he remembered the eeriness of the atmosphere in the empty hills even in full tourist daylight. "I can't let you go alone," he said.

"But I am going. You have no responsibility." She went quickly into her room, leaving Bernard torn on the one hand between disapproval of the whole ridiculous idea—coupled with a reluctance to return to a place which had so greatly unsettled him in a first visit—and, on the other hand, an old-fashioned compulsion to chaperon a female through a tricky situation. Gitta's indifference did nothing to resolve his uncertainty. In the end he decided that his anxiety on her behalf would be greater if he waited at the hotel alone than if he were with her.

Half a dozen taxis were parked hopefully outside the hotel, though it was difficult to imagine that the night life of Aurangabad tempted many tourists out after dark. The sun was already setting as they left and, by the time they reached the deserted range of hills which contained the caves, night had fallen. The driver looked uneasy as he asked how long they would be.

"Not more than one hour." Gitta had no sympathy for his loneliness as she switched on her borrowed flashlight. The sound of the taxi's radio followed its passengers for a little way as they walked cautiously along the steep track. As it faded, a new sound took its place: the mournful wailing of a single pipe. Gitta switched off the flashlight as the flickering light of a small fire came into view.

"It's best to be open," Bernard said definitely. "Trying to sneak in would be asking for trouble. He may even be armed. I've got enough money to sweeten him. Leave it to me."

"You take the torch then, and walk straight up to him. I'll be behind you as far as the Kailasha. If he does refuse to cooperate, keep him talking for as long as you can, while I'm inside, in the dark."

Accepting her instructions, Bernard approached the guard noisily. The man rose to his feet, suspicious, and proved to speak no English. This was the first time Bernard had encountered this problem in India: he applied himself to solving it. "Looking around" was too vague a concept; so he produced a notebook and pencil, indicating with a crude representation of an elephant that he wished to sketch in the Kailasha. He handed over money as a fee rather than a bribe, taking agreement for granted, and indicated on his watch the half-hour period which he wished to buy.

The guard replied fluently and incomprehensibly. Bernard deduced a general agreement and they shook hands on whatever had been arranged. Leading the way to the Kailasha, the guard unlocked an iron grille which was fastened across the entrance, and disappeared in barefoot silence. The sad sound of the pipe began again.

"Thank you for fixing it." Gitta appeared from behind a pillar.

"He hasn't got much to worry about," Bernard pointed out. "There's nothing that anyone could pick up and steal, since it's all part of the solid rock; and he'd hear if anything was broken or defaced. I'll hold the torch for you. What do you want to see?"

"The inner chamber." Gitta led the way in and up to the higher level. She moved slowly around the walls, sometimes only looking at the carvings which covered them, sometimes stopping to feel them. When she reached the relief of Siva dancing she stopped, moving her hands over the surface as though she could absorb its shape through her finger tips. Bernard waited uneasily. He could resist the eeriness of the temple as a whole; but in this innermost chamber he was acutely conscious of the existence of the Siva lingam, even though it was invisible now in the darkness. The single section of stone which absorbed Gitta was exciting to him as well, just as it had been in the morning.

"What is it about this?" The darkness had changed Gitta's voice, which now was soft and wondering. "It's not beautiful. It's not even perfect." Her fingers touched the rough edge where one of Siva's arms had been chipped away at some time during the past twelve centuries. "And yet . . . You feel it too, don't you, Bernard?"

"Yes."

"And the pose. As you said, it's barely possible. Unless it was that I needed a firmer support than you could give me." She took a step back, out of the light. "Or perhaps to show a god dancing needs more than a physical position. It's a state of mind. And Siva is only one aspect of the god—only a third of the whole. You'll have to be part of the dance, Bernard. Vishnu, the preserver, working to keep things as they are. Those who are alive, you will help to live longer."

Emerging hypnotically from the darkness, her voice flickered as erratically as her shadow, whose movements reflected the trembling of Bernard's hands. He put the flashlight down on the floor. He knew what he wanted, although not why; but until Gitta summoned him he was unable to move. By the light reflected off the wall he saw her step backward into the alcove, where the Siva lingam stood as an obscene altar.

"Which part should I take?" she asked. "Brahma or Siva? The creator or the destroyer? Or are they the same? And if I lead, will you follow? Because this is a dance that I haven't forgotten."

Using the Siva lingam to support her back, she began for the second time that day to copy the pose of the carving. The slowness of the movement increased its mesmerism. Her shoulders arched backward. Both arms raised themselves over her head and continued until her fingers pointed down toward the floor, straining to extend the tension of her body. Her long wraparound skirt fell apart from its fastening at the waist. She was wearing nothing beneath it.

Bernard took a step forward. This was why she had come. As he fumbled with his zip he tried to pinpoint the moment when he had known, but there was no time. Already he was pressing forward. She gasped once as she accepted him and then let her head fall back between her arms. Her stretched body was hard, like the stone she was imitating. There was no softness or tenderness; nothing womanly except the fact that she was a woman.

Somewhere in the distance the wailing of the pipe faltered. When the sound resumed it was close, and coming closer. Gitta raised her head a little and her arms came around to encircle Bernard's waist with a fierceness equal to his own. Excitement and panic brought a bitter surge of sickness to his throat as the impulse to finish quickly and escape fought with the desire to extend as long as possible something which could never happen like this again. But in fact he had no choice. He was imprisoned by the force of his own passion, by the unyielding strength of Gitta's arms and even, ludicrously, by the trousers crumpled around his ankles. The music came closer and stopped. Bernard surrendered at last to Gitta and did not after all care that the guard was certainly watching.

Afterward, Gitta was gently businesslike. It was she who retrieved the flashlight, who gave the guard a second tip, who took Bernard's hand and led him up the dark path toward the taxi which waited to drive them back to the hotel. On the balcony outside their two rooms she said softly, "Thank you, Bernard," and touched his shoulder with her hand.

Gitta closed her bedroom door, but Bernard, unsettled, remained on the wide balcony, a foreigner in his own life as well as in a country more easily reduced to a tidy map. For a little while he stared up at the black starlit arch of the sky. Then he turned one of the shabby cane chairs to face the window of Gitta's room, and sat down. The skimpy curtains did not meet perfectly, so from time to time he could see her, bare-shouldered, crossing the room. Motionless in the darkness, he tried to collect his thoughts.

"Who knows what may be waiting for you in Aurangabad?" Gitta had asked in Bombay. Had she known the answer even as she asked the question? No, it was not possible. It was the place, that one particular spot, which had imposed a kind of demoniac enchantment upon them both. It might have been true that Gitta had been hoping to discover the magic of the place, but she had not known in advance that she would succeed.

"Wishes come true," Gitta had said as well, when she was trying to disguise her belief in magic with a varnish of rationality. But how could this evening's events possibly have fulfilled any wish of Bernard's? Unless—was it conceivable that unconsciously he had been seeking to understand the man who was his true father: Robert Scott, who had claimed to find India even more bewitching than the beautiful woman who loved him? Robert had spoken of a kind of enthrallment; and his son, hearing the words repeated by Alexa, had been unable to understand them. But Bernard had chosen to come to India and had held to his choice even when it entailed a temporary separation from Helen. Was it, beneath all the other reasons, because he wanted to understand? Had he, without knowing it, wished to be bewitched?

No, that answer made no sense. And Gitta's behavior was equally impossible to explain in terms of wish fulfillment. At home in Ireland, when she booked her flight to Aurangabad, surely not even her wildest imaginings could have anticipated what had actually taken place. She had not at that time known that a man called Bernard Lorimer existed. But if he were to be honest now, he had to doubt whether she had been aware of him as an individual that evening. In a particular place and for a particular reason that he did not understand, she had needed a man and he had been on the spot. It should have been a humiliation, but that would come later. He had not yet escaped from the spell of the cave.

The light went out in Gitta's room. Could she see through the crack that he was still there? Was she even bothering to look? Gradually, staring at the closed door, he took a grip on himself. He had not very often, in all the years of his marriage, been unfaithful to Helen, but on those few occasions it had been on his own initiative. The reversal of roles by which it had so definitely been Gitta who called the tune was one of the most disquieting aspects of a peculiarly unsettling day. What had already happened was beyond recall, but now the situation was back under his own control. He could choose to follow Gitta into her bedroom. Or he could stay outside; and that, too, would be his own choice.

Half an hour passed in which he did not move. Then he stood up, a crumpled man with a crumpled face, but his own master again. A little stiffly he walked to his own room and closed the door.

The next day they flew back to Bombay, arriving in time to join the rest of the party at lunch. Michael, looking tanned and fit and enthusing about Annapurna, was sitting with the others. In the moment before he caught sight of Bernard, he opened his eyes in astonishment at the sight of Gitta being warmly greeted by Stephen Clyde. There was too much else to talk about for Bernard to take note of this at the time. Only later, when they had left the table and exchanged descriptions of their respective holidays, did he ask Michael why he had looked so surprised.

"It was the sight of Steve Clyde as a welcoming husband," Michael explained. "I arrived at the hotel last night, to be sure of not being late, and thought I might as well take up your offer of Helen's bed.

That didn't go down too well at Reception, since you were away. Steve heard the argument and came over—and within about thirty seconds I was being offered a place in *his* bed instead."

"That's disgraceful!" Bernard was genuinely shocked; but Michael, unworried, waved the topic away.

"It's flattering to be wanted," he laughed. "And after all, it's easy enough to say no, isn't it?"

Twenty-four hours earlier Bernard would have agreed. Now he was guiltily silent, and uneasy that Michael should have discovered that he had spent two nights away with Gitta. But then, no one who saw her could possibly imagine that the brief trip had any purpose other than sight-seeing. As long as Bernard himself did not dwell on the subject, Michael would not give Gitta a second thought—except as Steve's unlikely wife. Certainly there was no reason why he should mention her to Helen. Already he had left the subject.

"So all in all, did the holiday live up to your expectations?" he asked.

It was not an easy question for Bernard to answer. What had he expected? Eighteen days of sight-seeing in an interesting and unfamiliar country? He had certainly not been disappointed in that. But the question which he had put to his fellow travelers earlier in the holiday still had to be answered in his own case. Why had he chosen India? Had he intended to prove to himself that there was no such thing as the magic of a place, that a country could not cast a spell over an intelligent human being? If so, he had failed. However strongly his reason denied the thought, he recognized emotionally that the cracked carving of Siva dancing which had been his father's christening present had in a wholly irrational way drawn him to visit its homeland. And there was no reasonable explanation for what had happened there.

While he was still struggling for an answer, he remembered what Gitta had said about the hidden potential of everything in nature. Would it be fanciful to extend that thought, to consider that even a holiday, a simple package tour, might contain the hidden possibility of producing an experience which was—in Gitta's words again—a kind of perfection? But to think of last night's aberration as perfect was disloyal to Helen. And—to return to Michael's question—what had happened at Ellora might have been part of Gitta's expectation, but was certainly none of his own. He gave the tourist's normal answer.

"Absolutely," he said. "It's been marvelous. Mind you, now I'm looking forward to being home again."

In only a few hours' time they would all be on the plane and flying toward London. He would shake Gitta Clyde by the hand in the terminal at Heathrow and would never see her again. The episode at Ellora was closed.

XI

In the summer which followed Bernard's return from India, all the prophecies which Dr. Chandra had made in his presence were fulfilled. The daytime temperature in much of the subcontinent remained above a hundred degrees for several weeks, causing hundreds to collapse of heat stroke. So many bullocks died in the drought that when the rains at last arrived there would be few animals left to pull the plows. Not many farmers, either, still had the strength to cultivate their land, and most of them had sacrificed the grain which should have been kept for seed in order to keep their families alive. In at least three of the Indian states, more people had already died of famine in a few weeks than during any previous summer.

The statistics, briefly recorded in the press, troubled Bernard, filling him with sympathy and prompting him to give generously to the agencies which were organizing relief. Nevertheless, every week that passed diminished his feeling of involvement. A holiday was, by definition, an experience quite separate from the normal events of his life. He had always been a man who enjoyed the moments through which he was living: the pleasures of the past were stored in his memory, but he saw no need to draw on them when they had no relevance to his own present life.

So he did not too often allow himself to be disturbed by the contrast between India's parched soil and his own luxuriant garden, in which roses filled the air with fragrance around the rich green lawns. Even before his return from India Helen had managed to shake off the lethargy which had overcome her for so long after her operation. Once again she was slim and elegant and as businesslike as ever before in the organization of Bernard's domestic and social life. This summer, in addition—as though to compensate for the months before the hysterectomy, when she had been anemic and too often tired—she brought a new kind of carefree enjoyment to their lovemaking. Bernard several times congratulated himself quietly on the success of a marriage which had survived so many years without staleness.

In the autumn they took a holiday in France, enjoying sunshine and gourmet meals in each other's company. Now the trip to India was merely the last holiday but one, and all memory of Gitta Clyde had vanished from Bernard's thoughts.

Toward the end of the year a business crisis faced Bernard's company in the United States, where an antimonopoly suit would, if successful, threaten an important drug patent. The New York lawyer recommended that the company chairman should appear in person, and reluctantly Bernard agreed to fly out. The court proceedings dragged on—not longer than he expected, since his expectations had always been gloomy—but longer than he liked to be away. It was with a mixture of irritation and relief that he was at last able to book his ticket for the return journey to London in November.

The flight was uncomfortable. Battling against headwinds, the plane was late in arriving over Heathrow and was then kept circling for another half hour, bumping through the buffeting storm clouds as darkness fell and the ground below became patterned with the bright lights of motorways and runways. When, at last, they were allowed to land, it was almost two hours behind the scheduled time.

There was no sign of Helen at their usual meeting place, just outside the customs hall. That was unusual, for she always liked to meet him at the airport herself, and to her many other virtues she added that of punctuality. But perhaps she had arrived earlier and had gone off for a drink or cup of coffee; she would return as soon as the number of his flight clicked into the "baggage in hall" slot on the arrivals board. He waited for ten minutes before making a quick inspection of the bar and the coffee room, and then asked for a message to be broadcast on the public address system; but without result. He rang first the London flat and then the Cambridgeshire house, but there was no answer from either. Obviously she must be on the way.

He continued to wait, but now to his tiredness and impatience was added anxiety lest she should have had an accident. Only when a hour had passed did he take a taxi into London, wishing that he had done so earlier.

The flat was dark and empty. On the hall table was a neat stack of letters which had been addressed to him in Cambridgeshire and must have been brought from the house by Helen. Bernard looked quickly to see whether they included any message from her. Then, exhausted by the strain of his negotiations in the United States as well as more immediately by the stuffiness of the plane, he lay down on the bed to wait with his eyes closed until Helen returned to explain how she had missed him.

He was awakened by the sound of a closing door and found that he had slept in his clothes for ten hours. His head ached and his whole body was stiff and dirty. Helen would need all her charm to soothe away his feeling of neglect and malaise. But no one called out in greeting or came into the bedroom. Instead there was a sound of scrubbing in the kitchen. Rubbing his heavy eyes awake, he went to investigate.

The intruder was Jenny, who came in twice weekly to clean. Bernard had never before been in the flat during her working hours, although he had communicated with her by notes. She proved to be a very black and very beautiful young woman who looked up, startled, when he appeared without warning, wearing no shoes.

"I thought it might be my wife," said Bernard, although he could not seriously have expected to find Helen scrubbing the floor. "You don't know where she is at the moment, I suppose?"

"She was here Thursday." Jenny's voice was soft and completely English. "When she left, she was going to stay with some friends. But she didn't say where. Would you like me to make you some breakfast?"

"A cup of coffee is just what I need." He needed a bath even more, but that could come afterward. Picking up the pile of letters from the hall, he carried them to the table.

Within five minutes Jenny had produced fried eggs and fruit juice and toast as well as the coffee. Bernard ate appreciatively as he looked through the mail. All the envelopes had been opened. It was understood between them that Helen would deal with his personal correspondence whenever he was away for more than a week: they had no secrets from each other. On the top of each letter or invitation was a neat note in her handwriting to say how she had answered.

At the bottom of the stack was a card which, unlike the others, had been replaced in its envelope. It had originally been addressed to him at the registered office address of his company and forwarded to his home in Cambridgeshire from there. An unfamiliar handwriting had addressed the envelope and marked it "Personal." The Irish postmark was also unfamiliar. To the outside of the envelope Helen had paper-clipped a brief note: "When you read this one, you will know why I am not here to greet you."

Bernard stared uneasily at her message for a few seconds. Helen's absence was deliberate, then. There had been no accident, no mistaking of days or times. Whatever it was that he was going to read now, he was not going to like it. Worried, he drew the card out of the envelope. The note it bore was as brief as that clipped to the outside, and as menacing.

"A shout of joy! Your child is born, perfect. I will send you an invitation to the christening." It was signed by Gitta.

Bernard's first reaction was one of disbelief. She was too old. Surely she was too old to have had a baby. He tried to remember how Gitta had looked, and uneasily the suspicion grew that he could feel sure only that she was not young. Because she took no pains with her appearance, because she was ugly and lacking in any sort of sex appeal, she could be in almost any other period of her life except that of youth, moving without change between thirty and fifty. And women even in their forties were able to bear children, even if not many of them chose to do so.

As disbelief faded, a feeling near to panic invaded his mind at the thought that he was responsible for the existence of a child. He had spoken to Gitta about the dangers of world overpopulation, but that had never been more than a rationalization of his real belief: that to inflict life on a human being was as unforgivable a crime as that of taking it away. When he had taken such care to avoid that responsibility inside his marriage, it was monstrous that he should have been trapped into it in such an accidental way.

But of course it was not an accident. Panic gave place to anger as he realized that Gitta must at some point deliberately have chosen to have the child. Although abortion was doubtless illegal in Ireland, she could have come to London; she could have asked Bernard for help. To remain silent until it was too late was a positive action. Perhaps not even the conception had been accidental. Gitta had said more than once during the holiday that women needed to create, that she approved of reproduction. Wasn't it likely enough that she wanted a child herself and that Steve had proved unwilling or inadequate?

Rage closed Bernard's throat. He stared with disgust at the congealing egg on the plate in front of him and stood up, sweeping the whole of his breakfast to the floor with a furious gesture. It had been humiliating enough to know that in the caves of Ellora he had been the fortuitous instrument of Gitta's need for a man. But to realize that she had not expected pleasure from him, but had only demanded a stud, was insupportable. When Jenny knocked softly at the door to see what the crash had meant, he stood in her way, blocking the doorway so that she could not come in.

"You can go home now."

"I come for two hours." Her eyes looked past him to the sticky mess of egg and marmalade and broken china.

"I said you can go."

"Thank you, Sir Bernard. I'll just clear this floor first."

"Get out!" shouted Bernard, shocking himself, since it was his habit to be polite to employees. He could tell from the hurt and indignant expression on her face that she would not come back.

As the front door of the flat closed behind her, Bernard picked up the note to read it again. His eyes were unfocused by anger so that the words this time were illegible. It didn't matter. He remembered them clearly enough.

For perhaps ten minutes he paced up and down the flat, flinging open doors because no one room was large enough to contain him. He prided himself on his ability to handle difficult situations smoothly, but he had no idea how to deal with one woman whose motives he did not understand and another who had run away. Outraged and at a loss how to deal with the situation, he went back to bed.

He was awakened by the telephone. In the few seconds which he needed to clear his head, someone in another part of the flat answered the call. Bernard picked up the bedroom extension in time to hear

Helen's voice telling his secretary that yes, he was back, but very tired: she would ask him to ring the office later.

Bernard lay still, needing a moment in which to be sure that neither Helen's earlier absence nor her return now was a dream. Then he got up and opened the bedroom door.

Helen, the telephone call concluded, was clearing up the mess he had made. She looked up, not smiling, and waited for him to speak.

"Ten minutes," said Bernard. "I'll be with you in ten minutes." He was unshaven and, after sleeping in his clothes at the end of a long journey, suspected that his body was smelly as well as dirty. It would be a mistake to embark on the inevitable argument at such a disadvantage.

After a quick shower, he shaved and dressed in clean clothes, choosing a smarter suit than the probable routine of the day required, as though it would be helpful to present himself to his wife as a prosperous, well-dressed, confident businessman. But still she did not smile. Sitting stiffly on a dining room chair, she needed no words or gestures to make it clear that he was not to kiss her.

"One makes the gesture of walking out," she said. "But then one has to be practical. There are always details to discuss, aren't there?"

"I hope not," said Bernard. "Not the sort of details you seem to imply. I agree that we need to talk."

That was easy to say but difficult to do. He sat down opposite Helen, hoping that she would speak first so that he could answer specific accusations rather than make a general speech in his own defense. His silence was to some extent successful.

"I take it I don't need to apologize for opening the letter," she said.

"Of course not. It's what I expected."

"I worked out the dates. This Gitta, I take it, is a girl you met on that trip to India."

"Yes. Not a girl, though."

Helen waved the irrelevance away with her hand. "Have you always used your trips abroad like this?"

"No. And I didn't that time. I'd like to tell you what happened."

"I don't want to know," Helen said. "Good God, you can't think that I want to hear the details. I just want to be sure that you understand why I'm going to leave you. I wouldn't like you to think that it was anything as petty as jealousy about a holiday affair."

"Helen, you don't mean that. You mustn't leave. It wasn't an affair. I understand that you're upset, and I'm sincerely sorry about it. But this wasn't anything important. There's no need to be dramatic."

"Not important! There's a baby, and you say it's not important!"

"The baby hasn't got anything to do with you and me. Gitta's a married woman. If she had the baby, I presume it's because she wanted to."

"But she told you about it. She intended you to be involved."

"I don't precisely understand why. Perhaps she wants money. Well, she can have money. I've got enough."

"My God, Bernard, this is your child! You're its father. You can't simply cut it out of your life with cash."

"I don't understand what's upsetting you. In particular, I mean. I've said I'm sorry about Gitta, and I am. Terribly sorry."

"I wanted children," said Helen. Her voice was pitched lower than usual, as though she were controlling a wish to cry; she turned her head a little away from him. "When I was young, before we were married and in the first years, you knew how much I wanted children. But you didn't. You had strong views, if you remember, about the wickedness of forcing life onto someone who doesn't ask to have it. My views were strong as well, but I could only argue a personal need, not some great moral principle. In a conflict like that you were always bound to win. How could I bring a baby into our family if I knew that you wouldn't love it, that you'd be angry with me for forcing it on you?"

"You make it sound as though I sprung it on you. I made it clear what I felt before we were married. You can't pretend—"

"Yes, all right, I had to choose. You or children. I was in love with you and I chose you and until now I've never complained about that. Now it's too late to reopen the argument. The choice doesn't exist anymore, not for me. But if you were going to have a child after all, it should have been mine." She turned to face him at last, shouting slightly. "Do you understand me? It should have been my child."

"It wasn't intended," said Bernard. "An accident."

"There were never any accidents between us, were there?" Helen said bitterly. "You were careful enough with me. No passion without protection. But you can take a risk with a stranger." She brought her voice under control and continued more calmly. "I've never been jealous before. Not even when I knew something was going on. But I'm jealous of a woman you loved enough to be careless with. And I'm so jealous of her child that I shall think of it every time I look at you. That's why I'm leaving you. Now. I shall go to the house. You can phone me up when you want your things and I'll keep out of the way while you get them."

"Helen! Be reasonable!" But as he moved toward her she too stood up, ready to step back if he came nearer.

"No," she said. "I can't be reasonable. This hits me in the stomach, not the head. When I think of you creating that baby, I want to be sick."

Bernard took no notice. He understood his wife's distress, but it was time for him to convince her that he loved her, that nothing else was important. He put his hands on her shoulders. Helen pulled her right arm back and then swung it sharply to slap him hard on the cheek.

The blow was a fierce one, and painful, but it was a different kind of shock which made Bernard drop his arms to his sides and stare in incredulous silence at his wife. In all the years of their marriage they had hardly ever quarreled even in words; certainly there had never before been any blow struck on either side. For a moment it seemed as though Helen were equally shocked by her own action. But she did not apologize. Instead, she picked up the tray which she had loaded with the debris of his own earlier loss of temper.

"How do I make it clear?" she asked. "I'm not in a civilized mood. If you touch me again you'll get this lot in your face."

She moved away quickly, not wanting him to accept the challenge. Bernard watched as she carried the tray out of the room. He stood without moving until he heard the front door close behind her. Then, oppressed by the impossibility of solving his private problem, he abandoned it and went into the office.

In the course of a busy day he made one domestic decision. He would not attempt to get in touch with Helen for a week. This would allow her anger and disgust to fade a little. When jealousy had moved from her body to her mind it might be possible to offer an explanation. And perhaps by that time she might be feeling lonely enough to imagine what it would be like to spend the rest of her life alone.

In the course of that same day he asked his secretary to discover

Gitta's address from the agency which had organized the tour to India. What he should do with it was another matter. She apparently had no telephone and he could not spare the time to travel to a remote country district of Ireland. If he were to write, Steve might see the letter, and it was no part of Bernard's intention to cause Gitta the same kind of trouble that she had already brought on him, angry though he might be. If the baby was to be kept out of his way, nothing must happen to disturb its mother's marriage. The Gitta problem was, for the moment, as insoluble as the Helen problem.

The next day's post brought him a printed invitation to a private view. An exhibition of new sculpture by Brigitta Keenan was to open at a gallery in Grafton Street in a week's time. Bernard stared at the card in puzzlement. He had little interest in art and was on no gallery's regular mailing list. He was just about to throw the card away when the name which had been on his mind for the past twenty-four hours thrust itself out from the black italic letters of Brigitta.

So the card explained itself and might also explain a good deal about Gitta. At last she was answering the question he had been trying to ask throughout their holiday together. Sculpture was, presumably, the ruling passion which he had so signally failed to identify in her personality. But by now he was no longer interested in her tastes and talents. The invitation represented only an opportunity to meet and ask for explanations, and an excuse to postpone any decisions until the meeting had taken place. Bernard noted the date of the private view in his diary and propped the card up on a ledge in the flat as though there were a danger that he might forget the occasion. The real message which it bore him, he had completely failed to understand.

XII

The gallery was crowded with sleek young men and expensively dressed older women, each holding a glass of champagne; the high-pitched sound of their chatter bubbled out through the double glass doors. Bernard paused on the pavement outside to amend his expectations of the evening. The card of invitation had been a printed one. It had been quite ridiculous of him to suppose that Gitta had been proposing a private rendezvous when she addressed it to him—or, rather, added his name to a list. But art exhibitions were not an ordinary part of his life. He had not realized that a private view would be a party.

Lingering for a few moments before taking the plunge, he studied the single exhibit displayed in the window of the gallery: a bronze hawk. The almost invisible Perspex rod on which it was mounted gave it the impression of swooping through space. To express so much power and movement in a stationary object was an extraordinary achievement, thought Bernard. As he stared into the window he could feel himself subconsciously amending all his earlier opinions of Gitta and beginning for the first time to understand her; but he was not prepared to let admiration for her skill mitigate his resentment of her behavior.

He opened the door, and the noise shrieked round him. One of the suave young men pressed a glass of champagne into his left hand and a pen into his right so that he could enter his name and address in a book. Then he was free to make his way down a spiral staircase to a lower floor. He paused halfway down to look around for Gitta, but she was nowhere to be seen in the main exhibition room of the gallery.

Once he had established that, he allowed himself to consider the exhibits, sipping his champagne as he moved through the crowded room. Even his untutored eye was able to recognize that Gitta's strength lay in her talent for suggesting movement. There were a great many birds: sweeping, darting, hovering birds. He recalled how he and Gitta had watched birds together on the balcony of the hotel at Aurangabad and how the three crows had posed for them. It was a visual memory which until that moment had quite vanished from his mind.

As he moved from one work to another he forgot for a little while the anger which he had so justifiably borne toward Gitta. She had behaved thoughtlessly; but perhaps that could be explained by the strain of pregnancy and the birth of a baby which her husband might have good reason to disown. Instead, for a few moments, he felt sympathy for a woman who, during all her adult life, had been unable to move freely—and who had directed her talent instead to depicting movement in more fortunate creatures.

Had he been honest with himself, Bernard would have recognized that he had almost forgotten his earlier impression of Gitta. Now that she had revealed her true self, it was difficult to remember how reserved, even secretive, she had been. Seeing her talent on display, he forgot that he had found her dull. He remembered, certainly, that she was not beautiful, but not that she used her unattractiveness as a positive defense, to keep away all those for whom she had no use.

So he experienced an unexpected feeling of warmth toward her as he moved into a second room. When he encountered Gitta, as he was bound soon to do, he would not quarrel, but merely arrange a time and place where they could talk privately. He looked around from the doorway; but she was not in this room either.

Here, the work was in a different style; not birds, but playing children—groups of small bronze figures bursting with energy. One in particular caught his eye. Four spiky runners were bunched together in a race while the fifth with a desperate effort breasted the tape to win. Bernard stared at it for some time and was interested enough to wonder how much it would cost. There was no price on the bronze itself. He looked around the room again and saw Steve approaching.

It was interesting to notice what a difference the surroundings made. Standing by Gitta's side at Heathrow, Steve's appearance had seemed odd, but here he was in his proper element. His stylish blond hair was fairer but not more elaborately waved than that of most of the other young men who leaned languidly against the walls; his purple velvet jacket and matching bow tie looked restrained beside the extraordinary outfits worn by some of the middle-aged women. And his handshake, as he caught sight of Bernard and came across, was firm and businesslike.

"Is Gitta here?" Bernard asked him.

"No. She'll come tomorrow. She can't stand these occasions. She hates the people who only sink the champagne and don't look at her work, and she hates the people who do look but pass on. It all hits her as a personal rejection. But that's only a first-night reaction. After this, everything will be more relaxed and she won't mind about people who come in to look around and then go out again; she'll just hope they enjoy it. Tonight I'm standing in for her. I act as her agent, as you probably gathered earlier."

"No," said Bernard. "I didn't gather anything. I didn't even know about this"—he waved an arm to take in the whole exhibition—"until I saw the preview card."

"It's true that she doesn't like to talk about what she's doing. I think she feels that to discuss it would waste the energy which should go into the actual work."

There was an awkward pause. Bernard wanted to ask about the baby, but saw clearly that he must wait for Steve to mention it first; equally clearly Steve's mind was only on the exhibition. "Do you like the show?" he asked.

"It's most impressive. In quantity as well as quality."

"She doesn't bring her work to London very often. Ireland suits her. Plenty of space. Peace and quiet. No distractions. Favorable tax laws for creative artists. She gets dug in and doesn't want to move. I have to bully her from time to time, or no one would know she existed. This exhibition represents about five years."

"I like this one." Bernard pointed at the racing children. "Is it still for sale? And how much would it be?"

"Didn't they give you a catalog upstairs? Here you are." Steve produced a list of titles and prices from his pocket. "This is number twenty-four."

Bernard studied the price, which seemed reasonable enough to someone who had no idea what such objects normally cost. "If I think about it and come back tomorrow, what are the chances of it still being available?" he asked. The excuse for returning when Gitta would be on the premises was probably unnecessary, but Steve accepted it as easily as it emerged.

"Two gone out of an edition of twelve," he said, and Bernard saw now that two small red spots were stuck on to the base of the group. "It's not likely to sell out tonight. But before you think too much about this one, Gitta told me that if I saw you here I was to make sure that you had a look at her Siva. It's in the tiny room through the arch. Nice to see you again. If you decide that you are interested in anything, have a word with the girl at the desk."

Bernard watched him move toward the stairs, smiling to welcome a new arrival. He himself pressed on through the lower gallery toward what was little more than an alcove. No one else had come as far from the champagne as this and as he turned a corner the high-pitched chatter was cut off as abruptly as if a door had been closed. He took one more step and stopped in amazement.

The walls of the alcove were black and a ceiling spotlight pointed down at the single exhibit. There was no need to look at the catalog to know that the statue would be called Siva Dancing. Here, re-created in three-dimensional bronze, was the stone relief which had so greatly moved Gitta at Ellora. It was also Gitta herself, her body strained back over the lingam, her arms stretched over her head—but now there was no supporting stone, so that the figure was held in the dancing pose only by the strain and strength of its own muscles. The tension in the movement was so great that Bernard found it painful to study. In any case, he was not at this moment capable of considering the bronze as a work of art. The sight of it seemed to have winded him not only emotionally but physically. He leaned against the wall until his heart should stop pounding.

At first it was memory which overcame him—the memory of that ludicrous and ecstatic moment when he had seemed to be under a spell, unable to free himself from the mysterious bondage of the shad-owed temple at Ellora. But as he struggled to bring his emotions under control, the remembrance of that extraordinary episode was banished by a new thought; was it a suspicion or a hope? He stared more intently at the statue, and the supposition became a certainty. This bronze, this Siva, was the child which had been conceived during that second dark visit to the Kailasha temple.

Everything fitted. Gitta's card must have referred to the perfect casting of the bronze. Tonight's preview was the christening to which she had promised to invite him. Steve had not mentioned a baby because there was no baby. With a deep sigh, Bernard let out the breath he had been holding.

Chief among his emotions was relief that there was not after all a living child; it did not occur to him to doubt his certainty that he was right now and had been mistaken before. Later he would no doubt be angry again with Gitta for misleading him, and for the damage she had done to his marriage. But at this moment the memory of the desire he had felt for her in the darkness was so vivid that Helen's jealousy seemed justified, even if she had founded it on a misunderstanding. At the same time he was conscious of another and less familiar feeling. This was a statue which he longed to possess.

By comparison with the intensity of this need, his earlier interest in the racers revealed itself as merely a casual whim. If he had bought them, it would have been only through a sense that he ought to purchase something, and that piece was as good as any. The little bronze group had pleased his eyes, but Siva hit him below the belt. This, he felt as he circled the solitary figure, this was perhaps how a father felt at the first glimpse of his child. He no longer wondered why Gitta had chosen such an unfortunate metaphor as he acknowledged the same reaction of awe at perfection, of pride in being partly responsible and of a deep determination to protect.

Before anything else he must find out if he could own the work. He looked anxiously to see if it carried any red spot: none was visible. In respect of this item the catalog was unhelpful, giving neither the size of the edition nor the price. Details, it announced, could be obtained from the desk.

As he turned to go, the entrance to the alcove was blocked by a small group: two young men and one elderly woman with straight blond hair, wearing a silver trouser suit. They, like Bernard earlier, seemed transfixed by the quality of what they saw.

"That's quite something," said one of the young men to the woman; while the other wrote in a notebook. "If you're seriously interested, this would be the one."

"Excuse me." Bernard pushed rudely through the trio and hurried up the stairs to ask the price of number 49. The girl at the desk studied him for longer than seemed necessary before she answered with another question: "Are you Sir Bernard Lorimer?"

"Yes. What's that got to do with it?"

"The price of Siva Dancing is three thousand pounds, sir."

Bernard stared at her unbelievingly. "But that's ridiculous!"

"The bronze that you've seen is the only one that will be cast, apart from Miss Keenan's own," explained the girl.

"But even so. Compared with the others . . . I mean, you presumably know about prices. Don't you agree that this is exceptionally high? She's not Henry Moore, after all."

"I believe there are special circumstances, Sir Bernard. The money from the sale of this bronze is going directly to a famine relief fund in India, to buy a machine for deepening wells."

"You asked my name," said Bernard suspiciously. "Is that price a special one for me?"

"Only in the sense that I'm not giving anyone else a price at all. Miss Keenan told me to say that it was reserved, until you'd had time to see it and decide whether you were interested."

That made some sense. Bernard swallowed his indignation while he considered what to do. "So you could hold it for a day or two while I think about it?"

"Of course, Sir Bernard."

"I'd like to have a word with Miss Keenan before I decide. When will she be here?"

"Tomorrow afternoon."

"And what time does the gallery close?"

"Half past five."

"I'll try to come before then. But would you be kind enough to ask her if she could wait here until six, in case I'm held up?"

"I'll give her the message." The girl wrote it down, making no promises on Gitta's behalf. Steve came up to stand beside him.

"Did you see the Siva?"

"Yes," said Bernard. "It's very powerful."

"The best thing she's ever done. It ought really to be kept available for a museum. The Tate. That's why we haven't put any details in the catalog. Gitta thought that you might like it but only if you didn't have to share it with anyone. If she's wrong about that—the not sharing—we could have a normal edition cast; twelve copies, say. It would help to spread her reputation, and of course it would enormously reduce the price to you."

"I hope to talk to her tomorrow," said Bernard. "Tell me. She works at this sort of thing all the time, does she?"

"Seven days a week," said Steve. "Ten hours a day. It's her life. The only thing that has the slightest importance for her."

"It was something I wondered in India. How she spent her time. But then, I never understand what women do with themselves all day."

"This particular woman would make any good trade unionist throw up his hands in horror at the length of her working week."

"I'd like to take another look," Bernard said. "And then I'll hope to see Gitta tomorrow."

He went down the spiral staircase for a second time. The alcove was crowded now with people circling the bronze. Bernard stood in the archway, listening to their comments.

"Is it male or female?"

"Neither, darling, it's divine."

"What, with that nasty mischievous look on its face?"

"The god of destruction, that's why."

"I suspect that gods don't have backbones, then. Could you bend like that, pet?"

"You'd have to hold me up."

"Come on, then. Back you go."

Bernard turned away. He was not going to have his statue gooped over in museums by people like that. By the time he reached the top of the stairs he was already making plans to raise the money.

XIII

Deliberately the next evening Bernard waited until after half past five before returning to the gallery. In the brightly lit window the hawk still swooped on its unseen prey, but the reception hall was in darkness. Angry at the possibility that Gitta had chosen to evade the meeting, he rapped sharply on the glass door. A dark figure rose from an invisible seat and came to let him in.

"Hello," said Gitta. She was wearing the same black sweater and trousers in which Bernard had first seen her at Heathrow, but there was a brightness in her eyes which had not been present at that earlier meeting. "You've come to see Siva again, have you?"

She led the way down the spiral staircase and through the dark exhibition rooms. The spotlight in the alcove was already switched on. Someone had set two stools side by side in the entrance, but Bernard remained standing.

"You're expecting compliments, I suppose," he said, staring at the creature's odd, mischievous face. "Well, of course it's good. Marvelous. But you've made me very angry."

"Why?" asked Gitta; and then answered her own question, revealing the sphere in which her conscience must at some point have troubled her. "You mean that I've used an experience that ought to be private and transformed it into something public, on display? If that worries you, I'm sorry." She did not sound very sorry.

"I don't think you understand how it feels to be really angry. If you did, you wouldn't dismiss it so lightly."

"Oh, I understand well enough. The anger I feel at being crippled is what flows into the movement I carve or model. Other sculptors may be inspired by touch or eye, but I need an emotional stimulus to set me off. In a way, you were right in one of your first guesses, when you realized that I wanted to dance. This is the only way I can do it. Siva moves on my behalf. So something positive comes out of an old frustration. Anger is a creative emotion."

Bernard contradicted her, not troubling to be polite. "You've done a lot of damage. Anger is destructive."

"Is there any difference? Those old Hindus with their three-headed gods saw creation and destruction as aspects of a single whole, and I agree. Destruction is a part of creation. An essential part. I break down the clay before I can begin to model. Or I destroy the shape of a piece of stone in order to carve a new shape from inside it. Something had to be heated and pressed out of shape to form that quartz I showed you. And no one could make use of it, or even see it, until its shell had been broken."

"You destroyed a good deal more than clay or stone to make the Siva Dancing, didn't you?" he accused.

"Your peace of mind, do you mean? I'm sorry if you think so."

"Rather more than that. My marriage. My wife read your note— and not unnaturally misunderstood it."

"I sent it to your office," said Gitta, disturbed as she recalled what she had written. "And I marked it personal so that your secretary wouldn't open it."

"I was away from the office when it arrived. The details of what happened aren't important."

"They are to me, if you're accusing me of meddling deliberately."

"No, not that." Bernard's anger was changing as he put it into words. Had Gitta after all been right in describing it as a creative emotion? He could no longer tell the difference between fury and passion. Gitta's closeness excited him even while he was unable to forgive her.

"Well, I really *am* sorry," she said. "But surely the misunderstanding can be put right easily enough."

"It's too late for that. Because of course it was founded on the truth. And *I* misunderstood what you wrote as well—took it literally. So I admitted more than I can explain away by suddenly pointing to a piece of bronze. The situation has the essential ingredient of destruction—that what has been destroyed no longer exists. The trust has gone."

Was he complaining? Did he still care about Helen's feelings? Too many details now reminded him of the evening in Ellora: the same cavelike darkness broken by the single beam of light; the enigmatic Siva; and a woman who, now as then, was not the dull tourist he had first met but someone who sparked with an inner electricity. Bernard stepped forward and took her into his arms.

There were differences as well as similarities. It was good that the gallery was empty, with no guard to watch or interrupt. But it was not good that Gitta was unresponsive. More than that, she fought him off —and she was strong. What should have been an embrace became a humiliating struggle. It attacked Bernard's pride that Gitta should have had her own way in Ellora but should refuse now to accept his initiative. He became rough and clumsy and was tripped by one of the stools, whose presence he had forgotten. Still holding tightly to Gitta, he pulled her down with him as he fell. He heard her gasp with pain as her crippled leg twisted beneath her, but it was not so much this that brought him to a halt as the difficulty of pulling off her trousers as she lay beneath him on the soft gallery carpet. At Ellora she had dressed more conveniently.

"Not in front of the children," said Gitta. Instinctively Bernard looked up at the statue. Gitta took advantage of his inattention to make a slight movement away, but then was still again. "You'll have to help me up," she said.

Only then did Bernard realize that he had hurt her. He put his arms under her shoulders to lift her onto one of the stools. Gitta used both hands to move her leg into a more comfortable position, stretched out straight in front of her, and for a few moments she continued to clasp it, breathing deeply with her head down.

"I don't understand," he said, reluctant to apologize. "If something as marvelous as this Siva could come from a temporary encounter, just think what you could create if we had a more permanent relationship."

Pale and tight-lipped, Gitta looked up at him. "Some things can't be repeated," she said. "The atmosphere at Ellora was—unusual; and we were both sensitive to it, just for a moment. But here in England we have nothing in common."

"Don't you think that any two people can make a relationship work if they both want it?"

"Perhaps." Her voice was flat. "But I have no interest in relationships. None at all. I use Steve to protect me from them. I'm not interested in anything but my own work. I have a need to create, and for that I have to be emotionally free. I take what I require from other people and I have nothing to give in return. I told you all that in Bombay. You should have believed me."

"Yes." Bernard was suddenly tired. He would not have expected that Gitta would hold the power to hurt him so deeply. Staring at the Siva, he experienced again the protective emotion that had overcome him on the previous evening. If this was only a part of how a parent felt toward his child, he could understand Helen's anger at her deprivation. She would never forgive him. His loneliness made Gitta's attitude even less tolerable. "It doesn't occur to you that you might owe me something?" he asked.

"We never made any kind of bargain."

"You think it was fair simply to use me?"

"As fair as the way in which millions of men use millions of women. As you've used your wife, to have sex without children. Well, that's not my business. I took what you gave me and this is what I made of it. For you, if you want it. And *only* for you, if you want that as well. If I put a price on it, that's so that a few hundred people can perhaps stay alive for a little longer. Vishnu, the preserver. Wasn't that how you saw yourself? Would you like the bronze?"

"Yes," said Bernard. "I'll send you a check." He turned to go, but then paused: the habit of gentlemanly politeness was hard to break. "Do you want me to help you up the stairs?"

"No, thank you."

He would have liked to have the last word, to leave on some stylish phrase which would restore his own self-esteem or damage hers. But the selfish concentration of her interest made her invulnerable. Nothing he could say would emerge as more than spiteful. For such an extraordinary relationship to end with a triviality only increased its oddness. He felt his way up the twisting staircase and let himself out of the dark gallery.

XIV

"But I'm going to Libby's party," said Helen.

"Going where?" asked Bernard. The telephone connection was distorted by clicks and crackles.

"To Libby's party." The crackling stopped without warning just as Helen shouted to overcome it, making her voice sound untypically strident.

Libby's party would be in London. "Come and dress for it here," Bernard suggested. It would be a step back toward normality if Helen were to change at the flat, as she had always done in the past before an evening out in the city.

"I don't see anything to be gained by it." She spoke without enthusiasm, but did not absolutely refuse.

"There's something I need to talk to you about," Bernard told her. "And something I want to show you. Could you call at the office at five o'clock. You'd have plenty of time to change afterwards."

"All right." The answer came grudgingly, after a long pause. And Helen's reluctance to allow him much of her company showed itself again when she arrived at his office already dressed for the party. The fact that she had done her hair and made up her face and put on jewelry and a long dress all before leaving the country house at three o'clock in the afternoon was in itself a snub, telling him that she was not prepared to visit the flat even for her own convenience. She made it clear that he was not to kiss her, even in the way which she would have let the most casual of her male acquaintances kiss her at the beginning of a social evening.

Making the best of the situation, Bernard took her out to a taxi and gave the address of the gallery in Grafton Street.

"You're not interested in art," Helen said.

"There's something I want you to see. I'll explain afterwards."

They reached the gallery ten minutes before it was due to close. Helen looked round curiously as Bernard hurried her down the stairs.

"I'd like to know what you think of this," he said when they reached the alcove, empty but for the dancing Siva. He stood back in the archway while Helen, still puzzled, walked slowly around. The red spot which signified that he owned it of course meant nothing to her.

"Well?" he asked.

"I don't like it. It's evil."

"Mischievous would be a better word, don't you think?"

Helen shook her head. "It's nastier than that. Who is it?"

"Siva. The Hindu storm god. The destroyer."

"I believe you. A horrid adolescent boy tearing wings off flies."

"Not really. He destroys bad things more than good. Disease, for example, and infertility."

"A fertility god? I can believe that too." She circled the bronze again and this time Bernard kept beside her. "I wouldn't want him looking at me in my own drawing room."

Out of the corner of his eye Bernard saw Gitta walk past the alcove on the far side of the exhibition room, pause, and turn back toward them. He had not expected her to be there again this evening, and gripped Helen's arm in alarm and warning. "That's the sculptor," he whispered. "Just so that you don't say anything rude too loudly."

"Male or female?"

Bernard, who had once experienced the same doubt himself, was unreasonably annoyed that Helen should share it. There was no time to answer, for Gitta had already joined them.

"I brought my wife along to see the Siva Dancing," he said. "Helen, this is Miss Keenan, who made it."

"Do you like it?" asked Gitta as she shook hands. Bernard listened with interest to hear whether Helen would be polite or honest.

"It's very powerful," she said. "I don't think I can say that I exactly like it. I find it disturbing."

"That's what I intended. As your husband may have told you, the
idea for this came from an eerie temple in the Ellora Caves."

"In India, you mean?" Startled, Helen glanced toward Bernard.

"Gitta was a member of the same party." Bernard deliberately used
the name with which Gitta had signed her note and waited to see
what would happen. Nothing could make the situation much worse.

Helen's expression changed from puzzlement to incredulity. She
stared speechlessly at Gitta, taking in every detail of her unbecoming
hair, her weathered skin and flattened profile, and her unstylish
sweater and trousers.

Gitta too was reacting to the unexpected meeting. "Your husband
did me a very good turn," she told Helen. "I expect he told you. We
went to a temple with the guide, on the normal tourist timetable, but
then I wanted to go back again at night. It was a spooky enough place
even by daylight. I don't think I should have dared to go alone after
dark, but I did very much want to see a particular carving again. So
Bernard agreed to come along as protector, when he could have
stayed comfortably in the hotel. I'm more grateful to him than I can
say; I couldn't have made this without his help. I think of him now as
a kind of godfather to it."

By pretending not to know that Helen had read her note, she
presumably hoped to explain it away. Bernard stared at the two
women as their conversation continued. In this trite social situation
Gitta's electric vitality had disappeared. As well as being ugly, she was
dull. Helen—at this moment stunned by the flow of irrelevant words
—was not only beautiful, expensively dressed and carefully groomed,
but human in a way that seemed not to apply to Gitta. Helen was a
woman who could be hurt, who *had* been hurt. Bernard would have
liked to hurt Gitta, but lacked the power to do so. All he could do—
more to defend himself than to attack her—was to rid himself of any
interest in her. His success in this was a victory for her, not for
himself.

Gitta now was explaining the process by which the bronze was cast
and the anxiety she felt as she waited for the mold to be opened. "It
must be rather like having a baby. Not that I ever have. But one hears
that almost all mothers ask whether the baby is perfect before they
bother even about whether it's a boy or a girl."

Helen's mood had changed. She was no longer merely taken aback.

From the way her hands clenched into tight fists Bernard could see that she was angry. The situation portrayed by Gitta was true, but of course Helen knew it in a deeper sense to be a lie. He had better separate the two women before the inevitable quarrel erupted.

"We must be getting along," he told Gitta. "I only brought Helen in to look at the Siva. I didn't expect you to be here."

Even that last remark could not save him from Helen's fury. As soon as they reached the pavement she turned on him.

"How dare you! Do you think I'm an idiot? Did you really believe you could set up that oh-so-innocent explanation, so accidental, so spontaneous, and expect me to forget that you'd already admitted the truth?"

"Of course not." Bernard took her arm and propelled her around the corner, so that any scene would not be visible to Gitta. A restaurant he knew was just opening for the evening there. It was too early to eat, but they could talk more peacefully over an aperitif.

"I don't want—" began Helen; but Bernard insisted.

"Libby's party isn't for hours and we need somewhere to sit. I can explain what happened then."

Reluctantly she went in and waited while he ordered drinks.

"You've answered your own question," he suggested. "Of course I'm not such a fool as to ask someone to tell you a lie after admitting the truth myself. I didn't expect to see Gitta there. I didn't *want* to see her. I never want to see her again, and I don't imagine I ever shall. I certainly didn't ask her to tell you anything."

"Why should she bother to lie, if you didn't ask her to?"

"It wasn't a lie. That bronze, the Siva, is the child she mentioned in her note."

"I certainly gathered that was what I was supposed to believe."

"It's true," said Bernard.

"You mean there's no baby?"

"No. Just the Siva. That's why I took you there to see it."

"When did you find out?"

"At the private view on Monday. I realized what Gitta had meant as soon as I set eyes on the bronze."

"But until then you'd assumed she was talking about a real baby, just as I did. So it wasn't impossible. You did make love to her while you were in India."

"Just once. In that temple, on the night she described."

"Then she was lying about that."

"Implicitly, yes. Not in so many words. When I met her again, I told her how furious I was because her note had caused so much trouble. Meeting you unexpectedly, perhaps she thought she could put it right."

There was a long silence. Then Helen let out the deep breath of her anger in a single sigh and picked up the drink which until then she had ignored. "I don't really understand," she said.

"I'm not sure that I do either. It was odd, what happened in the temple. Gitta called the atmosphere eerie, but it was stronger than that. As though centuries of magic and ritual were trapped in the air."

"It's an original excuse. I can imagine the headlines of a divorce court report. ' "Enmeshed by magic," says drugs boss.' "

Bernard let that go and pressed on with his own argument. "She used the atmosphere—to get her idea of the statue straight. She used me as well. To say it straight out, she seduced me."

Helen's laughter, loud enough to make the waiters turn toward them, mocked his humiliation. There was no sympathy in her voice as she asked for another drink. "I don't know that it makes much difference," she said when it arrived. "There's no baby, but there could have been. You seem to have conducted your private fertility rites without regard to the consequences."

"As people have done for thousands of years. It's only within comparatively recent times that any choice has existed."

"It's a comparatively recent time that we're discussing. The fact that Gitta's baby is made of bronze instead of flesh owed nothing to any forethought on your part." She paused as a waiter appeared with menus and lingered within earshot.

"Since we're here, we might as well dine," Bernard suggested.

"I don't want anything. There'll be food at Libby's party."

"You won't see it before ten at the earliest. Have something light to be going on with." Since she did not seem prepared to choose, he ordered trout for them both, knowing that she liked it. "Couldn't you look at this in a different way?" he asked as the waiter moved off. "You'd have had more cause for indignation if I'd planned this, or hoped for it; if I'd taken a packet of contraceptives out to India and remembered to slip them in my pocket before setting out for the temple that night. Surely you must realize—I mean, you've seen Gitta now. Do you really believe—?"

Helen's laughter was higher in pitch than usual, suggesting hysteria rather than amusement. "You're not exactly gallant. But I accept your point. You found her sudden irresistibility as startling as I do." She pushed her glass forward for a refill. Bernard tried to fathom her expression. Was the storm over? Had she forgiven him for his holiday indiscretion? But then, Gitta had been almost irrelevant to the real cause of their quarrel.

"Would you like to adopt a child?" he asked. He spoke abruptly, but the thought had been in his mind all day. If it would solve any problem for Helen, it need create none for himself. He had enough money to keep the inevitable disruption under control.

Helen's face, which for a few seconds had seemed amused and almost friendly, froze into a white mask. "*What* did you say?"

"We could adopt a child. More than one if you liked. I do see that I've been selfish about this. And since it's too late—"

"What makes you think you'd like other people's children when you didn't want your own?"

"They'd be children who existed already. I wouldn't have to feel responsible for bringing them into the world. I recognize, of course, that for you it would only be a second best, but—"

"Do you?" Helen buried her head in her hands.

"Yes. It's odd. When I saw that statue . . . Well, I know it's only a piece of metal. But when I first saw it, I had a queer sensation. Almost as though it were my own child. It made me understand how perhaps you felt."

"Twenty years," said Helen. As she lifted her head, Bernard saw that she was crying. "We've been married twenty years, and in all that time you've never given a moment to sympathizing with how I felt. Even now it's taken a strange woman to jolt you into understanding. It was children of my own that I wanted. Now it's too late. I tried to convince you years ago how strongly I felt that children were a necessary part of a marriage and a home. But one can't go on arguing the same point for twenty years. If there's a deep disagreement inside a marriage, someone has to give in. I did give in. I accepted the situation. Probably I could have continued to accept it indefinitely—but only if you were consistent. If you change your mind, you make all those years a waste."

The tears were running down her cheeks. She dabbed at them with a table napkin. Then she stood up.

"Where are you going?" asked Bernard.

"To put my makeup straight. And then to the party. Libby won't mind if I'm early."

"But stay and have dinner first. Look, it's just coming."

"For twenty years," said Helen, "you've been making all the decisions. I've been living your life. Now it seems you don't find that wholly satisfactory. Too bad! It's my turn to be self-centered now. I've made it clear that I'm not eating with you, and you haven't bothered to listen. For the third time, I don't want dinner and I don't intend to have it. I do want to go to the party, and I'm going."

"May I come with you?" asked Bernard, standing beside her.

"You'd better ask Tommy. I've arranged to go with him. But I don't recommend it. I think I shall probably get drunk, and you might not like to see that."

"Will you come back to the flat tonight?" he asked.

"That depends what address Tommy gives to the taxi."

It was a moment before Bernard could control his voice. "You are rubbing my nose in it, aren't you?"

Helen shrugged her shoulders. "I expect I shall be sorry tomorrow. I'll come round and talk again if you want me to. But I don't think you realize how angry I am. I have to work it out. I can't just calmly tell myself to forget it."

"Do you think I'm not angry too?" demanded Bernard. "To be used as she's used me?" He choked on the thought and then forced himself to be calm again, quoting what Gitta had claimed, although he had been unable to believe it. "Anger can be a creative emotion. We could use it to make something new out of our marriage, not to destroy it."

"I take no responsibility for what has happened to our marriage," Helen said. "And if anything new is coming out of it, it's a life in which I make my own decisions."

"All right. I accept that."

"Yes," she agreed bitterly. "You'll let me make my own decisions as long as they fit in with your plans."

"Helen, I'll try." The headwaiter came questioningly forward as they moved toward the door. "Just a moment," Bernard said to reassure him; and then, to Helen, "I'll get you a taxi."

"Even hailing a taxi is something I can manage for myself if I try very hard."

Bernard gripped her hand. "Come back to the flat afterwards," he said. "Please. Even if you're drunk. Even if it's not till after you've been home with Tommy. I don't care about any of that. If I can just feel sure that you'll come."

"It's a snag, isn't it," said Helen, "when people take over their own lives? You can't be sure that you'll get a happy ending when you only have the power to write half the script, because the other person's happiness may lie somewhere else. I don't promise anything. I haven't decided anything." She moved away and then, remembering something, turned back and took a small object from her evening bag. It was the quartz stone, the two halves fastened together with sticky tape. Bernard had kept it in the house as an ornament, open on a shelf to catch the light: a holiday souvenir. "I brought this," she said. "I don't want anything from India in my home."

The door of the restaurant swung behind her as she walked away. Bernard, no more hungry now than Helen had been, paid the bill and went outside. A need to quarrel took him back to the gallery, closed by now. He rattled at the door, but no one came. Frustrated by the absence of anyone on whom he could release his anger, he clenched his hand around the knob of quartz, squeezing it as though that pressure might be enough to sublimate his aggression. Then he took it from his pocket and hurled it with all his strength against the window in which the bronze hawk swooped.

The glass was of a quality strengthened to keep out burglars and bullets. It was the quartz which shattered, littering the pavement with its tiny crystal teeth. Bernard stared at the mess and at the smoothness of the unharmed window, almost wishing that a policeman would appear to accuse him. At least then he would have the chance to explain his feelings. But no one was interested. More tired now than angry, he went back to the flat.

Sooner or later, he believed, Helen would return. It was because she loved him deeply that she had been so deeply hurt by something which a different woman might have shrugged away. In a permissive age, they were curiously old-fashioned in their views. Other couples took marriage more lightly, or did not trouble to marry at all. Bernard and Helen had married for life. Illogically, it was at this very moment when he most desperately feared she might leave him that he was most sure she would come back in the end—as though the fear were the price he must pay for her eventual forgiveness.

There was another price to be paid as well. As sincerely as though she were present to hear him, Bernard promised himself that if Helen returned he would never be unfaithful to her again. And yet he had not completely subdued the unexpected, unwanted stab of desire that each viewing of the Siva Dancing inspired: the wish that he could after all father a child, flesh of his own flesh, a new creation to be for a little while possessed and then to inherit all his own possessions. What was the use of owning a fortune when he had no family to enjoy it after he and Helen were both dead? He had always believed that to bring a new life into the world was an act of selfishness. Now he longed to be selfish in just that way; but if he were to remain loyal to Helen for the rest of his life he could never be a father. It would be too late for him just as it was already, more finally, too late for her.

Too late for his grandmother as well, he realized, weariness sending his thoughts off at a tangent. Alexa had already suffered the death of her only son without an heir. The realization that her grandson was equally determined to remain childless must have pained her. For the first time it occurred to Bernard that the family was dying. There had been no legitimate births to record in the family Bible since Asha's name was entered in 1941: the one illegitimate baby who had arrived later—a half sister of Asha's—had been taken to the United States by her father while she was still tiny, and was unlikely ever to be heard of again.

Nor did it seem probable that the family would acquire many new members in the future. Paula Mattison's marriage to a politician had been childless. He had died not long ago after a car crash, and Paula had returned to her native Jamaica. Even were she to remarry, she must be over forty by now. Only Asha, of all the Lorimers, was of an age to bear children. Did she realize her responsibility for the future of the Lorimer family?

Well, Bernard knew that he was the last person who would have the right to remind her of it. He made an attempt to discipline his thoughts, while recognizing that their very inconsequence was protecting him from the pain of thinking about his wife. Jealous and unhappy, he sat without moving through the longest night of his life: but Helen did not come home.

X V

All morning Alexa had promised herself that she would get up before her visitors came, yet she was still in bed when Helen arrived at three o'clock. There were days—and sometimes even whole weeks nowadays—when she simply lacked the energy to move. On her ninetieth birthday she had told herself firmly that standing up against old age was merely a matter of willpower and that she would stay on her feet until some specific disease, with symptoms and a name, laid her low. But over six years had passed since that ninetieth birthday, and more and more often nowadays she found herself succumbing to the temptations of warmth and comfort which the bed offered.

Though her body might be losing its strength, her mind was still quick to draw conclusions from what she observed. She was pleased to see Helen, but immediately alarmed to discover that she had come alone. Bernard often visited without his wife, but it had never before happened the other way around.

"What's happened to Bernard?" she asked sharply. "Not ill, is he?"

"Bernard's never ill." Helen bent down to kiss Alexa. "He's been staying at the flat, that's all, and I've come from the house. So we drove over separately. He'll be here soon."

He arrived at that moment, looking more disheveled than usual. Helen, so capable and well ordered, had never managed to make a smart man out of her husband. Alexa stretched out a hand to greet her grandson but was disconcerted to find that for the first moment or two he hardly seemed to notice her. Instead, he stared at Helen as though he had not expected to see her there and was not sure what to make of her presence.

That impression lasted only for a moment. Then he gave his grandmother his usual hug and sat down on the other side of the bed from his wife. But Alexa was still conscious of an unusual atmosphere in the room. The two of them were watching each other and talking separately to her, through her, instead of chatting normally: and yet there was no hostility, as far as she could tell, in their wariness.

"Did you ever meet Michael Laing?" Helen asked unexpectedly.

Alexa searched her memory and recalled a friendly young man with a warm smile and a thick beard.

"He came with you once, didn't he?" she asked Bernard. "Ilsa's son. A nice lad. I liked him. But he was too clever for me."

"He's too clever for most of us." Bernard laughed as he made the comment; but it was part of this prickly afternoon that he seemed to be looking for some significance in Helen's question.

"I'm glad you liked him," Helen said—speaking, as before, to Alexa rather than to her husband. "I felt I ought to check it out with you, since you're the head of the family. I want to draw him closer into the family circle. To adopt him."

Alexa's astonishment at this statement was not great enough to blind her to the fact that Bernard was equally startled. She left that fact to be considered later, while she gave her own reaction.

"But he's grown up," she pointed out. "Surely you can't adopt an adult."

"I'm not talking about any kind of legal process," Helen said. "I don't know that age actually does make any difference, but I wouldn't want to do anything which might affect his relationship with his father. They're very fond of each other, although they live too far away to meet often. But you see, although Michael may have a father, he hasn't got a mother and he hasn't really got a maternal family. I know Bernard is a sort of cousin, and our house is always open to him, but all the same . . ." She smiled at Alexa in the strained manner of someone trying to laugh off a subject which in fact was bringing her near to tears. "One day he'll get married and have children. I want there to be a firm understanding between us that I can be the grandmother to his children. They'll need someone like me, and I need them. Michael understands that. We've talked about it." Upset, she buried her head in her hands—Helen, who was always so calm, never seeming to be even mildly perturbed about anything! Alexa glanced anxiously at Bernard, but he was already on his feet. Quickly he moved around the bed to stand behind Helen, his arms encircling her while he bent to kiss the back of her head and neck.

Alexa kept very quiet. Whatever was happening between them was none of her business. She watched as Helen pulled herself together, dabbing her eyes and giving one last sniff.

"Sorry," she said—to Alexa again rather than to Bernard. "It's still that beastly operation, you know. More than a year ago, and in a quite different part of the body, but I still don't seem to have my tear ducts under control. You'd think that a man who spends his life inventing new drugs would have come up with something for lachrymose ladies, wouldn't you?"

"Kiss me," said Bernard. He pulled Helen up and around into his arms, raining kisses on her as she buried her head in his shoulder.

For a second time Helen looked apologetically at Alexa as she pulled herself away. "May I use your bathroom?" She took the answer for granted and went off to repair her makeup. Alexa waited for Bernard to explain.

"We had a slight tiff," he said. "Well, not slight at all. Entirely my fault. I've been worried. I think this means that she's decided to forgive me. I don't deserve it, but—" His smile showed his relief.

"And this business about Michael? You're happy with it?"

"It's a second best," Bernard said. "That's my fault as well. But it's the best of the second bests. Yes, I'm happy with it."

"And it's not as though Michael were a stranger." Alexa's thoughts moved off along their own track. "After all, he *is* a Lorimer. Kate's grandson. Part of the family circle already. I'm glad you and Helen want to tighten your particular link with him, but the blood tie is there already. That's important."

"But you know—" Bernard checked himself in midsentence, leaving Alexa impatiently curious.

"What do I know?"

"Does it really matter?" asked Bernard. "The blood tie, I mean? Isn't it enough if there's love and friendship?"

"It's nearly enough," Alexa told him. "But not quite. Love and friendship can both die. But if you're someone's son, or grandson, that relationship is part of you until you die yourself."

"Yes," agreed Bernard. "Yes. You're quite right. It matters very much." He looked toward the door as Helen appeared there, her hair smooth and her lipstick and eye shadow neatly reapplied. "Do you mind if we go out for a breath of air in the garden, Grandmother? Just for a minute or two?"

"Take your time." Alexa waited for a moment after they had closed the door and then, as secretively as though it were a forbidden activity, embarked on the adventure of getting out of bed. She threw off the blankets and moved her legs carefully around, a little at a time, until they hung over the side of the bed. This was the dangerous step, the moment of first standing up, letting her feet take the weight; it was all too easy to topple forward as her ankles gave way. Usually she only undertook the maneuver when her companion was standing ready to support her if necessary. But today she accomplished it successfully alone, feeling for her slippers and wrapping round her the silk kimono which served as a tea gown.

The tea tray was already laid. She switched on the electric kettle. As she waited for it to boil she ran through in her mind—as though on a tape recorder—the last few moments of her conversation with Bernard. There was something in it which did not quite connect. Bernard had abandoned a thought in midquestion and had never returned to it. Was there something which she ought to know and did not? Were there secrets which they thought she was too old to understand? Well, it had not taken her long to realize at the beginning of the visit that something was up between Bernard and Helen. She was not senile yet. They ought to trust her with the truth.

She intended to press the point, but when Bernard and Helen returned, hand in hand, they made it clear at once that there was to be a change of subject. Whatever the cause of their quarrel, they had made it up. Twenty years of love and friendship had proved strong enough to overcome a few weeks of estrangement, and their lighthearted relief made it clear that they had no wish to continue the earlier conversation. As they chattered—to each other now and not through her—Alexa allowed her own thoughts to return to Michael Laing. Because she hardly knew him, she had never given much thought to his place in the Lorimer family. But Ilsa's son must be her own great-great-nephew. Pleased at her success in working this out, she gave no further thought to the question of what it might be that she did or did not know.

Helen and Bernard stayed longer than usual that day, as though they found a special happiness in postponing the other happiness of being alone together. But they left at last, leaving Alexa to the next stage of her daily routine. In the past few years it had become important to her to reserve special times of the day for special occupations, so that there was always something to which she could look forward. At six o'clock every evening—to fill the empty period when tea was over and dinner not yet in sight—she liked to study the deaths column in the *Daily Telegraph*.

Tonight as usual she worked her way through the list of names, hoping for an identification which would spark off an hour of silent reminiscence or provide an excuse to write to a widow. But her recognitions were less and less frequent nowadays. Even friends and singers who had been a whole generation younger than herself had already departed. At a quarter to seven, disappointed, she allowed the newspaper to drop to the floor. No one she knew had died this week.

XVI

Brad Davidson was buried in San Francisco, the city in which he had been born and had spent the whole of his life—except for his wartime years in England. The arrangements for the burial were made by his daughter, Ros, and it never occurred to her to advertise the news of her father's death in a British newspaper. She had never heard the name of Lady Glanville mentioned, so there was no possibility of her feeling an obligation to write a letter to an old lady in England. Brad had had a great many friends, and in addition there were many charities with reason to be grateful for his generosity. The church was crowded for the service, and Ros had no sense that anyone was missing.

Only at the very end, when the last hand had been shaken and the last condolences acknowledged, was she overcome by a feeling of desolation at her bereavement, increased by loneliness because she had no family to support her. Brad had left her a fortune, but he had bequeathed her no brothers or sisters. Her only cousin had been killed in Vietnam. Now she had no living relatives at all.

There was Lee, of course, and she tried to shrug off her depression, telling herself that Lee would be enough. He had been standing a little apart, watching her protectively as she murmured thanks to everyone who had come. Now he came to put his arm around her waist. "Time to go home, kid."

Even before they were married he had called her "kid" whenever he most sincerely intended to express affection. She had never minded before. It was odd that for the first time the word should grate on her ears—as though, with her father dead, she had overnight become in some way more adult. But, grateful for his sympathetic company, she gave no sign of objection.

He drove her not to the house in which they had lived since their marriage, but to Brad's home on Russian Hill. Ros had moved back there five weeks earlier when it became clear that her father was dying. Now it had the cold, uneasy feeling of a house without life. All the impedimenta of illness and nursing had disappeared, as had Brad himself, and nothing yet had filled the emptiness. Ros was affected by the atmosphere herself, so she was not surprised when Lee gave a shiver of misgiving as he hurried to pour her a drink.

"We should get a good price for this house," he said. "The furniture, too. Dickie Delaney's got his eyes on one or two of the grandfather clocks."

"Long-case clocks." Ros, grateful for the drink, corrected him automatically. Brad had always been meticulous in his description of his father's collection. "I don't want to sell them."

Lee looked at her in surprise. "Collections are a special thing, kid: you know that. Sure, those clocks must have meant something to your grandfather. But why should *you* need to be told eighteen times when it's time to go to bed?"

"The family fortune was founded on clocks," Ros reminded him. Davidson Security Systems, Inc., in which she had just inherited a controlling interest, had grown from the talent which a penniless clock repairer had diverted to the invention of locks and safes. By now, a hundred years later, the company used electronics rather than keys and cogs to produce its timing and surveillance systems. But the beautiful—and very valuable—collection which her grandfather had built up remained as a part of the family's history as well as his personal memorial. "If you don't like having them here, we could move them into the boardroom." She hesitated, knowing that she was about to startle him. "I don't want to sell this house either, Lee. I'd like to live here. But even if you don't fancy that, I shall hold on to the property."

"Live here, in this mausoleum!" He had the grace to blush as he realized the hurtfulness of the word, but pressed the point anyway. "It's so old and dark and—and empty. We have a beautiful home, full of sunshine, with a pool and a view, and you want to live *here!*"

"I like the oldness of it," said Ros. "We don't need to sell anything. This is a city house. The pool and the sunshine and the view can still be there for weekends. But when do we ever have time to lie around on working days?"

"You won't go on working," Lee pointed out. "You're a very rich woman now, baby. You can afford to take things easy."

This was not the moment to make it clear to her husband that she had no intention of retiring from her work in the family firm in order to live off its profits. Ros knew that Lee would disapprove of her business plans and chose to finish one argument before beginning another. "The house feels empty now, but we can soon change that," she pointed out. "All it needs is flowers and friends and—well, just us, enjoying ourselves. And how about the stress we'll save ourselves when we don't have to drive in and out of the city every day!"

Lee made no comment. He would wait, Ros guessed, until they were in bed before raising the subject again. Lee was marvelous in bed, but had not yet recognized that his wife made decisions only by daylight. And the house was hers. Lee could refuse to live in it, but he could not force her to sell it.

"I didn't see Angie at the service," he said abruptly to change the subject. Angie had been Mrs. Brad Davidson for eight or nine years.

"She's two marriages on by now. I suppose my father was only a very small part of her life. She hasn't seen him for twenty years."

"But you'd think she'd want to support *you.*"

"She was only my stepmother, remember. Not the same as being the real thing." For a few moments Ros became withdrawn, remembering her unhappiness on the day when Angie walked out. She had been nine years old at the time and, with the egoism of childhood, had believed that it was herself rather than her father who was being rejected. It was only then that she had learned from Brad that she had been born—before her father's marriage to Angie—to an English mother.

"Tell me about her," Ros pleaded then: but Brad shook his head.

"She loved you very much," was all he would say. "We were all so happy together for a little while. I met her in London, during the war, and that was where she died. It was a sad story. I try not to think about it. We'll have to look after each other from now on, hey, honey?" He never mentioned her mother again. Now, on this day of bereavement, Ros felt for the first time the double shock of being an orphan. She had been deprived of a mother's love by fate, but it was Brad's unwillingness to talk which had deprived her of the ability to love her mother's memory.

Later that evening, reluctant to let her father go, she wandered around the room which Brad had used as a home office, pulling open drawers which would have to be emptied. One of them, she discovered, was stuffed full of letters and snapshots, the personal souvenirs of a long life. Curious—and yet ashamed at what seemed the invasion of a dead man's privacy—she turned them over one by one.

Many of the photographs were of Ros herself: she smiled at the memories they recalled. But right at the bottom of the drawer was one she had never seen before. It was a snapshot of a young woman smiling down at the baby in her arms, while a blond three-year-old girl tugged at her skirt. On the back Brad had written: "Barbary at Blaize, with Ros and Asha."

Ros stared at the photograph with an intensity of feeling brought to a head by the loss of her father. Why had Brad never allowed her to see her mother's likeness? There could be no doubt that Barbary must be her mother. But who was Asha, and what had happened to her?

Lee appeared in the doorway, anxious to take her to bed and comfort her for the sadness of the day. Needing to be loved, Ros put the photograph back in the drawer and went upstairs with her husband. But the next day she set in train an inquiry to discover from the British registry of births, deaths and marriages the name of the woman whom Brad Davidson had married in England at some time during the war in Europe. Several weeks passed before the answer came through. No such marriage had taken place and so no name could be provided. Without a surname it was impossible to track down the woman who had been christened Barbary. Looking at the brief report, Ros was forced to recognize that she would never know what had happened to the other little girl in the photograph: Asha.

PART IV

Ancestors
1975-1977

I

Looking back, when it was all over, Asha saw the Ancestor as a harbinger of trouble, so closely did the bad times follow on his arrival in her life. But as she carried the old man's portrait home on a sultry July Saturday in 1975 she regarded the gift from her elderly great-aunt only as an inconvenience, not as a malign influence. The picture was heavy and it was awkward to carry, no more.

On any other day of the week her taxi could have taken her all the way from the railway station to her front door, but today the Saturday market had closed the street to traffic. Never before had the Portobello Road seemed so long—or so crowded with tourists. They clustered around the market stalls, fingering souvenirs and enthusing without discrimination over silver or pinchbeck, rare books or fairground relics. They sat down in the middle of the road to rest their poor feet. In a score of different languages they complained of the heat. Because they were not looking for anything in particular they wandered aimlessly without caring whom they jostled. One of the nurses who looked after Lady Glanville had as a kindness wrapped the heavy Victorian painting in brown paper and this—without offering any great protection against a swinging handbag or an aggressive elbow—made it almost impossible to carry. Flagging in the heat, Asha retreated down a side street to rest for a moment.

If only she could have had the car there would have been no problem. But Ranji's cricket that day was also in the country, and he had promised a lift to three of his teammates. Neither of them had anticipated, of course, that she would return so heavily laden from her regular fortnightly visit. Asha gave a loud sigh and stooped to pick up the Ancestor again.

"Carry your bag, miss?"

"Chris!" Any friendly face would have cheered Asha at this moment and the appearance of Chris Townsend, who taught art at her comprehensive school, lifted her spirits immediately. He was wearing nothing but a smile and a brief pair of swimming trunks—appropriate to the temperature if surprising for a street in the middle of London.

"I saw you from my sunbathing roof," he said. "No one else in the city has such fair hair. Paler than blond. I recognized its shimmer even though I couldn't see your face. There's a refrigerator full of cold beer only twenty yards from here. Come and sample it. Then I'll put some clothes on and lug this object back to your place."

Ranji would not be home for hours. Asha accepted the offer gratefully. "I didn't know you lived here," she said.

"I squat here. A man with a salary on the Burnham Scale and no working wife can't afford to live anywhere." He led the way into a terrace house which from outside appeared derelict, its ground floor windows covered with sheets of corrugated iron. A tiny front garden was littered with empty Coke tins, broken glass and the red boxes of a takeout chicken shop, while all the exterior paintwork of the building had peeled away to reveal rotten gray wood. The stairs inside were dark and musty. Then he opened the door of his room on the first floor.

For a moment Asha stared in astonishment. Then she began to laugh. Chris had painted three walls of the room in a dazzling white. The fourth wall was covered by a bright mural of stylized flowers and butterflies. As though in a jungle, tiny men and women wandered naked among the stems of the flowers. Asha examined the wall with delight while Chris disappeared into his kitchen for the beer.

"I thought squatters were all hippies," she said when he returned.

"The hippies get the publicity. People like me, who want to be left alone, keep rather quieter."

"How safe are you?"

"It's almost foolproof. The council bought the whole terrace, scheduled it for complete modernization and then found that it had run out of money. If it put tenants in from the housing list, they'd sue for essential repairs. It can't even afford to demolish. A caretaker like me is just what's needed. No one recognizes my existence officially, in case vacant possession should ever be required, but a considerable number of blind eyes are turned. What have you got?"

"A flat above a shop. Oh, this is what I needed!" She took a long drink of the cold beer and then sipped more slowly.

"What are you carting about here?"

"The portrait of an ancestor. I have a great-aunt who's getting on for a hundred. Until a few months ago she was incredibly spry. But now she's had to move into a nursing home. And she can't have her own furniture there, as she did before. So when I visited her today, she gave me this."

"May I see?"

"Of course." Together they tore off the brown paper. Chris leaned the portrait against one of his white walls and they both stepped back to look at it. Although Asha had seen the picture often enough on the wall at Blaize, this was her first chance to study it with the possessive eye of an owner.

Dressed in black and with his thick white hair yellowed by varnish and the passing of time, Asha's ancestor stared out of the frame with piercing greenish-blue eyes. Asha stared back with slight uneasiness, not sure that she wished to share her flat with such an autocratic personality.

"Who painted it?" asked Chris.

"No idea. Can't you tell me?"

He fetched a magnifying glass and went down on his knees to study the canvas before announcing that it was unsigned. Moving it away from the wall, he found a small label attached to the back of the frame. "1877. J. J. Lorimer, it says here."

"That's the sitter, not the artist. Aunt Alexa's father, John Junius Lorimer. Founder of the family fortunes, which unfortunately seem to have got lost sometime in the last hundred years. Can't you tell from the style of the picture who painted it?"

"I might if it were someone well known or idiosyncratic. No clues here, though. Probably a provincial artist."

"Pity. I hoped I could make my fortune by discovering that I owned the eighteen-seventy-seven equivalent of a Giorgione."

"No such thing. Eighteen-seventy-seven wasn't exactly a vintage year in Bristol. Have you ever had *your* portrait painted, Asha?"

"No."

"You must let me have a go one day. That dazzling hair! And your complexion is so fair as well. Translucent. A technical challenge. I'd like to do a series. Asha by Renoir. Asha by Bonnard. Asha by Picasso. We could storm the Academy together."

"What about Asha by Townsend?"

"You've put your finger straight onto my Achilles' heel," said Chris sorrowfully. "I haven't got a style. If I had, I shouldn't be wasting my time at a crummy old comprehensive school. I have an enormous talent for imitation. That's quite useful for a teacher. I can show my pupils how to achieve any result that's ever been achieved before. But apart from that—" He shrugged his shoulders; and Asha, not liking to pay compliments out of ignorance, evaded the subject.

"It's not a crummy old comprehensive," she said.

"I withdraw the phrase. A progressive, well-organized, well-equipped, friendly comprehensive school which is four times as big as it ought to be and lacks both discipline and academic standards but otherwise is in every respect perfect."

"Given the system—" began Asha; but Chris interrupted her.

"And who gives us the system? Why should a handful of politicians who don't live here and would never dream of educating their children here have the right to say that we must have two thousand children in our school? Have you ever met a single working teacher, Asha, who genuinely believes that a school the size of ours is any good?"

"The range of subjects—"

"Was never a problem in a school of five hundred until one reached A-level courses. A sixth-form college would deal with that, and allow our sixteen-year-olds a bit of responsibility in what's left of the school. And then, instead of altering the exam grading system so that nobody exactly fails, we might be able to improve our teaching so that a few kids actually pass." He checked himself, smiling at his own indignation. "Asha, I haven't seen you since your appointment was announced. Congratulations. I was glad it was you. Promise of higher things later as well, I imagine."

"Thanks." Three days earlier Asha had been appointed deputy head of Hillgate Comprehensive School. The promotion—as Chris suggested—implied that she would be well placed in two years' time to apply for the headship when its present holder retired. But the Governors had not formally mentioned such a possibility and so it had not seemed necessary for Asha to volunteer the fact that her own plans for the next three years included a baby.

Somehow there had never been a convenient time for starting a family. Ranji—younger than herself—had still been a student at the London School of Economics when they married, and they had both agreed that it would be wise to wait until he had graduated before thinking about babies. Five years later he had suggested that the right moment had come, for by then he was earning a reasonable salary. But it happened that Asha had just been promoted to be head of the history department and was anxious to consolidate her new position; there was, after all, plenty of time. In 1971, after three years in the job, she would have been willing to take a break from work; but that was the year in which Ranji gave up his salaried employment in order to start and run his own business. It seemed a sensible precaution then to hang on to the one job which guaranteed a monthly paycheck.

But now, at thirty-four, she was aware that the risks of motherhood would increase with every year that passed: she must not wait much longer. Three terms as deputy head would let her put into effect plans which a weak headmaster had been dodging for too long. But if she were to start a baby next March, say, she could leave in July. The thought gave her pleasure, but she kept it to herself.

"Another beer?"

"No, thanks. I must get back."

"Why?"

"Just as I was leaving for school yesterday morning," said Asha, "a bookcase fell over. None of our walls or floors is truly vertical or horizontal. The bookcase had probably been doing a Leaning Tower of Pisa act for months, and one more book on the top shelf was the last straw. I didn't have time to cope with the mess before I went out, and when I came home again I was absolutely whacked. You know that end-of-the-week feeling."

"I know precisely the feeling," Chris agreed.

"So all the mess is still there. But weighing heavy on my conscience by now."

"Hang on, then." Chris dressed himself in shorts and sandals. He picked up the portrait as though it weighed nothing and followed her out. Asha noticed the care with which he locked the door behind him.

"You can't trust anyone these days," he explained. "Turn your back for a moment and somebody's squatting in your property."

"Disgusting!"

"Yes. Absolutely disgraceful!"

Asha went ahead, forging a path up the middle of the road. The crowd was thinner now, although tourists were still posing for photographs with monkeys or parrots on their shoulders, and two young men with guitars and a collecting hat were the center for a sing. Freed from her heavy load, she was able to move more quickly than before, and they soon reached her home.

The shop beneath the flat was divided into half a dozen tiny booths. The woman nearest the door, a specialist in sporting prints, looked at the portrait with interest as Asha felt for her key.

"Going into the trade then, dear?"

"No. Strictly private. How are things?"

"Tricky. Easy to buy these days, but hard to sell. All those banks and companies collapsing; it's made people nervous. I saw Ranji on Thursday when I was on my way to a sale; but not to speak to. We must have been on the same train, but I didn't catch sight of him until we arrived at Cambridge."

"Cambridge?" Asha, her key now in the lock, tried to keep the incredulity out of her voice. On Thursday Ranji had gone off to work at his regular time and had answered her evening query about the day with his usual "Nothing special." But her surprise was nobody else's business. "I hope you found something worthwhile at the auction," she said instead, and led the way up to the flat.

"I have some beer too," she said as Chris propped the picture against a wall.

"Actually, I wouldn't say no to a cup of tea. And before you put the kettle on, why shouldn't I help you get these books back?"

"Why should you?"

"Because any chore is less choring with two people than with one; right?"

"Right!" said Asha, pleased. "Ten seconds while I get out of my aunt-visiting clothes." She returned to the living room wearing jeans and a T-shirt.

"You look about sixteen!" exclaimed Chris. "Don't let the sixth form ever see you dressed like that, or discipline will shatter. Now tell me, is this to be a botch job or shall we do it thoroughly? We can put everything back as it was before, and one day it will tip again. Or we can slice a bit off the bottom of the bookcase so that it leans back on the wall."

"I've got a plane," said Asha. Chris, trained to handle a variety of tools and materials, did the job with speed and neatness. When he had set the tall bookcase up again she fetched a cloth and cleaned it.

"You know where everything goes," said Chris. "I'll bang the dust out of the books and hand them up to you."

It was a dirty task. As the dust flew, Asha was ashamed to think how long it was since she had done any spring cleaning. Not this spring, certainly. But because they chattered as they worked, the shelves were restocked in an amazingly short time.

Two hours later Chris stood up to leave. "That was good," he said. "Not just the tea. Those terrible staff rooms are like railway stations. Always people coming and going. One never properly converses." He paused, staring at the portrait he had carried in. "I could clean that, you know. It mightn't make the old boy look any more handsome, but at least he wouldn't be dark yellow."

"I hardly think he's worth it."

"There'd be no charge. It wouldn't need much more than patience. And a room to work in. Nothing at school is vandalproof."

"We have an attic." Asha took him up the narrow staircase which led to the top of the building.

"It's a studio!" exclaimed Chris. "Here's London full of desperate artists searching for anything that would serve to paint in, and you let a real studio stand empty."

Asha saw that he was right, although it had not occurred to her before. As well as an ordinary window, there was a large skylight in the north slope of the roof. But she had her own plans for the future of the empty, spacious room. One day it would be a nursery.

"Sorry," she said. "I mean, certainly you could use it to clean the Ancestor, if you're really prepared to do that. But I'm not going into the landlady business."

"Oh, well!" He shrugged his shoulders. "Anyway, this would do fine for giving the old chap a scrub. But not while this sunbathing weather lasts, and then I'll be away for the holidays. The first rainy Saturday morning next term, I'll be round." He moved across to the window and stared out. "You'd have a lot more sun if that tree came down," he pointed out. "It's far too close to the house."

Asha came to stand beside him. "Its doom is already written." She opened the window so that they could lean out, and showed him that the tree was one of a long line of elms. Although this was full summer, the arms of the three trees farthest away stretched bleakly upward, bearing no foliage at all, and on the boughs of the next two the leaves had turned brown and begun to curl. "It's the Dutch elm disease," she said. "They're all dead or dying except ours, and that can't last long. We had the Parks officer round to see whether there was anything we could do and he said it was hopeless. They're touching root and crown. The beetles which cause the trouble don't need to fly; they can just step from one branch to another. There could be two million tiny beetles on the move out there—terrifying thought! Our tree is the end of the line, so it may be good for one more season; but after that it will be for the chop. I find it sad. They're more than a hundred years old, those elms; they were here before the houses."

"It's a mistake to believe that everything should go on forever," Chris said. "A mistake to which the British are especially prone. It's necessary to let some things die—institutions, buildings, systems, trees—in order that something new may be nurtured. And better to plant a new tree in a suitable position than to keep alive an old one which should never have been allowed to remain so close to a building. I'm surprised to find that you're sentimental."

Asha was surprised herself, when she thought about it. She clapped her hands cheerfully. "You're right. Let the ax fall. Let the sun flood in. I shall paint the whole attic white, like your beautiful squat, and then invite you to put another marvelous mural on one wall—to be paid for in beer and frivolous chatter."

"Done!" Chris held out his hand to seal the bargain. It was odd, Asha thought, that although they had been colleagues for three years, this was the first time they had ever enjoyed a sustained conversation alone together. The good humor which his company had induced in her survived his departure by at least an hour. When Ranji returned home, pleased because he had taken three wickets in his cricket match, it was with no intention of nagging that she casually asked the question which the seller of sporting prints had put into her mind.

"What took you to Cambridge on Thursday, Ranji?"

I I

Why should a simple question upset Ranji so much? At first he even pretended that he had not been out at all, but had spent the day as usual in his office. Probably he pointed out, all Indians look alike to an English observer.

Asha didn't believe him. She and Ranji very rarely quarreled. There were times when the strain of her working day took Asha herself over the brink of irritation; but Ranji was so gentle and sympathetic that he could always soothe her before she came to the point of losing her temper. Today, though, she was worried by his prevarication. Was he having an affair with someone in Cambridge? It hardly seemed likely. Ranji had never in the past shown any inclination to chase after other women and their marriage was so happy that there seemed no reason why he should start now. But the thought did cross her mind, and it was perhaps Ranji's sensitivity to her feelings which made him at last confess: "Well, if you want to know, I was looking for a job."

The unexpected answer turned her questioning to puzzlement. "Why do you want a job when you've got your own firm?" For the past five years Ranji had run a contract cleaning business. He employed a predominantly Indian work force to provide regular office cleaning and also—more lucratively—to clear up new properties after the departure of the builders and maintain them in immaculate condition until a tenant had signed a lease. Sometimes, when he recognized a bargain, he took over the lease himself and sublet at a profit, but this kind of gamble was only a sideline: it was the service he offered which provided his main income.

"I *used* to have my own firm," Ranji corrected her. "That was three months ago. The property market collapsed last year. Perhaps you didn't notice."

"What difference—"

He sighed before beginning a patient explanation. "As soon as prices slumped, the banks got cold feet and called in the loans they'd been almost forcing on people a year or two earlier. The loans were secured on properties which couldn't find a buyer and weren't in any case likely to realize the inflated values placed on them; but they were put on the market anyway, and so prices fell again. Two of my most important customers went bankrupt and most of the others had to cut down on their expenses. I was left with bad debts and no new work coming in. And *I* had a bank loan as well. My bank manager didn't have the sense to work out that he was more likely to get his money back from a going concern than from a man on the dole. He read my balance sheet and saw that it didn't balance. So he demanded repayment of the loan. I couldn't pay, of course. He put a liquidator in to discover what assets I had."

"Ranji, does all this mean that you'll be made bankrupt?"

"Yes, indeed. And since half my assets are claims on other companies which are now bankrupt themselves, it's difficult to see how I can earn my discharge."

Asha took his hand and squeezed it sympathetically, wondering if there was anything she could do to help. "Do you think Aunt Alexa—?"

"No," said Ranji. "This isn't the sort of amount she might keep in her piggy bank. Even after I've handed over everything I've saved in the past five years there'll be thousands of pounds still owing, and if I borrowed it, I might never be able to pay it back. Besides, she doesn't even like me. You can forget that idea."

"Darling, I'm so sorry about this. Buy why didn't you tell me? You must have been worrying about it for weeks."

"Oddly enough," said Ranji stiffly, "confessing to one's wife that one has made a mess of things is not the most morale-raising of occupations. I agree that I ought to have told you. But I was waiting for something positive to put against it. Such as, 'I'm afraid the business has gone bust but I've landed an absolutely super job, so we'll be back to living on two steady salaries again and isn't it simply marvelous!"

"That's fine as far as other people are concerned. But I'm your wife. Anything that happens to you is happening to me as well. I want to share everything with you. Even the bad days."

"Well, you know now."

Asha kissed him affectionately, understanding that the deception which had sparked off their argument could be explained by his shame. Yet even as she forgave him for the small untruth she was aware in the back of her mind of a niggling annoyance, too petty to be put into words. Instead of leaving the flat at his usual time every morning during the past few weeks, and keeping away during his normal working hours, could Ranji not have contributed rather more time to the running of the household—taking over some of the chores, or at least sharing them, instead of leaving them to a woman who was still doing a tiring day's work? The bookcase, for example. Ranji, like herself, had been in the flat when it toppled over. But only Asha had genuinely needed to hurry off to work that morning, and only Asha had been genuinely worn out in the evening.

She had enough sense to know that this was not the moment to criticize him. "Did you get the job?" she asked.

"Which job? I've applied for dozens. Nowadays, no one's allowed to put 'white skin preferred' in a newspaper advertisement, but that doesn't stop the preference from existing. And running your own business isn't the best qualification for becoming an employee. People are afraid you may not be able to fit into a team. In any case, with so many firms going out of business, there are dozens of chaps with better qualifications floating around."

Worried and helpless, Asha could only kiss him again. "Ranji, darling, I'm so terribly sorry," she repeated. "From now on we must discuss everything together. I do hope it won't be long before you find something. And at least we shan't starve while you're looking." Too late she recognized that this was the wrong thing to say.

"Yes, indeed. It's just as well that I'm married to a successful career woman."

Asha did her best to ignore what seemed almost a note of grievance in his voice, and applied herself to the task of cheering her husband up. He was in no mood to discuss his job prospects any further, so she asked instead about the cricket match. It proved to be a tactful question. In return for Ranji's description of the wickets he had taken, Asha might have pointed to the neatly stocked bookcase, clean, upright, secure, as a token of her own achievement. Instead, she waited for him to notice it, and was disappointed. Nor did he inquire about her visit to the nursing home. Her niggling feeling of resentment returned and she held back her news until he should be interested enough to ask. Chris had carried the portrait up to the attic to await its cleaning, so there was nothing visible to prompt a question about her ancestor.

The last ten days of term were, as always, hectic. In school hours there were tests to be given and marked, books to be collected and all the special events which marked the end of the school year to be organized. In the evenings there was the usual last-minute rush of reports to be written. It was difficult for Asha—still working busily at nine o'clock one evening—to hear without irritation Ranji's inquiries about when she was going to get supper.

"Couldn't you?" she asked.

"If you'd thought to provide any food, no doubt I could try to cook it."

"Isn't there— Oh, I'm sorry. I was on dinner duty, so I couldn't get out to the shops. But we've got cheese and onions and tomatoes and plenty of eggs."

Ranji made a Spanish omelette and burned it. Asha picked at the meal without appetite. Her husband's inadequacy in the kitchen was largely her own fault. Neither in India nor as a student in England had he had the opportunity to learn to cook. Asha had been equally incompetent when they first married. They could have experimented and learned together. Instead of that, it had seemed a matter of pride that she should be responsible for all the domestic duties as well as doing her job. What a stupid, old-fashioned attitude! But she rather feared that it might now be too late to change.

"I *am* sorry to be so disorganized, Ranji," she said. "But the end of term is such an awful time. As soon as the holidays begin, I'll get things straight again. Just for this week, when I'm busy and you're not, could you give me a hand? If I make out a list, would you do some shopping tomorrow?"

"I have an interview tomorrow."

"All day?" But she could tell that what seemed to her a small and reasonable request was to him a humiliation. "Ranji, I understand how you feel. But it seems silly not to recognize that your commitments have changed. Why can't we adapt to the change—and adapt again when you get a job?"

"*If* I get a job."

Asha made no further comment. But that night she lay awake for a long time, unhappy with herself. For twelve years she had prided herself on her ability to do her work as a schoolteacher well and at the same time to be a good wife. Now she saw that she was only a good wife to a husband so much absorbed in his own business that he was glad to think of her standing on her own feet, having her own interests and responsibilities. In this changed situation her hard work was a reproach to him. What he needed now was the support of a clinging, fussing homemaker.

Paradoxically, though, he could only afford that kind of support when he was working. A few days earlier, in the empty attic, Asha had allowed herself to dream of babies in a nursery: but that dream could not be fulfilled until Ranji became a breadwinner again. So for the sake of their future family Ranji's period of unemployment must be as short as possible: and for the sake of his pride they must together do their best to earn his discharge from bankruptcy. There must be no more of the suppressed resentment which had spoiled the evening for them both. Asha saw that she must make it her responsibility to build up her husband's self-respect again—and, if possible, she must help him to find a job.

I I I

The school holidays began, and at once the atmosphere was lighter. With Ranji's lack of occupation admitted, they could spend whole days together, walking in the country or exploring the city like tourists. They were friends again. But beneath their happiness, Ranji's unemployment ticked away like a time bomb which might at any time explode to shatter his good temper and plunge him into gloom.

Since there were no longer any secrets between them, Asha was allowed to read her husband's file of advertisements and letters of application, and the discouraging replies clipped to each sheet. She sympathized with his resolve not to take unsatisfactory work just for the sake of working. He was determined to be a successful businessman and would consider only openings which led in this direction. But all over the country companies were cutting down on staff rather than taking on new employees. What could he do?

One way of earning a living was on view every Saturday from the windows of the flat. "How about renting a stall in the Portobello Road market?" Asha suggested. "Or a cubicle in one of the arcades? I could find out from the tenants downstairs whether anyone's thinking of giving up."

"Not a practical idea, I think." Now that the first humiliation of confession was over, Ranji did his best to show appreciation of Asha's suggestions and to control the easy reaction of sarcasm, but that did not prevent him from demolishing her ideas with decisive logic. "In the first place, I have no knowledge of the antique trade. In the second place, I have no capital with which to buy an initial stock. And in the third place, a bankrupt person is forbidden to borrow or to accept any kind of credit."

His tone did not allow for argument. Asha changed the subject, but the idea must have lingered in the back of her mind. It was Chris who indirectly tempted it back to the surface in a new form.

Chris arrived at the flat without warning toward the end of the summer holiday. "I've come to give Mr. Lorimer his bath."

"Come in." Asha was delighted to see him. "But what on earth have you brought with you?"

"If you remember, you promised that I could paint your portrait as a reward for cleaning your great-granddaddy."

"Did I? No, I don't remember."

"Well, you did. Not just one portrait, either. Asha by Bonnard, Asha by Renoir, Asha by Vermeer. What I have here is a perfectly frightful portrait of some Georgian squire, complete with a decent frame, which I was able to buy for less than the cost of a new canvas.

I propose to obliterate the old codger with some tasteful background and substitute a portrait of Asha by Gainsborough. And with that in mind I've persuaded one of your neighbors downstairs to lend you a dress." He was in the drawing room of the flat by now, unpacking a long gown of pale-gray silk shot with pink, and an overskirt of silvery lace. "The dress was made for someone so thin or so tightly laced that no potential customer has yet been able to make it meet round the waist. But since you're only going to stand still, no one will know that the bodice is held together at the back with tape and safety pins. Will you try it on straightaway, so that I can work out the pose?"

"I'm being hustled," said Asha; but she was smiling. The long holiday had enabled her to relax. Although her new responsibilities as deputy headmistress included such tasks as the drawing up of a complicated timetable, she had disposed of these early in the vacation and could feel the next few days to be truly free.

Slim though she was, she found that Chris was right about the impossibility of fastening the tiny buttons at the back of the dress. What he had not thought to mention was the extreme lowness of the décolletage. The tight cut of the bodice imposed its own line, pushing up her breasts in an authentically revealing eighteenth-century style. She flushed in slight embarrassment as she studied her appearance in the glass before making her way up to the attic.

"Gorgeous!" exclaimed Chris, taking the almost topless style for granted. "Absolutely super! Now. Stand as straight as you can, here. Head right up. You're a duchess at the very least. This chair is a parasol. Rest your hand on it languidly. One toe forward. Now look into the distance, over my head. Oh, Asha, marvelous!" He began to sketch the pose. "Thank goodness you haven't acquired a tan. All the way here I was wondering whether I might have to do Asha by Gauguin first. If I leave photographs with you, could you practice putting your hair up, dressing it round some kind of pad? Gainsborough's sitters wove their hair into a sort of bird's nest and then didn't wash it for a year, but all I need is an approximation. It will alter the shape of your face. I'll copy a balustrade and a couple of steps from one of the genuine pictures. Keep your chin up. No smiling. Haughtiness is the name of the game. Complete confidence in your own beauty and elegance."

His nonstop chatter made it clear that Asha must not reply, lest an everyday conversation should tempt her to relax the stiffness of her back, the tilt of her head. When at last she was allowed to move she stretched her muscles before taking a look at his work.

"You can't tell anything from a pencil sketch," he warned her. "This is only to help me plan the background."

"Will you really be able to make the picture look genuine?"

"I'm not attempting deception," Chris pointed out. "I'm using modern paints, and although I can produce the same texture and finish I shan't be as meticulous about brushstrokes as a forger would. Let's say that if you were to hang the finished picture on the wall of a stately home which didn't happen to possess any real Gainsboroughs, the casual visitor—not the expert, of course—might just think he was seeing one. And if you put it in your sitting room when it's finished and claim that it's an ancestral portrait—like old Mr. Lorimer, but prettier—I doubt if anyone will challenge you."

"I'm surprised you don't take that up as a second career," Asha laughed. "Painting mock ancestors for people."

"No business sense, that's my problem. I could paint them, but I'd never be able to sell them. And anyway, there'd be competition in the mock ancestor field." He gestured toward the painting which he had set down next to that of John Junius Lorimer: a primitive, two-dimensional portrait of a wooden-faced country squire in hunting pink. "Ugly old chap, but he must have been somebody's great-great-grandfather, and he was up for grabs. Anyone who was more concerned with inventing a past than acquiring a work of art could have claimed him as an ancestor."

"Was it very expensive?" asked Asha thoughtfully. An idea was germinating in her mind.

"Dirt cheap. If he'd had a fancy gold frame, that would have been a different matter. These dealers who go round knocking on doors, offering to buy pictures for the value of the frames—they may hope to pick up an unrecognized Rembrandt; but in the meantime they're buying what they claim to want. The pictures are mainly junk, and the countryside is full of them." As he talked, Chris began to dab the portrait of John Junius Lorimer with pads dipped into three bowls of strong-smelling liquids. Asha watched in silence, developing her inspiration, trying to find the snags.

"I often watch the tourists in the Portobello market," she said.

"Sometimes they only want a souvenir. But often I have the feeling that they're looking for a past. An American buys a Georgian silver teapot, and it links her personally with some stately drawing room. Buyers like that might be in the market for ancestral portraits—if only it could be made easy. The old masters in the auction houses are too expensive. But suppose—" While Chris continued to rub and dab, Asha pulled up the skirts of her long dress and sat cross-legged on the floor. The idea was taking shape.

"None of us has any capital." She was thinking aloud now. "So we couldn't acquire a large selection of old portraits. Not enough, anyway, to fill a gallery and attract buyers who wanted a choice. But suppose we did it the other way round. Collected orders first and filled them afterwards. Asking for a deposit with each order. Cash flow, that's what Ranji says is the most important thing in running a business."

"You're going too fast for me. What are you talking about, and who do you mean by 'we'?"

"You and me and Ranji. Ranji because he knows how to run a business. You because you know about pictures. And me because it's my brilliant idea." And because if we need to borrow money to start with, the loan will have to be to me and not to Ranji, she thought: but there was no need for Chris to know about the conditions of bankruptcy.

"And what precisely is this brilliant idea?"

"Well, just suppose. Suppose we were to print a leaflet and get it distributed in some WASPish part of the States. The leaflet would invite the reader to order an ancestral portrait. It would be clear from the start that it couldn't possibly be his real ancestor. But we'd take some trouble to find the right kind of picture. And if he bought it, he could say whatever he liked about it afterwards."

"It seems to me that we should be provoking terminological inexactitudes for profit," Chris said solemnly. "But go on."

"Well"—Asha was still thinking aloud—"to get into the scheme, the prospective buyer would send us information about what country his family originally emigrated from, and when. And he could send family photographs, so that we could look for a vague likeness. He'd pay a fee with his application. We'd call it a search fee and it wouldn't be refundable; but if he actually bought one of the pictures we offered him, his payment would be deducted from the cost."

"So you'd hand me a photograph of some Russian Jewish grandmother and send me out to scour the Home Counties for some face that could have been her father!"

"Don't be negative, Chris! This could work. We'd make it clear in the brochure that we'd mainly be drawing on British portraits. And in exchange for their search fee, we'd send people photographs of possibilities—three, perhaps, at different prices, to choose from. Seriously, wouldn't that make a nice little business? It would cost a bit for the publicity and the first half dozen pictures, but after that it ought to be self-financing."

"I see two prospects," said Chris. "Either the idea would be a complete flop and we'd lose any money we'd put into it: or it would be a success, and we wouldn't be able to cope with it. It's one thing to pick up a country squire like this just for the sake of the canvas. But to scour country sales and private houses with special features in mind would be a full-time job. Not to mention packing and insurance and all the filing and bookkeeping and registering as a company if one has to do that and paying taxes and God knows what else."

"Ranji could do all that. It would have to be Ranji's business. You and I would be consultants, taking a commission or charging for our time. If Ranji bought cheap pictures, they might need to be cleaned or restored, for example. You could do that, couldn't you?"

Chris had ceased to look doubtful and instead appeared to be considering some new proposition. "You mustn't think that I'm in any way encouraging this folly," he said after a long pause. "But I could fling one more mad idea into the pool. Earlier on you suggested that I could paint mock ancestors for people. Well, it's true: I could. If you sent out three photographs to a prospective buyer, two could be of portraits which were genuinely old but unlikely to show any resemblance to the buyer. The third could be of a picture painted by me, showing a face with a family likeness to any photographs the buyer submitted, plus period costume. Instead of Asha by Gainsborough, Mrs. John J. Doe by Gainsborough. Of course, it would have to be made clear from the start that that portrait would be painted by me now, in the twentieth century. No false pretenses."

"Absolutely not. Could you really do it, Chris?"

"You'd better wait and see how this one turns out. But yes, if I have any talent at all, it's for this. And as a matter of fact"—now it was Chris's turn to express enthusiasm—"it would be possible to build up a stock in advance. In America, you know, before photography, there were itinerant portrait painters. Primitives. They'd call at the richest-looking houses offering to paint the children of the family. And to save time, they'd carry with them pictures of children of various sizes in party clothes, finished except for the head. So Mamma would order a four-year-old boy and little Junior's face would be added to a white satin suit. If I bought myself a couple of shopwindow mannequins, I could have a few headless costume pieces ready by the time your first brochure drew blood."

"Is it possible, Chris? I mean, am I completely raving, or could we make it work?"

"I don't know whether a market exists," said Chris, more seriously than before. "I certainly don't know how we find it if it does. I have no capital to contribute, though I could run to the frames and canvases of my first offerings. I have a job, so for thirty weeks of the year my free time is limited. You also have a job, more demanding than mine. So *I* can't make it work. *You* can't make it work. It would all depend on Ranji."

Asha sat for a long time without speaking. Ranji must not have a second failure, and with such a speculative idea the risk of failure must be high indeed. It would be better if he could find himself secure employment. But then, every week which brought him only letters of rejection represented a failure—of a different kind, but equally hard to bear.

Holding up the skirt of her long dress she stood up and crossed the room to study the progress of Chris's cleaning work. He had just reached her great-grandfather's hair, which beneath the dark-yellow varnish proved to be white and curly. This was the portrait of a real person, with his own eighty years of history. Her aunt Alexa, no doubt, had tales to tell about the dramas of his life, his loves, his successes and failures. Asha found herself interested, excited.

"Could you find another canvas to use for your mock Gainsborough?" she asked Chris. "Leave the squire as he is, wooden face and all. With John Junius next to him—not to be sold, but as an example.

And then the fancy-dress picture of me when it's ready. We'll show all three to Ranji at once—to let him see the possibilities. After that, as you say, it would be up to him."

IV

Ranji considered Asha's suggestion for setting up a cottage industry more seriously than she had expected. No doubt what appealed to him most was the possibility of running his own business again, on however small a scale. Asha suspected that he felt no great enthusiasm for the prospect of working as a subordinate in a large company. He spent less time reading job advertisements and writing letters of application, and instead devoted much of the day to all the formalities which Chris had rightly guessed to be necessary at the start of a new venture.

Everything had to be done in Asha's name: her husband was not allowed to own a credit card or even a checkbook. In any case, Ranji was determined to earn an honorable discharge from bankruptcy by paying everything he owed, but was clear that this could only be done from the profits of a thriving concern; so the precarious income of the new venture must also be Asha's to start with. Inevitably there was a period of several months in which no receipts could be expected at all, while money had to be spent on printers' bills, postage, registration fees and Ranji's first buying expeditions to country auctions. Asha was careful never to show anything but confidence in his handling of the project—although sometimes, as she signed the documents and blank checks he put before her, she felt uneasy at the speed with which their savings shrank and their commitments grew.

It was just as well that nothing more than encouragement and signatures were required of her, for her first year as deputy headmistress was a punishing one, and as the end of the summer term approached she could feel herself wilting as visibly as the geraniums in her window boxes. The summer of 1975 had been hot enough: but the summer of 1976 rapidly carried England to an officially recognized state of drought. The huge panels of glass which chilled Hillgate Comprehensive School in winter had during the past six weeks transformed the building into a greenhouse in which pupils and teachers alike drooped listlessly. As she stood in front of a class of fifteen-year-olds on the last Friday in June, Asha—quite as fervently as any of her pupils—was longing to hear the sound of the four-o'clock bell.

This was her least favorite period of the week. She enjoyed teaching the school's sixth-formers, whose enthusiasm and hard work reflected the fact that they had chosen to stay on after they could legally have left. She also had a particular affection for the eleven- and twelve-year-olds who arrived bright-eyed from their primary schools and for a year or two remained obedient and appreciative. But the fifth form, overweighted with children who knew they would never achieve any paper qualifications and who sullenly sat out what they saw as their last year of imprisonment in school, provided the blackest spots on the timetable.

Every lesson was liable to become a battleground. Today's opponent was Leroy Wilson. She had asked him a question and he had replied insolently. When she repeated it, he turned his back ostentatiously and took out a comb. At least, for the moment it was a comb as he drew through his curly black hair the six pointed steel spikes which could just as easily become an offensive weapon. Asha recognized that he was pretending to threaten her—and knew that it was quite in the cards that the threat would become a real one. Four members of the staff already this year had been attacked by their pupils—quite apart from the headmaster, who had spent a week in the hospital after being visited by the father of a boy he had caned. Leroy Wilson was a burly West Indian who could easily overcome Asha in a struggle. All she had on her side was the intangible weapon of authority. She used it now.

"Leroy. Put that comb back in your pocket and turn round to face me."

The boy did not turn. She had not expected him to. Having made a first gesture of confrontation he would need some means of saving face before he could back down. Asha waited for only a few seconds.

"Leroy Wilson, I've asked you a question and you're going to answer it. The bell will ring in three minutes' time, but no one in this class is going home until you've given me a proper answer."

Now she would have to wait for the bell. It was a long three minutes. Asha stood beside her desk, studying the fidgeting but silent class.

Hillgate was perhaps the most multiracial school in London. Civil wars, revolutions, government repression and natural disasters all over the world were reflected in its register. There were Lebanese children, Arabs and Iranians: Greeks from Greece and Greeks from Cyprus; Turks, Irish, Vietnamese, Chinese and Pakistanis, together with South Americans who were almost certainly illegal immigrants. There were Indians from India and others—a quite separate group—who had never lived in the subcontinent but had arrived, penniless, in England after being expelled from Kenya or Uganda. Many of these had been prosperous in Africa and had taken a surprisingly short time to succeed in their new country. Their children, intelligent and hardworking, were Asha's most rewarding pupils.

But all these—and even the native English children—were minorities, for half of Hillgate's pupils were of West Indian descent. There were ten others besides Leroy in this classroom. If they stood up as a group and pushed their way out of the door, there was no way in which Asha could stop them.

The four o'clock bell shrilled out and from all along the corridor came the immediate sounds of shouting and the slamming of desks. Her own class instinctively stirred; but Asha, moving slightly toward the doorway, put up a hand to quieten them.

"Now, Leroy," she said. "I'm sure you don't want to stay here any more than the rest of us do. Turn round, please, and stand up. If you can't answer my question in your own words, you may read out the paragraph at the bottom of page twenty-eight."

There was one more moment of tension; then the boy shrugged his shoulders jauntily and gabbled through the paragraph. Asha thanked him and the class erupted noisily into the corridor. She let out a long breath. What kind of a victory was that? Her aim as a teacher—and her special ability—was to arouse enthusiasm as well as imparting knowledge. But in this section of the school she was unfairly handicapped by a curriculum and an examination system which had nothing to offer a boy like Leroy—and he had just enough intelligence to know it.

Well, the battle was over for another week. How delightful it would be if she could not make her leisurely way home, relax under a cool shower, help herself to a drink and enjoy a glass of wine with a meal cooked by someone else. She sighed again. Her actual program required her to get her skates on if she were to reach the health center before it closed for the day.

The council estate in which the center was situated had a bleak atmosphere. In winter the wind howled down forlorn concrete corridors: now the drought had brought a different kind of desolation. Dust hovered in the windless air and the sound of babies' crying came through a score of open windows. Notices forbade the playing of ball games on the grass, but there was no longer any grass. On one corner of the baked mud two girls in bikinis were stretching out to improve their suntans. Asha recognized the girls as Hillgate pupils, gigglers who were waiting impatiently for the time when they could leave.

Leave for what? Asha asked herself as she walked briskly on. It was a question which often worried her as she taught her least intelligent pupils. In a few months' time these girls, no doubt, would be shampooing hair or serving in a shop, spending their evenings at discos, doing their best to entice some poor boy away from his mates and his football matches in order that as soon as possible they should be able to escape from their parents, put their own names down on the council housing lists and end up—where? In another flat on this terrible estate? Could that really be anyone's ambition?

The trouble was that few of her pupils had an ambition at all. The white children were almost as apathetic as the blacks, who took it for granted that they would fail their exams and be offered the worst jobs. Unlike the bright-eyed, competitive Asians, most of these children were not prepared to make any kind of effort.

Asha had decided long ago that the difference must lie in the attitude of the parents. The Asians from Kenya and Uganda who had struggled back to prosperity in England knew that it was possible to succeed by hard work. They were determined that their children should do well and offered not only encouragement and discipline but also the example of achievement.

By contrast, the mothers of those two sunbathing fifteen-year-olds had probably thought school a waste of time themselves, and accepted the same attitude in their daughters without wondering whether a little more enthusiasm for education might not pay dividends in the form of a more interesting life. Asha wondered where it would ever be possible to break through the habit of apathy. For the giggling girls it was already too late; and they—no doubt very soon— would be the equally unsupportive mothers of the next generation of schoolchildren. The circle seemed closed.

With this discouraging reflection Asha reached the health center, a low brick building which changed its function according to the day of the week and the time of day. Room four had been a prenatal clinic in the morning but was now the family planning clinic.

Dr. Clarke did not, as usually happened, scribble a prescription while asking a few routine questions about Asha's general health. "Let's see," she said thoughtfully instead. "How old are you now, dear?"

"Thirty-five."

"And you've been taking the pill for—what?—thirteen years? I think I must advise you that it's time to stop."

"But why?" Asha was dismayed. Although she wanted to start a pregnancy as soon as it became practicable, the time was not yet ripe for her to abandon the regular salary which was supporting Ranji as well as herself. The first inquiries about ancestral portraits had begun to arrive in the spring, and the search fees which accompanied them made a welcome contribution to the new balance sheet; but Ranji had yet to make his first actual sale.

"As you grow older, the pill can produce a dangerous side effect of clotting in the blood. And although it hasn't been finally proved, the risk is thought to be greater for women who've been taking it for a considerable period. At thirty-five you're approaching the risk area on the first count; you've already reached it on the second. I'd be happy to discuss it with you again in a year or so. But for the time being I think you should consider the alternatives."

"But—"

"There are plenty of contraceptive methods which are nearly as reliable as the pill. We can see which suits you best. Or, of course, there's one completely foolproof way. If you've decided not to have a family, your husband might consider a vasectomy."

"We haven't decided that at all," exclaimed Asha. "I want to have children. It's just rather awkward at the moment. If I could keep on as I am just for a few months—"

"If you seriously plan to have a child, then I would in any case recommend you to come off the pill for a few months first; so that wouldn't affect my advice. And I do think, dear, that you ought not to stretch that 'few months' too long. I don't want to be alarmist, but with every year that passes there's a slightly higher risk of problems with a first pregnancy—risks both to you and to the baby."

Asha, aware of this, did not argue further. She allowed herself to be examined and was thoughtful as she walked home.

Ranji greeted her with good news. "We have our first orders! Two on the same day. A family in Virginia wants something like the mock Gainsborough which Chris did of you. And a Dutch woman from Pennsylvania has fallen for the hideous Pothoven family group which has been in the gallery across the road for a year. I took a four-week option on it before I sent the photographs and told her we could offer a genuine old master if she made up her mind quickly."

"I'm surprised she recognized Pothoven as being an old master."

"As well as the photograph of the picture itself, I sent the good lady a copy of Pothoven's page in our encyclopedia of art. It spoke most highly of the gentleman. So we have two customers."

"I'm so glad. Congratulations, darling." Asha sat down, encouraged by his satisfaction to raise the matter which troubled her. "Ranji, I've been to the family planning clinic." She told him what the doctor had said. "She was right. If we're going to have a family, we ought to start now. Or very soon."

"Soon, perhaps, if you wish to; but not now. How could we?"

"Well, if the ancestors are taking off—"

"We have two customers, that's all. And from the money they send I must buy the Pothoven, pay Chris to paint a Gainsborough, and pack and insure and dispatch the pictures. We're only acting as an agency, Asha. The client may seem to be paying a good price, but not much will stick to our fingers. And we must pay off the starting expenses first."

"But as more and more orders come in—"

"*If* they do. It's still a speculation. We need your salary."

"We'd have it for the first seven months of a pregnancy. I'd go on working. Then I'd get maternity benefit for a bit when I stopped. And my job would be protected by law: I could go back three months after the birth if we found we couldn't manage."

"It's all very well to have a job kept open. But how could you work with a young baby?"

"He could stay with you. It would only be in term time. You'd be working from home anyway, and babies sleep most of the day."

"I know nothing about looking after babies."

"Nor do I. We could learn together."

"But, darling—" Ranji gave a helpless laugh. "If you're to look forward to giving up your job, it's all the more important that I must work hard to get the business going. And you know that I'm *not* at home all day. How would I go to sales? With a cot on the back seat? Breaking off in the middle of an auction to make a bottle warm? I look forward as much as you to the time when we shall have our own family. But I must earn enough to support my wife and bring up my children. How can they be proud of their father if they see it is only their mother who pays for the food they eat?"

"Nobody cares about that sort of thing nowadays, Ranji."

"*I* care."

The decisive note in Ranji's voice startled Asha into realizing that she was not giving sufficient consideration to her husband's feelings. Bankruptcy and unemployment together could dent the dignity and self-confidence of even the most resilient man. It was understandable that Ranji should be reluctant to agree to a major change in their life together if this would result in yet another blow to his pride.

"The time will come, Asha. Be patient." The softness returned to his voice as he tried to comfort her; but she was not convinced.

"There are two ways of looking at time, Ranji, don't you see? If I were still in my twenties, of course we could wait until we were more secure. But I'm not young anymore and time's running out and soon it will be now or never." Her voice trembled, revealing how much the doctor's warning had upset her.

Ranji put his arm round her shoulders. "Have you had a bad day at school?"

"Yes. Well, no." It was only the last period which had proved a strain. Earlier in the afternoon a mock election had provided a lively current affairs session with her favorite twelve-year-olds, and in the morning she had been proctoring examinations. "No, a good day."

"And yet you're tired. This work is a strain for you. You earn your salary and you look after me and the flat, and that is two lives. When you have a baby, that will make a third. Three is too many—and there would be crying at night. You would be tired all the time. Besides, there would be extra costs. The flat, for example, isn't big enough for a child."

"The attic would make a marvelous nursery and playroom," Asha pointed out.

"Chris must have the attic for painting the pictures which would feed the baby, and for storing those I buy. We would need a bigger place to live. I can't get a mortgage until I'm discharged from bankruptcy. You wouldn't get a mortgage without a regular job."

"Perhaps Aunt Alexa—" A year earlier, Asha had been quick to recognize that her great-aunt could not be approached to settle Ranji's debts. It would be a different matter, though, to ask for support at the time of starting a family. But even as she spoke, Asha was doubtful. The rise in the cost of living during the past two years might at last be adding substance to the complaints of poverty with which Alexa had greeted every income tax demand for the past thirty years. Asha stood up and began to wander thoughtfully about the flat. It was true that there would be no room for a baby unless the attic could be used. She went up the stairs to the top floor.

The attic was lighter than she remembered it. Crossing to the window, she saw the reason at once. The Dutch elm disease had reached the end of the line of elms and brown, curled leaves were falling unseasonably in a steady, rustling shower from the nearest tree. Well, no doubt the extra light was good for Chris's painting. He had set up his easel in the center of the room, surrounding it with a clutter of reference books and jam jars full of long-handled brushes. A dummy, bald-headed and bare-legged, wore a cravat of which Beau Brummel would have been proud, with a brocade coat which Asha recognized from the school production of *The Rivals*.

Around this central area the pictures bought by Ranji on his country expeditions were neatly racked, with empty frames stacked in one corner. And all this was quite apart from the space downstairs which had been taken over by filing cabinets and a desk. Ranji was quite right. They would need to find either a new nursery or else a new studio, storeroom and office.

It could do no harm to find out what Alexa's financial position was. Asha had never asked for anything before—and she did not intend to ask now if it seemed that a request for a loan would cause anxiety. But if it should prove that her ninety-nine-year-old relation was nursing a small fortune—well, at least she could test the water. Asha went to find Ranji again.

"You remember it's my Oxford Gaudy weekend tomorrow," she reminded him. She had cleared the engagement with him several weeks earlier. "I'd like to take the car, if that's all right." The car was her own, and she had paid for its MOT test, service and road tax and for the gas in the tank. Asking for permission to use it was part of the process of keeping up Ranji's morale during his bankruptcy: a reassurance that he was still the head of the family.

"There's a good train service to Oxford," said Ranji. Probably he had hoped to drive himself to wherever he was playing cricket.

"I'm not going straight there, though," Asha told him. "And the cross-country journey would be hopeless. I want to call on Aunt Alexa on the way."

V

The ground-floor room of the nursing home in which Alexa would spend the rest of her life was spacious and light. From her bed she could look out at the grounds of the manor, while on a wide shelf beneath the window, house plants clustered in a thriving indoor garden. The shelf continued along the wall which faced her bed, supporting a remote-control television set and Alexa's own record player and stereo speakers, as well as her large library of records. There had been space for very few of her personal possessions in the room which now constituted her whole world: she had chosen to furnish it with music.

Little in Alexa's surroundings changed from visit to visit. The room was always clean and sweet-smelling, the flowers were always fresh and the bedside table stocked with whatever drink was appropriate to the season. Today a jug of fresh lemon juice stood beside a thermos flask of iced water. Asha gratefully accepted the invitation to pour herself a drink, for the day—like every other in the past two months

—was blisteringly hot, unrefreshed by any breeze. As she handed a glass to her great-aunt, her eye was caught by a change in the scenery.

"What's this?" she asked, crossing to the window. In the middle of a group of house plants stood a bronze statue of a dancing figure.

"Turn it away from me," Alexa commanded. For many years the tone of her voice had been imperious, and this effect was heightened by the breathlessness of old age, which clipped her speech into a series of staccato statements or instructions. "Nasty sly face. I don't like it looking at me. Let it look out of the window. That'll give a nasty shock to anyone who stares in!"

"But what is it?"

"Siva Dancing, Bernard calls it. A nasty heathen god."

"Were you too polite to tell him you didn't like it?"

"He didn't bring it as a gift. Asked me to keep it as a favor. So I didn't have to pretend. Wouldn't have let it stay if I'd known it was going to annoy me. But it's all right like that, I suppose."

"I still don't understand—"

"Bernard bought it off some sculptor. And Helen can't stand it. Won't have it in the house. He doesn't want to sell it. So he asked if it could lodge here. Hopes Helen will come round to it later, I suppose. I think it's something to do with that bad patch they went through a while back. Seem to have made it up now, though. I'm glad about that. Especially for Helen. Bernard's got his work. But when a woman doesn't have children and doesn't have a job, she needs a husband. Just to talk to, you know, as a friend, even if the rest isn't so important anymore."

"Do you think she's sorry she didn't have children?" From the earliest years of her childhood Asha had been on affectionate terms with her cousin Bernard, in spite of their difference in age. But she had never become intimate with his wife. Helen, calm and elegant, seemed content with a life devoted only to gracious living: the smooth running of a country house and a London flat. Asha, always busy, found it hard to imagine how Helen spent her time. The two women had little to talk about when they met.

"Of course she's sorry," said Alexa without hesitation. "But she can't start now. Not after a hysterectomy. So there's no point in her weeping about it."

"How old were you, Aunt Alexa, when Pirry was born?"

It took a moment for Alexa to work it out. "Thirty-six."

"And it was all right, was it, having a baby at thirty-six?"

Age had robbed Alexa of mobility but had had no effect on her intelligence. "Thinking of starting, are you, dear?" she asked, bright-eyed with interest. "Yes, thirty-six was all right. Pirry was a beautiful baby. Something you should remember, though. Nobody tells you at the time. Then they say you should have known. This pill you all take. Makes you feel you're in control. You can decide when you don't want a baby. So you think you can decide when you *will* have a baby. Not always so easy. I used to think it unfair. Girls who didn't want babies were landed with them. Those who did want one sometimes couldn't manage it. You young ones, you've only cured half the problem. Remember that."

"You mean that you can't always start a pregnancy straightaway? I know that."

"That's part of it. The other part is that pregnancies go wrong. No one warns you. They don't want to frighten you. But it happens. It took me three years to have Pirry. One baby died. Then a miscarriage."

"You must have wanted him very much."

"Pirry was the price I paid for a happy marriage. Piers wanted an heir, and I was in love with him. Whatever he needed, I wanted to give him. But in a different marriage I could have been happy without children. Had my own career, you see. Like you. It seemed worthwhile to me. Does yours?"

"Yes," said Asha. "Yes, it does. Most of the time, at least."

"I know how you feel," said Alexa unexpectedly. "Time passing. This year, you still have a choice. In five years' time, not. You're tempted to do what's possible now just because it won't be later. You need to be very sure, dear. And clear about *why* you want children, if you do. If I'd chosen to have Pirry to look after me in my old age, I'd have lost out, wouldn't I? But I had him to make Piers happy, and that was all that ever mattered."

There was a quick tap on the door. A nurse looked in, smiled at Asha and closed the door again.

"They're good girls," Alexa commented. "I'll say this for the Brownlows." Mr. and Mrs. Brownlow were the owners of the nursing home. "They charge the earth, but they pay well. So the nurses stay. I like that. No chopping and changing just as you've got used to someone. Every afternoon one of them pops in for a chat. When you get to my age, you don't have many friends left to come visiting."

"You can manage the charges all right, can you, Aunt Alexa?" Asha had hoped for a lead of this kind. "You're not worried about money?"

"Always worried about money since that wretched socialist government after the war. But it was Pirry who played me the worst trick. Promised that he'd survive me, and then died. Only fifty-two. And he knew what it would mean."

"Yes, it was rotten for you, having to leave Blaize."

"It wasn't just Blaize I lost. You wouldn't remember. There'd been a house in Park Lane as well. Bombed in the war. We had compensation, and a good price when we sold the site for a hotel. But the lawyers said all that money was the equivalent of the house. Part of the entailed property. Pirry and I, we could use the income from that capital. But when Pirry died, it all went with the title. When you've had a fortune and lost it, it's harder than if you'd always been poor."

"But you've got enough to pay the bills, have you?"

Alexa's bright eyes sparkled with triumph. "I did well there," she boasted. "Bought an annuity when I was ninety. Dirt cheap. They didn't think I'd live so long. It was enough until I came here last year. But the costs keep going up. It's all the fault of the Arabs, they tell me, being greedy about their oil. I'm having to break into my savings, a little every quarter. But there's enough to last me until I'm a hundred and two. After that I shall have to throw myself on your mercy."

"I'll start saving now," Asha promised her. "The Aunt-Alexa-hundred-and-third-birthday fund." She stood up. "I must go now, Aunt Alexa. Sorry it's been such a flying visit. But it's my Gaudy weekend."

"Gaudy? What's Gaudy?"

"Old Girls' reunion for Dame Eleanor's College. It happens every year, a week after term ends at Oxford. I've never been before. But if I stay on at Hillgate, I have a chance of being head next year. It's one of the things I've got to decide in the next three months, whether to apply. If I do, I need to make contact again with the dons. We've never sent anyone to Oxford or Cambridge. It's difficult for us to compete with schools which give special coaching for the entrance exam. But we've got one or two clever children coming up into the sixth form. I need to establish a little general goodwill. So in a way it's a working weekend."

She bent over the old lady and kissed her affectionately. There was no need to put the question which she had come to ask, for her great-aunt had answered it already. Alexa had done far more than her duty in bringing Asha up, and nothing more must be expected.

V I

Dame Eleanor's College—standing sturdily aloof from the contemporary fashion for coresidence—was still an all-female institution. Its red-brick walls had a no-nonsense look to them, possessing none of the mellow stone charm of the men's colleges. It had no tradition of history to be trapped in peaceful quadrangles. But as though in compensation, the architect had set the building's widespread wings in landscaped grounds which had grown to become one of the most beautiful gardens in the university. Pausing only to unpack the evening dress which she would wear for the formal Gaudy dinner, Asha left the room allotted to her and stepped outside onto the terrace.

The summer drought had attacked Oxford as fiercely as London, but with a different effect. The Portobello Road, dusty and dirty and littered with empty Coke tins and half-naked bodies, had been made sordid by heat: but here the shimmering sunshine created an idyll. Summers of the past were preserved by memory in just such a state of perfection, but had perhaps at the time proved more disappointing. The college lawns, although parched, were smooth and tranquil; thirsty roses bloomed extravagantly over pergolas or against walls; dry terraces were dotted with the silver or scented leaves of Mediterranean bushes. The heat had hurried forward the autumn flowers, so that Michaelmas daisies mingled their blues and purples with those of wisteria, delphinium, buddleia and lavender. Large specimen trees provided cool circles of shade: and quiet corners, gardens within a garden, offered a restful privacy, whether to undergraduates and their books or to the older women who today might choose solitude to remember how they had been young here.

A chattering of voices and clattering of teacups drew Asha toward a less peaceful area: trestle tables round the Principal's lawn were stocked for the occasion with plates of egg sandwiches and cream cakes. Among the crowd of white faces was a familiar black one. Surprised and delighted, Asha hurried forward. She had not seen her Jamaican cousin since Paula returned to her homeland as a widow a few years earlier.

"Paula! Marvelous to see you! I didn't know you were in England."

"Asha, hi! I tried your room earlier, but you hadn't checked in. This is a flying visit to set up a help and information service—so that Jamaicans who are planning to emigrate can find out what conditions are really like before they decide. I signed up for the Gaudy as soon as I knew that I'd be within striking distance of the old alma mater at the right time"—Paula had been a scholar of Dame Eleanor's College in the nineteen-fifties—"and they promptly invited me to make one of the speeches tonight."

"What will your speech be about?" asked Asha as they loaded their plates with éclairs and meringues and settled themselves on a garden seat.

"They wanted me to talk about discrimination. Sex and color both, I guess. But it's not something I've suffered from much. Not in England, at least. At a certain level it actually helps to be black. But the theme I prefer may fit in with their suggestion. Expectation. Why do so few women reach the top in business and politics and the professions? Is it really discrimination? Or is it because they don't *expect* to succeed? Ability on its own isn't enough; they need a mixture of self-confidence and ambition and determination. But why should I waste my arguments on you when you'll hear it all this evening?"

The evening belonged to Paula. Almost to a woman the senior members of Dame Eleanor's College proclaimed by their dresses and hairstyles their lack of interest in personal appearance. Paula outshone them all. As an undergraduate she had been conspicuous by her elegance and wit. Now, in her late forties, her brilliance with words had not changed and her appearance was even more dazzling. Her personality sparkled as brilliantly as the sequins on her tailored jacket. Asha, laughing with the rest, felt a possessive excitement which took her to Paula's room after the formal part of the evening was over.

"There's something I want you to do for me," she said. "Will you come to Hillgate and give a talk to our school-leavers—see if you can put a few stars in their eyes? They've taken their exams and they're killing time until they're allowed to escape from school. They're bored and they're unambitious. Someone like you could inspire them. Not just by repeating the things you've said tonight. But by being yourself —black and successful. It's an aspect of expectation you didn't mention. The exceptional boy or girl can construct a ladder to success in his imagination. But most children need to see someone standing on the top rung, to show that it can be done. We've got a great many black children at Hillgate. But it's hard to find black achievers to show them. Someone like you—"

"Why are they bored?" interrupted Paula. "Why are they unambitious? What are you doing to our children in your schools, Asha? I see kids in Jamaica *longing* to learn. Not always clever, but full of enthusiasm. Their parents support them. I may not approve of a boy getting a whipping from his mother if he has a bad mark at school, but it surely does encourage hard work. If anything, Jamaican kids are *over*-ambitious, wanting to achieve more than their capabilities allow. And the parents who leave Jamaica for England must be the ones with the most initiative, not the dullest. What is your school doing to their children?"

"It's failing them. They're being defeated by people with good intentions."

"Elucidate!" Paula, always ready for an argument, threw a pillow onto the floor and sat on it.

"Well, take Oxford. A center of academic excellence. The top of one of the ladders to success. You and I and every one of the women here tonight had to show ambition and determination at the age of seventeen or eighteen to get a place here in a fiercely competitive field."

"And what have the people with good intentions done about that?"

"They've looked at the losers instead of the winners. No one must fail—so no one can win. It started reasonably enough with a move towards equality of opportunity, but somehow it's changed into equality of achievement. The children themselves have lost the urge to compete. They're almost ashamed if they turn out to be better than the others at something. And so the whole atmosphere of the school works *against* achievement, not for it. The teachers have given in and no individual child is strong enough to fight the system."

"Are you going to change the system, then?"

"I can't do it from underneath," said Asha. "I'd have to be the head. Even then it wouldn't be easy. We'd still have to take the children we were allotted—so many from each band of ability: always more duds than geniuses. But our eleven-year-olds arrive for their first day at Hillgate full of enthusiasm. We must keep that alive, not drown it."

"So you'll make them compete with each other for seven years and then send them to Oxford!"

Asha laughed ruefully. Hillgate pupils rarely achieved the A-level results which qualified them even for the local polytechnic. "Just to see *one* here would be enough to show that it can be done. But there are other goals. We have bands and orchestras, for example: we lend instruments and arrange teaching. But we don't enter the children for the grade exams. That would be turning pleasure into work—and they might not pass. So a child who turns out to be talented can't get into music college because he hasn't got the right certificates. And then we have a good many natural athletes. Why shouldn't we try to produce Olympic swimmers as well as Oxford scholars? When I think of the drab streets and narrow lives from which so many of the children come . . . We must open all sorts of doors so that they can step through and look up. But first, they need ambition."

"It's a dangerous policy." Paula, although sympathetic, was laughing. "As your well-intentioned governors will point out. Once your whole sixth form is inspired with a passionate desire to become Nobel Prize winners, Olympic champions, concert pianists, those who still end up collecting garbage may feel more resentful than if they'd never thought of anything else."

"Ambition doesn't have to be tied to a job. A man can empty dustbins and still win boxing matches at his local club. The lazy children and the stupid children will dodge any attempt to help them anyway. But we should offer a ladder to anyone with a head for greater heights."

"Never let anyone undervalue you, Asha," said Paula, smiling. "All those speeches about how women must use their legal rights and aim for positions of power. You're almost there already. When men talk about power, they mean the power to make money or run the country. But as head of Hillgate you'd have the power to alter the lives of thousands of children. You'll take the job, won't you?"

"I shall apply for it." Asha knew that success could not be taken for granted. But the governors had demonstrated confidence when they appointed her deputy head. She had a good chance.

That night she lay awake for a long time in her narrow student's bed and thought about the future. Everything Ranji had said on the previous evening had been sensible. She had a full life. She enjoyed her work and was good at it. She would enjoy even more a post with greater responsibility and she would be good at that as well. It was indecision which had upset her and made her tetchy. But Paula, just by being Paula, had shown her the way ahead. More cheerful than she had felt for many months, Asha sank into sleep.

VII

On the other side of the world another young woman had also reached a turning point in her life. Outside the San Francisco courtroom in which the case of *Travis* v. *Travis* had just been concluded, Ros Davidson shook hands with her lawyer and walked briskly away so that she would not need to speak to Lee. The divorce had been amicable, in the end, but both of them had been bruised by the six months which preceded it. The waiting automobile carried her swiftly to the offices of Davidson Security Systems, Inc., where receptionists and security guards and secretaries all greeted their executive president as Miss Davidson. They were not making a special point about the morning's events. In the firm which she had inherited from her father, Ros had never been known as Mrs. Travis.

In a sense it was the firm which was responsible for the breakup of the marriage. Lee had felt himself humiliated by being kept in second place—not because there was any other man to threaten their marriage, but because his wife was also his boss. Although ultimately it was his behavior which provided the legal grounds for divorce. Ros knew that much of the fault was her own.

Her father had warned her, as soon as he realized that she was serious about a young man for the first time. "You're a beautiful girl, honey, and every man who sees you wants you. But this one has his eyes on your money as well."

"Then you could shake him off by disinheriting me."

But she knew as well as Lee did that Brad Davidson was devoted to his only child. She was certain one day to enjoy his fortune. To Ros, who was willing to share, Lee's attitude promised security in the marriage. If he wanted money it would be there for him to have long after the rosebud beauty which had earned Ros her name faded away.

Both Brad and Ros had misjudged their man. It was not money that Lee wanted, but power. While his father-in-law was still alive, the young husband indulged his wife's curious determination to work full time in her family business as a whim which would be cured by the arrival of the first baby. But no baby appeared and after Brad's death Ros had taken over not only her father's stock but also his presidential chair.

Even then, Lee assumed at first that she would only be a figurehead. There were a good many people in the company as alarmed as he at the prospect of a young woman assuming executive control, but the fears of the others were gradually assuaged. Only Lee's resentment remained. Ros gave him his own sphere of the business and the vice-presidency that went with it, but she would not surrender the final authority—and this, it soon transpired, was what he had wanted all the time. If Lee had taken his revenge by running after one eighteen-year-old girl after another—and he had—it was from a need to show who was master. But he had lost that battle, too, on the day Ros decided she would rather be lonely than either tolerant or angry.

Would she be lonely? On that first afternoon, finding it difficult to settle at her desk, she stared out of the window, across the bay, watching the scudding clouds. In family terms she had been completely on her own since the death of her father: it was a fact she deeply regretted. But she had friends, and business colleagues; and her work would fill any other gaps.

That evening one of her friends had arranged a party for her, so that she would have cheerful company on the first night of her new life. Dickie Delaney was there, making sure that she noticed him, but not forcing himself obtrusively on her attention. Several other unattached men were less restrained: but Ros went home alone.

That was when it hit her, as she stepped inside the house which was so ridiculously large for a single woman. In the huge master bedroom she looked silently down at the wide pioneer bed which had belonged to her great-grandfather—the bed she had shared with Lee. In the six months since he left it had seemed a luxury to sleep in it alone but now, suddenly, she wanted nothing in the house which was associated with her ex-husband. She spent the night in one of the guest rooms. In the morning she called Dickie Delaney.

The appointment she made was for the evening, but Dickie could not resist one question.

"The house on Russian Hill?" he asked in his soft Irish brogue. "Please God, Rosie my darling, let it be the house on Russian Hill."

It was tempting to tease—to offer him only the cottage at Lake Tahoe or the summer villa by the sea. But that would spoil his day. Ros smiled over the telephone. "Yes," she said. "The house on Russian Hill."

Dickie Delaney was in the business of selling life-styles. He could not, like some interior decorators, be hired to tart up a room with new drapes and wall coverings and cushions. Nor could he be asked, like some antique dealers, to display furniture and *objets d'art* for his client's choice, for he carried no stock. When he agreed to do over a house he would personally fly off to find everything that was needed. He knew exactly where to go and he was not interested in any patron who was likely to quibble about the cost.

Ros guessed that even before the party he had been expecting her call. Dickie had his finger on the social pulse of the whole West Coast. It was his business to know who was moving into any of the houses which aroused his enthusiasm, and also who was moving out. But he had tact as well as taste. He always waited to be asked.

He arrived punctually that evening carrying a case which was no doubt full of photographs and samples; but as he looked around the paneled hall he struck a dramatic pose.

"It will be a crime!" he exclaimed. "What you're after having here is a perfect example of San Francisco's Mining Millionaire Period. It should be a museum. I can't touch it."

"Sure you can," said Ros. "Who wants to live in a museum? And according to my father, the real museum piece was a house on Nob Hill which was damaged in the earthquake. The family only moved here in nineteen-oh-six. This is a Johnny-come-lately house. If it's a crime to touch it, I'm sure you're ready to be a criminal."

"With a free hand? Rosie, my darling, a free hand for Dickie?"

Ros shook her head. Dickie did his best to keep his clients so diverted by the extravagance of his conversational style that they would not notice what power they were delegating, but she intended to retain at least the right of veto; for Dickie, unsupervised, was quite capable of transforming her substantial city mansion into an Arab harem quarter or a Russian monastery. "I shall be keeping my grandfather's collection of long-case clocks. The setting needs to be appropriate."

"Let me show you, then." In the drawing room he produced a set of painted sketches. The rooms they showed were unmistakably her own, transformed. Ros's astonishment turned to amusement as she realized how long ago he must have taken it for granted that the commission would eventually be forthcoming.

"For the clocks, you see, the style should be French or English," Dickie explained as he spread the sheets in front of her. "I can't exactly see you in Louis Quatorze. But I've been waiting a long time to find someone who'd appreciate an Adam room."

"I'm not sure—" began Ros, admitting ignorance rather than objecting, but the sentence died on her lips as he set in front of her a sketch of her own dining room. At the moment it was dark and heavy, furnished with the solid pieces which had been fashionable at the turn of the century. In the picture, by contrast, twenty-four elegant Chippendale chairs encircled a mahogany table with rounded corners which made the shape appear delicate in spite of its great length. Behind alternate chairs the long-case clocks stood like silent footmen against a wall of palest pink which had been given an appearance of paneling by rectangles of white beading. The carving on the doors and the white plasterwork of the ceiling and frieze had been delicately touched with gold and in the center of one of the long walls was depicted an obviously genuine Adam fireplace.

"There's a country house falling to the ground at this very moment in England," Dickie told her. "I have an arrangement with the demolition foreman that the fireplace is to be mine. The chairs are in

London, waiting for me to take up my option, and the table is in
County Cork, owned by a family which doesn't know where its next
penny is coming from. What the room will need then is fine pictures.
One over the fireplace and one at each end. There was a Gainsborough I tried to bespeak for you when I was in London last month. But
it belonged to a museum and they wouldn't sell, not even for real
money. I've photographs here of one or two paintings which will be
up for auction in the next month or two, but they're not right: not
quite right. Don't worry. Somewhere in the world must be exactly
what we need. I'll find them for you. Trust Dickie."

He shuffled the photographs in front of her as he spoke. Ros agreed
with his rejection of them all, but her eye was caught by a folded
brochure printed on a glossy art paper. "Hang an ancestral portrait on
your wall!" it commanded in Gothic type. She picked it up to study
more closely. Like a marriage bureau, it provided a selection of illustrations to show the possibilities. The largest was of a slender young
woman in eighteenth-century costume. She looked at Dickie inquir-
ingly.

"I brought that back with me from London," he told her. "There's
an antique market there in the Portobello Road. You'll have heard of
it. Out front it's a tourist trap. But behind the scenes there are some
important pieces moving. The leaflet was on display in the gallery
which is holding the chairs for me, and since I was on the spot I
called in at the address it gave. You can't tell anything from a black-
and-white shot like that. It *might* have been a Gainsborough." He
laughed at himself. "It had been painted a few months back by a
young fellow in a garret. Not a bad effort at all, at all. But not right
for you here. You should have the Real McCoy."

"Right!" agreed Ros. Nevertheless she did not return the leaflet to
Dickie when he left, but read it through with care and interest. Since
she had no living relatives, it would be amusing to invent some dead
ones. An ancestor or two in the Adam dining room would provide an
interesting conversation piece. She would enjoy making up histories
for them and inventing their descendants. After all, she could claim a
Scottish grandfather on one side and an Irish great-grandfather on the
other. And an English mother. Ros went thoughtfully into her den
and picked up the picture of her mother.

She had had a copy enlargement made of the snapshot she had

found after her father's death. This might be enough to provide a likeness for the enterprising English businessman and the artist working away in his garret. Once again Ros studied the reproduction of the painting which looked so much like a Gainsborough. For a moment it seemed to her that there was a likeness already between the illustration and her photograph. She laughed the idea away as an example of wishful thinking. All the same, her transformed dining room would not be a genuine Adam room, so why should it matter if the pictures in it were twentieth-century? Before she went to bed that night she had come to a decision. She would leave Dickie Delaney to develop his plans without interference. But once the main part of his work was done and she could see where there were gaps to be filled to her personal taste, she would buy herself an ancestor.

VIII

The photograph caught Asha's eye as soon as she arrived home from school on a miserable February afternoon. At first she was merely curious as she looked down at the picture—which Ranji must have placed on the table especially for her to see—but then she studied it with puzzled intensity. A young woman with a baby in her arms was smiling at the camera, while a fair-haired little girl tugged at her skirt.

"Where did you find this?"

"Do you recognize anyone?" Ranji came to stand beside her. "My goodness, you're soaking. Take your mac off before you drip all over my documents."

"That's me in the photograph," Asha said, obeying his instructions. "And my mother. I've never seen that particular snap before, but there are others of us together when I was about that age. But who is the baby? Where did this come from, Ranji?"

"It's one of three photographs sent by a potential client. Does the name Ros Davidson mean anything to you? Or Brad Davidson, her father?"

"No." Asha turned the photograph over and read a typed slip stuck to the back. "The original of this was labeled 'Barbary at Blaize, with Ros and Asha.' "

"Ros Davidson, of San Francisco, is the baby in that picture. And she says that the woman holding her, Barbary, is her mother. Barbary, Asha, Blaize—such unusual names! There can't be any doubt. Ros Davidson's mother must be your mother."

"It isn't possible." Asha was hardly able to speak.

"It must be so. The photograph . . . What happened to Ros, Asha, after your mother died?"

"I don't know." She sat down, numbed by shock.

"You must remember having a baby sister."

"I don't remember anything." Without warning Asha burst into tears.

Ranji took her hands to comfort her. "Tell me," he said gently.

She needed a moment before she could control her voice: the tears ran down her cheeks as she spoke. "One day when I was five my mother took me to school, just in the ordinary way. When we reached the corner she kissed me goodbye as usual. I ran on to the gate, and turned round, and we waved at each other, as usual. I went into school and—and—"

For a second time she began to sob. Ranji's arm hugged her shoulders. "You'll feel better if you tell me the whole story," he said.

Asha gave a single deep sigh and dabbed her eyes dry. "My grandmother came to fetch me from school that day—but she didn't take me home. I was frightened and wanted my mother. I can remember screaming and screaming until my grandmother locked me into a room and said I could come out when I was quiet. I never saw either of my parents again. I can remember every minute of that day, Ranji. But nothing at all about my life before it."

"You remember your mother, surely?"

"Not as a real person. I only know what she looks like from photographs. I couldn't tell you anything that we ever did together. All I know about my first five years is what Aunt Alexa has told me."

"Did she explain what happened to your parents?"

"They both died."

"It can't be as simple as that. One of them might have died while you were at school that day, but not both. Do you really not remember anything at all about a baby called Ros?"

Asha shook her head. "It's not a selective forgetfulness. All those years have disappeared." She stared again at the photograph taken on the terrace at Blaize. "I think I need to have a chat with Aunt Alexa," she said.

Alexa was not alone when Asha arrived at the nursing home on the next Saturday. A young man holding a notebook sat beside the bed. His clothes—a T-shirt, gym shoes and the bottom half of a track suit —were more appropriate to an athletics stadium than to a nursing home, but Alexa, usually quick to criticize slovenly dress, appeared to have established a cordial relationship with her visitor.

"This is Peter Langley," she announced in a businesslike way. "Peter, my great-niece, Asha. She's far too young, of course, to be any help to you."

"What sort of help?" asked Asha as she shook hands.

"Peter works on the Bristol *Evening Post.* He's helping me to prove when I was born."

"But surely you know."

"Yes, of course I know. But the Queen doesn't know. You do realize, don't you, dear, that I shall have my hundredth birthday in March. The Queen is supposed to send me a telegram. Matron wrote off some weeks ago to give her warning. But a secretary wrote back asking for my birth certificate. It's not as simple as they seem to think. A hundred years ago people didn't always bother with birth certificates. Even if they did, you couldn't expect a poor orphan to keep such a thing."

"How on earth have you managed all these years without one?" asked Asha, laughing.

"You poor child! Brought up in a bureaucratic age. Without papers you don't exist. When I married Piers, I was allowed to decide for myself whether I'd ever been born or not. And since then, the certificate which shows that I'm Lady Glanville has been enough for most people. But not for Her Majesty, it seems. Well, I know *when* I was born, so I had to find out where, to get a copy of the certificate. Bristol seemed the most likely place. I wrote to the editor of the *Post* and asked if one of his young men could look into it for me."

"It's fascinating," said Peter, his voice conveying a greater sense of awe than seemed likely from his appearance. "Lady Glanville has been telling me all about her parents. I did a series of pieces on local history a year or so ago, so of course I knew something about the collapse of Lorimer's Bank in the eighteen-seventies. But to meet someone who was indirectly responsible for it . . . !"

"That's going it a bit, surely!" exclaimed Asha. "Aunt Alexa, what *have* you been saying?"

"Well, dear, my father was John Junius Lorimer. There's no denying that. And I was born only eighteen months before the crash."

"That hardly makes you responsible for it!"

"There was a lot of gossip at the time," Peter said, "about what had happened to all the bank's assets. John Junius Lorimer was accused of embezzlement. One fact which emerged out of all the rumors was that he'd spent a lot of money on some jewelry which couldn't be found when his possessions were sequestrated. Lady Glanville's just been telling me what happened to the jewels. I hope you'll let me write about all this, Lady Glanville, as well as finding a birth certificate. Reporters always hope to find themselves writing history— history in the making. Mostly, though, it turns out to be school fetes and court reports. What you've been telling me really *is* history—and I don't think anyone's known it before."

"Write anything you like, dear boy. And come back if there's any more you need to know." She held out her thin hand in dismissal.

As the door closed behind him, Asha looked suspiciously at the bright-eyed old lady. "You're not having him on, are you, Aunt Alexa? Bribing him with juicy tidbits so that he'll do the dull slog for you?"

"The jewels are real enough," Alexa said indignantly. "Rubies and diamonds. I keep them in the bank. I'll wear them on my birthday, if you like. Then you'll see how people dressed for parties a hundred years ago. Still, you don't want to talk about old family matters, do you, dear?"

"As a matter of fact, I do." Asha managed to keep her voice steady. "I want you to tell me about Ros."

Alexa was not easily disconcerted, but the directness of the request made her pluck at the edge of the sheet with nervous hands. "What do you want to know?" she asked at last.

"Everything. The truth."

Alexa thought for a moment before nodding. "Yes, it can't do any harm now. Pull me up a little, will you, dear?" Asha arranged the pillows to give her more support. "Well, then. Your mother and you were in England, waiting for you to have an operation, when the Japanese invaded Malaya in nineteen-forty-one. Your father was caught out there. Someone I'd known as a boy in San Francisco—Brad Davidson—came to England during the war and visited me. He met Barbary, your mother. They fell in love."

"And what happened to my father? You've always told me that he was taken prisoner by the Japanese."

"We learned that much later. But at the time your mother thought he was dead. She wasn't the only one to make that kind of mistake. You mustn't blame her for what happened, Asha. She and Brad thought they'd be able to marry when your father's death was confirmed after the war. They set up house together and Ros was born in nineteen-forty-five." She made a helpless gesture with her pale hands. "Then your father came home."

"I don't remember him at all," said Asha.

"He was very ill. He'd been treated appallingly by the Japanese. He found out about Brad and Ros. A normal, healthy man might have been able to understand and forgive. But your father had been—well, damaged. He was vindictive. Stole you from your mother."

"At school," said Asha. "He sent my grandmother." They had reached the beginning of her own memory.

"That's right. Then he died. He'd been dying all the time, in a sense. His will left us in a terrible muddle. He didn't want your mother to have you back, you see. So then it was her turn to become ill. She couldn't find out where you were, not at first. When she did, she had to go to court for custody."

"What happened to Ros?"

"Brad wouldn't let his baby go when Barbary went back to her husband. He hoped that if he held on, your mother would come back to him. That was part of the reason for her breakdown, that she seemed to be losing both her little girls at once. It was the strain and the unhappiness that killed her. She was a sweet girl, Barbary, and very honest. Determined to do whatever was right. But when she saw right on both sides . . ." Alexa shook her head and fell silent, perhaps remembering that time. Not wanting to tire her, Asha refrained from putting any more questions; but the story was not yet complete. "So Ros was brought up in San Francisco," the old lady said with a new briskness in her voice. "She wouldn't remember her mother. I was sorry for her, the poor little girl. I left her the rubies."

"The rubies?"

"The Lorimer jewels. We were talking about them earlier. After the war I made a new will. I left the rubies to Ros and the money to you. I'd forgotten about that. I must change it. Ros doesn't even know who I am—and there may not be much money left. You've been a good girl to me, Asha, dear. You deserve to have anything I've got. I'll wear the rubies for my hundredth birthday. But you can have them after I've gone. Or even after the party. If I just slip them to you, perhaps we could dodge these terrible taxes. I'll ask my lawyer."

"You're very generous, Aunt Alexa. But I've made you tired. Have a good rest." Asha kissed her goodbye. As she drove thoughtfully back to London she gave no further thought to the rubies. Instead she probed her memory, endeavoring to mesh her own recollections of childhood with what she had just learned.

Ranji was interested to hear her great-aunt's revelations. "While you were gone, a thought occurred to me," he said. "Just for once we could sell a real ancestor if we chose." He pointed to the portrait on the wall. "I remember you telling me that you were descended from the old gentleman through both your mother and your father. So Ros Davidson must have a line back to him as well through her mother—*your* mother. I think Miss Davidson is not exactly on the breadline. She wrote on the notepaper of Davidson Security Systems, Inc., a company of which she appears to be executive president."

"She's my half-sister! I'm not going to let you—"

"Ssh, ssh. Don't get so indignant. I'm not going to rip her off. We can send her all the usual possibilities. You have better photographs of her mother, so Chris could produce a lifelike costume piece. I'll try to find her a swashbuckling seventeenth-century slave-trading sea captain. But—unless you feel sentimental about it and don't want to let it go—we could also offer her a genuine eighteen-seventy-seven portrait of John Junius Lorimer of Bristol. I am only suggesting that it would hardly be unreasonable to charge a stiffish price for something which would be exactly what we claimed it to be: a contemporary portrait of Ros Davidson's true ancestor."

Asha stared at the portrait of her great-grandfather. It was true that the nineteenth-century autocrat of Lorimer's Bank with his somber clothing and imperious gaze was out of place in their flat. And this would not be the same as selling John Junius to a stranger. Ros had almost as much right to provide a home for the portrait as herself. "We ought to ask Aunt Alexa, though," she said.

"Why? She gave the picture to you. She doesn't expect to see it again. We don't need to tell her that we're selling it."

Asha considered for a moment longer. "After the party," she said at last. "There's going to be a party for the hundredth birthday. I've been told to invite all the family. Not that there are many left. She might want John Junius brought back for the day. But after that, I wouldn't mind."

"It would take that long to arrange, in any case."

"Aunt Alexa will probably want me to invite Ros," Asha suggested. "I took her by surprise today. When she thinks about it, she'll want to find out how I knew the right questions to ask."

"The timing could fit neatly. I send the usual portfolio for a new client, plus a photograph of the genuine article here. In view of its high price, I ask if she'd like to inspect it personally. In the meantime, while I'm putting everything together, you'll be writing Ros a personal letter, telling her who you are and everything you know about her place in the family. And asking her if she'd like to come to the party."

Asha nodded in agreement. "I should think she'd be thrilled. Aunt Alexa knew her father, Brad Davidson, at the time of the San Francisco earthquake, apparently. All those years ago—isn't it incredible!" She looked again at the portrait of the Bristol banker. "I think of John Junius as existing way back in history. He was born in eighteen hundred. He must have cheered the news of Waterloo while he was still only a schoolboy. But he held Aunt Alexa in his arms when she was a baby. When she first started getting excited about this centenary birthday I only felt that I should humor her by making the arrangements. But I'm beginning to understand her feelings. Not that it's anything to be proud of, living to a hundred. But it's certainly *interesting.* Yes, I'll write to Ros."

She smiled to herself as she sat down at once to compose a letter of introduction and invitation. Ros would be as thrilled as she was herself to learn that she had a sister, and just as sorry as Asha was that they had not grown up together. But it was not too late for them to become friends. Asha felt no doubt about the answer she would receive. Ros would come to England for the party.

IX

"The rubies," said Alexa. "I shall need the rubies on the day before the party. Will you collect them for me, dear? They're in the bank. For safekeeping. Tell the manager I want them out for two days."

"I doubt if he'll take my word for it." Asha added yet another note to her list of final instructions. It was fortunate that the date of the celebration fell within the school's Easter holiday. "You'll have to give me a letter of authority. And the bank receipt."

"I put those jewels into safe deposit in nineteen thirteen. You don't expect me still to have a receipt, do you? Young Dangerfield will arrange it." Three generations of Dangerfields had handled Alexa's legal affairs since she married Lord Glanville. Asha had met the current representative of the family firm, a pleasant young man, when Alexa's move to the nursing home was under discussion. "And ask him to come with you when you bring them here. So that I can arrange for you to have the rubies instead of Ros. If anything needs to be signed, he can bring it the next day. I've invited him to the party."

"Where are you holding this party—in the Albert Hall?" As the date approached, Alexa had become generous with invitations. "Why do you want the jewelry a day early, Aunt Alexa? Wouldn't it be safer if I brought it actually on your birthday?"

"That nice young man from the Bristol paper is bringing a few of his friends along on the day before. They want to ask questions and take photographs, ready to appear on the eighteenth. He put in a lot of work, you know, finding out where I was born. This will do him good in his job. And I shall enjoy reading what they say. He'd like me to be all dressed up, as if the party had started. So I need the rubies."

"I'll fix it." Asha's mood was one of brisk efficiency. Her appointment as head of Hillgate Comprehensive School from September had been confirmed, and her head was full of plans for changes. Compared with the problems involved in taking over an unwieldy educational establishment and setting it on a new course, Alexa's requirements were child's play.

On March 17 Asha and Mr. Dangerfield met at the City bank in which the jewel case was kept and together went through the formalities of extracting it from the strong room.

"Lady Glanville was hoping to slip this to you after the party tomorrow," said the lawyer as he drove the valuable cargo toward the nursing home. "She thought she could avoid capital transfer tax. If she'd made the gift fifteen years ago it would have been perfectly legal. But I'm afraid I can't be a party to what she has in mind now. And the bank records of ownership can't be changed retroactively. I'm sorry to be unhelpful. If I'd known that the jewels existed, I would have given her advice earlier. But as it is . . . She's going to instruct me today about changes in her will. I'll do my best to have the codicils ready for signature tomorrow."

"I didn't know the jewels existed any more than you did, until a few weeks ago," Asha told him. "Are they insured while they're out of the bank?"

"Special cover for two days, and they have to go back to the strong room overnight. I won't tell you what value I've put on them in case it makes you nervous. One of the conditions, incidentally, is that Lady Glanville mustn't be left alone while she's wearing them. Either you or myself must be in the room all the time."

Asha nodded. She was still thinking of the birthday itself as the big occasion, so the scene which greeted them on arrival took her by surprise. Peter Langley's "few friends" proved to be a squad of reporters and photographers large enough to cover a royal tour. The matron, anxious, was lying in wait for Asha.

"I wouldn't let them in until you came," she said. "You must make it clear to them what it means to be old. Just because Lady Glanville is bright and able to talk doesn't mean that she's strong. You know how quickly she tires. And she's overexcited already about tomorrow's party. I've asked the nurses to play it down, but they're excited themselves."

"I'll see that this doesn't go on too long," Asha promised. "Let me have a word with her first. Then I'll make a timetable for the interview." She tapped at Alexa's door and went in. Mr. Dangerfield was closing his notebook as she entered, so presumably he had been given his instructions. Asha bent over to kiss the old lady. "You look marvelous," she said.

It was true. The soft waves of her snow-white hair made it apparent that a hairdresser had come to her room that morning. And he must have brought a beautician with him, for the nurses would not have been able to create such a delicately smooth complexion on the face of a woman about to celebrate her hundredth birthday.

"White of egg." Alexa could read her great-niece's thoughts. "Old stage trick. Only good for a couple of hours. But I didn't see why the photographs should show me looking like an old crone."

"You've never looked anything but beautiful." As she paid the compliment, Asha's eye was caught by the jewel case. Its three velvet-lined drawers had been unlocked and pulled out to reveal their contents. She stared in astonishment at the rich display.

The main piece was a necklace which at the front divided into three tiers of rubies, from which hung a pendant in the form of a rose: a single large ruby, surrounded by petals made of smaller stones, was set in silver and edged with diamonds. This rose design, on a smaller scale, was repeated in a pair of delicate drop earrings. In the third tray of the jewel case was a tiara. Yet another rose of rubies in its center was surrounded here by trembling leaves outlined in diamonds. Asha had learned that the Lorimer jewels were valuable. She had not expected them also to be so beautiful.

"Will you help me put them on, dear?" Alexa asked. It took a little time. Asha had never handled a tiara before and she and Alexa were equally nervous about disarranging the newly created hairstyle. The necklace was more easily fitted. Alexa had chosen a bed jacket of pale-pink chiffon, so sheer as to be almost transparent. Fitting into the décolleté lines of her lace-edged nightdress, the necklace appeared from a distance to be resting on smooth young skin. Alexa had always known how to make the best of herself.

"Five minutes' rest now," commanded Asha, when the earrings were also in place and the final effect had been approved. Leaving the lawyer to fulfill the insurance condition, she went out to talk to the waiting journalists. She told them firmly that Lady Glanville would become confused and quickly tired if they all crowded into the room at once. It was agreed that the photographers should go in first and leave without arguing when Asha told them that their time was up.

While the cameras were flashing, she chatted with the reporters and was amused to find that Peter Langley had appointed himself Alexa's press agent, issuing his rivals with a curriculum vitae to guide their questioning.

"What have you left out?" she whispered to him when the others were not listening. "What's the revelation which your readers and no other will discover tomorrow?" She could tell from his grin that her suspicions were well founded.

"The Bristol bank crash," he confessed. "It's not part of her career. But it's an interesting piece of social history, and the birthday is a peg to hang the story on."

"I hope you're not still arguing that her birth was responsible for a financial collapse a hundred years ago!"

"Well, it might have been, you know. At this distance of time, who can tell what really happened? Now if only her father had kept a diary! He must have been a fascinating character. On the face of it, so eminently respectable, so fabulously rich—model husband, solid banker, connoisseur of art, city benefactor. And beneath it all, the secret of life: the Italian mistress, the illegitimate daughter, the valuable gifts, the cooking of the books. Then the wheel of fortune turns full circle with the collapse of the bank, the ruin of the community, the disappearance of the jewels; it's a marvelous story."

"Which you've already sold."

"Naturally. With your aunt's full approval. I've persuaded her, incidentally, to let me ghost her memoirs. Her memory is incredible, and it's important that people who've been famous should set the facts down. They owe it to their descendants."

"She'll never have any descendants, I'm afraid."

"Well, posterity, then." He looked at his watch. "Time to change shifts?"

Asha had intended to allow her aunt another rest before the questions began, but Alexa's eyes were bright with excitement. As she recalled her youth, she almost seemed to be young again in reality, and her pleasure in the occasion was infectious. She had long ago mastered the art of being interviewed and her reminiscences poured out without any great regard for the questions which prompted them.

It was she as much as the journalists who protested when Asha at last announced that the session must end. An actress to the last, she kept the bright smile on her face until the door closed on the last of her visitors. But her fingers were fidgeting with the sheets in a sign of tiredness and her exhaustion was evident as she allowed her head to fall back onto the pillow.

"You were marvelous, darling." Asha bent over her with a kiss of congratulation. "May I just take the necklace off?" She undid its fastenings and then gently eased out the delicate earrings and removed the tiara, marveling at the value of the stones she was handling. How impossible it was to visualize a world in which rich women had worn such fortunes around their necks each evening as a matter of course—a world of which Alexa was a survivor. "May I try them on?" she asked. "Just for a second, before I put them away?"

"No." Alexa softened the sharpness of her answer with an affectionate pat of the hand. "No, dear, I don't want you ever to wear them. Tomorrow I'll sign the new will, and then they'll be yours one day; but you're to sell them. Send them straight from the bank to an auction house. Promise me you'll never put them on. They bring bad luck, these rubies. I don't want you touched by it."

"Aunt Alexa! I never knew you were superstitious!"

"I'm not with anything else. Not with these, even; not superstitious. Just stating a fact. They've always brought bad luck. People have died because of them."

"Then why did you choose these particular jewels to wear today, Aunt Alexa? You must have lots of others."

"Most of the others went when Pirry died. Glanville family heirlooms. The lawyers said I couldn't keep them. I've sold all my own. Except these, because I'd forgotten all about them. Until you talked about Ros. As for wearing them today . . ." She was silent for so long that Asha thought she had forgotten the question. "When I was young, Asha, I had great ambitions. Didn't someone once define hell as the place where you find all your wishes have been granted? It wasn't like that with me. I got what I wanted—my career, my husband, my son, my little opera house—and I enjoyed having it all. But now—what does an old lady look forward to? Celebrating a hundredth birthday. A bunch of grapes and a telegram from the Queen. Ridiculous ambition! It's served, though, for the past few months.

Tomorrow, it's over. Achieved. What then? I'm not saying that I want to die. Certainly not. But if I try to look forward . . ." Again she fell into silence.

"I accuse you of being a sensationmonger," Asha said cheerfully. "You sent for the photographers and you put on the jewels and you hoped that you'd drop dead on the spot through some kind of magic. That's what you wanted, wasn't it? A sensation on the front page of all the newspapers. Well, it hasn't happened. You're going to go on bullying these poor nurses here until you're the oldest living person in England. After that, you'll have to take on the Georgian peasants who claim to be a hundred and forty. *There*'s an ambition for you. I shall tell Matron to put you on a yoghurt diet at once." As she spoke, she arranged the rubies in their velvet-lined drawers. Closing the case, she bent over the bed to kiss Alexa goodbye.

"Have a really good rest this afternoon," she said. "This has only been a preview. You'll need all your strength for the real thing. I'll be back at three tomorrow, ready for the party."

"Ah yes," Alexa murmured. "The party." Her eyes were already closing in sleep as she squeezed Asha's hand. "Thank you for arranging everything, dear. You're a good girl. I'll see you tomorrow, then, at the party."

X

"I'll escort you back to the bank." Peter Langley made the offer as Asha closed the door of her great-aunt's room.

"There's no need," she began; but then remembered that she had come in Mr. Dangerfield's car and required transport if not protection.

"Lady Glanville's insurance company would see a need," Peter suggested. "You and that little box are an invitation to muggers."

"No one's ever mugged me before," Asha claimed cheerfully.

"Perhaps you've never before been in possession of something so much worth stealing."

"Who would know that I am now?" She answered the question in her own mind. "You're not suggesting that one of your journalist friends—"

"Certainly not. A more honest bunch of chaps you'd never find. All the same, it *is* faintly possible that they may have adjourned *en masse* straight from here to the nearest pub. It would only take one loud voice commenting on Lady Glanville's sparklers to make some local villain prick up his ears. There's no point in arguing. Mr. Dangerfield and I have agreed that you must have a protector. And he's decided to trust me, since he's got an appointment to keep."

Asha, pleased, responded with vivacity to Peter's enthusiastic chatter as he drove her to the bank and laughed at his exaggerated sigh of relief when she had exchanged the jewel case for a receipt.

"Five past one," he said. "Marvelous timing. Lunch?"

"I'm afraid I can't. Ranji will be expecting me."

"You mean that at this moment he'll have the soufflé rising for you, the casserole bubbling, the zabaglione whipping?"

"No such luck. I mean that at this moment he'll be looking at the clock and muttering because I promised to be home before one. To get lunch for *him.*"

"You've been delayed," said Peter. "The press conference went on longer than you expected. You can't possibly get back before three. So he'd better boil himself an egg and you'll make it up to him at suppertime. There's a telephone on that corner."

Asha hesitated for a moment longer and then succumbed to temptation. She dialed her own number, but found it engaged. A quarter of an hour later she tried again from the restaurant. Ranji accepted the lie in silence; probably he was already sulking over her lateness. Asha sighed to herself at the thought of arguments to come, but resolved that since she would have to pay for her outing later, she would at least enjoy it now.

"Your great-aunt really was quite a girl, wasn't she?" said Peter. "She showed me her scrapbooks. All the reviews of her performances. And the photographs! In every generation there seem to be a few women who are outstandingly beautiful. She was one of those, wasn't she—quite apart from her singing. There's one photograph in the scrapbook that I remember in particular, from her twenties. She's wearing a long pale dress of some satiny material. Cut very low—you can see what lovely breasts she had. And very tightly fitted at the waist; such a slim waist. Long hair swept up and coiled like—like a crown, with jewels in it. It's a posed photograph, of course; artificial, you might say. But she looked like a princess. Perfectly, absolutely beautiful." He was silent for a moment, indulging his admiration. Then his eyes twinkled as he looked up at Asha. "You could look like that if you wanted to."

"Don't be silly."

"Oh, I realize that you don't want to. You like to appear business-like, efficient, competent, because your professional success depends on that look—just as Lady Glanville, when she was an opera singer, needed to be glamorous. But—while she was wearing those rubies, I imagined how good they'd look on you, with your marvelous complexion. Your hair's as beautiful as hers must have been once. You're as tall and as slim as she looks in the photograph. If you took your glasses off —sorry for the cliché—and wore a dress out of Lady Glanville's Edwardian wardrobe and posed for a photographer, you could produce as stunning an effect as she did. It's a question of style. Some generations have it. Ours hasn't. But you're beautiful in a way which would fit into a good many of the old patterns. Hasn't anyone told you that before?"

Asha felt herself flushing. Chris had said something of the sort when he first asked to paint her. But even the success of his mock Gainsborough portrait had not made Asha think of herself as a beautiful woman, and neither did Peter's compliments now. "You're embarrassing me," she said.

"Sorry." He accepted her wish to change the subject. "What did surprise me in Lady Glanville's scrapbook was her support for the suffragettes. I mean, of course, the suffra*gists.*" Asha guessed that he had received the lecture which Alexa invariably delivered to those who used the popular newspaper term. "Have you inherited Lady Glanville's feminist principles as well as her beauty?"

"I can't have inherited anything at all from her," Asha pointed out. "I'm not a direct descendant."

"But you must have an ancestor in common somewhere."

Asha thought of the elderly Victorian gentleman whose portrait would soon be on its way to the United States. "Yes," she agreed. "That Bristol banker who interests you so much. I should think he'd have had a fit at the thought of letting women vote. He would have

expected the females of his family merely to do good works and practice amateur talents and display his wealth in their clothes."

"Without ever having to worry about money. Don't you sometimes
regret that those days are gone? Wouldn't you like to sit back and feel
that your husband or father was entirely responsible for your comfort?"

"We're talking about a very small section of society," Asha pointed
out. "And although the men may have been financially responsible for
their wives and daughters, it was the servants who actually provided
the comfort. What I do regret is that, as the servants disappeared
from the middle-class scene, it was the women who took over their
jobs. So that now we work outside the home as a matter of course,
we're still left with the responsibility for the domestic support system.
I'm generalizing madly, but you know what I mean. Husbands nowadays are happy to take on the chauffeur's chores—to wash the car and
tinker with the engines. But in most families it seems to be the wife
who's replaced the cook, housemaid, gardener, interior decorator,
laundrymaid, nanny, governess and housekeeper—and all in her spare
time."

"That's changing, surely."

"Is it? Well, I'm glad to hear that a young man thinks so."

"Women are so formidably efficient," Peter suggested. "It's hard
for a man to tackle the wallpapering when his wife has demonstrated
that she can do it better. You need to look incompetent occasionally.
And the other side of it, of course, is up to you as a teacher. Do you
give your boys a chance to learn cookery, for example?"

"It will be one of next year's innovations." Asha was pleased that
she could give a positive answer. "Cookery classes for all first-year
pupils. And no sex segregation in the options later. Boys and girls
alike can choose to type or sew or cook or do carpentry or metalwork."

"And will you—" Peter's face shaded with apology. "I ought to
warn you that I seem to be interviewing you. That wasn't the idea
when we started talking, but we seem to be moving that way. Do you
mind?"

"I'm not worth a page in your notebook," laughed Asha.

"Oh, but you are. You're about to become a very powerful woman.
The lives of more than a thousand children in your hands. Their

futures, their ideals, their happiness. Did that Bristol ancestor of yours ever have as much power as that?"

"He had enough to ruin a whole community," Asha reminded him wryly. "As you've already discovered, when Lorimer's Bank went bust, the whole of Bristol went bust with it. I hope I shan't achieve quite that effect." But she was interested to hear Peter repeating almost word for word the opinion with which her cousin Paula had encouraged her to apply for the headship.

"Different kinds of power, agreed. All the same, you know what I mean. You'll be able to impose your philosophy of life on the impressionable young. It's a matter of public interest to know what that philosophy is."

"I'm afraid I'm not feeling philosophical today." Asha turned the conversation away from herself, asking Peter about his work. Only at the end of the meal did he return to the subject of her family.

"I hope you don't feel that I've—well, 'used' Lady Glanville," he said. "When her letter came in, asking if someone could trace her birth, the editor gave me the time to do it because of her title, really. He thought the hundredth birthday might rate a paragraph if she was a local girl. Discovering that she'd been so famous was a piece of serendipity and I have rather battened onto it—making Fleet Street work through me, until today. It's done me a lot of good professionally. All quite deliberate. But all rising out of the fact that I thought she deserved it. I wouldn't like you to think—"

"She's loved every minute of the fuss," said Asha. "Talking about the days when she was young and famous. I don't remember her ever being as excited as she was this morning. And knowing what will be in all the papers tomorrow is the best birthday present she could have had. I should have thought of it myself. I'm grateful to you, so I'm glad if you found it useful."

"I gather you don't like compliments," said Peter. "But she's lucky to have you; you realize that? So many old ladies find themselves alone in the world. All their relations are dead or don't want to know."

"It's the other way round," Asha told him. "I've been lucky to have her. Peter, I must get home. I'll see you again tomorrow. The great day. Thank you so much for the lunch."

Ranji's lunch had been baked beans on toast. He had left all the debris in the kitchen to prove it.

"I'm sorry about that." Asha realized guiltily that it was half past three. "I'll do something special tonight."

"Have you had anything to eat yourself?" Ranji asked.

"Yes. Peter Langley took me out, since I was so late anyway." Admitting that her meal had been less frugal than Ranji's helped to ease her bad conscience at the pretense that she could not have returned to the flat at a reasonable hour.

"Where did you phone from?" he asked.

"When I spoke to you, it was from the restaurant. I tried before, at about one o'clock, but the line was engaged."

"That would have been while I was talking to Matron. She said you'd left some time earlier; she expected to find you here."

"I had to take the jewelry back into safe deposit." The defense was true, but she noticed that Ranji showed no sign of the irritation which might be justified. "What did Matron want?"

"She had some news for you, Asha. Really, she wanted to tell you herself. When the nurse went in to get Lady Glanville ready for lunch, she found her dead."

Asha had been running water into the pan to soak away the burned layer of baked beans. She set it down and turned, speechless, to stare at Ranji.

"Overexcitement and overtiredness, Matron said. It would seem she was trying to shift blame from her own shoulders. Though why she should need to make excuses after keeping the old lady alive for so long, I can't imagine." He came into the kitchen and stretched past Asha to turn off the tap. "It's a shock, darling, I know. Sit down for a minute." He offered a handkerchief to mop up the tears which were flowing down her cheeks. "She'd had a good run, Asha. Ninety-nine years and three hundred and sixty-four days. Nothing to cry about."

"But she was so much looking forward to her party tomorrow."

Ranji smiled affectionately as he put an arm around her shoulders, hugging her. "You make her sound like a five-year-old in a frilly birthday frock, wondering what her presents will be."

"That's how it was, in a way. When I was a little girl she looked after me. But these past few years, when she couldn't manage, I've had to look after her, or arrange for someone else to, just as though she *were* a child. And like a child she'd set her heart on enjoying all the fuss. Seeing what the papers say, getting her telegram, blowing out the candles on the cake. She'll be so disappointed."

"Asha, sweetheart, she's *dead.*"

"Yes. Yes, of course." The first shock of hearing the news was succeeded by the desolation of believing it. Ranji, sympathetically, did not disturb her thoughts until with a last sniff she indicated that, although unhappy, she was ready to talk again.

"I promised Matron you would call back to discuss the funeral."

Still shocked and distressed, Asha moved toward the telephone. But before she rang the nursing home, she dialed another number. Alexa's birthday, had she lived, would have been reported in style in the national press. Now the birthday party would not take place, but that was a news story in itself—and the journalists and photographers who had crowded her room would not let their material go to waste. Had she died six months earlier the fact might have been reported only briefly, because she had reached the pinnacle of her fame so very many years ago and few people still alive would remember Alexa Reni's voice and beauty. But tomorrow, if Fleet Street were alerted in time, she would receive the kind of obituary afforded normally only to royalty. Asha would not now be able to hand over the centenary present which she had already gift-wrapped; but instead she could give her great-aunt the reviews of a lifetime.

Alexa would have appreciated that.

XI

Ros Davidson slept late on the morning after her flight from San Francisco to London. It was half past ten before she rang room service for breakfast, and not until eleven o'clock did she unfold the morning paper which came with the tray.

England had lost the Centenary Test, whatever that might mean. This fact—apparently the most important item of world news—was recorded by a heavy headline and a large photograph of a man called Lillie bowling a man called Knott in Melbourne, Australia. Ros passed her eye quickly over it and concentrated instead on another photograph, lower down the page. Above the caption "The Singing Suffragette" it showed a beautiful young woman in the dress of 1912, carrying a Votes for Women banner. Ros nodded approvingly to see that her relative's hundredth birthday rated the front page—until her jet-lagged eyes focused more clearly on the small print and she learned with dismay that Lady Glanville, who had once been Alexa Reni, was dead.

Stunned by the news, Ros read the front-page story and then turned at once to the obituary columns. Asha's invitation to the birthday party had explained Lady Glanville's relationship to Ros's mother but had only briefly mentioned how famous the old lady had been in her youth. With increasing frustration at the discovery that she had arrived too late, Ros read the exceptionally full account of Alexa's life.

How tantalizing it was to have missed by such a very short time the opportunity to talk to Lady Glanville. Worst of all, she had lost her best chance to learn about her own mother. Asha would probably not remember much from her infancy. Ros had been relying on the old lady to recount the whole of Barbary Lorimer's life history.

The deep disappointment which swept over her as she pushed the newspaper aside made her briefly angry that her father had never told her the truth while he was alive—had never mentioned that she had a great-aunt and a half sister living in England. It was all to do with trying to forget the heartbreak of her mother's death, she supposed: but her ignorance made her feel curiously lonely—and, at this moment, affected by a greater sense of bereavement than would normally be caused by the death of a stranger. She sighed to herself and considered what she should do now that the day could not adhere to its original program. The first thing was to make a telephone call to her half sister.

Asha's voice was both friendly and businesslike as she made clear her wish to arrange a meeting as soon as possible. "I know I oughtn't to make a visitor do the traveling," she said. "But I'm tied to the telephone. Would you mind?" She gave detailed instructions about underground lines and the way to walk from Notting Hill Gate station. Ros listened politely and took a taxi.

It set her down in a scruffy street, outside what appeared to be a shop. Ros checked the address doubtfully; but even before she had time to ring the bell a door opened at the side of the shop and a tall, slim woman with long pale hair was holding out both hands in welcome.

Not even for the first moment were they strangers. Each of them separately had longed to have a sister and their delight in finding each other was mutual. As they went up the stairs together they held hands like friends reunited after a long parting.

The rooms of Asha's home were more spacious than the neighborhood suggested. If Ros had expected something grander, that was probably because of the connection with Lady Glanville. The furniture was not stylish, but it was comfortable; and the coffee she was offered at once was freshly ground as well as freshly made.

"You're upset," she said, looking more closely at her sister's pale face as the tray was set down on a coffee table. "You and the old lady were close, I guess."

Asha nodded. "I keep reminding myself that she was so very old, that this was bound to happen. But all the same . . ."

"It hit me too," Ros told her. "Sure, I can't weep for someone I never met. But I've always wanted to be part of a big family. I was raised rich and pampered, but that one thing was never on offer. I want you all to think of me as kin. But most of all I want to hear just everything about you, Asha. Right from the beginning. And especially how we came to lose each other. Your letter didn't explain that."

"I only found out recently from Aunt Alexa," said Asha. Ros listened intently as her sister passed on the details she had learned, and then asked questions to bring Asha's career up to date.

"So we're both boss women," she commented as she heard about the promotion to headmistress which would take effect in September. "You're going to run a big school, and I already run a company. Only because my father gave it to me; but that doesn't alter the fact that I'm in charge and that's how I like it. With different fathers, it must be from our mother that we've inherited the taste for being in control."

"According to Aunt Alexa, she was shy," Asha said. "But of course she was still young when she died. And it's true that the Lorimers as a family are pretty strong-minded. Come upstairs and I'll show you our great-great-grandfather—a boss figure if ever there was one."

Ros stood up to follow, but her eye was caught by a picture on the wall: a full-length portrait of an aristocratic young woman in a gown of gray lace and pink satin. It was the picture whose illustration on the Ancestors leaflet had first caught her notice. "Is that another ancestor of ours?" she asked. "There's a likeness to you, although not to me. It's beautiful. And so clean." She wondered why Asha did not answer and tried to interpret the mischief in her smile. Puzzled, she studied the portrait again. "You?" she said incredulously.

Asha's smile broadened as she repeated the pose. With her head held unnaturally high she pointed a neat toe forward and turned the knuckles of one hand to rest on her hip while the other was supported by an invisible parasol. "Ranji told you, didn't he, when he answered your letter, that one of the alternatives on offer was a painting of yourself in period costume. This is the prototype; we show it to give clients confidence that the result will look good. And just up these stairs is the man who painted it." Asha led the way up into a very large, light room. "Meet Chris Townsend. Chris, my sister, Ros Davidson."

The young artist was not standing at his easel but sitting astride a painter's donkey with a canvas propped in front of him at a slight angle. He turned his head to smile at them and set down the brush he was using.

"Please don't get up." Ros moved to stand behind him. "May I look?" She studied the photograph of a bespectacled sixty-year-old businessman which was fastened to the unfinished painting. Then she compared it with the kilted figure striding mistily across the canvas. "I don't believe it! It's impossible—but it's exactly him."

"He reckons that he's descended from one of the ancient kings of Ireland, and who am I to argue?" said Chris. "He only sent me a profile, so a profile is all he can have. But the costume is genuine, at least. And I feel like being Turner this week."

"Will you paint me?" asked Ros. She was not normally impulsive, but this unusual day was proving to be both exciting and frightening. People died, people lost touch—even relations as close as sisters. Perhaps it was still the effect of jet lag, but she felt her life to be shadowy and shifting. A portrait would put her on record as having existed, would fix her in one period of her life. And this young man was good. If he would allow her to commission him she could feel all the pleasure of being a patron and perhaps later enjoy a second pride in watching him grow famous.

Chris twisted around to stare at her more closely. Ros, never shy, lifted her chin and flashed brightness into her eyes.

"Certainly I'll paint you," said Chris in a businesslike manner. "I'll need half an hour's camera session with you before I start, and then three four-hour sittings, with a gap of at least three weeks after the first one—unless you want a run-of-the-mill effort just from the photographs. What period have you in mind? And have you a favorite artist?"

"The period is now," Ros told him. "Me now by you now."

"There's no such thing as me," said Chris. "Asha would have warned you of that if you'd given her advance notice. My talent is for appearing to be someone else."

"I don't believe you." Ros studied the mock Turner again and thought of the "Gainsborough" downstairs. "Sure, you have that talent, but you could do it straight. Could I have Blaize in the picture, do you think? Is it still standing, Asha?"

"Oh yes, Blaize is still there," Asha assured her. "Aunt Alexa will be buried in the churchyard on the estate. If you come to the funeral, you'll see the house."

"I've no rights in Blaize," Ros admitted. "So it mustn't steal the show. It's been a kind of dream castle, that's all, ever since I was nine. I knew I was a baby there because I'd seen a photograph: but I didn't know what or where it was. What I'd like is Blaize in the background, misty like the moor behind your Irish king. With me in the foreground, very clear. Not a photographic style, but in modern dress and recognizable."

"I can tell you're sisters." Chris pretended to be gloomy, but he was smiling. "Bullies, the pair of you. Everything to be just the way you want it. Well, when I look at the Ancestor I can see where you both get it from."

Ros turned at the reminder and saw that the picture of John Junius Lorimer had been set up on an easel for her to inspect. She had already seen a photograph of it, but that had not prepared her for the imperious eyes which stared directly into her own.

"I see what you mean. A strong picture of a strong man. Will you be able to give me a family tree, Asha? Your husband's letter just said that he was the great-grandfather of my mother. I want to know everything you can tell me about my mother's family." She gazed at the old man's face for a few moments longer. "Think of all the things he must have done in his lifetime—all the people he must have loved or hated."

"Everyone's life is a story, isn't it?" suggested Asha.

"Right. I was thinking just that this morning when I read Lady Glanville's obituary. Oh, Asha, I truly do wish that I'd had time to meet her. To miss it only by a day! That's really tough. All my life I've been starved of ancestors and relations. You've no idea how I'm going to cling from now on. You'll never be able to shake me off."

"I don't want to. I may have a full head of ancestors but, like you, I'm short of relations. And especially of sisters. Are you interested in buying John Junius, then?"

"Oh, yes," said Ros. She put an arm around her sister's waist, hugging her close. "If you're willing to sell, I've come here to buy." She stared into the old man's piercing green eyes, giving as good as she got. "I guess not everyone would want a personality as strong as that in the room. But I can cope with him. I'm a Lorimer as well."

XII

Alexa had expressed the wish to be buried in the little churchyard at Blaize. The parish church had been built by the Glanvilles many centuries earlier for their own convenience: a fair distance from the village but very close to the house. Asha thought it would be tactful to telephone the present head of the family before making arrangements for the service, and was invited to Blaize to discuss her plans.

The Lord Glanville who greeted her proved to be a plump and pleasant young merchant banker. He made it clear that he welcomed an opportunity to bring to an end the obscure feud between the two branches of the Glanville family. "I'm sure my father never intended Lady Glanville to leave Blaize so precipitately after her son died," he said. "Her belief that she needed to vacate the house immediately was all of her own making. Father found himself cast as the ogre of the piece without being given any opportunity to discuss the situation."

"Aunt Alexa and your grandfather had a bitter quarrel," Asha told him. "Over eighty years ago it must have been, but she never forgot it. I don't know exactly what happened." And now I never shall know, she thought. There would be no further chance to explore the remote history of Alexa's life.

"I imagine you often visited your aunt while she was living here," Lord Glanville said. Asha had not quite been able to control the movement of her eyes as she noted the changes which had taken place since she was last at Blaize. The drawing room itself looked far larger now that it no longer contained a grand piano. The room had formerly been crowded with photographs of Alexa in her various operatic roles. Now the only display was of silver cups and medals and trophies in the shape of horses. A large Stubbs hung on the wall which once had displayed the portrait of Alexa's father.

"I did more than visit," Asha told her host. "I was brought up here. This was my home until I married."

"Then welcome home. Let me give you a drink. I asked the vicar to drop in so that you could fix everything up in comfort. We spend a small fortune every year on heating that church and it's never anything but arctic. What kind of funeral are you planning?"

"A very small one. While she was alive, Aunt Alexa made plans for a memorial service to be held in London. More of a concert than a service. An opera singer will sing one of her favorite arias. And the violinist, Leo Tavadze, was a protégé of hers once: he'll play something. She thought some of the ex-pupils of the school might perform as well. But I was only to choose the good ones. 'Nothing but the best.' It was always her motto. That service will be a public occasion. But the funeral itself will be very nearly confined to family. I imagine that some of the old tenants here may want to come. And one or two of the nurses who were looking after her when she died asked to be told the date. But that's all."

"I'd be glad to offer any members of the family a drink or a meal or whatever's appropriate to the time after the service. Will you bring them back here?"

"That's very kind of you. It will be most welcome. There won't be many."

She had certainly spoken the truth there, Asha thought to herself four days later as she introduced Lord Glanville to the few remaining Lorimers, and the thought saddened her. It was natural enough that such a very old lady should have outlived all her friends. But Alexa must have hoped, earlier in her life, that her family circle would expand, increasing in number with each generation. It had mattered to her that the family should live on.

That was one reason why she was so pleased when Bernard and Helen drew Michael Laing—who was here with them today—more closely inside the family. And it was because they all knew how much it meant to her to believe that the Lorimer line was still strong and would flourish in the future that none of them—not even Michael himself—had liked to reveal the fact that Ilsa had not been his real mother. He was the youngest person in the room now, but he was not a Lorimer by blood. No Lorimer babies had been born since Ros, who was now thirty-two.

Would there be any in the future? Ros was not too old to become a mother. But she had made it clear to her sister that her greatest satisfaction came from the successful running of her own business. Children would be an interruption to her work and would tie her to their father with a degree of permanence which she found unacceptable. Since she had chosen to be childless while she married, it was unlikely that she would change her mind now that she lived alone.

That left Asha herself. In practical terms she alone would decide whether the Lorimer family lived or died. Without formulating the thought so precisely, she must have been aware of this for a long time already. It was hard to understand why she should suddenly feel overwhelmed by the burden now as she looked around at the tiny group of people in their black funereal clothes.

Perhaps it was because the sight of the family assembled in Lord Glanville's drawing room made its contraction clearer than a mental count could ever do. But even as she persuaded herself of this, a second emotion swept over Asha: a desolate loneliness triggered off not by the smallness of the group but by the place in which it was reunited. As though it were yesterday, she remembered her arrival in Blaize when she was five years old. She had tried to be brave, but the tears had streamed down her face as she cried aloud, "I want my mummy!" Her mother was dead. It was Alexa, already seventy years old, who had gone down on her knees beside the orphaned child and promised to look after her. In every sense except that of giving birth Alexa had been Asha's mother, and now Alexa was gone. Asha put up both hands to cover her eyes but was unable to press back the tears which repeated a thirty-year-old memory in a present sadness.

The others were chatting over their drinks with as much animation as if this were a cocktail party: they did not notice her sudden distress. Only Ranji, quickly sensitive to her feelings, excused himself to the vicar and came across the room. He did not speak but took her in his arms and held her tightly so that her hands, still flat over her face, pressed against his chest.

"Sorry," she said at last, sniffing herself under control. "Silly."

"Not silly at all. Absolutely natural. Stay here just a minute while I tell everyone we're going."

Asha dried her eyes and said her goodbyes. Ros had already been invited to drive back to London with Bernard, who remembered her as a baby. She kissed Asha sympathetically and promised to call her next day.

In the car Ranji did not speak but took hold of Asha's hand and placed it on his knee, stroking it gently from time to time as he drove. When they drew up in front of the flat she tried to explain something of what had upset her.

"When I was a little girl, Aunt Alexa was all I had," she said. "And in these last few years, she's really only had me. When I'm ninety-nine, I shan't have anyone."

"You'll have me," said Ranji. "I shall be ninety-six only. I'll drop you here. You can be getting into bed while I park the car."

"Bed? I'm not ill. When I cried, it was only—"

"Other things can happen in bed beside being ill," Ranji reminded her. "I love you very much, and especially when you cry. That beautiful woman needs comforting, I say to myself. Go and make the sheets warm for me."

Asha watched him drive away. It would take him a few moments to find a space in the residents' parking area and to walk back. She went upstairs to the flat and into the bathroom. With one hand already stretched toward the cupboard in which she kept her contraceptives, she stopped to think. Did she really care that the family was dying out? Was she truly afraid of being lonely, of having no one to love her as she had loved Alexa? If so, this was the moment when she could take a chance. Ranji, in romantic mood, would not stop to check that she had taken precautions. And if, later, he learned that she was pregnant and accused her of not consulting him, it would be easy to say that she too had been excited—that after all the years of taking the pill and not needing to worry, the more recent routine had been forgotten at this less usual time of day.

No. That would be cheating—and there was no need to lie. Ranji had never said he didn't want to start a family, only that they should wait. Well, she had waited: eight months had passed since they last discussed the subject. In any case, this would be an isolated occasion, a gamble of a sort, nothing more. Too much of her life was predictable, running to a well-organized timetable. It was necessary once in a while to open the door to the unexpected. Her knowledge of the possible consequences would add a touch of danger to their lovemaking and change it from a routine to an adventure. She could feel herself flushing with excitement as she closed the bathroom cupboard. Smiling, she moved toward the bedroom, unfastening her clothes as she went.

XIII

On a warm evening in June Ros flew into Heathrow for the second time. For her first visit in March she had allowed only the few days needed to make the acquaintance of her sister, attend Lady Glanville's birthday party and inspect the picture of her ancestor. A business meeting in San Francisco made it impossible for her to extend her stay by more than a day on that occasion—just long enough to allow Chris his first sitting—but before she left she made arrangements to return in the summer for a real vacation. Now Chris could finish the portrait and she would give herself time to explore London as a conscientious tourist.

Even in the bustle of Terminal Three's crowded arrival hall Ros recognized at once what had happened to her sister. She hardly waited until Asha had welcomed her with a kiss before producing a laughing accusation: "You're pregnant!"

Asha's expression of delight at the reunion changed to amazement. "How can you possibly tell?" Automatically her hand stroked her smooth, unbulging skirt.

"You have the radiant look that writers of magazine stories describe in such gooey detail." That was not wholly truthful. It was a mixture of triumph and secretiveness in Asha's smile which aroused suspicion. "I notice you're not about to deny it."

"I make no comment," said Asha primly. Then she grinned. "In other words, you could be right, but I haven't broken it to Ranji yet."

"Because you're not sure? Is sisterly intuition speedier than pregnancy testing?"

"Oh, I'm sure enough. Waiting for the right moment, that's all. What sort of flight did you have?"

"The best sort: uneventful." Ros took the hint to drop the subject of pregnancy. She had no wish to spoil the pleasure of the reunion by stumbling into some kind of marital minefield.

For this visit she had made arrangements to rent a service apartment, more spacious than the guest room offered by her sister and more comfortable than a hotel. Asha drove her there from the airport. The luxurious building was almost unnaturally silent, with double-glazed windows to insulate all its rooms from the noise of traffic. The doors of the elevator made no sound as they opened and closed, and the thick pile of the carpet stifled their footsteps as they followed the receptionist along the third-floor corridor, turning two corners before they reached the door of the apartment. Quietness had been Ros's primary specification when she made the booking, and her request had been honored.

"There's something we have to talk about right away," Ros said after the receptionist had shown them the apartment and left. She made herself comfortable on a sofa in the sitting room and gestured Asha to do the same. "Lady Glanville's rubies."

"What about them? They're your rubies now. You've been told that, haven't you? I ought to have let Mr. Dangerfield know in March that you were here in England. But your visit was so short, and there was so much to be done after Aunt Alexa died. I didn't think about it

until he wrote to find out whether I had an up-to-date address for
you."

"The rubies should have gone to you," said Ros. "Mr. Dangerfield
told me that. If Lady Glanville had lived just one day longer they
would have been yours. And you knew it."

"It was extremely unprofessional of Mr. Dangerfield to say so. The
law doesn't take any notice of ifs."

"He only told me because I asked him right out. We had a long talk
on the telephone. It didn't seem right that something so valuable
should go to me, a stranger, when you'd been so close to Lady Glanville. I reckoned that she must have forgotten what she said in her will
—and that she'd have changed it if she remembered. When I put
that to Mr. Dangerfield, he admitted that she was just on the point of
altering the will. Why didn't you challenge it, Asha? An old lady on
the eve of her hundredth birthday—a court might well have considered that the will didn't represent her true wishes."

"Aunt Alexa was never senile," Asha pointed out. "To the very last
minute of her life she knew exactly what she wanted. Besides—" she
seemed for a moment to be struggling for a clear understanding of her
own feelings. "I wasn't brought up in the expectation of inheriting
any kind of family fortune. I always knew that Blaize and all the
Glanville jewels and trust funds would be whisked away as soon as
Pirry died. I think Aunt Alexa herself for a good many years had
forgotten that the Lorimer rubies existed. Certainly I only saw them
for the first time on the day she died. So they aren't some kind of
heirloom that I'd been expecting to get. And there's another thing.
She lived as a rich woman for a lot of her life, but by the time she
died she hardly had anything left. Whatever I did for her in those last
years was because I loved her, not because I hoped to inherit anything. She knew that, and I knew it, and that was the right way for
things to be. If I'd tried to dispute the will, I'd have spoiled that
relationship—even after it was over. Do you understand? The rubies,
as jewelry, mean nothing to me. I couldn't ever wear anything so
valuable. And as a token of love I don't need them either, because I
know what she felt."

"I get all that," Ros agreed. "But they have a third value that you
don't mention. Hard cash. I'm not asking you what I should do, Asha.
I'm telling you what I've decided. When I called Mr. Dangerfield I

first of all asked him to find a way of making you the heir. Some of what he told me I could hardly believe. If I got it right, he was saying that so long as all the beneficiaries agree, they can carve up an estate any way they like and the hell to what the person who's dead wanted." Ros allowed her face to reveal what she thought of such an unbusinesslike arrangement.

Then she continued more briskly. "At first I thought we could deal with it that way. But one more point came over loud and clear. If you had inherited the rubies directly from Lady Glanville you would have had to pay some kind of tax—was it capital transfer tax?—on their value. And it wouldn't have been peanuts. So because the money which she *did* leave to you didn't come to much, you would have had to sell the jewels before you could pay the tax which entitled you to own them. Well, that's what Mr. Dangerfield said. I won't tell you what I think about such a crazy system; he got me to believe it in the end. So it wouldn't help for me simply to sign away my rights. Okay, then, we agreed another plan. I accept the legacy. I put the whole set of jewelry up to auction—in London, because if it got around California that I owned that kind of property I'd have gunmen lining up for the right to break into my safe. Once the rubies have turned into cash, I pay off any British taxes and then I make a money present to you. Mr. Dangerfield said the tax law wouldn't catch a gift from a foreigner."

"Ros, I can't possibly—"

Ros silenced her with a wave of the hand. "You don't get to have a choice," she said. "Look at it this way, honey. I'm a very rich lady. I don't need more money. If I knew I was going to die tomorrow, I wouldn't know what to do with what I have. Well, my employees would find that they owned a cooperative and a couple of charities would clap their hands. Lady Glanville wanted you to have a gift of money in memory of her. I intend to see that her last wishes are carried out. Now then, when is Chris going to let me sit for him again?"

She was amused to see how completely her eloquence on the subject of the rubies had silenced Asha. Ranji, she guessed, would have no sentimental doubts about accepting the offer: and Asha, realizing that, had no choice but to give in with a helpless, affectionate laugh and kiss of thanks.

It was as well that Ros had arranged a leisurely visit, for disposing
of the rubies proved to be a protracted business. Mr. Dangerfield—
moving with what in legal terms was lightning speed—had already
negotiated the tax liability on an agreed valuation, but Ros had to
establish her identity as well as her claim. On the day that probate
was granted she acquired theoretical ownership of her legacy. The
actual hand-over took place later, toward the end of her stay in England. Escorted by Mr. Dangerfield to the bank manager's office, she
signed a set of papers to release the jewel case from the strong room.
Its contents were displayed to her while she compared the pieces with
the written specification. A second set of papers arranged for the
valuables to go immediately back into safekeeping until they were
auctioned in the autumn.

"I won't see these jewels again," Ros said. "Someone from
Sotheby's will come to photograph them and prepare a description,
but I'll be gone by then. I'm going to ask you both to wait a moment
longer. Just once, I want to wear them."

She took the necklace from its velvet-lined drawer and fastened it
around her neck. Slipping from her ears the thin gold rings which she
wore by day, she replaced them with the delicate drop of ruby roses.
Only when it came to the tiara did she hesitate. It was the lawyer who
unexpectedly offered to help.

"I remember how Lady Glanville wore it," he said. "May I?" Ros
felt him slide the tiara into her hair and settle it firmly. "I held a
mirror for Lady Glanville as well, but—"

The bank manager, without speaking, opened a coat cupboard
which proved to have a looking glass fixed inside the door. Ros had
expected English professional men to be stuffy, but these two were
taking obvious pleasure in her childlike enjoyment of dressing up. She
produced a camera from her handbag.

"Would you?" she asked Mr. Dangerfield. "Something for the family album. Well, two or three. The flash is automatic."

The lawyer glanced at the banker and received a nod of permission.
Within a few moments the jewels were back in their case and a
security guard had returned them to the strong room.

"Crazy, isn't it?" commented Ros, describing the incident to Asha
a few hours later. "My father falls in love with a married woman in a
foreign country and thirty-five years later I'm wearing a set of precious

jewels given me by someone who never saw me after my first birthday."

"You didn't wear them!"

"Just once. Why not?" Ros looked curiously at her sister, whose expression displayed a momentary alarm. But Asha did not explain. "As soon as they're printed, I'll show you the pictures to prove it. Talking of rubies, I had a call from someone called Peter Langley, who said you knew him. He's working on a biography of Lady Glanville, right?"

"Yes. She asked him to help her write her memoirs, but she didn't leave herself time. Now he plans to do a kind of family history. A hundred years of the Lorimers. He knows a lot about Aunt Alexa's father—the man in your portrait."

"First he's writing a newspaper piece about the rubies. I guess that's faster money than the book. He'd read Lady Glanville's will when it was probated, so he wanted to interview me as the current owner. I said he could stop by. This is to check him out with you."

"He's a journalist, yes. And honest, if that's what you're asking. If he'd wanted to steal the rubies he could have knocked me down and run for it in March. All the same . . ."

"All the same?" For a second time Ros noticed a doubt in her sister's eyes, but again was given no explanation.

"Oh, I'm sure it's all right. I don't like that kind of publicity myself. I've told him not to mention me in any of his articles, though I don't suppose I can keep out of the book. But in four days' time you'll be gone, so I don't suppose it can do any harm."

The phrase was a curious one to use about a simple newspaper interview, but Ros did not press the matter. She had other business at Asha's home, for her portrait was finished. Chris was clearly nervous as she and Asha appeared in the attic to inspect the painting, but Ros found no difficulty in expressing enthusiasm. He had painted her sitting on the ground, as though on a hilltop. Blaize—misty, as she had asked—stretched across the background: but Ros herself, her hands clasped around one knee, had been depicted in strong browns and reds. There was nothing wistful in the pose to suggest that she was pining for Blaize. Instead, Chris had perfectly caught in her expression the firmness with which she was accustomed to make important decisions. "I like it," she said.

That, of course, was not enough. It was necessary to praise every aspect of the work, to exclaim over details, to assure Chris that he did indeed possess a distinctive style.

"How soon can it travel?" she asked him.

"It should really have time to dry. But I'll put it in an airtight crate together with John Junius so that it can't get knocked or dusty." Ros had left the Victorian picture behind after her earlier visit so that it could be packed together with this new one. "I'll bring the crate round to your apartment the night before your flight."

That time was not far off. On the day that Peter Langley's article appeared—illustrated by the photograph of Ros wearing the jewels—she took Asha and Ranji out to dinner before returning to the apartment to pack. This was not a task which demanded much time or thought at the end of a trip and she was in bed before midnight. Her flight was booked for the next morning. She had enjoyed her vacation, but she looked forward to returning home and was in a contented mood as she slipped easily into sleep.

Ros did not consciously hear the noise that awoke her in the middle of the night but, once disturbed, had no doubt that there had been a sound. With wide-open eyes she stared into the darkness, holding her breath and listening. The silence was so complete as to be almost unnatural. Was someone on the other side of the door listening as intently as herself? Could mere imagination be enough to make her skin prickle with uneasiness?

It was not imagination. There was a second sound, so faint that it would have been inaudible had she not been waiting for it: the sound of a well-made, well-oiled door whispering over the thick pile of a carpet. From the bed, set into one end of the L-shaped bedroom, Ros could not see the door, and its opening admitted no light: but she was quite sure that someone had come in from the sitting room. Moving as stealthily as the intruder she began to move a hand toward the bedside telephone, but then changed her mind. The instrument had an old-fashioned English dial instead of a speedy press-button face and she had already noticed that the emergency number was, ridiculously, the one which took the longest to dial. Long before she could complete a call she would be heard and interrupted.

So instead she lay still. Her mouth was dry—too dry to scream, even had there been any chance of anyone hearing—and her heart pounded so loudly that it must surely be audible. But she did her best to control her breathing, exaggerating it slightly in the hope that she would give the impression of being deeply asleep. The burglar would soon discover that all the drawers were empty and then, please God, he would creep out of the room as surreptitiously as he had entered. His quietness, suggesting that he hoped not to disturb her, was the only reassuring factor in a terrifying situation.

The wait seemed interminable. In San Francisco Ros kept a loaded pistol in her bedside chest. But knowing that to carry a weapon would be illegal here and on the plane, and believing England to be a less violent country than her own, she had brought nothing with which to protect herself. In any case, she had once in the past been robbed at gunpoint, in her own car, and believed that passivity, although humiliating, was often the safest policy.

A drawer was slammed back into place and a man's voice swore violently. In spite of her attempt at self-control, Ros could not resist a gasp of alarm. She grabbed at the telephone, knowing that her pretense of sleep would no longer be accepted, but before she could lift the receiver she was seized from behind. One hand covered her mouth, pressing her head back so roughly that she felt her neck must break, while the other grabbed an arm and twisted it painfully behind her back. She tried to struggle, kicking out frantically, but her attacker was too strong. Still kicking, she was turned face downward on the bed. A knee on her neck pressed her head into the pillow so that she could not breathe. As she struggled—not now to escape but to avoid suffocation—she was hardly aware of the wire being twisted around her wrists. But a sharp tug brought her feet up behind her back to be tied to her hands, stretching all the muscles of her body. By the time the pressure on her neck was released she was trussed like an animal, unable to move her arms or legs. Her gasps for breath mingled with sobs of pain.

A hand covered her mouth again as she was turned on to her side and the bedhead light was switched on by a man dressed in a black sweater and jeans. A dark stocking over his face flattened his nose and thickened his lips but was not sufficiently opaque to dull the glitter of his eyes.

He held a knife for a moment in front of her face. When he was sure she had seen it, he lowered it until the blade touched her neck. Ros lay still, not daring even to swallow the lump in her throat.

"Keep quiet," said the man. "Or else." He pressed the knife against her skin as he took his other hand away from her mouth. Ros kept quiet.

"The jewelry," he said. "That's all I want. Tell me where it is and I'll take it and leave you alone."

"What jewelry?" As soon as she spoke Ros realized that the question was a mistake.

"Don't play games. The rubies."

"I don't have them. They're not here."

"I saw the picture in the paper. They were round your neck. Where are they? I'll find them anyway, but it'll be better for you if you tell me."

"I wouldn't keep anything like that in a rented room. They're at the bank."

"You're packed for traveling and it's Sunday tomorrow. You must have taken them out. Come on. Where are they?"

"I promise you—" But the man was too angry to listen and Ros, seeing how short was the fuse of his temper, was even more frightened than before. She watched apprehensively as he felt in a pocket. Did he mean to torture her? But what he produced was a wide piece of adhesive tape which he pressed firmly over her mouth. Then, muttering under his breath, he left her and went into the sitting room.

Now that he no longer troubled to be quiet, Ros could follow his actions in her imagination as he broke open her suitcases and flung out the contents. There were pauses, when perhaps he was opening a toilet bag or discovering her jewel roll, which did not in fact hold any valuable jewelry. She could hear him muttering, as well, and the fear that his anger was a form of madness pumped through her body with each beat of her heart. Her stomach was turning, and that in itself terrified her, for if she were to be sick with her mouth so firmly sealed she would choke on her own vomit.

Without warning he was back, pulling her on to the floor so that he could strip the bed. He tore the cases off each pillow and lifted the mattress to see what was hidden beneath it. The wire cut into her flesh as, half lifting her and half dragging, he carried her into the sitting room and tugged the plaster from her mouth.

"Last chance. Where are they?"

"Waiting to be sold." It was urgent that she should tell him everything before he silenced her again. "They're going to be auctioned. The bank's keeping them until the sale." If only she were able to show him the receipt; but she had given it to Mr. Dangerfield, with authority to hand the valuables over to Sotheby's. "You have to believe me. Why should I let you kill me for a few jewels if I could hand them over? They're in the bank. That's the truth, God help me."

"They're in the crate, aren't they?" Ros felt sick again as she realized that he refused to believe her. The wooden crate in which the two pictures had been sealed up for the journey was the only container left unopened. He held up a small ax which she recognized by its red blade. She had last seen it in a case at the end of the corridor, kept ready for emergency use in the event of fire. "You think I won't dare use this because of the noise. But there's no one to hear. I shan't ask again. Where are they?"

"In the bank. Please. Please. No, please." As the plaster was pressed back again Ros tried frantically to persuade herself that the man had nothing to gain by harming her. But somewhere inside the panic which now overwhelmed her was a small cold center of recognition that she was going to die as certainly as if she had been sentenced to execution. To die for no good reason. Part of her mind seemed to be outside the scene and watching it, as though this could not possibly be happening to herself. Murder victims were always other people. But her body knew the truth, voiding itself on the carpet and jerking convulsively as she strained against her bonds.

She heard herself moaning and made one last effort to bring her terror under control, to reach a calm acceptance of whatever was going to happen to her. But it was impossible. The man had abandoned his first attempt to prize the crate open and now, crazy with frustration, brought the ax crashing down into the wood. Surely someone must hear. Surely someone would help. But there could not be much time. The trembling of her body grew more violent as he twisted the ax out of the wood and raised it to chop downward again. And again. And again.

And then, reaching the limit of fear, she became still, no longer shuddering, no longer conscious of her stretched muscles or the tightness of the wire which trussed her. All the bones in her body seemed to have dissolved. As though her throat were already cut and her blood already drained away she felt herself sagging down into the thick pile of the luxury carpet. The crazed blows continued to beat down on the splintering wood. Ros closed her eyes and waited.

XIV

At seven o'clock on Sunday morning London was lazily relaxed. There was no traffic on the streets and the few pedestrians who had risen early to choose their Sunday newspapers strolled at a leisurely pace as they studied the headlines. Asha, on her way to Ros's apartment, moved more briskly, although there was no hurry. Ranji would not be bringing the car around until nine to drive Ros to the airport; this earlier walk was only to give the two sisters time for a last chat and a cup of coffee together.

There was no one about in the silent entrance hall of the apartment block. Part of the service it offered was the impression that there was no one else alive within several miles. Remembering the racket of the Portobello Road and the perpetual yelling of children in the school playground, Asha felt briefly envious of the peace that money could buy.

Stepping out of the elevator at the third floor, she walked along the carpeted corridor, reached the door of Ros's apartment and put out her hand to ring the bell. But her arm fell back to her side as she saw that the door was not quite closed; and its frame was damaged.

Asha froze. Common sense told her that she should turn away at once and hurry to find help or at least company. Her brain gave instructions and her body, numbed by alarm, refused to obey them. Instead, she held her breath, listening for some faint sound which would speak of danger or need: but all the suspense was in her own mind and not in the heavy, undisturbed air. If she were to ring the bell, would there be a cheerful shout from Ros, an apologetic explanation of how she had locked herself out of the apartment and forced her way in? Asha tried to make herself believe in the possibility; but failed.

Like a puppet controlled from above she lifted her arm again. This time it seemed far heavier than before. The door opened silently as she pushed it: the curtained room was still and dark. Without moving her feet she leaned forward to feel for the light switch.

What she saw did not surprise her, because she already feared it; but that did not reduce the shock. Still without moving she forced her eyes to survey the chaos of the sitting room. The chairs and sofas had been overturned and their cushions scattered on the floor. The drawers of every piece of furniture lay face downward on the floor. Ros's three suitcases—no doubt placed neatly near the door after being packed for the journey—had been opened: their contents were strewn over the carpet. The wooden crate containing the two portraits had been hacked open with an ax, which was still embedded in the wood. Asha gave a small cry of anguish as she saw that there was blood on the blade.

Sure by now that no living person was waiting for her in the apartment, she forced herself to step inside. Her feet crunched on cosmetic jars or stepped softly on clothes. Behind one of the upturned sofas she found her sister's body.

Her muscles tensed as she tried to contain her horror, recognizing that a single groan, a single shudder would be enough to trigger off a total lack of self-control. One reaction, though, could not be controlled. With an irrational reversion to childhood rules she turned away, trying to leave the room before she was sick—as though it were possible to inflict any greater contamination on the bloody scene. But there was no strength left in her legs, and in the doorway of the apartment she fell forward on to her knees, vomiting and sobbing for breath. How was it that no one heard? Long after her body had, surely, emptied itself, she continued to retch, doubling up in spasms which became steadily more painful. She tried to crawl away from the mess and found that the carpet of the corridor, like that of the sitting room, was stained with blood. Had she trodden too near to Ros and brought a trail out with her? No. The blood was her own.

The spasms continued and the pain grew until even her distress was not great enough to shield her from it. And the distress itself took on a new dimension, because now another life was at risk. "Ranji!" she called, between each agonizing contraction of her muscles. But Ranji was not due to arrive for more than an hour. Unable to move, Asha watched her blood soaking into the thick pile of the luxury carpet and knew that he would be too late to save his child.

She must have fainted, because when she next opened her eyes she was in a hospital bed. One arm lay stiffly by her side, attached to tubes dark with blood. On the other side of the bed Ranji held her hand with both his own, kneeling on the floor with his head bowed so that his forehead touched her wrist. She called his name faintly and at once he was kissing her. He had been crying, she saw as after a little while he pulled himself up to sit in a chair.

"Oh my God, Asha, I was so frightened. When I saw what had happened, I thought you were dead as well."

What had happened? Asha did not remember. She stared into Ranji's eyes as though she could read in them the history of how she had come to be here. Dead as well? As well as whom?

No sooner had she asked herself the question than the answer imprinted itself on her eyes. As vividly as though she were back in the apartment she saw again the white-satin nightdress stained with blood, the wrists and ankles so swollen that they almost concealed the wire which bound them, the half-severed head of the sister who had been unknown to her for so many years and now was lost forever. As strongly as though she were seeing that picture for the first time she felt her stomach muscles contract and cried out not only because of the hideous memory but from the pain of her involuntary retching.

Ranji must have been warned, because he held some kind of dish ready as she hung her head over the side of the bed. Only a little dark-green bile emerged. He wiped her mouth gently clean as she collapsed back on the pillows, exhausted.

"Don't think about it," Ranji pleaded; but she could not think of anything else and even as he tried to comfort her he must have realized that. When the ward sister stepped through the curtains which screened Asha's bed from the rest of the ward and announced that a policewoman wished to speak to him, he refused at first to leave.

"It's really your wife she needs to talk to," Sister told him. "I said she'd have to wait a bit and she agreed to that if she could get some immediate information from you about Miss Davidson."

"I'll be all right," whispered Asha. "Come back again."

He squeezed her hand as a promise and rose to his feet. The nurse was about to follow him when Asha called her back. "Sister! I'm pregnant. Will this—?"

The nurse looked down sympathetically. "I'm sorry, dear. I'm afraid you lost the baby."

Asha's eyes flooded with tears—and yet she had guessed even before she asked.

"It was early days, wasn't it?" Sister said. "This won't stop you trying again. You'll need to build up your strength. But in two or three months . . ."

Asha dabbed at her eyes with the sleeve of the white hospital nightdress. "Does my husband know?" she asked.

"He saw that you lost a lot of blood before he found you. After we'd examined you here, we told him that you'd had an internal hemorrhage." She gestured toward the transparent tubes which continued steadily to feed their contents into Asha's arm. "People get alarmed if they see the drips without any warning. He was so concerned about you that he didn't ask about the baby."

"He didn't know. I'd meant to tell him today, after my sister—my sister—" She began to cry again. "I don't want him to know now," she managed to say at last. "It will only upset him more."

The nurse nodded neutrally. "Could you cope with the policewoman?" she asked. "If you felt able to get it over, we could give you a sedative. A really good sleep is what you need now."

"All right." Asha waited, numb with unhappiness, until the policewoman arrived, acompanied by Ranji. "I can't tell you anything that you didn't see for yourselves," she said. "It was all over before I got there."

"What time was that?"

"About quarter past seven."

"Did you meet anyone inside the building? In the hall or corridor? Or did you hear any movement, as though someone might be keeping out of your way?"

"No. Nothing."

"And in the street outside. Was anyone moving unusually fast, behaving suspiciously, wearing bloodstained clothing?"

Asha shook her head.

"I'm sorry that I have to ask this kind of question, but did you touch your sister's body? It would help if we knew whether it was still warm then."

"I didn't touch anything except the door and the light switch. I just looked." Unbidden, the picture of what she had seen returned. Her eyes seemed to flood with blood. In a room which suddenly darkened she did not hear the next question and was only aware that one had been asked because of the anxious expressions of her two visitors when she drifted back into consciousness. "Sorry. What was that?"

"If you could describe the room," said the policewoman, reluctantly businesslike. "The position of everything you remember."

Asha did her best, while the policewoman checked the details against her own observation later in the morning. "I've nearly finished," she said when this was done. "But can you suggest what the intruder might have been looking for? Would Miss Davidson have had a lot of money on her?"

"She used credit cards more than cash. And she was on the point of leaving England. She'd settled the bill for the apartment, and we were going to drive her to Heathrow. She'd hardly have needed any more sterling at all."

"What about other property? Were the pictures in the wooden crate valuable?"

"Not to anyone outside the family. And they weren't stolen, were they?"

"The intruder might have been disturbed. But what attracted him to the apartment in the first place? This wasn't a casual breakin and a quick snatch of anything lying round. The search was thorough—and angry. There must have been something specific he expected to find."

There was a long silence. Asha remembered the uneasiness she had felt at Ros's casual mention that she had tried on Alexa's jewelry. It could not be a coincidence that Peter Langley's article—illustrated by a photograph of Ros wearing her legacy—had appeared on the morning before Ros's murder. The jewels were in the bank and the receipt was in Mr. Dangerfield's safe, but the article had not mentioned this.

"The rubies," Asha said—so faintly that Ranji and the policewoman were forced to lean toward her in order to hear. "Yes. He would have been looking for the Lorimer rubies."

X V

For two days already the scream of the chain saw had pierced its way through to the living room of the flat. Asha and Ranji had learned to close their ears to it; but Mr. Dangerfield, paying an unexpected call, reacted to the sound with startled alarm.

"There's a row of elm trees between this row of buildings and the next," Asha explained. "The last of them died of Dutch elm disease this summer, and now the council has realized that they're dangerous as well as dead. So they're all coming down. Coffee?"

"Thank you very much." The lawyer sat down and opened his briefcase. "I thought I might see you at the auction yesterday."

Asha's hand trembled as she poured out the coffee. Three months had passed since Ros's death and her own miscarriage, but the mere allusion to her great-aunt's jewelry still made her shudder. "Not interested," she said briefly.

"But as you'll see, they've brought you in a very handsome sum." Mr. Dangerfield set two sheets of paper on the table in front of her. Glancing at the first, Asha saw that it was the printed form on which Sotheby's had typed the amount for which the lot had been sold. The other sheet was covered with handwritten figures. No doubt it contained Mr. Dangerfield's calculation of the tax to be deducted. She did not bother to study it.

"I don't want anything to do with the rubies," she said, setting down the cups and saucers so that their rattling should not betray how much the subject upset her. "As far as I can see, they came into Aunt Alexa's side of the family dishonestly and they've brought nothing but trouble ever since."

"No one's expecting you to have the jewels themselves," Ranji reminded her. "It's only money."

While Asha continued to shake her head, the lawyer leaned forward in his chair. "It's certain that Lady Glanville intended to bequeath the jewelry to you," he said. "It was unfortunate that her wishes should have been frustrated by a matter of hours, but at least

Miss Davidson didn't make the same mistake. Her instructions were completely clear, confirmed in writing and signed. I was empowered to act as a trustee in putting the jewels into the auction, paying all charges and taxes out of the proceeds and handing over the balance to you. The legal transfer was effective before Miss Davidson's death and I am obliged to carry out her intentions."

"But you can't make me accept," said Asha. She turned to her husband, sitting beside her on the sofa. "Ranji, I'm sorry if this seems unreasonable. But anything we did with the money would always remind me of Ros and what happened to her. No one can force me to take it, surely?"

"It's enough to buy a house," Ranji pointed out.

"How could I ever be happy in a home bought with this money?"

"Or it could pay off my debts. I could apply for my release from bankruptcy. Then I would be able to put the Ancestors on a proper business footing." There was a note of appeal in his voice which at last penetrated Asha's almost hysterical reaction to every mention of the rubies. How selfish she was to think only of herself!

The two men waited as Asha, without speaking, forced herself to consider the question more rationally. Any money handed over to the official receiver to pay off Ranji's debts would be effectively removed from her control. It would disappear, bringing her no direct benefit. There would be no acquisition, no object or building tainted by Ros's death to act as a permanent reminder of unhappiness. And Ranji's creditors, innocent victims of the market collapse for which he in turn had not been to blame, deserved to be recompensed. "I see," she said slowly. "Yes, of course."

With her mind made up, she looked straight into the lawyer's eyes. "Then will you draw up something for me to sign, Mr. Dangerfield? I want to transfer my interest in the jewelry to Ranji, so that the auctioneers hand over the sale proceeds directly to him."

"You realize, of course, that a very considerable sum is involved and that you have no legal liability for your husband's debts? As long as this money remains your property the receiver can have no claim on it. But if it becomes part of your husband's personal assets . . ." Mr. Dangerfield's voice expressed no disapproval. He was merely making sure, as a good family lawyer should, that his client understood the consequences of her decision.

Asha hardly bothered to listen to him. She was aware only of Ranji's hand squeezing hers in a tight grip of gratitude, of Ranji's brown eyes brimming with love as they looked down into her own.

She had been wrong to think that the gift would bring her no benefit. Her husband was an honest, honorable man who felt the shame of his debts keenly. Thanks to Ros, he could recover his self-esteem and these past two unsatisfactory years could be put behind them and forgotten. The heirloom which had touched so many of the Lorimers with misery would at last, in the very moment of passing to strangers, bring happiness to the family. She smiled back at Ranji, mouthing the words "I love you" in silence so that Mr. Dangerfield would not hear.

"I shall be happy to arrange it," the lawyer said. "And to present the case for discharge from bankruptcy if you would like me to do that."

"I'll leave you to fix it up together," Asha said, for the telephone was ringing. She took the call in the dining room, which had become Ranji's office. To her surprise, the caller was her cousin Paula.

"Another flying visit," Paula said. "I've been invited to give evidence to a race relations commission. I'll tell you all about it when we meet. Can I see you this afternoon? For a walk in Hyde Park, perhaps?"

Asha hesitated. "It's the beginning of the school year, Paula. All the new children who are coming up from their primary schools to start at Hillgate will be arriving at two o'clock. I'm taking an assembly at three, to give them a pep talk. But this evening—"

"Five minutes," said Paula. "Just five minutes between two and three o'clock, in your room at school. Could you spare me that?"

"Yes, but—"

"See you!" Paula rang off before Asha could insist on a more leisurely meeting. She went back into the drawing and found that Mr. Dangerfield had left.

"More coffee?" asked Ranji, pouring it out.

"Thanks." She pulled a cushion onto the floor and sat down on it. Years ago, when she had first known Ranji, this had been her way of indicating that she was ready for a serious conversation. His smile suggested that he remembered this.

"When Mr. Dangerfield was here, I said that I couldn't bear to buy a house with the money from the rubies," she reminded him. "But all the same, we might consider moving, don't you think? The one thing to be said for an oversize school is that it entitles its head to an oversize salary. We could afford a mortgage."

"Why would you like to move?" Ranji was not opposing the suggestion.

"The Ancestors business is really taking off now, isn't it?" The summer tourist season had brought a rush of orders to Ranji's fledgling business. People who had read the brochure in the United States, but were reluctant to commit themselves by letter, had added the studio to their list of London sights. Chris had needed to spend the whole of the long summer holiday in the attic studio to meet the demand for modern costume pictures and every spare corner of the flat was filled with old canvases which Ranji had bought at sales. "There are so many people calling and telephoning. And when I went up to the attic this morning I felt that it didn't belong to me anymore. It's Chris's studio. The dining room is an office and the landing is a storeroom and—well, the flat isn't private anymore."

"Is that the only reason you want to move?"

"Yes. To have a home just for the two of us."

"For two only? Or are you thinking of three? Asha, that day—" He paused, not wishing to upset her, but Asha knew which day he meant.

"Yes," she admitted. "I had a miscarriage. I was pregnant."

"I thought so. So much blood. I didn't like to ask you then, but even earlier I'd been waiting for you to say something."

"That very day I was going to tell you."

"Was it an accident—the pregnancy, I mean?"

"No."

"So do you want to try again?"

"No." Asha's answer was definite. "I made a misjudgment, Ranji. It was after Aunt Alexa's funeral. I was upset and—well, I can't explain in any way that makes sense. I felt that the family ought to be kept alive. And I seemed to be the only person who could do anything about it."

"So you took a decision as though you were the head of the family. You ought to have asked me." He spoke reasonably, without anger.

"Of course I should have discussed it with you. I'm sorry. On top of that, it was sloppy thinking. And a wrong decision."

"So what do you think now?"

"I think now that to bring a child into the world for no better reason than to provide my ancestors and myself and you with descendants would be unforgivable. And I think also that I'm of more value to the world as a teacher than as a mother. I could bring up one or two children of my own well enough, no doubt. But as a headmistress . . . This afternoon, Ranji, I shall welcome more than three hundred children to Hillgate. Most of them come from poor homes, with narrow horizons. I'm going to open their eyes to new worlds—and open doors so that they can step through. I've been given the power to influence their lives, and I have a duty to use it. There are going to be a lot of changes in that school."

"And if I were to say to you that I would like to have a child, two children—?"

"I wouldn't believe you." She checked herself and glanced at him, wondering if she was wrong to claim such a definite knowledge of his wishes. But if he had felt any passionate desire to become a father he would have made that clear long ago. She saw now that when he agreed in the previous year that they would have a family one day, it was only in order to please her, to promise what she seemed then to want. "It's too late now," she told him. "And you're *not* saying that, are you?"

Ranji did not answer at once, and for a moment Asha was anxious. Then he looked at her with the sweet smile which had won her heart fourteen years earlier. "Just testing," he said. "You still see yourself as head of the household, I think. But I love you all the same."

XVI

Asha stood at the window of the head teacher's study. Waiting for Paula, she watched the new children arrive at the school gates.

How young they seemed! They had all passed their eleventh birthdays, but expressions of anxiety or expectation gave each of them a look of vulnerability. A few wore shabby clothes with an air of either shame or defiance, but most were overdressed. In every family which could afford it, the change of school had been signaled by the buying of new clothes—with an eye to long life. The sleeves of new blazers reached almost to fingertips, while some of the girls walked proudly in navy-blue raincoats whose hems flapped around their calves. Poor little things, efficiently waterproofed on a hot September day.

As well as being overdressed, they were overloaded, made lopsided by the weight of a bulging shoe bag or an overstuffed briefcase. Unfortunately for posture, the old-fashioned school satchel was still out of fashion. But Asha was glad that this first arrival at a new school had been treated as a special occasion. It meant that the parents were on her side. Unconsciously she clenched her fists, silently promising not to let them down.

Some of the children were accompanied on this first afternoon by mothers or older siblings; but any nervousness on the part of the new pupil was less than the fear of being thought a baby. Goodbyes were swift and at some distance from the gate. And then there was no time for loneliness. As each youngster stepped inside the playground, an older boy or girl moved forward from the reception group waiting by the door. The newcomer was led to a list pinned to a blackboard, where each name had a cloakroom number and classroom letter.

It was on Asha's own insistence that the school had been opened a half day early. In the past she had felt sorry for the eleven-year-olds who found themselves milling around among almost two thousand children in a huge building, and who spent the whole of their first day in a state of anxiety or panic about where they were supposed to be and how to get there. Now they would feel looked after as they hung up their clothes and found their desks and met their class teachers and the other children who would become their friends. After Asha herself had welcomed them all, they would have the chance to explore all the buildings, with guides to help them, and to learn a few of the school rules without being swamped at once by the whole burden of orders and prohibitions.

A taxi drew up outside the school gate, and a smartly dressed black woman made her way briskly through the cluster of eleven-year-olds. Asha moved away from the window and opened the door of her study, ready to welcome her cousin. "Paula!"

"Asha, hi! Great to see you. And special thanks for letting me intrude on your working day. Something's different. What is it?"

Paula stared intently. "You've put your hair up. Very elegant. Makes you seem older. But then, you never looked more than seventeen before, so perhaps that's the idea."

Asha laughed her agreement. "Right! I've even acquired an M.A. gown to add dignity and authority. Look at this! Not for everyday wear, of course. But in an hour's time all the new children will be waiting in the assembly hall, and I intend them to notice my arrival."

"Good for you. It's one of the points I'm hoping to get across to the commission tomorrow. Jamaican children actually *like* authority and discipline in the classroom. One of the things that throw them when they come to England is to find schoolteachers saying matily, 'Call me Charlie.' I hope you're hiding a cane in that cupboard!"

"What is this commission, Paula?"

"Your government's latest effort to investigate race relations in England. We're due for a stormy encounter tomorrow morning, I think. *I* want to discover whether our people who've emigrated to England are being treated decently, but I suspect that the commission wants to find out how we in Jamaica would cope if any large repatriation scheme was put into effect. I'm moving into politics in a big way now. When I was sixteen I decided to be Prime Minister of Jamaica one day, and it's time to get going. I've done a lot of local broadcasting, so people know my name. But I mustn't hold you up now with my chatter. I've only come to ask a single question."

"Why were you so keen to ask it here instead of spending the evening with us and having a proper talk?"

"I'm taking you both out to dinner this evening," Paula said. "But I wanted to see you first when Ranji wouldn't be around."

"You'd better sit down." Asha felt suddenly chilled. "Is something wrong, Paula? Something affecting me?"

"It's tricky," said Paula. "I'm breaking a confidence, you see. Ranji specially asked me not to say anything to you. But then I thought, if I have to take sides between you and him, I'd always choose you. Naturally."

"Why should you have to take sides?"

"I hope I don't. But I wondered whether perhaps you were splitting up."

"No, of course not. We're very happy together."

"Then that's all fine and dandy and I'm sorry I spoke."

"You'll have to go on now," Asha said quietly. "What was it that Ranji didn't want you to tell me?"

"That he was offering me the portrait of old John Junius Lorimer —the one that used to hang in the drawing room at Blaize. He wrote to ask me whether I'd like it. But if I took the picture, I wasn't ever to tell you that I had it. My first thought was that maybe you'd walked out on him and he was disposing of everything that reminded him of you. Oh God, Asha, what have I done?"

Asha struggled to control the trembling of her body. She could feel the blood draining from her face. Something in her head was roaring as it had roared on the day she pushed open the door of Ros's apartment, and if she had not been sitting down her legs would have collapsed beneath her as they had collapsed then. She was staring in Paula's direction, but all she could see was a bloodstained ax half buried in a wooden crate.

It must have been a moment or two later that she was aware of a hand pressing her head down between her knees. "Do you have a bathroom?" Paula asked. "Cold water?" Asha indicated a door and a moment later her cousin came back with a wet towel. "Crazy!" The coldness was pressed firmly down. "I'm sorry, Asha. Why couldn't I do what I was told? I should have asked Ranji, of course, not you."

"It's all right." Taking a grip on herself again, Asha saw that it would be best to dispose of the subject. "Quite simple, really. That portrait was in Ros's room when she was killed, you see. It was damaged by the same ax . . ." She had to make an effort not to cry. "When I saw Chris repairing the canvas afterward, I remembered . . . I asked Ranji to get rid of it, any way he liked. I thought he'd sell it, to a stranger. But perhaps he felt it ought to stay in the family. If he'd given it to Bernard, I would have seen it when I visited. He must have decided that Jamaica was safe."

"Until I put my big foot in it. I *am* sorry, Asha."

"Ranji's very good about that sort of thing," Asha said. "He's sensitive. And kind. I must stop letting memories upset me. I'm glad you've agreed to look after our ancestor." She forced herself to laugh. "Talk about the wheel of fortune turning! That picture started life in its owner's immensely grand mansion. It's never gone out of the family, but it's moved to a tenement, back to another stately home, down

to a nursing home and my untidy flat, and now it's on its way up again
—off to the home of a future prime minister of Jamaica!"

"Whose other ancestors were slaves." Paula laughed as well as she
made her own contribution to the unexpectedness of it all. "So as far
as you and Ranji are concerned, everything is hunky-dory. I'm glad."

"There *was* a bad patch," Asha admitted. "Ranji had problems at
work. And I—I think it was all my fault. When I met Ranji he was
young and shy and flat broke. He would never have dared to push me
into marriage. I did all the pushing. Mostly because I was so much in
love with him—but partly because Aunt Alexa went on about it so."

"You held the purse strings then, I suppose. You were in a position
to push."

"I suppose so. But it didn't seem right to go on in the same way
after he graduated and started earning. Perhaps I was still a bully, but
I bullied him into being the boss instead, if you see what I mean. I
thought that was what he'd expect—a supportive, domesticated, obedient wife. Well, he did, of course; but at the same time I was working as hard as he was and *I* needed a supportive 'wife' as well. It was
crazy of me to impose a pattern of marriage which was the opposite of
what I really wanted. Talk about digging a trap for oneself! He was as
much in love with me as I was with him, after all. He would have put
me on a pedestal and gone down on his knees to scrub the floor all
round it if I'd told him on the first day of the honeymoon that that
was how we were going to live." She sighed in mock regret. "Too late
ever to get back to that, of course."

"So for fourteen years you've been curbing your natural inclination
to dominate—and now you're a headmistress! What does Ranji think
about that?"

"I expect he hopes that I'll work out all my bullying tendencies in
school hours and be especially sweet when I get home." Asha laughed
lightheartedly at the idea. "Or perhaps he never really wanted to take
on all the responsibilities I pushed on him." Only a few hours earlier
Ranji had accused her of acting as though she were the head of the
household. He had seemed to be asking for a denial—but he might
not necessarily have wanted the denial to be true.

It was too complicated to explain, and yet she wanted Paula to
understand the importance of the day for her. "All my life, you know,
I seem to have been surrounded by people with great talents. Inside

the family, I mean. Aunt Alexa was born to sing and Aunt Kate was born to heal people and Ilsa was born to make music. I remember Ilsa telling me once that composing was a vocation, not a career. That set me on the wrong track for a long time."

"How so?"

"Well, it gave me the feeling that vocation was tied to some form of creation—symphonies, books, pictures, babies or whatever. I didn't have any qualifications in any of those fields, except perhaps for motherhood. What I understand now—but I didn't then—is that you fulfill a vocation by drawing out the talent that's inside you and using it—even though it may not be a creative talent and it may never make you famous. It's what I'm hoping to offer the children here; but I had to practice on myself first."

"So you discovered that your vocation was for teaching?"

"No," said Asha. "I have a talent for teaching, and I enjoy it, and until now it's been my career. But my vocation is for running things. For seeing goals and working out how to achieve them. Taking responsibility and making decisions. It took me a long time to find out. But now I'm sure. To discover—after a lot of dithering—what you really want and to realize that you've got it: it's exciting!"

"You rejected the idea of motherhood, then?"

"That was part of the dithering," Asha admitted. "The feeling that I had some kind of responsibility to keep the family going. But this job is more important. And besides—" Asha was suddenly shy. "Ranji and I—I love him so much. I don't want anyone to come between us. Some marriages are completed by children. But I think that others are damaged by them. We shall be happiest as two adults, relating just to each other."

There was a knock at the door, and a seventeen-year-old boy announced that everything was ready. Paula helped Asha to put on her academic gown and hood and they walked downstairs together. As Paula left through one of the main doors, an eleven-year-old West Indian boy burst in through the other, panting with panic because he was so late for this important first day. Skidding to a standstill, he looked helplessly around the large entrance area at all the anonymous doors.

"Over there." Asha indicated the way to the assembly hall. She moved in the same direction as he scuttled inside, but paused for a moment to allow the disturbance of his arrival to subside.

There was a glass panel set in the upper half of the door. Through it Asha could see the new boys and girls, trying not to fidget as they sat in rows under the watchful eyes of their class teachers. Her lips parted in a smile as she studied them. These children, starting their secondary school lives on the same day that she began her career as a headmistress, would be her special pupils.

Asha straightened her shoulders, nodded to the prefect who was waiting to open the door for her, and moved with slow dignity up the steps and across to the center of the platform. As she walked, her mind was still on the earlier conversation with Paula about their common ancestor. It was not only in the hanging of his picture that the changing fortunes of the family had revealed themselves. In the hundred years since his death all the social values which he took for granted had been turned on their head. What would an elderly Victorian have thought of a marriage in which the wife, rather than the husband, took the major decisions as well as bringing in the higher salary? Could he have seen his great-granddaughter today, John Junius Lorimer would have been amazed at her calm authority and dismayed by the decisiveness with which she had cut herself free from the burden of dynastic responsibility.

Yet one family tie could not be cut. It was from her Lorimer ancestors that she had inherited the spirit which made her determined to succeed in her own ambitions while refusing to accept anything but the best efforts of others. Such a legacy was less easily renounced than a material fortune: a painting or a collection of jewels.

Forms scraped and feet scuffled as the year's new intake rose untidily to its feet. As Asha waited for the silence which would follow the moment of shuffling and fidgeting she looked down at the three hundred and twenty young faces in front of her and could not restrain a smile of love.

These were her children.

The best years of her life were about to begin.